SAVAGE DOMINION

BOOK ONE
SAVAGE DOMINION

SAVAGE DOMINION

BOOK ONE
SAVAGE DOMINION

LUKE CHMILENKO
GD PENMAN

Wraithmarked
CREATIVE

Editor: Dominion Editing
Cover Illustration: Mansik YAM
Cover Design and Interior Layout: STK·Kreations

Trade paperback ISBN: 978-0-9991920-7-8
Ebook ISBN: 978-0-9991920-8-5

Worldwide Rights
1st Edition

Published by Wraithmarked Creative, LLC
www.wraithmarked.com

To our Friends and Family,
thank you for your endless love and support.

CHAPTER 1

Throughout the eons of human history, men have done a lot of really dumb things to get laid. When you put that into context, going for a ten-mile hike for a first date when you are as athletic as a cabbage probably doesn't even make the top ten. It is one of the dumbest things I'd ever done personally, but on the grand scale of things, it doesn't even register.

The forest that she took me to was actually pretty gorgeous—if you're into heavily wooded areas and bugs. The sun was filtering through the leaves, making the path beneath our feet green and golden in alternate patches. In the distance, I could hear a stream gurgling by. If I'd been an outdoorsy kind of person then this would probably be my idea of heaven. Since I was more of a stay inside and play video games until three in the morning kind of person, I was less than enthusiastic.

Needless to say, the actual date part wasn't going so well. It was pretty apparent I'd lied when I showed up to the hike in a T-shirt, jeans, and sneakers instead of whatever boots and beige explorer gear I was somehow meant to know I should be wearing. The fact that I was dripping with sweat and panting for breath after the first slight incline probably gave away the game a bit too.

Maybe I could have salvaged the situation, laid on some charm, and made it funny, but that panting thing was no joke. She was mad, and she was hiking up the path like she planned to stomp right through it.

"Hey..."

Every so often she stopped for me to play catch up, but by the time that I did, I was so out of breath I couldn't say anything.

"Uh…"

She stormed off again just before I got a word out, and I had no choice but to traipse on after her.

"So…"

There was a gentle breeze rustling through the trees as we continued to climb, yet I seemed to be burning up. Ever notice that you can't feel your lungs unless something has gone wrong? They don't ever feel pleasantly cool when you're just relaxing. It's only when you start putting some work in that they start to complain.

Which, in my case, made me feel like I'd been huffing napalm, leaving me looking like a partially boiled lobster. A lesser man might have just watched a nice butt wiggling up the trail ahead of him and accepted the day was a total bust, but I kept on going. Momma didn't raise a quitter after all. This was just going to be a funny story for our hypothetical grandkids someday. My perseverance in the face of adversity was sure to win her over any minute now. She'd respect me for carrying on even though I was completely out of my element, throw herself into my waiting arms, and kiss me until sundown. Then she would carry me back down to the car over her shoulder because my legs had turned into jelly.

The ground finally started to even out after we'd reached the seven-thousand-mile mark—also known as the top of the ridge that we'd been heading up. I never thought I could be so happy to see some dirt packed flat, but there I was. I was so overjoyed that I didn't even notice the path widening out into a clearing until I almost walked right into the back of my date.

I pulled up abruptly behind her, and in the moment before my brain caught up to what was going on, it fed me some weird little details. Some of the hair had finally wisped out of her ponytail, and she was standing really still like she was trying to not even breathe. There was even a bead of sweat running down the side of her neck, which I took as a win. Sure, I'd dripped out enough saltwater to fill a manatee enclosure, but she was sweating too, so this hiking thing was hard for everyone. It wasn't just me.

About then my eyes managed to focus on what had brought her to a dead halt. There was a wolf on the other side of the clearing.

Wolves are a lot bigger than you'd expect. That was the first thing I noticed. Next, I spotted the size of its teeth since it was snarling at us. It took a while to look away from those yellowed fangs and stop imagining just how much damage they could do. The fur along the length of it was thick and rich with a swirl of browns and greys. There was a smell hanging over the whole clearing—like a wet dog but acrid, sharp, and musky. The whole thing was surreal. I didn't even think there were any wolves in the wild around here, let alone frothing, growling, furious wolves that were bigger than me.

I wish I could say that some heroic instinct kicked in and I jumped forward to protect my date—maybe I would have, had I been given enough time for my exhausted brain to catch up—but the wolf didn't give us that chance. In one bounding step, it closed the distance, drool trailing from its jagged jaws.

Finally, my body decided to move, and I threw myself to the side, shoulder barging my date into the dirt and catching the wolf's jaws on my arm instead of her throat. Guess those hero instincts were in there somewhere, but I didn't have much time to be pleased because there was a wolf gnawing on my arm.

That was going to hurt really soon, but for that initial moment, all I felt was the heat inside his mouth. The wolf snarled at me, and I screamed right back at him. My date was scrambling back to her feet, but I had enough presence of mind to yell, "Run!" at her before the wolf started yanking on my arm like I was a rag doll.

She stood there staring at me for just long enough for me to think she wasn't going to listen, expressions washing over her face too fast to follow, then that good old-fashioned survival instinct kicked in, and she ran for her life back down the trail.

Good. That was one problem taken care of. Sure, I was about to become a snack, but at least the girl who'd spent all day aggressively ignoring me was going to be alright. The pain was coming now, nauseating waves of it every time I felt the teeth grinding on my bone. My screaming probably wasn't so defiant anymore. Nothing could have prepared me for the sensation of the bone cracking when the wolf got a good grip and really bit down.

I punched the wolf in the face. Then when it still didn't let go, I punched it again. I might have been twisted off balance and dragged halfway into the undergrowth before I realized I could fight back, but now I was ready. I was hurting, and I was angry, and this overgrown Chihuahua was not about to have me for dinner.

The next swing hit it right on the nose, and it let go of me with an undignified little yelp. We both jumped back from each other, then started to circle each other like it was a boxing match. I just wasn't sure I'd make it through another round.

We'd completely swapped places by the time it occurred to me that I could run for it too. Guess running never came naturally to me. When it came to fight or flight, I had always seemed to be missing the second part. I never wanted to give anyone the satisfaction of seeing me scared, even when it got me my ass kicked.

For once, it looked like fighting was the right choice. With the trail at its back, the wolf turned away from me, looking for easier lunch that wouldn't whack it with a rolled-up newspaper. The trail that my dearest darling date had just run down. Damn it.

I had one hand still working right, so when the wolf turned to run, I grabbed onto his brushy tail and pulled. That earned me another yelp and the undivided attention that I probably should have been doing my best to avoid.

The wolf spun on the spot, snapping at my wrist and catching a mouthful of tail instead. My throat was sore from all the panting and screaming, but I still managed to bluster out, "Too slow, bitch."

Maybe he understood English, or maybe he was just angry about biting itself on the tail, but either way, he came for me, and my jelly legs had no choice but to move where I told them to.

Even if I managed to get past him, I couldn't lead him towards my date, and I was pretty sure that a hungry wolf could outpace me on a flat surface even on the best of days—he was cheating, he had two extra legs—so the trail ahead was out too. That left only one other option.

I dove into the underbrush and made a run for it. If I could get a bit of distance and climb a tree, the wolf would be screwed. Of course, that would require me to move faster than a creature that was chasing me down through its natural habitat, when my natural habitat was the sofa seat closest to the bathroom so I wouldn't have to walk too far. I tripped over a root about ten seconds into my sprint and sprawled on my face.

The wolf obviously expected more from me, and he shot right by and had to make a U-turn to come back at my face—my face which now happened to be at a convenient chomping height. I had to fling myself to the side and swing a wild haymaker into the impending jaws of death just to keep the wolf from my throat.

It was like punching a furry brick wall. It turned the wolf's head so the bite missed, but that was it. The rest of the big hairy beast still rolled over me like a train. Flat on my back, looking up at the clear blue sky above me, I caught a glimpse of the moon. It wasn't meant to be here today. Neither was I. My ears were ringing. Maybe shock was kicking in.

The wolf darted in, faster than I could follow, and this time its teeth found my throat. With a bite strong enough to shatter bone, those teeth didn't need to be needle sharp to hurt me, but that was still the first thing I felt, before the wet and the heat and the pain; that first sharp touch on my skin before I jammed my hands in his mouth to keep the jaws from closing.

The wolf bit down anyway. No matter what I shoved in the way, it could still bite through, but instead of the rip and tear it had gone for, it got a mouth full of crunchy little hand bones that it had to try and grind through. It was like biting into a chicken wing wrong and feeling the bone splinter in your mouth.

Except in this scenario, I was the chicken wing in question.

With my hands busy being chewed to shreds and an angry wolf on top of me, the only thing I could do to get it off me was head-butt the mangy mutt right on its wet nose. With a strangled yelp, it jumped off, paws hammering me back into the scrubby plants all over again.

I rolled and was up and running before I had time to realize that pushing off with my hands was going to be an agonizingly bad idea. There was no time to stop and scream, so I did it while I ran, yodeling through the woods at top speed with the wolf literally snapping at my heels until my breath ran dry.

All that I could hear was the hammering of my heart, the whipping of leaves by my ears, and the wolf. Always the wolf. His ragged breath. The steady beat of his paws on the ground. The long growl that rumbled out of him as we ran.

Then one moment, just as abruptly as the wolf had appeared, he was gone. I staggered forward a few more steps before tripping over something and falling in a heap. I twisted, expecting the wolf to be on me again, but it was just standing there. Hackles up. Teeth bared. I shuffled my back up against what I'd assumed was a mossy tree. Its cool presence informed me it was actually a rock. There were eight of them, all covered in so much moss and lichen that you couldn't even see the color of the stone. They loomed in a circle that I'd just fallen into the middle of.

A circle that the wolf wouldn't, couldn't enter.

If I wasn't so grateful that I wasn't currently being treated like a dollar store chew toy it probably would have been unsettling. Outside the circle, the wolf bayed and barked, drooled and paced, but not once did it try to come inside. I'd beaten it. I'd won. I started to laugh, but it hurt too much. My hands were a mangled mess of gristle, blood, and bone, and reaching up to my neck with what was left of them, I found it was slick with gore too. The bite that I'd stopped short hadn't stopped short enough. My shirt was soaked in blood, and the sun in the open sky above the circle was getting dimmer by the second.

It took so much effort now just to look around. All the stuff I'd taken for granted was suddenly arduous. I knew that I was dying—I wasn't dumb. Nobody bled this much and survived. However, there was still one last thing I had to do before I died. My eyes locked on the wolf, still snarling on the other side of whatever invisible barrier was keeping it out. All that work and he wasn't even going to get a taste of my delicious man meat.

Straining with all my might, I lifted both of my arms and curled all but one finger on each hand as tightly as I could, grunting through the pain. I kept those middle fingers raised at that wolf for as long as I had the strength. Eventually, they started to wobble and drift as my eyes fluttered shut, and heavy darkness overtook me.

So that was what dying felt like. In case you wondered.

CHAPTER 2

Death is not the end.

I remember a lot of people worrying about that back when I was still alive, so I thought I'd clear it up. Everything went dark, then everything went light again, blindingly bright for just a moment, then I was hanging there above my body, looking down on it and wishing that I wasn't. It wasn't pretty. I mean, I wasn't much of a looker to start with, but the wolf had really done a number on me. Bits were dangling that were not meant to be dangling, and the whole thing just looked wet and gross. It made me glad I wasn't in the body anymore. There was no pain, and there was no fear—those were functions of the body I'd inhabited. Instead, there was just me.

Ghosts are also a thing as it turns out. I was dead but not gone. There aren't many things you can call that other than ghosts. Tearing my attention away from the meaty mess I used to occupy, I looked to the wolf, only to discover that he'd wandered off sometime between the darkness, the light, and my haunting beginning. I couldn't see any sign of it. Next, I found my attention drawn to the stones, which now seemed to glow faintly blue in the day's dying light. I already knew that there was something strange about them when the wolf wouldn't come in, but now I was wondering just what fresh hell I'd landed myself in. I was just starting to think that I could do with some sort of advice on what to do next when I saw a robed figure hanging in the air just beyond the circle's perimeter. I glanced quickly over the scythe and the anorexic hands that gripped it and found myself staring into the dark recesses of the hood, from which a voice echoed out, *"Your time in this world has ended. Come to me, and I shall take you on to the next."*

When capital "D" Death tells you to do something, obeying is almost automatic. I felt myself moving before I even had time to think. I'd nearly made it out of the circle before I realized something. Even Death couldn't come in here. "What happens if I don't?"

For a moment, the wraith froze in place, then, as soft as a sigh, Death said, *"Then you will linger here for all eternity. Forgetting more and more of what you were—doing nothing, changing nothing—until only your awareness remains. It is that fate which I labor to spare you all."*

Lingering for all eternity with nothing to do but look at these rocks did sound kind of dull, and it wasn't like I was going to get less dead by hanging out next to my corpse. So I tried to shrug, found I was missing the required shoulders, and drifted on over.

Death moved off between the trees almost as soon as I'd started to follow. Keeping up wasn't a problem now that I passed through everything like it wasn't there, but it was still kind of rude. Besides, I had a lot of questions. This was my first time being dead. "So what happens next?"

"You do not know? Most mortals are brimming over with opinions."

Every time I nearly caught up, he put on a new turn of speed. We must have been flying along at thirty miles an hour now. "I think I'd prefer to know what is actually coming instead of guesswork."

Death stopped dead, and I almost rammed into the back of him. *"Most mortals I reap pass into whatever world their actions have destined them for. You are different. Your circumstances necessitate intervention."*

Uh-oh. "What kind of 'intervention' are we talking about?"

"Divine."

I didn't like the sound of that either. I'd never been big on religion while I was alive, and now that I was dead, I didn't really want to change that. Every story I'd ever heard about a person getting some divine intervention usually ended up with someone on fire, in a whale, or having some internal organs becoming external. It was that last one that was concerning me right now. Sure I was dead, but that didn't mean I wanted some big alligator-looking dude weighing my organs to decide if I was a good enough guy to not be eaten by miscellaneous nightmare beasts.

Why did my mind go there? See where your mind goes when you drop dead.

In either case, I was just starting to reconsider the whole lingering for eternity bit when I realized we'd stopped for a reason. We were in the middle of nowhere now—even more the middle of nowhere than where we'd started out from. This place was as barren as a desert with none of the exciting sand dunes and scorpions. Just an endless blank expanse. Except for the golden gate that hung unsupported and open ahead of us. It wasn't a pearly gate with a neon sign flashing "Heaven ahead", but it looked promising enough. There were no screaming souls of the damned pouring out or anything. Maybe I had found the time to be a good person in between movie marathons and MMO raids?

Stepping through the auric arches, it was like someone had switched out the lights on the whole universe. The only reason I knew Death was walking by my side was that he hissed, *"Stay close. This is no place for spirits to be lost."*

I couldn't see anything, but I supposed that being insubstantial meant that I wouldn't be stubbing my toe or banging into anyone in the dark anyway. I felt myself moving, even if I couldn't see it, then in the distance, I began to make out a shimmer of golden light. From the refractions, the hall that we were moving through began to take shape.

It was huge. Impossibly huge. So big that no human hands could possibly have wrought it. If we had footsteps they wouldn't even have echoed in so wide a space. The marble was dark and seamless, with only a hint of distant stars buried somewhere deep down within it. There were no clear cuts or joints, no sign that the stone had been worked at all. It was as though the whole place had just sprung into being fully formed.

Hanging back really was a bad idea. Big D seemed to have no intention of slowing or even acknowledging me now that I was here. I guess I was just a work friend. I had to hurry after him or risk being left behind in the hollow darkness. Yet now that we were coming closer to the light, I realized that neither one of us was actually alone. There was a train of four wisps following in his wake, only visible now that they were coming into the light of whatever golden sun lay ahead of us. Were they more people like me, all requiring divine intervention to find their final resting place? Was that what I looked like? Just a little puff of light and substance hanging in the air? Was that all that was left of me?

That mental rabbit-hole would have to remain unexplored because I soon found myself distracted by the shiny. The hall had continued to open out into an even grander chamber, and standing at the center of it all was the source of all light in this place.

The gods.

Each one of them was bathed in radiance that made the brightest day back on Earth look like it was thick with fog, the colors in my memory appearing faded and mute in comparison. But even as bright as their aura was, it could not compare to the light that poured from their eyes. Looking into them would have blinded me if I still had the anatomy for it. I was formless, impervious, and I still caught myself flinching.

While I could sense more gods watching from the wings, there was only a trio waiting for us at the center. The tallest and grandest wore a crown. He was more or less everything you'd expect from a god—towering, muscular, flowing white robes, and lots of gold filigree. He even had the big white beard, although it seemed that there were little embers glowing at the end of each wavy hair. In one hand, he held a spear that was even taller than him, in the other a golden sphere that glowed almost as brightly as his eyes. It could very well have been a small sun for all I knew about how the universe worked. Maybe stars were like handbag dogs for the gods?

Beside him, and back a step on either side, were the other two gods. On his left was the most beautiful woman I had ever seen—so picture-perfect that she didn't look real. Every line and curve of her face and body were porcelain pristine, accentuated, and masked in equal parts by the diaphanous, silky white gown that she wore. Here too was more gold. A circlet at her brow and filigreed details worked into her clothes. It was difficult to tear my eyes away from her to look at the third figure.

What this one lacked in height compared to the central god, they made up for in bulk. There was gold aplenty to be seen, but none of the white robes for this one. They were clad from head to toe in plate armor, shining blinding-bright in the light of the others and emitting their own solar glow from six holes in the helmet's faceplate. While you could have mistaken the middle god's spear for something decorative, this one had flails looped short in their hands that were clearly meant to be used, the spiked head of each hidden by the flames burning wildly within.

Death stopped before the gods without deference. Then he turned back to we mere mortals and pointed to the gods, each in turn. "*Eosphel, King of the Dawn. Hemeraphel, The Noon Queen. Bilaphel, The Purifying Flame. These gods rule the Solar Court. They shall have their pick of the four of you.*"

Hemeraphel's white mask of a face creased into a benevolent smile. A hand slipped from her trailing sleeves and beckoned us forward. I had automatically tried to do what Big D told me to because it was wired into my brain, but I wanted to obey the Noon Queen because it might please her. I wanted her to turn that smile on me. More than anything, I wanted her to choose me. To make me hers in whatever way this afterlife intervention allowed.

Only the surprisingly solid arm of Death stretched across my path brought me to a halt. "*Not you.*"

Before I had the opportunity to object, Eosphel raised the golden sphere above his head, and his booming voice rolled over us all. "Behold Amaranth."

The little sun went supernova, exploding out to envelop the entire room in flames and light. It was only once we were inside the corona that I could see again, and there, hanging above Eosphel's hand, was a world. It was detailed in the same golden glow that poured out from the gods, but it was still clearly a little planet that we were looking at, and as we gawked, it grew larger and larger until we were drifting across its surface as it rotated.

"Look upon Amaranth, first of all worlds. The world of which all others are mere shadows. It is the holy land where the great matters of the Courts are settled."

It took a little time to understand what I was looking at. The little image of a world was spinning by so fast, and we were so high above it that making out details would have been a struggle anyway. The fact that everything was being displayed in the same golden color really didn't help much. There were mountains and rivers, forests, and plains. It looked a lot like Earth used to before we built all over it. There seemed to be a few deserts in unexpected spots, but beyond that, it didn't seem like anything special.

"When there is order in Amaranth, there is order throughout the cosmos. When there is chaos here, all worlds fall to it. Amaranth is key to mastery of the universe."

We dipped in closer to the surface now, and the illusion that this world was wild and empty washed away. There had been buildings, even cities, once upon a time, but they had since fallen into ruin. Colossal statues were hidden beneath the grime of ages, long broken and forgotten. Everywhere I looked, the world had grown back on top of what people had tried to build there. Layer upon layer of civilizations laid down in strata to support this latest wilderness.

"That mastery is the very reason that there are strict rules that govern conduct upon Amaranth. Gods of neither court may walk upon it. Nay, all of our great works there must be done through our agents, the Eternals."

The world stopped spinning.

We stood on the crest of a hill, overlooking a vast battlefield. Down amidst a confusing sea of swarming creatures, a single man in armor stood tall and unmoved. He was no bigger than the host buzzing around him, but he filled up our sight all the same, the only real looking thing in the glowing illusions laid out before us. Yet even he didn't escape the divine light entirely, and when he turned our way, we could see it blazing in his eyes—just the same as it did in the eyes of the gods.

"This is the fate that we offer unto you lost souls. Hearken to us and be born again into a living world. Be granted bodies once more that not just match those that you bore in your previous lives, but are better in every way. Bodies that are empowered with our divine might, so that you can bring order to the world of Amaranth. You have all felt the icy touch of oblivion upon you, but you need not feel it ever again. In exchange for your servitude, each of you shall be granted the most glorious boons. Not the least of which is life everlasting."

I don't know what I did to win this jackpot prize, but I wasn't going to let it pass me by. "I get to be a badass warrior for all eternity? Where do I sign up?"

Eosphel fell silent at my interruption, and I had a horrible flashback to a timeshare pitch that I'd once been tricked into sitting through with the promise of a free brunch. The brunch hadn't even been that good. The gentle golden light that the king was wreathed in flared to life like somebody poured gasoline on him. I was getting the distinct impression that gods weren't used to being interrupted.

The flare lasted for just a moment, then he seemed to get it back under control and press on with the sales pitch as if I weren't there. Probably a good thing, all things considered.

"The four of you have been chosen by the fates. Your deaths were not wasted as so many are but instead were sanctified. Each of you passed from your mortal forms on holy ground. Know now that even the manner of your death needed to be righteous for you to be ushered into these halls. Even in this, there are strictures and limitations to ensure that only the truly worthy are called."

That explained why the place wasn't packed. A lot of people died all day every day throughout the world, but how many did so in weird stone circles in the middle of nowhere? Five in a day seemed about right.

Wait, there were five of us newly dead here, weren't there?

Eosphel was still blabbing on about divine providence and the virtues of service, so I took a second to do a recount. There was Big D, me, the gods, and four other glowing wisps. Five dead people in total. If the gods couldn't do basic arithmetic that also explained a lot about the universe.

I tuned back into Eosphel's grand proclamations just in time for some of the juicy details. "Within Amaranth, you too shall be bound by the strictures of the concord we reached with the other Court but empowered by them too. Your world was tainted thoroughly by chaos. So much so you could not even perceive the fundamental nature of your own selves. In Amaranth, you shall truly know the new self that we here shall forge. All shall be revealed to you. The very sacred geometry of the cosmos laid bare."

The big golden display shuddered and shifted, and suddenly, we were surrounded by a circle of people standing to attention and drifting in a slow orbit. There were a pair of good old-fashioned humans amongst them, but they were an afterthought compared to the cornucopia of fantastical other races that had just appeared. There were lizard people, dwarves, elves, and then some hulking horny beast that towered over the rest. We weren't just coming back from the dead, we were going to fantasy land. I just wished I had a mouth so I could grin.

Sure, dying sucked, but if you gave me the choice of anywhere to go when I died, then this would have been it. Keep your hundred virgins and your magic sherbet, I'll take dungeons and dragons any time.

"Amaranth was the first world of the cosmos, and the echoes of its people find their way into the dreams of all other worlds. You may know these creatures as myths, but they are more real than the shadow creatures that you once lived as. To be reborn, we shall name you and shape your spirits in their form. Look upon them now and choose your future."

All the other wisps darted around taking in the sights, but once again, Death held out his arm to keep me back. I was getting really tired of that, so I darted out of reach to join the tour. What was he going to do, kill me?

I decided to get the boring ones out of the way first. Humans. Just looking at the glowing construct was enough to set off the booming voice of Eosphel in my head.

"Mankind is the youngest people of Amaranth, born into the world during the Revelation of Araphel. Though lost and confused, they swiftly took up the banner of righteousness and joined the war against the Void God, making many see them as the saviors of all free folk."

Oh, my gods…

"Despite their natural disadvantages compared to the other races, they have become more numerous and prosperous than any other."

This was…

"Though they have none of the other races' unique abilities, they have the adaptability to excel in any..."

So... boring.

Why wasn't there an option to skip the fluff? Show me the stats. Damn it. Give me the delicious crunchy numbers. I concentrated on the weird symbols hanging beside the human's display, and the god of no-inside-voice cut out. Thankfully.

Race: Human
Starting Attributes:
Potency: 10
Celerity: 10
Vitality: 10
Piety: 10

Starting stats. When they were talking about Amaranth being bound by rules, they meant game rules. Whatever game the gods were playing on Amaranth, it was a crunchy-stat based one.

Beneath the stats, another little row of symbols appeared.

Racial Ability:
Curiosity:
Filled with a curious and cunning spirit, there is little a human cannot discover or learn if given enough time.
Effect: Humans gain an extra rank when unlocking a skill for the first time and gain additional experience across all skills.

Yawn. Generic humans were generic. Come on game designers, humans are so many weird and wonderful things, why did we always get such dull racial abilities. Come on! We could heal from almost anything. Why didn't we get regeneration? We could make friends with wolves and wildcats. Why didn't we get animal handling? Humans were the weirdest animal on Planet Earth, and somehow, when the time came to make games about us, everyone came up with "oh they can learn stuff." At least it wasn't a flat experience boost.

Dwarves were up next—at least they were liable to be a bit more interesting. "The Dvergar were once known as the Godseekers. The Dvergar had no gods of their own. While the other races lived on the surface in clear view of the sun and moon, they dwelled beneath the earth, yearning for the same care that the heavens granted their terranean kin. In their desperation, they delved deeper and deeper beneath the surface of Amaranth, answering the siren call of the beast below."

Dwarves that delved too deep. What a shocking twist. At least this beast below was a bit more exciting.

"Darkness made flesh, he seemed the perfect god for those who dwelled forever beneath the stone. They fell at Araphel's feet. Yet Araphel's hunger for conquest was not sated by mere Dvergar. His designs were upon all of creation. His worshipers became his slaves, toiling in the Flesh Forges to create abominations for his all-conquering army."

So the dwarves were the bad guys in this world. That was actually a bit of a twist.

"Amaranth was consumed by war. Civilization was ground to dust. Though oathbound to Araphel, in the dying days of the Revelation, the Dvergar turned on him, yet even with their waning power added to the armies of the Free Folk, they were no match for Araphel's divine power."

At least that explained the state of Amaranth when we did our slow pan over it. The whole place got dark lorded all over.

"When the Revelation ended, the Dvergar were a ruined people—ashamed in equal measure for the doom that they had unleashed on the world and for the oaths that they broke to halt that doom. They retreated to their mountain holds, bitter solitude, and inevitable decline."

Well, that was just a barrel of laughs. I was about to move on in search of a more upbeat storyline when the same little symbols formed in the air between the male and female-looking Dvergar. Symbols that I could now, somehow, read.

Race: Dvergar
Starting Attributes:
  Potency: 11
  Celerity: 5
  Vitality: 18
  Piety: 6

Racial Ability:
  Toughness:
    Made of sterner stuff than mere flesh, the Dvergar are resilient to the point of inflexibility.
    Effect: Dvergar have a natural armor value equal to half of their Vitality score. This is cumulative with other armor.

And a rapid swerve back into boring territory. If I wanted to spend eternity being an immovable object then maybe that would be tempting, although I'd probably just cut out the middle man and reincarnate as a rock instead. I'd had enough boredom and drudgery in my first lifetime. This was my afterlife, and I was going to have a good time.

Next up, the clock struck elf-o'clock.

"Most beloved of the Solar Court, the Alvaren were masters of the Arcane. Devoted to defending their world from chaos, they were often defined by their opposition. When first they arose in Amaranth, they fought the Wyrms to a standstill. During the Revelation, they were the first to take up arms against the Void God and his evils, leading the Free Folk to many of their victories against him."

The defenders of the universe schtick was appealing, but the magic thing didn't really tick any boxes for me. Standing far away from things I didn't like and muttering at them aggressively was how I'd wasted my first life.

"Through the early millennia, the Alvaren dwelled within the forests of Amaranth, but by the time of the revelation, their civilization had crystallized into city-states, differentiated from those settlements of others not only by their size and complexity but also by their mobility. Each great castle floated amidst the clouds in the sky, traveling to where its rulers directed, giving them a commanding tactical position from which their war-hawks took flight."

Flying mounts changed things up in the Alvaren's favor. I'd played enough MMOs in my time to know how much running around was involved. Sure I had eternity, but that didn't mean I wanted to be hiking for all eternity. After the day I'd had, I wasn't sure I could think of a worse fate.

"Yet as the greatest of his enemies, it seems that the Alvaren suffered the worst of Araphel's death curse. Others may have been laid low by the backlash of the Void God's own destruction, but the Alvaren and all of their cities vanished without a trace. For an Eternal to choose their form is to remind Amaranth of a bygone age of glory but also the sorrow of the world's greatest loss."

So they went extinct, which meant all that handy infrastructure had probably vanished right along with them. Great. Real handy.

Race: *Alvaren*
Starting Attributes:
  Potency: *8*
  Celerity: *12*
  Vitality: *8*
  Piety: *12*

Racial Ability:

Grace:

> *To the Alvaren, mind and body are one. Thought becomes movement. Movement becomes art.*
>
> *Effect: Alvaren have a movement speed double that normally provided by their Celerity score.*

Running fast. Great. Love running. Live for running. The Alvaren would do as a fallback option if nothing else looked appealing, but they weren't at the top of my list.

Next up were the lizard people, which I was leaning towards before I'd even started. I've always kind of liked lizards anyway, and if I didn't have to be human anymore, I wasn't sure why I'd want to be one of the sort of the almost-human-but-not-quite Dvergar or Alvaren.

"Slaves to the Wyrms, the Inyoka are bound to the cause of chaos by the same yoke. As a race, they were bred from beasts to sentience in abject servitude. Outside of the secluded domains of the Wyrms, the Inyoka are rarely seen, and when they are spotted it is by misstep. They travel only to spread their master's byzantine plans behind the scenes. They rule nowhere yet are the power behind many thrones."

Damn it all. I wanted to go on fun-filled lizard adventures, and this world was giving me nothing but suspicion, slavery, and spies.

"The Inyoka served as meat for the grinder in the Wyrm's long war against the Alvaren and likely would have continued to be mass-produced if so many of the swamps where they were spawned had not been purged by arcane fire. By the time of the Revelation, the Inyoka's numbers had dwindled until they could field no army at all, with all of their race devoted exclusively to the physical care of their overlords."

More slavery and misery. I suppose that if I was a better person, I might have made myself into an Inyoka and fought back against their wyrm-riddled oppression, but just the thought of everyone assuming

I was lying and sneaking around all the time was exhausting. I was not good at lying. As the lead up to my untimely death had demonstrated. I didn't like lying, I didn't like liars, and I wasn't entirely convinced that my brain was wired right to keep track of a whole pack of lies all at once. Don't ask me if your ass looks fat in that outfit unless you want to know the truth. Even when I do manage to bumble out a lie, without fail, it blows up in my face a few minutes later.

Race: Inyoka
Starting Attributes:
  Potency: 7
  Celerity: 14
  Vitality: 9
  Piety: 10

Racial Ability:
Regeneration:
  Blessed with an unmatched healing ability, an Inyoka can recover from the deadliest of wounds and afflictions in short order.
  Effect: Inyoka naturally regenerate health at a rate equal to their vitality score every minute.

I'd heard enough about that one. Sure, none of the other races could heal naturally without intervention, but that just meant that the world had to be chock-full of doctors, healing potions, magic ponds, and all that jazz. On to the big horny boys.

"The Chagnar Faun, firstborn of Amaranth, are hunters at heart. From the first moonrise, they swore themselves to chaos and lived as little more than beasts, reveling in bloodshed and slaughter. Yet for all of their much-vaunted martial prowess and strength surpassing all other races, they have still been bound to the will of their betters time and time again. Serving first as menial laborers for the Alvaren Empire, before betraying their masters to fight as the vanguard of Araphel. Humans, Alvaren, Dvergar, and even the Wyrms themselves eventually fought back against the Void God's horde, but never the wicked Faun."

I was wrong. The Dvergar weren't the bad guys. These were the bad guys. Yet something about the way that Eosphel had told the story had rubbed me the wrong way. When it was the Wyrms lording it over the Inyoka it got called slavery, but when it was the Solar Court's favorite pointy-eared darlings, suddenly it became "menial laborers."

I truly cannot stand a lie.

"After the revelation, with their new god defeated and their promised reign of destruction reduced to naught but a dream, the Faun found themselves outcast once more, offered not even the meager comforts of servitude to the other races. They became the horrors of bedtime tales and the creatures of nightmare; cannibalistic beast-men intent on consuming all ill-behaved children."

It sounded less like the Chagnar Faun—the proud warrior race I'd been looking for—were evil, and more like they'd been given a chance to escape eternal servitude under the Alvaren and put all their money on the wrong horse. If anything, I had more respect for these guys than I did the Dvergar. Even the Dvergar themselves admitted that they were ashamed that they broke their oaths to this evil god Araphel. Yet the Faun, who kept their promises, were treated like monsters for it?

"In the wild places of the world where they still dwell, perhaps these legends of savagery hold true, but the reality of the Faun rarely holds up to the tales when they come down from their feral realms. Still, they can find a place in the civilized world as mercenaries and thugs for hire. A kindness that they have not earned, and treatment far better than loyal servants of the adversary deserve."

Race: Chagnar Faun
Starting Attributes:
  Potency: 18
  Celerity: 7
  Vitality: 11
  Piety: 4

Racial Ability:
Relentless:

> *The Faun are the greatest hunters on Amaranth, known for pursu-*
> *ing prey for days or even weeks at a time before closing in to strike.*
> *Effect: Faun are immune to fatigue—their Attributes do not degrade*
> *over time without rest.*

So they were strong as hell and built for head butting wolves. Exactly what I wanted out of my second life. It sounded like a lot of people wouldn't like me if I was a Faun, but on the other hand, it sounded like they were the kind of people I didn't want to associate with anyway.

This was a big decision if I was going to be one of these things for the rest of my life. I drifted back a little to look at the Chagnar Faun in all their glory. Both of the example Faun stood at about seven-feet-tall, and that was with the natural forward hunch of their shoulders. Their bodies were so broad-shouldered and thickly muscled it was hard to tell which was meant to be the male and which was the female, though I guessed that the one wearing a top was probably the lady. Maybe they didn't even have genders. I wasn't going to go lifting any loincloths to find out.

I couldn't make out much coloration in this glowing display, but the details of their faces came through clear enough. A thick head of hair flowed back from behind the thick ridge of their brow, and great dark ram's horns curled back around their ears on either side. Like all of the previous races, this particular Faun was movie-star pretty. Intense stare... broad jaw... this was a face I could learn to love.

I turned to Eosphel before I could second guess myself, "Hey, Dawn King, I've chosen my new body."

Once again Eosphel seemed to seethe at the sound of my voice, turning so slowly to glower at me that I wondered for a moment if he'd even heard me speak.

I thought that his voice had been loud and annoying before, but now it felt like someone had turned him up to eleven.

He roared, "You are not worthy!"

CHAPTER 3

You aren't worthy. Any of the other wisps might have been shaking in their incorporeal boots when they heard that, but for me, it was almost a relief. I already suspected that I'd been brought along by accident, and this just confirmed it. Whatever special hoops a person had to jump through to get reincarnated as an awesome divine warrior in a fantasy world, I was pretty sure that getting gnawed on by an angry dog and falling down in the wrong place wasn't it. Death crossed the room in the blink of an eye, positioning himself between me and the glowing golden gods with sleeves outstretched. *"This one is not for you."*

That was enough to draw a little huff of surprise out of everyone, even the gods themselves. What was I here for if it wasn't for this?

Eosphel looked confused, and Bilaphel looked menacing, more so than usual. The only one that seemed to comprehend what was going on was Hemeraphel. She'd brought a delicate hand up to her perfect lips to hide a gasp. "It cannot be. The Lunar Court has not had a champion in…"

Death cut her off. Cutting people off mid-sentence was his specialty, after all. *"Three thousand six hundred and forty years. Time has no meaning. This one died on moon-hallowed ground. Marked by a beast."*

The silence stretched on and on. If these gods were the Solar Court, did that mean that the Lunar Court that I was heading for was the opposition? I was already planning to be a Faun, at least in part, out of spite towards the Solar Court being dicks. If I was allowed to play for the other team then that sounded more than fair. I looked around the shadowed periphery of the chambers for the gorgeous moon maidens and silver knights I was expecting and was rewarded with something else entirely. There was a shimmer of light coming towards me, eye-shine from the approaching gods, but the one leading them in had far too many eyes. I could count eight of them in all, clustered together and blazing with the pale light of the moon.

A spider as big as all the other gods combined scuttled into the chamber, every chitinous leg making a clatter like high heels on the marble. The wisps and gods all reared back from this monstrosity in horror, but not Death. I suppose he had nothing to fear. It wasn't like he had any insides to be turned into meat soup for a giant bug.

"*Baal Gharron, The Weaver that Binds.*"

I was frozen in place, not out of arachnophobia, although holy crap that was a big spider, but because I'd just realized this was the side I was signing up with. Something else slithered in from the shadows, long and serpentine, almost invisible outside of the Solar Court's glow apart from the tell-tale shimmer of scales.

"*Losna, The Conqueror Wyrm.*"

That thing was a straight-up dragon. It might not have had any wings on display, and it may have been weirdly elongated and snake-like, but there was no questioning that there was smoke trickling out of its mouth.

I was waiting for the next one to come out and complete the trinity of big scary monsters to balance out the shiny happy Solar Gods in the middle of the room, but whatever was out there in the shadows just went on lurking. I got the odd glimpse of eye-shine, just to let me know that *something* was out there, but I had no real idea of its size or form.

The spider seemed to be the spokesperson for the Lunar Court. She was the sociable one. Figures. "This one is ours. Ours. We claim him. It is our right. Loathe us. Revile us. We are gods all the same. Our rights are the same. He is ours."

Her voice was as rich as chocolate despite the undercurrent of anger. Deep but profoundly feminine. Like some sort of jazz club singer. Seductive and smoky. I had to remind myself that same voice was coming out of the giant bug that had scuttled over to peer at me like I was the last fly at the buffet. In the light, her chitinous hide shimmered like an oil slick.

Despite appearances, Baal Gharron seemed to be fairly reasonable. Unlike Losna, who'd reared up beside us and started to bellow. "Shred your flesh. Make you scream. Make you bleed. Beg for death."

I didn't have time to unpack all that, and it seemed like the rest of the gods were used to the crazy threats because they just ignored the dragon god entirely. Bilaphel rattled the chains of his morning-stars a little, but the others acted like Baal Gharron was the only one in the room. Hemeraphel stepped out between the two sets of gods with her hands held up placatingly. "This matter can be settled with words. There is no need for such accusations."

It was only when I caught myself staring at her hands and thinking about how elegant her fingers looked that I realized there was something strange going on in my response to her. She was messing with my mind. Almost involuntarily I drifted back, closer to the spider's embrace. Baal Gharron seemed pleased. "Of course, my lovely. My sweetness. I am sure it was just an accident that you were trying to poach our first Eternal in millennia. An accident."

Eosphel scoffed, "You think that we want that bitter little soul?"

Rude. Baal Gharron pressed on seamlessly, legs edging forward to surround me in a tall, crooked fence of safety. "Then it is settled. This Eternal is ours. Settled, my sweetness."

I got the impression that this argument wasn't really over, but they didn't want to keep it going when they had guests. So, like all squabbling families, they pretended that the offending party didn't exist.

Eosphel turned back to his own flickering wisps and started taking their orders for custom-made bodies, and the looming monster clucked over me like a mother hen. "All that they have told you is a lie. Lies. History is written by the victors, and for oh so long the Solar Court has ruled over Amaranth. When first the terms of engagement were agreed, all was equal, but the longer that the Solar Court's stagnation set in, the fewer of your kind came to us. Rare treat, my sweet."

This close, the giant spider face was somehow even more terrifying, but it was still the only friendly face around, so I tried to stay upbeat. "Well, I'm here now."

"You are here, but we have precious little time to share the truth with you. Truth. Your coming was hidden from us."

In the center of the room, the first of the Solar Eternals was already being consumed in a pillar of golden sunlight, the distant silhouette of a body gradually taking form within. Baal Gharron pressed on, all her many eyes fixed on that shadow. "Know only this, whatever the Solar Eternals seek to achieve, it is your duty to stop it. Stop them. The Solar Court means to paralyze all of existence in their hunt for perfection. Chaos is the only remedy. You must bring that chaos. You must break down the walls they have built. You must set Amaranth free. Chaos, my sweetness."

"No pressure then?"

Suddenly Losna was there, weaving through the spider's legs and snarling. "Mock your gods? Kill you! Rend your soul. Make you dust."

Up close, the serpent had a hell of a lot of teeth. Whiskers too, like a catfish. In normal circumstances, I probably would have freaked out at that thing snapping an inch from me, but my weirdness meter had been so overloaded that this didn't even seem to register.

Baal Gharron seemed oddly pleased with me, her mandibles rubbing together in delight as she said, "You have seen the races of Amaranth and heard the lies that the Solar Court spin about them. Have you chosen a form? A fleshy form, my sweetness?"

"I want to be a Faun. Definitely. I never want to be too weak to stand up for myself ever again."

She let out a soothing rumble that I realized was a laugh. "A wise choice. The Chagnar were the first race of Amaranth, living joyfully in anarchy. Joy, sweetness. They were the first to worship us, and they remain our most devoted. You really were meant for us, little one."

From amidst the pillar of light, the first of the Solar Eternals emerged, tall, lithe, and beautiful. She was an Alvaren with straight jet-black hair long enough to flow down and hide her nakedness. Guess somebody fell for the sales pitch on that one—hook, line, and sinker. Her skin was so white that she looked ethereal, even here amongst literal ghosts. The next wisp zipped past her bare figure and plunged into the pillar of light without hesitation. No body, no hormones, no ogling. That was interesting.

Still, I wasn't quite ready to take the plunge back into the world of flesh just yet. "Okay, I get that we're tight for time here, but can you two give me a quick uh… tutorial for this whole Eternal thing?"

Losna was still close enough that his brimstone breath was fluttering the flames of my spirit. "Enough questions. Make flesh. Bind spirit. Slay foes. Please Patron. Earn Glory."

I drifted away from the crazy dragon until I was brushing against Baal Gharron's closest leg. Weird to think of a giant spider as soothing, but any port in a storm, right? "You shall speak in tongues so that all may know your words, sweetness. You shall know the touch of death, but only for a moment before you are reborn beneath the earth of Amaranth. Once a shrine has been built in your honor, you shall return there, but until then, all of the world is your grave and the soil from which you shall spring renewed. Flesh and blood and bone, alive."

Better build a shrine fast if I didn't want to end up doing the grand tour of the whole planet. "Okay, so I respawn. Does that cost anything?"

Like an encouraging kindergarten teacher, the giant spider bobbed her head along as I spoke. "All of your Glory shall pass from you with each death, sweetness, a bounty for your slayer. Wealth and plunder shall pass from you also. Physical possessions shall remain where your corpse has faded."

The second Eternal emerged from the pillar of sun-fire. A Dvergar. Half the height of the Alvaren girl but twice as broad. His skin was a rich chestnut brown, his beard not quite long enough to hide his dangling Dvergar-hood. I was stuck staring for a moment before I jogged my mouth back into action. "Glory?"

"When you are made an Eternal, we are not only granting a fraction of our power, we are setting you on the path to godhood. When your deeds echo throughout Amaranth, Glory is the reward, sweetness. Through crystalizing your Glory, the Pillars of Divinity are empowered, and you ascend."

And I don't lose Pillars when I die, just unspent glory. I was pretty sure I'd played a game like that before. The gamble of spending your experience fast instead of saving up for something better. "So I get my god powers by spending glory?"

"You ascend through the Tiers of Glory and the Pillars of Divinity, but your "god powers," as you call them, are skills. Skills that mortals could never achieve, sweetness."

Another mechanic to learn. "So there are skills too?"

Losna was inching closer and closer to me the longer we spoke, a glow building in his throat. I didn't want to be here when it came out. I didn't think that I could die right now, what with me already being dead, but I was fairly confident that dragon fire wasn't going to do anything good to me.

Baal Gharron was keeping up that ignorance is bliss act, ignoring the serpent in our midst, dribbling venom to sizzle on the floor. "All that live can improve their skills with practice and develop new ones by investing the experience that they have earned into knowledge, sweetness. You shall outlast them all, so you are limitless."

I tried to move farther from the Wyrm, but I found that the comforting interlock of legs behind me also served as a cage. I was trapped in here with the dragon, trying to maintain focus. "Experience and glory are different things?"

Losna was growling so loud I had to strain to hear Baal Gharron's answer. "Mortals can learn and grow, but Glory comes only unto the divine. Divine like you, sweetness."

Okay, Skills, Experience, Glory, Pillars. I'd played much more confusing games than this before. "What about the stats—the Potency and Celerity and? …"

The spider's great fangs snapped forward and latched onto Losna's neck. The serpentine body bucked and flailed, but everywhere it had coiled around the spider's legs it now found itself trapped. She gave one firm shake, then dropped the dragon god to the ground where it lay limp and seething. "As your skills improve and evolve, so in harmony shall your attributes grow, sweetness. In this, mortals are limited in what they can achieve, Eternals are not. You are boundless, my sweetness."

Writhe as it might, the wyrm did not rear up again, lying before the spider goddess in a display of submission, but it did hiss. "Time through. Flesh now."

The insane dragon god had a point. The last of the Solar Eternals was being stitched together as we spoke, and I didn't want to miss the last bus to Amaranth. "Okay, I'm ready. Let's do this. Do I get to choose what I look like or is it—"

Baal Gharron interrupted me. "We shall weave flesh to best suit your spirit and bind it with a name, my sweetness. You shall be mighty, and fearsome, and ours. Ours. Your skin shall be the grey of long shadows, and your eyes shall burn with the moon's fire."

"Is that optional because if I could go incognito sometimes it might be—"

This time I was cut off by the sudden blinding light surrounding me—so bright I could see nothing beyond it. So bright that I felt like it was tearing what little was left of my soul apart. Who I had been was gone. What I was going to be came scorching out of the light. Everything that made me *me* remained, but everything else seared away. My old name was the last piece of me to be burned away. It was the capstone on the complete destruction of what I was before, and the deepest hole in the foundation of what I would now become.

The light faded, and I was left looking down into Baal Gharron's face. Giant as she was, I was level with her now. I reached up with my new, thick fingers and touched the blackened tips of the horns I could just barely make out at the periphery of my vision. When I brushed them with my finger, I could feel them stretching all the way up to my skull where they were rooted. That was going to take some getting used to. I drew in my first breath with my new lungs and tasted the vanilla and acrid venom in the air.

Muscles rippled beneath my skin—more than I'd ever had in my last life, and more than any bodybuilder I could remember seeing either. My skin was grey, but it shimmered with an almost metallic hint. Not grey like a dead thing, but grey like a mineral. Like I was a mountain that could move. A force of nature. My new voice was much deeper, not gravelly but resonant, like the pounding of a war-drum. I reached out and cupped the spider-god's mandible-clacking face between my hands. "Thank you."

Baal Gharron seemed startled, jerking her face out of my grasp. Maybe touching gods was frowned upon. Maybe I was about to get smote. Smitten? But when she bashfully replied, "You are welcome, my sweetness," while brushing at her face with a forelimb, I realized that if spiders could blush, she would have been pink.

Now that I had flesh again, I could feel the heat radiating out of Losna's face. It was like being next to an open blast furnace. The same went for my body as well now that I had all the glands I needed to feel properly intimidated by the dragon and properly worried about searing my eyebrows off, assuming I'd grown some. Another thing to check out later. A glance down revealed plentiful wiry black body hair, so singeing hair wasn't off the agenda completely.

Losna's interest in me seemed to have switched now that I had a body, and their eyes raked up and down me with something like hunger. I caught myself trying to cover my nether regions with my hands. The wyrm barked. "Patron now. He must choose. Must choose me. Look at him. Built for slaughter. Blood and war. Mine. Mine."

Once more Baal Gharron tried to fend her compatriot away from me so that the grown-ups could speak. "Each of us is a god of chaos, my sweetness, a god of the wild and the moon. Yet each of us governs a different aspect of chaos."

Losna went on barking behind her legs. "Mine! Mine!"

The spider did not sigh, but it seemed to be a struggle. "Losna is the god of war. To accept his patronage means your greatest victories will be won on the battlefield. His gifts will make you stronger, faster, and more skilled with the blade and the bow the more Glory you bring to him."

That sounded good, but I wasn't sure I wanted to be beholden to a deranged lizard for all of eternity. "What about you?"

"Me? My sweetness? I am the one that the Solar Court hates the most because I am the one whose power commands them most frequently. I am the ties that bind all living things. The bondage that cannot be escaped and obeys no logic. I am their love and their hate and their passion above all else. Passion, my sweetness. The one thing that no demand for order can crush."

So my only options were snakey-fights-a-lot or an eternity of whips and chains. At least this new body could pull off an all-leather outfit.

Baal Gharron pressed on without a breath. "My patronage gives you influence over those you meet. You will change minds with words, with thoughts, with just a look, my sweetness. You shall inflame passions. Turn foes into friends. Rule over others by the strength of your heart. Your heart."

Heart power. Great. Just what I wanted when I got this bad-ass warrior body.

"*There is another choice.*"

That sounded like the voice of Death again, but that particular spooky scary skeleton seemed to have vanished somewhere in the middle of my reincarnation. Maybe all that life being created offended him. Or maybe I just couldn't see him now that I had a body again. I didn't even have a chance to thank him. How much are you meant to tip your reaper?

Losna and Baal Gharron had fallen silent. As had all the other gods and Eternals. Silence echoed through the halls, broken only by the soft padding of leathery feet somewhere off in the deep shadows. "*There are three great gods of the moon. Not two.*"

That voice. It was coming closer. Each step setting the ground trembling. Each breath rumbling with a growl. A smell swept through the halls ahead of the coming of the god—a smell rich and earthy, sharp with pine sap. The forest seemed to flow into the spaces between the marble walls, filling everywhere with the scent of the wild. I opened my mouth to make a dumb-ass remark and realized that I didn't have any to make.

The wolf opened its eyes, and the moon shone out, blinding bright. Baal Gharron and Losna were dwarfed in the shadow of this looming darkness. My new body barely came up to this god's shaggy chin.

"*I am Chernghast, The Wolf that Waits. I am the inevitable.*"

The stare, the voice, it all paralyzed me, pinning me in place as the wolf stalked ever closer. Chernghast was still almost invisible in the darkness. Only the hint of white when his eyes or his razor-sharp teeth shone out betrayed his approach.

"*When you decide, I shall be your patron. You shall have powers unmatched. Known as mercy to some and dread to others. You shall stalk Amaranth in my place. You shall be death, you shall grow strong on the taste of it, and death shall follow with you.*"

He was close enough now that I could see him clearly. Baal Gharron had scuttled off, and Losna had slunk away like a worm. I didn't even see them go; I couldn't turn away. Even the glow of the Solar Court gods had dimmed in Chernghast's presence. He was the wolf that all other wolves were based on, the one that they all dreamed that they would be when they grew up. His body was muscled and sleek beneath a coat as black as night. I could barely even think when he was this close. Terror vying with some other emotion that I'd only briefly brushed against in my past life. Awe.

I was nodding my head. What this guy had was what I wanted. Power radiated off him. Enough to silence even the Solar blowhards with nothing but his presence. "*You must say the words. You must ask me to take you.*"

My mouth was dry and my lungs quivering, but I managed to wheeze out the words he asked for. "Be my patron. Please. I want you to. I...I need you to."

Those big white eyes filled up my whole world. The light of the moon pouring out of this ancient forest god and into my head, filling me up, lighting me up. His voice was there in my head with the light. Echoing. Deafening. Maddening. "*You shall be alone in Amaranth. The only Lunar Eternal to be born in millennia without reckoning. You shall be bound to death, loved by death, empowered by death. But the charnel path cannot be walked with others. You shall have no family, no brothers or sisters. Only yourself. Destruction shall be your gift and your only companion. So this I name you, Maulkin. Brother only to slaughter.*"

My ears were ringing, and my vision came back only slowly, first as shadows, then as shapes, then finally in full detail. Chernghast had gone back to his place in the shadows, Baal Gharron was looming over my prone body like a clicking mother hen. Even Losna seemed concerned for my welfare, in the sense that they'd coiled around my body in a wide circle and were hissing and spitting wrath at everyone except me. Aww, they really did care. I got back to my feet as fast as I could manage. None of the other Eternals seemed to have fallen down when they were getting named, so I had already managed to mark myself as the weirdo of the group. Although the whole "opposite sides of a celestial war" thing probably had an impact on our potential friendships too.

The room seemed a lot brighter now. All the shadows receded, and it only took me a moment to realize it was because light was now coming out of my eyes. I had wondered why they kept the place so dim before, but I suppose when you are one big flashlight, it makes sense to save on the electric bill.

You are mine now, Maulkin. Let us see what you are made of.

Knowledge suddenly burst like a pulsar into my head, setting me staggering all over again. I knew things I had no way of knowing. I knew Amaranth. The scents, the sounds, the taste of the water, and the sound of the wind. More than that though, I knew myself.

Maulkin – Chagnar Faun of the Lunar Court – 1st Tier of Glory
Statistics:
   HP: 300/300
   Devotion: 200/200
   Glory: 300
Attributes:
   Potency: 18
   Celerity: 17
   Vitality: 11

Piety: 4
Skills:
None
Traits:

Relentless: *The Faun are the greatest hunters on Amaranth, known for pursuing prey for days or even weeks at a time before closing in to strike.*
Effect: *Faun are immune to fatigue, their Attributes do not degrade over time without rest.*

Acolyte of Chernghast: *Chosen by the wolf that waits, you bear his invisible mark and walk the path that will someday make you the personification of inevitable death.*
Effect: *The presence of the dead reinvigorates you. For every corpse within your Sphere of Influence, all of your attributes are increased by 1.*

4 unallocated attribute points remaining.

It was me, broken down into numbers and words. Everything about me was there to see the moment I turned my attention inwards. The moonlight inside me illuminated it all. Concentrating on the bit about unallocated points to spend seemed to slow the world around me down to a crawl so I could focus on what I was doing. I didn't even need to give it a second thought. It was all going into Potency.

Attributes:
Potency: 22
Celerity: 17
Vitality: 11
Piety: 4

With a little flare of light behind my eyes, the number changed, and so did I. The muscles all over me thickened again, bulging and stretching out my skin in a sudden surge of raw power. I felt like I could tear this whole place apart with my bare hands, brick by brick. It passed fast, but I could already see how addictive that rush was going to get.

Eosphel was the one to spoil the afterglow, booming out, "Eternals, someday you may ascend to join us here in these celestial courts. Earn Glory, gain power, remake Amaranth in our image. Serve us well and ascend. Fail us, and fall into obscurity."

Stick and carrot all in one go. Maybe he was the god of pep talks and middle managers?

Baal Gharron nudged me to turn and face the braying ass, whispering in my ear, "Be ready, my sweetness."

"The time has come for your quests to begin. Farewell, Eternals."

Bilaphel surged forward, morning-stars sweeping in an arc, trailing light like comets. First, the Alvaren caught a blow right in her gorgeously sculpted face. It wasn't so pretty afterward. It was a caved-in gory mess, smoking at the edges. The body I'd just started admiring collapsed like a heap of wet noodles.

Her cut-off cry of surprise gave the others a chance to respond, but they weren't quick enough. The Dvergar tried to run, but Bilaphel clubbed him down with a backhanded lash as he passed. Blood splattered and sizzled across the marble floor.

The white-haired human woman and the blue-scaled Inyoka didn't run. They tried to stand their ground—for all the good that it did them. Bilaphel moved too fast for the eyes to follow. So fast that a trail of flames was left in their wake. The human was split in half at waist height by the arc of sun-bright flame. The Inyoka fared ever so slightly better, ducking under the first sweep of the morning-star only to be caught by the other across the chest. I could have lived a long and happy life never knowing what his insides looked like.

I wasn't going down like a chump to that flashy bronze dick. I might not have had weapons, but I had arms big enough to punch out a reasonably sized elephant. Let him come for me and see what happened to him.

Turns out, I should have been paying less attention to the tin-can man and more attention to the spider on my back. Baal Gharron's fangs slipped into my shoulder so smoothly I didn't even feel them at first, pulsing as her venom flooded into me. At once, the light in my eyes seemed to go out. Darkness rushed in all around me as I died for the second time in a day.

You'd think that practice would make perfect, but of my two deaths, getting dissolved from the inside out by spider venom was actually a lot worse. The two points where the fangs were stuck in me were blessedly numb, but it felt like lava was being piped into everything else. As fast as I'd gained all my new strength it faded away. I was only standing because she had me impaled.

"Die now, my sweetness. So sweet… So sweet… Die and live again. And again. And again…"

CHAPTER 4

When I woke up, everything stayed dark. The pain was gone. The burning and freezing vanished in a moment, but it was replaced with some new sensations that I didn't love either. Mostly weight, pressing in on me from all sides. Darkness, weight, and no air to breathe. My lungs were straining and heaving with no success. Where the hell was I? What the hell was happening?

I probably would have died all over again if it hadn't been for Chernghast's voice in my head.

Rise from your grave.

It all came back to me in a flash, and the second that I realized that I was buried alive, my arms started moving. Mechanically at first, then with more haste, more power. Muscles straining and groaning. Lungs burning all the way. When I broke the surface and my fingers found nothing but air and blades of grass, I might have let out a little moan of delight—if I'd had any air left to do it.

With one hand out, it should have been as easy as pulling myself up and out, but I had no such luck. No sooner did I breakthrough did something up there then grab onto my wrist, its claws digging into my skin. The rest of me might have still been stuck in the dark, but whatever was up there must have been too hungry to wait. It was trying to pull me up like a turnip.

Well, this vegetable was going to bite back.

I pulled back against the grip, using this new enemy's footing to haul myself up and pulling them off balance—they weren't as big as me. I doubted many people would be now. Once my head broke through the dirt, I gasped in my first breath of Amaranth. It tasted like soil and camphor. The sky above was vast, rich, and purpled with sunset. That was all the time I had for sightseeing before the fighting started.

Most of my grappler's slim body was concealed by a hooded sack-cloth cassock, but I could see the hand latched onto me. Scaly, pale as a flat-worm, and just as clammy to the touch. This dude had serious evil minion vibes.

I jerked my arm out of his grip, slamming both of my fists down onto the packed earth to haul myself up and out in one motion. The body-farmer skittered back out of reach, and I didn't blame him. Hauling something as big as me out the ground was a ridiculous show of strength that would have had me running for my life, at least in my old life, but I didn't wait to see if intimidation was going to work. I put my head down and charged.

Slick as oil, he slipped under my outspread arms, like he knew where I was going to be before I did. At this point, he probably did. This new body of mine handled like a boat. When I missed him, I plowed right by and slammed into the rocky outcropping that over-looked this little patch of dirt. With my bulldozer-like momentum behind me, a human would have snapped their neck like a twig. Instead, I just hit the rock with an echoing thump. It hurt, but it didn't drop me.

[Health 286/300]

"At this moment in time, I am not your enemy, Eternal."

Growling at the pain, I charged back in the first moment I could see straight. "That is…"

And missed again.

"Weirdly…"

And again.

"Specific…"

And again.

"Phrasing!"

I'd turned the first charge into a haymaker that should have snapped him in two. He sidestepped it contemptuously. Punch after punch I grazed by the frayed edge of his robes, never quite hitting. Always a moment too slow.

There was a tail swishing behind him for counterbalance, and every once in a while, I caught a glimpse of a scaly snout under the hood. When his scaled skin poked out into the dusk light he was opalescent, and some little bit of my newfound knowledge of Amaranth was whispering to me that paleness wasn't right.

Even now, the damn lizard didn't seem to be all that ruffled. "All truths can become lies with time, Eternal. I speak only of this moment when I would aid you, not do you harm. There are those who know me as the White Prophet. Such a name will serve at this time."

My blood was pumping, but I could see that I was getting nowhere throwing punches. This really wasn't fair. Giving me an awesome fighting monster body and then putting me up against literal gods and slithery lizard men that I couldn't even touch. "What do you want?"

"To guide you to your purpose. To instruct you in the use of your gifts. "

To point me at whoever he didn't like and fire me off like a cannon. Figures. It seemed that everyone in this new afterlife wanted to use me for something. "How did you find me? Even I didn't know where I was going to be...born."

"There are those of us in this world who can read the ebbs and flows of fate as others see the coming of the tide. Those who can look to the patterns of the past and predict..."

I let my fists ease down to my sides. My head still hurt, but I wasn't going to let this snake see me hurting. Predators pick off the injured first. The wolf had gobbled me because I was out of breath.

I wasn't going to make that mistake twice in one day. "You can see the future. Got it."

"Neither mortal nor god can see the true shape of things to come, Eternal." He gestured grandly to the sky. "I study prophecy and the stars, but those are but long shadows cast by the great events of the future."

"Prophecy, stars, shadows. Got it." I stretched my arms out to their full breadth and drew in a deep breath, finding that even after all my digging and punching, my arms weren't tired. I could get used to this. "So what is my first lesson? Let's get the tutorial out of the way so I can start whooping wyrms."

His eyes never left me. Yellow so pale they were almost white, but slit vertically with a line of black, they twitched and narrowed as he studied every detail of my face. "Let us first acquaint you with the limits of your new flesh and serve our second purpose also."

Demanding that I do his bidding less than a minute after I stopped trying to hit him? That was quicker than anticipated. "Which is?"

He gestured to the shovel laying in the long grass beside my grave. "We must retrieve the other Eternals before they expire."

Why does the new guy always have to do all the hard manual labor?

For all my grumbling, which now sounded so deep in my chest that it was practically seismic, I didn't actually mind the digging all that much. I expected it to be the same miserable slog as having to do hard work back in my old life, but with this body and the new rules of engagement the little aches pains and strains never showed up since my stamina was now governed by statistics rather than something more nebulous.

It also helped that in this world, hard work actually paid off. As I dug, there was a tickle in the back of my brain, the spinning of a counter up from the grand total of zero experience that I'd come into the world with. To start with, it clicked up by one with every shovelful of dirt. Then it slowed gradually until it was only clicking every fifteen or twenty. It had already jumped up from my abortive fight with tall, white, and handsome. Even when I missed, I'd ended up learning something from the attempt.

Hah, here I was. I'd been an agent of the gods for all of five minutes, and I already sounded like I belonged on a motivational poster. Next, I'd be dangling off a branch and telling people to hang in there.

The ground here was rough, layers of clay under the topsoil. There were dry grass and huge chunks of old masonry sunken down within that and lumps of stone that had to be pried out and tossed aside. Either I was even stronger than I'd thought to plow through all this on my way up, or the others were buried deeper. Or white-snake over there was talking a load of nonsense, and I was the only one popping up in this particular field. I was starting to believe that it was the last option when the blade of my shovel nearly went right through an upraised hand.

It was pale, slender, feminine. Probably not the Dvergar or the lizard. Yet there was a rosiness to that hand that didn't match up to what I remembered of the Alvaren. I grabbed the wrist and pulled, hauling up the skinny white-haired human girl that I'd caught a glimpse of back in the Celestial Court. Thankfully, the gods had seen fit to toss some rags on our bodies before we sprung up because this situation was awkward enough without nudity. Just like me, she came up swinging. Unlike me, she could actually hit the person who'd pulled her out of the ground.

She was basically dangling in my grip, so she didn't have much leverage, but she also had both her legs free and clear. She twisted her whole body, slamming a foot into my temple. On a human, it would have been devastating. In this situation, she probably hurt her foot more than she hurt me.

Sighing loudly, I dropped her on her head in the freshly turned soil, just to make a point. "Last time I'm helping you."

She'd turned the head-drop into a roll and was on her knees, ready to spring up again before she spluttered out, "You talk?"

"Better than you kick."

Her pretty little face had been all twisted up with stress and fury until now, but the minute I said that, it did what it was made for. Smirking. Maybe her eyes would have sparkled. Instead, they just flared white-hot for a moment.

When I held out my hand to help her up, she took it. "I'm Maulkin, I guess."

"They called me Mercy."

"Ironically?" I tried out a smirk of my own, wishing I had a mirror to see how it looked on this new face.

"Listen, pal, you're a big scary-looking monster, and I just got buried alive. That's enough to make anyone twitchy."

I handed her my shovel with a grin. "You can make it up to me by helping dig out the others."

One by one, we hauled up the Eternals from the Inyoka's little vegetable patch. I caught the other Inyoka by the tail and hauled him ass-first into his new life, then we moved on to the last patch while Mercy and the Prophet struggled together to pull the Alvaren girl out. We heard her more than saw her. It had been a couple of minutes now, and I was starting to worry about the little guy still under the ground. He wouldn't die permanently if we didn't get to him in time, but who knew where he'd pop up again.

The blue-scaled Inyoka and I didn't have much time for chatter while we worked. We traded names—he was Asher—but that was the extent of the pleasantries. I'd finally worked up a sweat, though there was still no weakness or real signs that I was starting to tire.

We must have been halfway down to the Dvergar when Asher dove to the ground and a shovel cracked into the back of my head.

I'm not too proud to admit I ate dirt. My thick skull saved me from serious injury, but my ears rang, and the force of the blow knocked me over. I was getting really tired of this crap, and I'd only been alive for a few minutes.

By the time I was up, everyone was yelling. The Alvaren was the one swinging for me, shouting something about me being "The enemy."

The other two Eternals were yelling right back at her, the albino snake man was sidling away, and despite all the noise that they were making, I couldn't help but notice that none of them were actually stepping in between the crazy lady with a spade and me. This was a new world, with new rules. Maybe she was right? Maybe we were meant to kill each other on sight. It didn't feel right to me though.

I used my own spade like a crutch to get back to my feet and groaned, "What was that for?"

The Alvaren's golden gaze snapped back to me, her eyes narrowed, and she charged. She cleared the distance faster than you could blink. At the last moment, she leapt. I barely got the haft of my own shovel up to catch the blade of hers as it descended.

New Skill Discovered! [Combat]
Combat: Rank 1/10
34 Experience Gained

Even with all my strength, the blow would have ripped the shovel from my hands, so I just let it happen. Instead of getting hauled off balance, I let the shovel fall away between our bodies and grabbed for her instead. She was quick, but not as quick as the Inyoka.

My arms wrapped around her lithe body, and I squeezed. Her arms were pinned to her sides. Her superior speed was useless in a bear hug. Struggle as she might, it was inevitable now. I cuddled her close until the bones of her ribcage started to creak, and the spade fell useless from her fingers. Her eyes burned huge, so close to my face

I was surprised I couldn't feel the heat. I certainly felt the heat of the rest of her pressed up against me.

Exerting this much pressure without going further and truly doing damage was harder than it looked. It was a constant balancing act between the danger of her slipping free and the natural instinct to crush the life out of her for sucker-shoveling me. I grunted, "If I wanted you dead, I'd have left you for the worms."

"What you want doesn't matter. The gods told us that you had to die." She strained against me, kicking my knees as if that were going to make me drop her. "So die."

The albino Inyoka finally stepped up. "The stars have aligned to bring you all here. Of all Amaranth, you have been born together, here. Do you not wonder why? Do you not wish to hear the answers that only I can give you."

She stopped wriggling and looked around at her fellow Solar Eternals, expecting them to jump to her defense. Shame I'd just hauled them kicking and screaming into the world, and their loyalties were a bit shaky. Mercy rolled her eyes. "We can always start murdering each other after we've heard what the White Prophet has to say."

Asher just shrugged. Murdering me or not murdering me, it was apparently all the same to him. Thanks for that, Asher. I'll remember that next time you're buried alive and digging sideways instead of up. Still, that shrug seemed to do the trick. She stopped writhing about and let me carefully place her down.

There was a long tense moment as I waited to see if she tried to kill me again, but when the attempted murder didn't arrive, I asked, "Can we dig up the little guy now?"

We were almost too late as it turned out. The shouting and spading match had stolen the vital minutes before the Dvergar began to suffocate, and it was only thanks to his species prodigious endurance that he survived until we could reach him. He couldn't even speak by the time we hauled him out, the poor Dvergar alternating between coughing up clods of dirt and weeping incessantly, leaving two little trails down his face that weren't covered in soil and a grimy-looking snot bubble on his stubbly lip.

The Prophet looked him over where he lay, tail lashing with concern. "Let us move him inside. He needs time to recover, and this is not a safe place."

I gave the Alvaren the stink eye. "No kidding."

Now that the initial panic had passed, I was able to take in the sights. I'd kind of expected some gentle starting area with a friendly village and friendly gnomes or something, but instead, we were treated to desolation. Beyond the scrubby grass and the withered old camphor trees hiding in the lee of the low cliff-face I'd faceplanted into, there really wasn't much to see. The dying light wasn't as much of an impediment as it could have been, thanks to my built-in torch eyes, but it still sapped visibility over by the shadowed horizon where literally anything interesting might have been hiding.

There were dark patches that might have been low cliffs or even a forest. The thing that stood out to me the most was that this was not some artfully designed theme park wilderness like the one I'd gone hiking in before or a pristine park with careful rows of trees and plants. No human hands, or any other creature's for that matter, had shaped this land. The rain and the wind had swept through, battering the earth below. The earth had stood up for itself where it could. And over the top of all that tumult, life had clung on.

As a troupe, we carried the Dvergar up and around the ridge, although I could probably have tucked him under one arm and been done with it. Beneath our feet, there were glimpses of stone protruding from the packed soil, worked and carved, then clotted up with moss over the years until they were indistinguishable from the shale.

Sitting back from the ridge, hidden from our view when we struggled out of the dirt, was a low-slung building. It was part ruin, part ramshackle work of hastily hammered together boards. The crowning achievement of the thing was a dome—the only pristine part of the construction—smooth and broken only by the telescope poking up out of it. An observatory.

Getting close, I could see the crooked hanging door of the place had been another late addition, but the stonework was still that same ancient work of engraving that we'd been walking all over. Great smooth whorls were cut into the stone, and I let my fingers trail over them as I ducked through the door. My skin was almost a match for the grey of the stone, and my thick fingers looked like part of the engravings for the moment I paused. Better not to think about that too long.

Inside, the floorboards had all rotted away, leaving that same scrubby grass and dirt. There was only one grand old room, patched all over the place and every part of it surrounding the colossal telescope. There was a little cot bed set up in one corner. It didn't have any covers on it despite the chill of the night air creeping in through all the little cracks and crevasses where the walls didn't quite join up, but that was probably a cold-blooded thing. There was a haphazard hearth in another corner, smearing the roof above it with soot. Everywhere else was a scattered array of bizarre instruments I guessed had to do with stellar observation, the tools surrounded by or partially covered by reams upon reams of yellowed paper. Stacked up on every flat surface in the place, I could see that they were all filled with scribbled ciphers and astronomical symbols that even my new brain couldn't decipher. Books seemed to be few and far between, treated with more reverence than the scribbled notes, and placed on high shelves that looked liable to fall off the wall if you sneezed too hard. Basically, it looked like some madman's shack, and if it weren't for the fact that the White Prophet was literally the first and only person I'd met on this planet,

I'd have been sidling towards the door about now, remembering that I'd left the cat on the stove.

The other Eternals, on the other hand, seemed to take the madhouse's appearance in stride. I saw Mercy make a face when we first got in the room, but the moment the duo of Inyoka turned to face us, she wiped it away fast. The Prophet started to ramble. "As all places and things are temporal and limited to the moment that we encounter them, so too is this one. I have been here but a short time, awaiting the precise moment of your coming."

"Yeah, the place hardly looks lived in." I couldn't help myself. Mercy snorted in a very unladylike way but managed to get her face straightened out before the Prophet looked her way again.

He ignored us, pushing back his hood for the first time and exposing his distinctly serpentine face. Asher looked closer to an iguana or something, but this pointed white face reminded me of a milk snake. "There is much that I must tell you. Much that you must know of the past before you can shape the future, but our time together is limited. You have come in a time of great crisis for this world, though most would deny it if they could. They would shelter in lies to protect their own power, pretend that all is as it always has been and doom is not fast approaching."

I clapped my hands, startling the Alvaren. "Okay, history lesson of doom. Let's have it."

She hissed at me. "Will you shut up? The sooner he is done, the sooner we can kill you."

"That really doesn't encourage me to speed things along as much as you'd think."

She lunged for me, and before Mercy and Asher could catch hold of her, she had one hand locked around one of my horns and the other pulled back in a fist.

On reflection, I probably should have just taken the hit and scored some sympathy points with the other Eternals, but this body was hardwired for action, and I really don't like it when people punch me in the face.

I bucked, jerking my head and horns up out of reach and hauling her off her feet. She let out a little yelp, and I was able to catch her by the arm as she fell. "We've got to stop meeting like this. I don't even know your name."

She wasn't so pretty when she was hissing. Alvaren faces seemed to be pretty narrow at the best of times, and the sneer-scowl combo made her look distinctly like a ferret. Mercy piped up. "She's Orphia. I heard Bilaphel name her."

The Prophet's clawed hands were there between us a moment later, pulling Orphia away when I gratefully released her, giving us both some breathing room.

The Dvergar had progressed to wheezing down on the ground, which was probably a sign he was getting better? Asher crouched over him, checking his airways were clear as best he could. "This one is Uthelred. Named by the Queen. He is unwell."

"Choking on dirt will do that to you."

Asher's tail lashed. "He breathes well. I mean his mind. The experiences of the day have damaged him."

Mercy shrugged. "Dying twice in one day would do that for you."

"This fate has oft befallen Eternals throughout history." The Prophet was stoking the fire, beckoning us all closer. "When the weight of memories becomes too great, Eternals retreat from the world. Some into their own minds, and some into the wild places where mortals fear to tread."

So we have trauma-dementia to look forward to. Fantastic. This gig is sounding better by the minute. I dragged my eyes away from the Dvergar, deliberately ignored Orphia, and faced the rest.

The Prophet sank down in front of the fire, coiling his tail over his crossed legs so it didn't burn. "May I continue?"

Begrudgingly, we all settled down for storytime like we were children. All except Orphia, who parked herself up on the stool by the verdigris-green eyepiece of the telescope. Holding herself above the rest of us. What a charmer.

The warmth of the fire was nice after the cold of the grave and the cool wind. A nap might have been in order if it weren't for everyone being out to kill me.

"The Dvergar wanted a god. In the light, we had the sun and moon to guide us, but deep beneath the earth, they sought out the Void. Araphel, the living darkness. He rose, a match for any one of the gods in their courts but bound by none of their rules. He walked Amaranth. He destroyed. All the powers of creation were arrayed against him but found wanting. No mortal power could match him."

"But somebody did." For a change, it was Mercy who butted in. "Somebody killed him."

The Prophet turned from his introspection to face her. "Nobody was there to see him die. Yet his influence seemed to leave the world, so all took it to be the truth that he had been slain. The story goes that some unknown hero confronted the dark one alone and slew him. There is a great blighted land where he was said to have died, and this can still be seen. The Rustlands. Still stained with blood. And at the heart of the blight, a sword, rusted from freshly forged to shards by Araphel's dying curse."

That sucked. Imagine that you finally got it together and killed the big bad dark lord only for it to self-destruct so hard that nobody even knew who won the fight.

"Each shard was taken by one of the peoples who had opposed Araphel. Each one served as their rallying banner and symbol in the days to come. Ownership of a piece of the Rusted Blade became the foundation of dynasties and empires. Yet now all have forgotten that it was once a real weapon. The only weapon to ever wound a god."

As far as clout went, holding a hunk of god-slaying metal probably helped anyone's street cred. I started trying to work out how many pieces there must have been. Humans got one, Alvaren, Dvergar, and Wyrms too, I'd bet. So that was four at least. Would the Eternals get one? Did we count as our own people? Maybe there would be a Q and A at the end of the mad lizard's ramble.

"What is not so widely known is this. Araphel returns. All of the stars and portents warn of his coming. Yet try as the learned might, they cannot convince the ignorant of their doom. He is coming back, and there are none who will stand to oppose him. The Alvaren are gone. The Wyrms hide in seclusion to wait out the age of mortals. The Dvergar cower in their hills, shivering at their last brush with the Void. The humans rule over much of Amaranth now, and they waste that sovereignty by squabbling amongst themselves."

I could feel Orphia staring daggers at me as she asked, "What of the Faun?"

"The Chagnar Faun? Most would welcome Araphel with open arms. A return to the past glories that they still dream of. You shall have no help from them."

With a sigh, the Prophet spread his arms wide. "So it is to the Eternal servants of the divine, that I must turn. You must make ready for the coming of Araphel. You must forge the Rusted Blade anew and turn the only weapon the God ever feared against it once more."

A big fetch quest. Not exactly original, but at least it was pretty straightforward. Find shards. Make sword. Kill god. Easy. I guess now was Q and A time. "How many shards are there?"

"From the histories of the free peoples, we have identified six distinct shards in all. Each granted to one great champion of each race and passed down through the generations."

Asher counted them off on his fingers. "Humans, Dvergar, Alvaren,

Wyrms, Eternals, and… Faun?"

The Prophet nodded, but there was no way that Orphia was letting that one slip by without comment. "Why the hell would they give the Faun a shard? They were the enemy."

"The Faun have no written histories, so I do not know for certain—and much of what we know about that time from other sources has been colored by more recent clashes between the free people. Perhaps it was a term of the peace treaty. Perhaps some few Faun fought back against their overlord and this was their reward. None can say for certain. The truth has been lost to time."

"I'd believe they extorted it before I'd believe in a hero Faun." Orphia scoffed.

That was enough for Mercy. "Are you kidding me? How can you already be racist when you didn't even know most of these races existed before today?"

"The gods were very clear about who we should trust, if you had only listened more closely to their guidance."

Asher sighed, and it made all the scales on his body ripple out of place and then back again, like a bird puffing out its feathers. "Can you please let him finish?"

The Prophet had been sitting silently, waiting for us to shut up. Good thing Asher was here, or he might have died of old age. "I shall share what I can with you about the last-known locations of the Shards, but first I would prepare you for your task more thoroughly. The powers of the Eternals are not widely known, but I have made a study of the few texts available so that I might better instruct you in the gifts that you have received."

This was starting to sound more like it. A quick blast of tutorial junk to learn how skills, the Divine Pillars, and Glory worked, and then we could get out there and start kicking ass.

The Prophet moved from sitting to standing in one fluid motion like he'd just come up out of a toaster. "Come with me, and your first lesson shall begin."

At his direction, I dragged the cot out into the middle of the room and revealed a trapdoor. It was thick old wood, not the new stuff that the building had been patchworked with. This had been part of the original structure before the prophet slapped an observatory on top. It took all my strength to haul the thing open. Stairs stretched down into the darkness, and he led us down in single file, Orphia at the front and me bringing up the rear with a Dvergar over my shoulder. A buffer of two sane people between me and the Alvaren seemed smart. I didn't want to give her any opportunities to stab me in the back.

Up on the surface, this building wasn't all that impressive. I mean, it was kind of impressive that it was still standing and that it could support the weight of the observatory dome despite being 50% stone and 50% crumbles.... Anyway, the point is, this place was like the proverbial iceberg—not a lot up top but huge beneath the surface. The stairs led into a long corridor which then twisted, turned, and branched out. If any one of us wasn't lost by the time we came to the big, dank cellar where we stopped then I would have been surprised.

"From my tomes, I have learned that you came from other worlds and lived other lives before being chosen to come here. There has been much debate about the meaning of this among scholars."

The cellar was different from any I'd ever known. The piles of miscellaneous crap and broken lawnmowers were missing. Even the big barrels of booze that I'd been hoping for were conspicuous in their absence. I'd been looking forward to seeing how wine-drunk a Faun could get.

The Prophet rambled on. "All that is known for certain is that the laws of those worlds were different from those here, and the life lessons learned differed along the same lines."

Now that we were stopped, my eyes began adjusting to the darkness, flaring a little more moonlight. It was definitely an empty room. The stone walls showed the same whorls as I'd seen upstairs, but the floor was made up of tiles instead of the flagstones or packed dirt of the previous corridors. A great big mosaic depiction of a dragon and a giant bird of prey wrestling with each other. Hot.

"Yup." Mercy was crouched down, studying the mosaic inch by inch like it was hiding secrets. "Things were definitely different back on Earth."

"Then let me be the first to share the most vital lesson to your survival on Amaranth." The Prophet ran a clawed finger over one of the great whorls on the wall, one indistinguishable from all the rest to my eyes but apparently special judging by the way that it suddenly started to glow green.

"Do not trust anyone."

The tiles of the floor, which had been solid as a rock beneath our feet just a moment ago, fell apart with the sound of shattering glass.

Every tile rained down around us as we plummeted into the darkness. The last I saw of the White Prophet, he was standing on the one patch of paper-thin tiles that hadn't moved as we tumbled into the pit below.

Then even my eyes couldn't pierce the darkness anymore.

CHAPTER 5

Did I mention that I was getting really tired of this crap?

We were only falling for a moment, but it seemed to stretch out endlessly. Mercy was tumbling head over heels, and Asher had spread-eagled himself to try to land flat. The only one falling with any sort of grace was Orphia, arms outstretched and feet pointed down—like she was falling on purpose.

I wasn't sure when it happened, but I'd wrapped myself around the Dvergar so that he wouldn't get mangled on landing. I guess I felt protective of the little guy.

We hit the stone floor together. I landed on my back, the rebounding dead weight of Uthelred hammering into my chest in a pincer movement of pain.

[Health 191/300]

From the moans around me, I guessed that the others had just been introduced to their health scores for the first time. I rolled the Dvergar off me with some of my very own grunts and grumbles. "Wish you'd wake up, little guy."

By the time that we were vaguely upright, the tiles were fluttering back up to form a distant roof. The room down here was bigger than the one upstairs, but rusted metal bars ran along the length of it, separating us from the extended part and the door that led out of this new prison. There was no gate on our cage, and judging from the bones scattered around the place, there was not meant to be. There was no way in or out now that we'd been dropped.

I scooped up a human skull and threw it at the roof, round about where the Prophet had been standing, but all it did was shatter and shower us all with bone meal. I didn't think it would actually work, but if I didn't try then I'd never be certain.

Orphia was quick to take the opportunity to blame me for getting dust in her hair. "Idiot."

"I didn't see you spotting the trap either." I was feeling sore and petty. Can you blame me?

Mercy had landed worse than the rest of us. She was still sitting down, nursing a bleeding nose and trying to will away the dizziness. Despite that, she was still aware enough to reach out and grab Orphia's leg as she charged at me yet again. There was quite the crunch when that pretty Alvaren face met the flagstones. Now both of them had nosebleeds.

They scrambled to their feet, ready to fight, but Asher was already there with his clawed hands up, ready to intervene. "This is not the time to fight amongst ourselves."

I liked the sentiment there, but honestly, it seemed like it was probably the best time to fight among ourselves. It wasn't like there was anything else to keep us entertained down here. Oubliettes don't get cable tv.

"What do you think you are doing?"

While Mercy and Orphia had the beginnings of a good screaming match, albeit one that sounded a bit nasal after their falls, I went to take a look at the bars. If they were as rusted through as they looked, they might not be any more of an impediment than a beaded curtain.

"From the minute we got here you've been looking down your pointy nose at us..."

The bars were pretty solid underneath the top layers of crumbling orange and brown—spaced close enough that even one of the waifish races wouldn't have been able to squeeze through. I took a hold of them and flexed my new muscles. All that Potency had to count for something.

"The fact that you are so ready to cast aside your divinely ordained duty, simply because it is convenient in the moment, is…"

I strained and strained with all of my strength, and I could feel movement in the metal. The bars thrummed with the pressure as my arms began to shake. I was strong now. I could do this. The old me might have struggled to open a pack of tortilla chips like this but I was Maulkin.

Sweat prickled my brow, but the bars did not bend. My shoulders began to scream, and still, the bars did not bend. With one last heave, I put everything that I had into pulling the bars apart, and…they did not bend. Whatever Potency I needed to bend metal with my bare hands, I just wasn't there yet.

I turned my attention inward, and once more the world around me seemed to slow. The nasal whine of Orphia's bitching turning into a solid bass note. I pulled up all the information that this new world provided me about myself but skimmed past the stats, racial attributes, and the single skill point I'd acquired in Combat. There had to be more here. We were Eternals from the moment we landed on Amaranth, it wasn't something that we earned with time, so surely they wouldn't have dumped us here, powerless.

I stopped on The Pillars of Divinity and gave it my full attention—the way that I had the Eosphel's holograms. Only a moment was all it took for the text to blossom out into a vision that filled my entire mind. I was on some great dark plane with only a few pinpricks of moonlight shining around my feet—a light so faint it would have been invisible if I were not surrounded by such deep shadows. There were seven pinpricks in all. Seven tiny stars on the ground. I closed my distance with the first of them, and that strange text that the gods used whispered up out of it.

Cosmos – The shaping of reality.

I stepped on to the next.

Omnis – The knowledge of all things.

These were the different pillars. The different types of power I'd be able to unlock with Glory.

Ascension – The rebirth of the self.
Primal – The creation of life.
Aether – The mastery of souls.
Creation – The building of worlds.
Artifice – The remaking of materials.

That last one was what I needed. Not turning into animals to seduce milkmaids, not throwing lightning bolts, and not making things; remaking things. Remaking things like metal bars.

I reached out to touch the light, and it flared to life at my attention. I could feel my hands shaking, even though I had no idea why. I reached out again, and the light turned solid at my touch. With the sound of crushing ice, it hardened into a crystalline pillar, thin as a thread for now, but it was sure to get thicker the more of my Glory I poured in.

Slipping back to view my mental character sheet once more, I could see *Artifice Tier 1* marked down there. I was committed to it now. But even with the Pillar active, I still didn't see any new powers. There had to be something I could use. Some reason for empowering a pillar to start with.

The big spider lady said that my powers would show up as skills once they were unlocked, so I jumped up to that. There were 314 experience points hovering there, just waiting to be spent. I didn't know how much of that came from digging, and how much came from listening to lectures, but either way. I wasn't letting them go to waste.

Skills began to roll out in a huge toilet-paper long list, every single starting skill that you could choose from listed out so fast that I barely had time to recognize them as words before a dozen more had flown by. I stopped the list at random, somewhere in the vicinity of "Igneous Arcanum: 100XP Per Rank" and then started over, concentrating only on the skills that seemed to be glowing with moonlight.

Artifice Tier 1: Rough Hewn Weapons
Artifice Tier 1: Rough Hewn Armor
Artifice Tier 1: Rough Hewn Architecture
Artifice Passive Ability: Sphere of Influence

The passive ability seemed to be tied to the other three, like unlocking them would give you it as a freebie. There certainly wasn't any way to invest in it directly. It would have been nice to say that I considered Architecture or Armor first, but I really didn't. Too many attempts had already been made on my life for me to pick anything else. I needed to be able to fight back, and that meant weapons.

The downside of these *Celestial Skills* was the price tag. Chernghast was whispering to me that they cost three-hundred experience points per rank instead of a hundred. Still, raw experience was probably easy to come by, weapons weren't. I poured my experience into *Rough Hewn Weapons* with a weird tickly sensation in my brain then suddenly I just knew how to use it. The same thing happened with *Sphere of Influence* without having to pony up any more experience, thankfully.

Opening up my eyes, I could now feel everything within that *Sphere* nearby, like my nervous system had just jumped a few feet outside of my body and could now take in all the information I needed from everything around me. I could feel the temperature and pressure of the air. I could taste the iron content in the bars.

It was hard at first, like the first time you moved a muscle you didn't know that you had. I had to strain to draw the iron out of the bars—and strain even harder to turn the small amount of actual metal into something resembling a weapon. I'd been imagining a big sword, like something an anime character would swing around, defying all laws of physics in the process. Instead, I got a cleaver. A hunk of raw metal flattened out into a rectangle and finished down on one side with a chipped and ragged edge. I guess proper swords needed more metal than I had to work with along with somebody doing less *Rough Hewn* work than I was. It didn't matter though. I had something I could use to fight, and three of the bars crumbled away to orange dust on the floor.

Time jumped back to its usual tempo, and I turned to the others just in time to see Mercy ducking under a kick. "Hey!"

My little shout didn't interrupt them for a moment. Orphia was still coming at the other woman with everything she had, and Mercy was still scrambling to get out of the way. Asher was just standing there watching them, and Uthelred was just lying there watching the wall. I was getting the impression I was the only one who was going to do anything.

I charged in to break up the fight, kind of forgetting about the big blade in my hand. It brought Orphia up fast when she saw it.

She backpedaled away from me rapidly, arms outstretched to pull Asher to safety behind her. I guess staying neutral meant he was on her side in her mind. "I tried to warn you fools! He is going to murder us all. He is the enemy."

I bent to give Mercy a hand up, which she took gratefully before we turned to face the other Eternals. "I've found a way out. We can unlock one of the Divine Pillars and pick out a starting skill, I used mine to remove some bars and make this. I can probably make some weapons for all of us if you just…"

"Drop the blade."

"Hey now. I haven't been trying to jump you this whole time."

"Drop the blade or we fight for it, this very moment."Orphia hissed.

The light seemed to have gone out in Asher's eyes. The sunlight dimming until it was barely a glow. His breathing looked like it had stopped too, but it was kind of hard to tell how fast he was meant to be breathing. Did lizards breathe the same as mammals? I wish I'd read more books before I died. Science ones. Not ones with dragons and chainmail bikinis on the cover. Well, more of them too.

Apparently, this wasn't the time for introspection. Orphia charged at me, leaping over the Dvergar, hands already reaching out for the cleaver. Since I really didn't want to cleave her pretty face in half, I did what she'd asked and dropped it. She dived after it, only to catch my foot in her gut.

[15 Damage]
Combat: Rank 2/10
32 Experience Gained

It was enough to knock the wind out of her and send her rolling back across the floor to thump into Uthelred, but somehow, she came up with the cleaver in her hand. She looked from it to me, and something like a smile spread over her face. "Now I have the blade, you are all going to listen to me. Now you are all going to follow my lead. Not that thing over there. He is an abomination. He is the enemy."

Mercy snarled. "He isn't the one threatening me with a knife or trying to kick out my teeth."

Asher seemed to have lit up again, and he was taking in the

whole situation with no small degree of interest. Uthelred still wasn't moving, which was honestly kind of fair—I wouldn't want to get up for this either.

"You will stand down, Mercy. I know that you have some strange fondness for this beast, but I do not have time to indulge it. He has opened a way out of this cell to win our trust and corrupt us into following his desires. I say that he shall remain here while we use it without the fear of ambush."

I wet my lips. "So what, you just want me to sit here forever?"

"I want you to die, but I am showing my new friends here that I am willing to compromise my desires and principles to service their needs."

Mercy let out a little snort. "The scary thing is, this probably *is* her version of a compromise."

If this was the only way to get out of this without anybody dying, then I was willing to go our separate ways. I didn't want to, but I figured I could give them an hour's head start, then start on my own adventure. "Alright, so I'll stay here, and you'll head out. Do you guys want me to make you some weapons first? I've got no idea what is waiting on the other side of those bars."

"Our safety is no longer your concern, Faun." I couldn't believe that rolling over and submitting was all it was going to take to calm her down.

Mercy pointed to Orphia's feet, her jaw still clenched. "What about the Dvergar?"

Orphia seemed to remember that he was there for the first time. She crouched down to look him over, seizing his wooly chin and turning his dim eye-lights to face her. "I have no time for useless people."

I wouldn't have thought that my haphazard cleaver had much of an edge on it, but it seemed to be sufficient to slit the Dvergar's throat from ear to ear when Orphia leaned her weight down on it. Mercy and I both let out a cry when we realized what she intended, but it was already too late. Crimson blood was arcing up out of the Eternal's neck to spatter across the dirt floor.

In those last moments, Uthelred seemed to find some life, jerking up and grabbing at his bleeding throat and then smearing gore on Orphia's pristine white skin when his dull fingers scrabbled at her. She rose back up to her full height with a sneer that robbed her face of any beauty. "Perhaps now you'll understand that I am not playing games."

Then a glow surrounded her like the dull purple-blue light of a plasma ball lamp, and her hair started to rise up as static crackled across her. She took notice, looking down at the sparks crawling over her clothes in confusion.

Asher stepped out into our line of sight. His hands lit up with crackling lightning, and his lipless jaws were moving without pause, mouthing out some secret language that I could not understand or even hear.

When he ripped his claws apart, the lightning leapt out and struck Orphia in the back, conducted through the cloud of ionized air that already enveloped her. Her pristine white skin blackened in an instant as the electrical burns spread, and her hair crisped and blew away. Most importantly of all, the light shining out of her eyes blinked out, and she slumped to the ground on top of her victim. Two dead Eternals in under a minute. We were off to a flying start.

Asher lowered his arms with a barely perceptible shudder. "Worth noting. Spells take longer than expected to cast."

Both Mercy and I were stunned into silence, but it was for very different reasons. Mercy was looking down at the remains of Orphia as her body went through all the stages of decomposition in a moment. Skin sloughed off. Meat shriveled. Bones crumbled to dust. When it was over, there was no trace that Orphia had ever been there at all—nothing but the rough-hewn cleaver that she'd taken from me.

It only took a glance to confirm that the same thing had happened to poor Uthelred.

Orphia deserved whatever she got, but I spared a moment to feel sorry for the little guy. Of course, this was all a bit overwhelming for a regular guy, it was just a shame that he was going to pay for that feeling with his life, repeatedly, until he got over it.

I was pointing at Asher without meaning to. "You learned magic with your starting experience."

"That is correct." He cocked his head to the side in puzzlement.

"And you're an Inyoka."

"That was also my choice, yes."

I took a deep breath, trying to keep my excitement under control and failing. "You're a lizard wizard!"

It was enough to draw Mercy out of her reverie with a groan.

Asher cocked his head the other way, oblivious to my grin. "Queerly phrased, but ultimately accurate."

Mercy was fighting a giggle and losing. Maybe she didn't want to encourage any more of my nonsense. I decided to move on before she tried to move me on.

That seemed to wrap everything up with the crazier Eternals for now, so I went back to the cell bars and rubbed my hands together. "So what does everybody want? I'm going to try and make that little chopper into something more substantial. You want knives? If we find some wood, I could maybe do a spear?"

"Are you really going to just go on as if nothing happened?" Mercy was scooping up the cleaver and carrying it over, a little crease forming between her eyebrows.

"Well, the way I figure it, we can have a big cry about one of the folks we came here with being a bit too stab-happy or we can get to work. Either way, we are still going to have to escape from this dungeon, so I figured I'd cut to the chase."

Asher called over from where he was experimenting with the electric discharging between his claws. "No metal equipment for me if you please, it may turn my lightning back on me."

"Chargrilled lizard is off the menu. Got it."

With a strain, I slowed time to a crawl and stripped the metal from the next pair of bars, letting it drop as misshapen ingots in a shower of iron before moving on to the next. Mercy tossed the cleaver on the heap of metal and stopped to watch me work as I made my way along, gathering more and more raw material for the veritable arsenal I was planning for us. Eventually, I couldn't ignore her stare anymore, so I gave my massive arms a flex and asked, "See something you like?"

"Okay, first off, yuck. Second, can you make me a bow?"

"Yuck? Yuck?! I'll have you know that I am the most attractive man in this whole dungeon."

"I'd rather lick the lizard. Bow and arrows? Can you do it?"

I closed my eyes and strained. This time the bars fell in a shower of arrowheads. "We'll need to find wood and string, but yeah, I can do it."

Asher was right by my elbow when I turned, and I nearly backhanded him out of pure surprise. "Whoa. Dude!"

"With all due respect to the pair of you, it would be better if you did not refer to me as a lizard. It is as inaccurate as calling you a donkey-bull or her a monkey, and while I understand such things are meant in jest, there may be others in this world who find casual racism less amusing."

I finally stopped and thought before I spoke. "It didn't even cross my mind. I'm sorry, man."

His tongue flicked out, tasting the air. "Asher."

"Sorry, Asher."

Mercy mumbled, "Sorry," too.

I wondered if you could unlock achievements in this world. *First Awkward Apology.* It would have taken me nearly three years before I got that one in my last playthrough of life, yet here we were barely an hour into Amaranth and I was already performing above expectations.

With Mercy's arrowheads and the metal fixings for her bow made, and something like a bowstring woven from what used to be my shirt, I turned my attention back to the cleaver and the little hillock of metal chunks I'd pushed together with my foot. No time like the present. I closed my eyes and wished for a great big sword, then I put my Artifice to work with a gruff grunt that Asher could have quite rightly pointed out sounded like a goat's.

I opened my eyes again when the cleaver had put on so much weight it was almost a strain for my new, buff body to lift it. It was still shaped like a cleaver, more or less, with one huge cutting edge stretching along all six-foot of the blade's length. I'm willing to admit I may have gotten a little carried away, but when you were as strong as I'd become, you sometimes want to flaunt it a little. Plus, I was willing to bet that my big chopper could stop a charging elephant with one whack at this point. I hefted the blunt side up onto my shoulders, leaned my horns back against it, and felt the cool metal sapping the day's aches away from the knot of muscles up there.

Mercy was staring up at the ragged edge of my giant sword with another little smirk on her face. "Compensating for something?"

"Compensating for how puny the rest of my teammates are."

We gave the place one last look over for anything of value and were about to head for the door when I let my new *Sphere of Influence* reach out one last time to seek anything hidden among the dried-up carcasses on the floor. The bones hummed at the touch of my power. I was such an idiot.

With a strain of mental effort, the ribs of the nearest dead man tore loose and began a slow orbit about me, fusing together as they passed. Vertebrae snapped clean of the spines that once held them and lengthened out as the force of my will pulled on them. There was no wood down here, but that didn't mean we lacked materials. By the time I was done, Mercy had her bow and arrows, little bone spurs stretching out of the tail end of each one to serve as a flight. They were rough as hell, but they'd work.

Weirdly, Mercy didn't look all that pleased when I handed her the pile of corpse-bits that were now her weapon. "And again, I say yuck."

"Suck it up, buttercup. If you find me a tree, I'll replace them. Alright?"

She muttered something about my ass and a tree, but even my new heightened senses couldn't quite pick it up.

Asher intervened before I could poke the bear. "Shall we proceed?"

The corridor leading out of the jail was laid with the same mildew-stained flagstones as the cell had been. The only thing that made it more inviting was the faint breeze that was drifting through it. The chill night air was calling out to us. Somewhere out there was a way out of this hole.

It kind of made sense for me to go first, since swinging my sword with either of the other two in front of me was liable to end in friendly fire. Plus, bows and spells didn't require getting all up in a monster's face. I was assuming that this dungeon had monsters in it. That was the deal with dungeons in all my substantial fantasy gaming experience, and I wasn't going to start doubting that truism until I made it through at least three underground installations without anyone trying to murder me. I was giving this one the benefit of the doubt and not counting Orphia since we brought her in with us.

The dark corridor twisted and turned like it was trying to mess up my sense of direction, and if it hadn't been for our light-filled eyes, we would have been completely screwed. Even as it was, Mercy had to shout out a couple of times to warn me before I accidentally tumbled empty-head first into a pitfall. I wasn't sure if they were deliberate traps or just holes caused by disrepair, but I couldn't see the bottom, and I didn't fancy finding out what we could hear living down there in the pitch darkness, chittering away.

Eventually, we came to a pitfall that was definitely deliberate, six feet across with no way around. The tunnel stretched on beyond it, but there was no way forward except to jump. I had been spoiling for a chance to try out all these new muscles, so I wasn't exactly mad about it. Mercy looked down into the pit with a grimace. "Just be careful."

With a laugh, I tossed my sword to clatter on the far side of the pit. "Please, I was made for this."

I took a run-up to the gap.

I made a mighty leap.

I immediately headbutted the ceiling with the horns I'd forgotten were there. Crap.

CHAPTER 6

Luck and reflexes came to the rescue, and I flung myself flat as I fell back towards the pit. My shoulders landed with a crunch on one side of the gap, with my heels on the other. I groaned. This was not my finest moment.

To add insult to injury, the already chortling Mercy stepped on my chest and strolled over to the other side. "Portable bridge. That's going to come in handy."

"Laugh it up. I can see right up your skirt from here."

She stomped on my gut when I said that, but it did make her move a bit quicker.

Asher followed her over with an apologetic little half-bow. The dick. He was at least quick about it—I barely had time to say, "I don't know what I'm looking at exactly, but I can see up your skirt too."

With everyone off me, I rolled over and crawled back up onto the side I'd started on. This time I remembered my height before I leapt and cleared the gap easily.

New Skill Discovered! [Acrobatics]
Acrobatics: Rank 1/10
41 Experience Gained

Mercy gave me a round of applause, and a slightly puzzled Asher joined in before I shook my head at him. Mercy was still grinning when I grumbled, "Yeah, yeah, people falling over is peak comedy."

Scooping up my sword and squeezing past the two of them without accidentally slapping anyone with it was another feat of acrobatics, even if I didn't get a skill up. Then without another word between us, we were on our way again.

It was only a few minutes down the dank corridor before Mercy decided to open a can of worms. "So do you guys remember who you were before?"

"I don't remember what I was called, but I do remember some stuff." I paused to step around another pit, sending flagstone shards tumbling down into the dark. "I guess I was just an average, yet totally awesome kind of guy, then a wolf killed me out in the woods, and all this stuff happened."

Mercy raised an eyebrow. "Why were you out in the woods?"

"Hiking date."

She raised her other eyebrow. "Somebody dated you?"

"Do I have to listen to this sass for all eternity? Is this actually hell?" I grumbled. "Yes, somebody dated me. I dated. It was a disaster. Fifty percent of the people on the date died."

Mercy really seemed to be having a good time needling me, so I didn't pry about how she ended up deader than a doornail. She pressed on. "How do you screw up hiking that badly? Isn't it just walking?"

I cut her off. "Hold up. Hold up. None of us are here because we made good life choices. This isn't the Maulkin Mystery Hour. What happened to you? Who were you?"

"I don't remember my name, and I don't know how I died. One minute I was scuba diving in some old Parthenon-looking ruins, and the next old skull face was there telling me I'd croaked."

I snapped my fingers. "Got to be sharks, right?"

"Probably an aneurism or something wrong with my air mix. I don't know. I don't really want to know. It is done. Right? No point worrying about it."

"Yeah, don't think about it." I brushed aside a particularly thick clump of cobwebs. "Thinking is just going to make you bummed out."

She snorted. "Wow, you really just explained your whole life philosophy in that one sentence."

"So, scuba diving? Were you like a spy on a secret mission or something? Highly trained shadow government ninja assassin?"

"I was a diving instructor, you giant dork."

"I did not care for my life before," Asher interrupted us. "I lived a life of servitude to my Wyrm. Diligent and mindful. Tending her aromatic gardens as she waged war on the other great serpents of the world. I served her there until my final moments, when the temple fell to invaders."

That was a conversation killer if ever there was one. Guess we didn't all come from Earth. We trudged onwards in awkward silence again, not even talking when the tunnel branched and then branched again. It was almost a relief when something big and hairy jumped out at me.

The corridor had just opened out into a room when a mass of teeth and fur lunged out of the shadows, aiming for my neck with its gaping jaws but meeting an abrupt, slightly panicked headbutt instead.

The thing fell back into the room with a squeal so high-pitched I was fairly sure only dogs could hear it properly, leaving Mercy to chime in as it retreated, "What is that?"

The thing leapt at me again just as I brought my sword around. Claws skittered over the flat of the blade and it rebounded again.

"I don't know Mercy," I replied testily, "why don't you ask it while it chews on my face?"

I didn't give the thing another chance to jump me, charging forward with my sword held level to the floor, the tip held in my off-hand to create a solid wall of metal between me and those teeth. The thing scampered back on all fours. It was about the height of a Dvergar, but where they kept all their hair together on their head, this thing was covered with it from toes to tufted ear tips. It had a flat piglike nose above gnashing needle teeth, and there were beady eyes in amongst the fur of its face somewhere. Combined with the large radar dish like ears, it made the critter look like a bat boy.

Maybe if there had only been one then we could have talked things out, but the hungry little bat-thing had friends along for the ride, and they came scrambling out of the dark holes that honeycombed the floor and walls. We'd strolled right into their nest.

They moved almost like a flock of birds, perfectly synchronized as they bounded across the uneven floor and leapt at me. It lined them up perfectly for my swing. I turned my body in a great clumsy pirouette and then swept them out of the air with my sword.

The blade was far from sharp, but it was still a massive hunk of metal being swung around. The bat-boys went flying away from us. I hauled my sword back up for another swing with a grunt of effort. Maybe I had made the thing a little too big.

Mercy's first arrow grazed past me to hit the first of the monsters to attack us square in the chest. Between my headbutt and that length of bone, it wasn't getting up again. Maybe I should have felt some pang of guilt about that, but the rest of them didn't really give me time.

I could feel the hair on the back of my neck stand up as Asher did something with his lightning. Shot by carefully placed shot, Mercy was picking off the stragglers that I'd only injured instead of killing. Time for me to put in some more work.

This time I took the fight to the bat-lings, giving them no chance to regroup or charge us. That first swing might have looked epic, but I knew for a fact that it was more luck than skill that made it connect. I brought my sword down on the first one that I reached like a guillotine blade and flinched as scorching hot blood sprayed up to coat my chest.

I could feel a distant hum in my head as experience points accumulated, but now was not the time for counting. I stamped on the next bat-thing's face as it tried to scramble to its feet.

As I spun, looking for another target to present itself, one of them leapt from a hole in the roof to land on my back, latching onto my trapezius with all those teeth.

[Health 167/300]

The little bat's throat started working, and those leathery lips tightened against me as it gulped at my blood and did its damnedest to give my new body its very first hickey. I wanted to pull it off, obviously, but the rest of the swarm didn't care about my opinions on the matter.

Wounded ones skittered back towards me with their fangs bared, not risking the attack but threatening it, keeping my attention divided. If I let go of my sword to deal with the limpet, they'd pounce.

A second impact rocked me forward onto my tiptoes, then the hypodermic teeth lodged in my shoulder eased out. A quick, wild swing startled the others back long enough for me to glance down and see one of Mercy's arrows embedded in my personal leech's back. Nice.

I had to shout to be heard over the screeching of the bat-things. "Thank you, Mercy!"

Another arrow flew by, catching a leaping furball as it pounced. "Really?" Then another arrow shot past, close enough that I felt the breeze. "Now you want to be polite?!"

There seemed to be no end to the little fur-bats. More and more of them swarmed out of the tunnels and pitfalls all around us. Each individually was no challenge, but together they made up a lethal collection of hooked claws and nipping jaws. In a war of attrition, we were screwed.

New Skill Discovered! [Bestiary]
Bestiary: Rank 1/10
22 Experience Gained

Hobs. They were called hobs. They lived in dark holes. Most people only ever encountered them in village wells or cave-side cliffs. They preyed almost exclusively on children. The sudden rush of knowledge came without warning, and I had to shake my head to focus on what I was doing.

Whatever Asher was up to finally popped off with a silent thunderclap that rocked everyone in the room. I'd been hoping for a big fireball or something, but I couldn't see any exciting new explosions. Maybe the spell failed? I had no idea how magic worked.

A mass of hobs came swarming up out of one big pitfall, and I wasn't having it. Using the flat of my sword to shield off scrabbling claws as I pushed forward, I drove them back. Step by step, I pushed, setting my strength against theirs and finding all of them to be wanting. Their heel claws screeched over the flagstones as they tried to find purchase, but no amount of nails on the chalkboard was going to stop me. I should have said something dramatic before I pushed them into the pit, but it wasn't like anyone was going to hear it over all the squealing, and one last heave sent them all tumbling head over heels back into the dark.

When I turned back to the room, there was a small army of hobs between me and the other Eternals, yet they weren't attacking. Their fur was also standing up on end, static crackling up between their big pointed ears like they were tesla coils. Whatever Asher did, it was confusing the hell out of them.

Good enough for me.

One by one, I batted the little puffball bat guys with my sword and laughed as they trailed showers of sparks behind them as they flew across the room. My very own private fireworks display.

None of the hobs actually sounded the retreat, but instead of rushing at us, they were now rushing away, scrambling back into their holes with stumpy little triangle tails tucked between their legs. Mercy fired off a few more times at any that looked like they might still have some fight in them. It was a pretty convincing argument for leaving us alone. "Yeah, you better run!"

Victory!
Combat: Rank 5/10
302 Experience Gained

Asher was still gathering a ball of lightning between his outstretched palms, and he seemed to be genuinely irritated that all the enemies were running away before he got to use it. His tail was lashing with frustration as he squeezed his palms together and the tiny storm blinked out. Mercy gave him an awkward pat on the shoulder. "Nicely done."

"I did not even cast my spell, only the preparation." He was staring down at the little sooty marks on his claw-tips with narrowed eyes.

I joined in, trying to perk him up, "Hey, man, whatever works, right? You won the fight."

He let out a little huff of irritation, then seemed to come back to us. "Indeed. Shall we proceed."

There was a multitude of hob-holes leading out of this room but only one corridor, so that was where we headed, always moving towards the breeze. I nudged Mercy as we walked. "Thanks for the save. That was turning into a nasty hickey."

"Still better than your last date though, right?"

I laughed despite myself, then fell back into a companionable silence as I turned my attention inwards. The fight had earned us no Glory, so I was no closer to unlocking another Tier of Glory—or the Pillar of Divinity that came with it. Plenty of experience though. 389 points of it. Enough to buy another Divine Skill if I wanted *Rough Hewn Armor* or *Rough Hewn Architecture*.

The trouble was, I didn't know how much use either of those was going to do us down here. There was no more metal for me to work with, so armor was out of the question, and if I started screwing around with the walls, trying to build us a way out of here, I was just as likely to dump the whole structure on our heads. I could hold onto the experience and wait for the next Tier Up, but there was no way of knowing how long that might take, and if I died in the meantime, I'd lose all of the sweet experience that I'd worked so hard for. It was a conundrum.

There were other options. I could always buy a rank or two in some non-divine skills to help things along in the meantime. Asher hadn't even touched his Divine Powers, and he was rocking magic powers. I went trawling through the regular skills looking for something that would make me better at hitting things with a sword.

Sword Skill was right there, but concentrating on it revealed that I needed a *Combat Skill* of 10 before I could unlock it. I wasn't going to blow all my experience getting *Combat Skill* up from 6 to 9, so I decided to take a look around other options. *Bestiary* hadn't been helpful against the hobs, but if we were up against something that spat acid or whatever, then knowing in advance would be vital.

I dipped into the knowledge skills and found *Dungeoneering* almost immediately. I needed it. Whatever it was. I needed it. There was a 100% chance of dungeons in my future. Concentrating, I felt my experience draining away as *Dungeoneering* lit up in my mind. Even after it was lit, I still kept that same focus, dumping even more experience in before I realized my mistake. To save myself the hassle of trying to work out how to suck experience back out of it, I just carried on to the next rank.

Skills:
Combat: Rank 5/10

Acrobatics: Rank 1/10
Bestiary: Rank 1/10
Dungeoneering: Rank 2/10

With two ranks in *Dungeoneering*, I expected to suddenly understand everything around me better, but instead, there was no sudden rush of knowledge. My eyes started getting drawn to details I'd missed before, but that was all. I could see a little mark in the stonework of a supporting archway that had once held a tripwire in place. I could see one of the flagstones up ahead was lower than the level of the rest, but lower on an even plane, telling me there had probably been a pressure-plate beneath it with springs that had now rusted away. Trap spotting was great, but I'd kind of expected more. Ah well, I still had 186 experience to play around with.

I was so used to gaming by myself that I had totally forgotten that I wasn't alone down here. "Hey, guys, I picked up *Bestiary* in the hob fight, and I just unlocked *Dungeoneering*. Don't want you wasting experience buying overlapping skills."

Mercy blinked at me. "Hob fight?"

"The little bat dudes, they're called hobs. And *Dungeoneering* mostly seems to help me spot traps so far."

Asher was silent for a moment, then finally asked, "Are we resolved to remain together?"

That actually stopped me in my tracks. "I mean, uh. I kind of assumed."

Mercy looked even more awkward than me, so I tried my hardest to be a grown-up about all this. "I mean, I like you guys, and we seem to work well as a team, and this whole world seems to be out to kill us so far. It kind of makes sense to stick together, right?"

Once again, Asher punctured the politeness. "As a servant of the lunar court, you are destined to be our enemy. Are you not?"

"I'm nobody's servant. I didn't ask for this gig. Just because they gave me eternal life doesn't mean they get to decide how I use it."

Mercy nudged me as she passed, still pressing on, even if the men had decided to stop for a heart to heart talk. "It doesn't feel like we are enemies."

I sighed. "How about this? We stick together until we don't want to anymore."

"Until destiny calls us to do battle with each other, we shall be companions," Asher intoned.

I patted him on the back a little too hard, sending him staggering along the corridor. "Cool."

His tongue flickered out. "Indeed."

Mercy called back over her shoulder. "If you two are done braiding each other's hair, we've still got a dungeon to escape."

Asher looked up at me with his head cocked to the side. "We have no hair."

I scratched at the top of my head. "I've got some stubble coming in, maybe you can braid it later."

"We do have all eternity to await your hair growth." Mollified, Asher moved on along the corridor.

We kept on keeping on, following whichever of the branching tunnels had the tell-tale breeze coming through it until eventually, we came to a cave-in. Beyond the heap of rocks, we could make out distant specks of starlight, but even with all of my strength, this path was going to remain impassable. It was the same problem that I'd had with *Rough Hewn Architecture*, if I went digging around I was as likely to collapse the roof as to get us through. Another death was not on the agenda for today, so we were looking for another route.

I took point again when we started backtracking, turning us left at every available turn and straining that new *Dungeoneering* skill to see if it could give us any hint on which way was out. There were more dead-ends everywhere that we went. Collapse after collapse. This place was ancient, and it looked like it had no maintenance in the last dozen centuries, so really all the parts that hadn't collapsed were the surprising part.

We came upon a new room and something felt wrong. I held out an arm to stop Mercy's relentless march forward and stared into the dim room, trying to work out why my senses were tingling. She bounced her forehead off my arm and snapped. "What?"

"Wait a second. My brain is trying to tell me something."

"First time for everything," she snarked back.

The room was like all the rest—dirty, dusty, and abandoned. The flagstones on the floor were the same. The brickwork on the walls. Nothing looked any different except the ceiling.

"Look up. The tiles."

We were staring up into the underside of another mosaic, this one depicting some great battlefield. Another trapped room was up above us almost close enough to touch. A chance to get closer to the surface if we could just work out how.

Taking a few steps into the room, I swung my sword up into the piecemeal stonework, earning me a nice jarring sensation and a metallic ringing that I'd bet I was going to hear for days. Guess brute force wasn't going to work.

I put down my still-vibrating sword, then grabbed Mercy by the hips to hoist her up. "Can you see a way to unlock the tile trap?"

She kicked me on her way up, grumbling all the way. "Damn it. Ask before you pick somebody up."

"I thought you were in a hurry."

She gave me one more halfhearted kick. "Do I even weigh anything to you?"

"Nope.“

We inched across the room with Mercy touching and tugging at every seam she could find. "I don't get how it works…at all."

"A wizard did it?" I sighed.

"So can a wizard undo it then?"

She let out a yelp when I dropped her, but she managed to find her feet rather than fall on her ass, so the punches she bounced off my back were mostly for show. "Hey, Asher. Think you can blow the roof off this thing?"

He was studying the ceiling tiles himself, walking around the walls of the chamber. "I shall make an attempt, but I have no way of knowing how the magics will interact."

Mercy and I retreated to a safe distance down the corridor, then she called out. "Do it!"

This was the first time I'd actually had the chance to watch Asher casting a spell, and I had to admit, it was kind of cool looking, even if it did take a while. At first, he just worked his hands back and forth like he was stretching out taffy as more and more static crackled between his fingers. Finally, when there were arcs of lightning leaping off him to ground themselves on the floor, he flung his arms up, and it roiled up in a wave of sparks that spread out across the ceiling, leaving the whole thing crackling with power. Unfortunately, though, it didn't work. Whatever held the tiles in place didn't so much as budge under the wizard's spell. I let out a sigh and was already stepping back towards the room when Mercy caught hold of the rope I was using as a belt. "He isn't done."

She was right enough. Asher's hands were in motion again, not whipping back and forth like before, but rolling over one another, jiving out to draw in another crackle of lightning from the air, then coiling over themselves once more. That same ball of lightning that we saw before was beginning to form between his hands, and now that it was self-perpetuating, he just held it there between his palms. Just waiting as the power gathered.

Maybe I should have gone for the magic thing after all, that looked badass. Maybe there was still time.

Once he was satisfied with the lightning gathered between his hands, Asher strained to pull them away from whatever gravity was holding the whole thing together. With a grunt of effort that I could just make out over the ozone hum, he hauled his claws apart.

The lightning leapt up into the charged ceiling, and for a moment, it seemed like nothing was going to happen at all, then suddenly, we were rocked by a thunderous concussion. The whole roof lit up blue-white for an instant. We had to blink away the after-images of that light, so we still didn't know if the spell had done its job or not.

The tinkling sounds of falling tiles was our first indication. When my eyes had adjusted to the dark again, the room had doubled in height. Asher stood in the middle of the raining tiles with what I had to assume was a smile on his face. It was hard to tell without lips. Yet almost as fast as our victory came, it was snatched away. The tiles lay on the flagstones for just a moment, vibrating in place before they began floating back up to trap us all over again. "Oh no, you don't."

Poor Mercy never saw it coming. She might have suspected I'd pick her up again, but she definitely didn't expect me to grab her by a thigh and bicep before launching her like a javelin towards the upstairs exit. She squealed as she flew, but she never lost her grip on that bow.

Asher was next, his eyes popping open as Mercy passed over his head. He didn't try to argue or fight me, he just let it happen. I hooked under his shoulder and tail, then launched him end over end on the same arc as Mercy. I scooped up my sword as I ran, slamming the blunt end of it down to crack the flagstones, and I pole vaulted up towards the all-too-solid looking tiles above me.

There was a nasty ripping sound as I passed through the razor-edged tiles. A sound accompanied by a fresh sense of wetness where they'd opened up my skin.

Acrobatics: Rank 2/10
41 Experience Gained

My graceful leap had been slightly spoiled by mincing myself on the tiles, but at least they were solid enough for me to make a painful landing on them rather than falling right back through and tearing myself some more new holes.

"Ow."

Mercy stomped over to kick me while I was down. "I told you to knock that off."

"Ow."

Asher crouched down beside me. "How badly are you injured? Can you move?"

He prodded at one of my lacerations with a claw. "Ow!"

Mercy rolled her eyes. "He's fine."

I grumbled to my feet, leaving bloody patches all over the place. My lovely new rags were entirely wrecked. I was going to have to pick up *Rough Hewn Armor* soon or I was going to end up naked. Meanwhile, my sword was sticking up out of the tiled floor, King Arthur style. The tiles that it had displaced were in an orbit around it, dipping in to crack off the metal every so often.

One good tug made me the rightful king of England—or whatever the Amaranth equivalent was—and we were ready to move on again. The trail of blood that I was leaving behind was new, but the passages were starting to look familiar. More and more of the flagstones were submerged in the dirt, and there were a few dry leaves here and there that could only have been blown in from the surface. We were back in the passages just below the observatory. We were nearly there.

When we rounded the corner and saw the stairs, there was palpable relief from the other two. Not me though, I still had my head in the game. I wanted to introduce the White Prophet to the business end of my new sword. "Get ready. With three of us attacking together there's no way he can dodge everything."

Asher cocked his head. "Who are we attacking?"

"The White Prophet?" Mercy whispered. "Promised to help us learn how to use our Eternal powers, then dumped us in a dungeon? Ringing any bells?"

"Have we not learned how to use our powers?"

That shut us both up for a moment. Was this all just a test? I really couldn't think of a better way to get a gang of newborn Eternals using their abilities to the fullest than by dumping them in a dungeon. I ran a hand over the stubble on my head, but it came away smeared bloody. "Alright, fine. We talk first. Then we make Prophet paste if we don't like the answers."

Mercy nodded tersely, and Asher seemed placated. "Let us proceed then."

I still couldn't resist the urge to charge up the stairs and give the pasty Inyoka a scare. He'd spent all this time one step ahead of us. I wanted to get my own back with a good startle at least.

We shouldn't have been surprised that the guy who knew the future was still one step ahead of us. Up above ground, in the observatory, there was no sign of him. All of the papers were in disarray, and the books were gone. It looked like he'd come right back upstairs, packed in a hurry, and then fled.

Asher took it all in with disappointment graven on his face. "Our fate…"

Mercy slumped down on the bed with a groan. "After all that, he's gone."

"Gone, but not forgotten." Down on his haunches, Asher started digging through the papers. "There are notes here that might guide our path. Interpretations of prophecy. Fragments of history. He told us of the Shards but not of their location or guardians. From these papers, perhaps we can discern where we should next turn."

I wasn't so confident. "Asher, do we even know anything he told us was true? I mean, the dude dumped us in a pit. Can we really trust any of this?"

"If he had intended our deaths then could he not have left us in the ground? And would a simpler tale not have turned us to his service far more readily than something so convoluted?" He had handfuls of scrolls, half-crushed in his desperate grip. "What was the benefit of his deception?"

Mercy had flopped back on the cot. "Some people are just ass-holes?"

Asher dropped the scrolls and turned to her with his tail lashing. "No. I refuse to believe that this was all for nothing. I believe in the Prophet's words, if not his methods."

"Alright, let's just calm it down. We've all had a hard day. Asher, why don't we have a look through the papers and see if there is anything that might help point us in the right direction. Mercy, why don't you have a nap and chill out."

Mercy rolled over onto her side. "Way ahead of you, boss."

Nobody had made it clear to us whether Eternals actually needed to do things like eat or sleep but from Mercy's snoring, we discovered that it was possible at least. After the day that we'd had, sleep sounded extremely tempting, but I couldn't leave Asher alone to his frantic scrabbling through the papers.

In a fantasy world, I'd been expecting Kingdoms and Empires all over the map, but from the papers we'd discovered, there didn't seem to be much in the way of royalty or nobility. There were notes here and there on long-dead dynasties, but for all the Lunar Court's talk of stagnation, the history of Amaranth seemed to be one of constant chaos and change. Most of the nations founded only lasted as long as a generation or two before somebody else swept in and built a new one on their graves. It made keeping track of any one object being passed hand to hand through the years practically impossible. I had seriously underestimated how little I knew about this new world. Everything seemed to either refer to some person I'd never heard of, someplace that hadn't existed for a thousand years, or some historic battle between two sides that nobody could even remember. It was infuriating.

New Skill Discovered! [Ancient History]
Ancient History: Rank 1/10

Sometime in the early hours of the morning, my attention span finally gave out, and I fell asleep, only to be nudged awake by Asher, who was trying to retrieve a squashed scroll from underneath me. Sluggish, I wandered over to the bed and gave Mercy a prod. "Move over."

She raised one finger in an entirely not-ladylike gesture and went on snoring. If I hadn't been so sleepy, I could have picked the whole bed up and flipped her off in return, but I really didn't have the energy. I slumped down to sit by the foot of the bed and let my head tip back until my horns rested on the straw mattress.

My only consolation in this arrangement was that Mercy was probably getting fleas.

CHAPTER 7

Thumping stirred me from my rest. For a disorienting moment, I thought that I was back home, waking up in my own bed with one of my roommates banging on the door because I'd slept through my alarm. Then my eyes opened, and I remembered the truth. It had not all been an awesome dream. I actually was a big buff Chagnar Faun.

Sweet.

The banging continued. Somebody was at the door of the observatory. I lumbered to my feet with a grunt and retrieved my sword from where I'd left it in case the Prophet had finally come back to face his comeuppance. Mercy was still snoring away like a wood-chipper, and Asher's manic energy had given out, and he lay curled up with his tail by his nose beside the cold ashes in the fireplace. Guess I was the butler. The thumping grew ever more insistent, and in my half-asleep state, I wondered about the state of the Amaranth postal service. I was reaching out to open the door when a stone axe-head splintered it apart an inch from my hand. Mail-men were aggressive in these parts.

"Wake up! Fighting time!"

A spear was shoved through the hole that the axe had made, stopping just short of me before being wiggled around and withdrawn. More blows hammered on the door, and more chinks of light shone through the new holes.

"Wake up!"

Asher was already at my elbow, making me jump again. "I am prepared."

Mercy was at my other side just a moment later, drawing back her bowstring and bitching all the way. "Is a decent night's sleep too much to ask for?"

"You slept longer than the rest of us put together. Are you trying to hibernate for the winter?"

"Don't think I won't 'accidentally' shoot you."

A whole board of the door was knocked away, and an elongated snout with all the color of a flatworm poked through. For a moment I thought somebody had descaled the Prophet, but this thing was half the height and three times as ugly as any Inyoka. Long ears flopped back onto its shoulders, and somewhere behind; the beady black eyes. Those sunken eyes were the worst part—they looked like the dried-up darkness of some dead thing.

My *Bestiary* skill provided me with the name Svart, but that was about it as far as information went. "They're svart."

"They do not look very intelligent to me." It took so long for me to realize that Asher was making a joke that the svart had broken through before I could let out a surprised laugh.

Mercy let fly before the first of them could scramble through the gap—a perfect shot, right through its forehead. Then on they came, pushing the corpse of their companion aside like it was nothing. The chaos as they scrambled and crawled over each other to get at us was enough to make me miss the intuitive synchronicity of the hobs. They were all armed with the same primitive weapons, little more than sharpened stones tied to sticks, but while the first spearhead had been plain flint, these ones were shining quartz. I charged in to bottleneck them in the door, only realizing halfway through my first swing that I didn't really have enough room in the observatory to swing a cat, let alone a great-sword.

My first hit clipped the leading svart in half at the waist, but if we'd hoped for any kind of fear or empathy for the fallen from the others, we were sorely mistaken. The rest came on regardless, and I couldn't get my sword up for another swing without gouging a strip out of the wall and getting tangled in furniture. "Damn it."

The svart seemed to have more sense than to charge me head-on, but now they tried to encircle me instead, jabbing at me with their spears while the ones I was ignoring darted in to hack at my legs with their little hatchets. I dragged my sword in a wide circle around me, trying to scatter them back, but now the rear half of their gang were slinking into the building and training their bows on us. "Damn it."

The first arrow grazed over the top of my scalp, deflecting off my horns without much damage, but the next one was aimed at Asher, and I couldn't have that. My hand shot out as if I was going to be fast enough to catch it. Instead, the arrow lodged right through my palm. "Damn it!"

I was not enjoying getting my ass kicked by these little goblin-looking assholes. It was embarrassing. If they'd brought a giant monster along to beat the crap out of me, I would have been fine with dying, but this was just sad. Mercy peppered the crowd with arrows, but there were at least five svart for each one of us, and more seemed to keep coming. Another of the runts dashed in with a knife aimed at a part of my anatomy that I really did not want to be stabbed—a part that I wanted stabbed even less than all the other parts of my body that I didn't want stabbed. They were getting cocky. I gave her a solid kick in the face.

She tumbled back, end over end, to bowl down some of the archers, sending their shots wide. I caught one of the thrusting spears and yanked the whole svart off his feet and into easy headbutting range.

My sword fell useless to the ground. I didn't need it. This body was a weapon, and so I slapped my pierced hand down onto the nearest svart head.

While it hurt like hell, it also slammed the arrow through the svart's egg-shell skull and into whatever reeking sponge it used for a brain. When I pulled my hand free, the arrow was gone. The hole was not, unfortunately.

The rest of the svart were losing their bravery now. Their eyes were turning away from me to dart to their companions, trying to guess who was going to be dumb enough to wade in next. That was when Asher's spell sparked off. There was no dramatic crack of lightning, no bolt from the blue, just a glowing static charge, clinging not to the enemy, but to me.

Whenever I came close to one of the svart, my personal electric cloud discharged with a little snap, crackle, or pop, surrounding them with the same nimbus as me. Asher was letting me light up his targets. A grin spread across my face, then I put down my head, scooped up my sword, and charged.

However the svart thought this was going to play out, they did not expect a face full of angry Faun coming right at them. The ones that couldn't scramble out of my way were bowled over, the rest tripped over their dead companions trying to get clear. Either way, they were all lit up with electricity.

I barged right out into the daylight and the open air, finally dragging my sword up from where it was trailing behind me to take a proper swing again. The stragglers of the svart warband were lingering around the entrance and regretting their lack of courage as my blade carved a bloody swathe through them all.

Pieces of svart tumbled apart, spraying the yellowed grass and ancient stonework with steaming black ichor. It didn't even smell like blood, more like antifreeze. Wretched things.

Inside the observatory, there was a thunderclap and a flash of blue light that sent the remaining living Svart scampering out with smoke rising off them, the few wispy white hairs on their balding heads alight.

Most of them, I caught on the backswing.

But a few of the lucky ones managed to scramble their way clear, leaping over the edge of the ridge, down to the disturbed earth where we'd first come into this world. Like hell were they getting away. After shooting me full of holes, trying to lop off my Chagnar Faun-hood, and beating the ever-loving hell out of me there was no chance I was letting any one of the runts run free.

I charged across to the drop-off with my sword raised, ready to make an epic leap and cut them down. Sadly, they'd brought a friend.

Whatever that thing was, my *Bestiary* skill was not up to identifying it. It sure as hell wasn't a Svart. It was almost easier not to look right at it and work my way in from the outside. I could see the Svart dangling from the chains that were meant to bind the abomination and let them steer it. They were ancient chains, once golden but now filthy with age, the links twisted by the immense power of the thing straining against them. Where the chains met flesh there was a golden band, still perfect and pristine, rubbed to a sheen where it pressed into the flesh that looked too smooth and perfect to belong on anything real.

My eyes started to hurt just looking at this thing, and it only took a moment for me to realize why. The golden seams in its marbled flesh were not metal, they were sunlight. The same light that filled up the Solar Eternals had been twisted and trapped inside this thing. The spark of divinity, bound in a puppet of meat.

The center of its mass was bulbous, pinched in by the gold of its restraints, but it was the only part of it that truly looked like a body. From slits within the lowest part of the abomination, claws like a cat's protruded, not to hook but to twist and turn like the limbs of some great insect. The top of the torso looked almost human but mirrored wrong, with a limb extending in each of the four cardinal directions. Each one was reverse jointed and ending in barbed sickle blades that seemed to be forged from the same material as all the rest, matching the skittering things at its base. At the top, where you'd expect a head, there was a perfect sphere, punched right through the center with emptiness, where others might have had a face. Bands of gold made their grinding orbit around that open head, two rings, crisscrossing through each other with a painful screech. Within that hollow, a tiny star was trapped. Burning with the divine spark.

My will to fight faltered for a moment in the face of that thing. I didn't even have words to describe it properly. There was something wrong with it. It was wrong in some fundamental way that made my empty stomach twist within me. Mercy and Asher caught up to me, each smeared with black blood. Mercy had restocked her makeshift quiver with the svart's arrows, and Asher was carrying one of their crystal-tipped spears. The same revulsion washed over them. Mercy shuddered. "What the hell is that?"

I opened my mouth to answer, but Asher already had the right answer. "That is not important. All that matters is that it is our foe, and it must be destroyed."

The abomination had no eyes, but I could feel the pressure of its attention on us then. The skittering claws that it had used for little more than to nudge the Svart away from its feet before now sprang into motion, proving just as capable of hauling it up the vertical cliff-face as across the torn-up soil of the Prophet's little graveyard.

It mounted the cliff and was coming right for us with its sickle-arms raised before any of us had a chance to think. The Svart that had been in its way were punctured by the skittering legs, and the ones hanging on to its chains were flicked free with a twist. Only some instinct that I didn't even know I had brought my sword up to block the descending strike.

Where those bone blades struck, they gouged wedges out of my sword. All those bulging muscles I'd been so proud of on my arms and back started screaming with the strain. My feet sank into the solid earth beneath me with the force of the blow. It was impossibly strong.

Asher danced back, already gathering a storm in his fist, and Mercy fired off an arrow into the glowing orb in the void of its head, only for the shot to vanish without a trace. The abomination spun gracefully on the spot, like some murderous carousel, trying to bring its other sickles to bear on us. My sword was ripped from my grasp and flung aside as I tried to stand my ground and protect the others.

When the other blades came around I had no way to block them, but I still couldn't let them hit Mercy. I launched myself forward, pitting raw strength against the abomination. There was no way I was going to win. No way that I was going to move that immovable object, but I didn't need to.

When my shoulder hit the closest claw leg, it gave away.

Those scuttling claws were too flexible to be fixed to solid bone. The whole abomination rocked forward before it could scuttle in a circle and find its balance. The blades ripped a pair of long gouges out of the earth instead of halving Mercy.

Time stopped for just an instant as the numbers beside Combat Skill in my brain vanished, and it flared with moonlight before settling, dark and dead. Set in stone.

I was back in the moment. The same leg I'd nudged now reared up to impale me. This thing was fun from top to bottom. I leapt to the side as the spike punctured the earth where I'd stood and managed to land on my sword, coming up armed and ready to rock.

Asher's spell sparked off, surrounding the abomination in a blue-white glow that seemed to drown out some of the flickering golden light from within it. My eyes no longer hurt to look at the thing. That was progress at least.

Stepping up to bat, I took a home run swing at the abomination's twisted torso.

My sword jarred to a stop. Like there was sheet steel under the spongy surface. Where blade bit into the pallid flesh more golden light oozed up to the surface. Like this whole thing was full of sunny delight.

Now that I had a half-a-second to look, I could see that the rest of the central tower was pincushion peppered with arrows. Mercy had been hard at work. No wonder the abomination was pissed at her.

It seemed to ignore me and the glowing hole I'd hacked in its side entirely. The spinning dervish of blades had come to an abrupt halt too. For a moment I kind of hoped that it was reconsidering the whole fight, then the star in its head sputtered to life, and a great golden gout of flame came rushing out.

Asher was the solar flare's target, and he was so lost in concentration that he didn't have a chance to dodge. The grass caught alight in a strip leading up to him, then his rags ignited with a whoosh and the force of the beam knocked him off his feet. The flames guttered and died a moment later, but Asher wasn't moving.

"Mercy! If he's alive, get him up." I ducked under one of the sickle blades as the whole thing sprang back into cyclone motion. "It is going after him. It must be scared of magic."

Arrows darted past me as I moved. The remaining Svart had finally found the courage to follow their pet up the ridge. Just what we needed. More trouble.

I didn't even try to meet the abomination's next attack head-on. Not when I was this close. Instead, I swung with all my might at the place where the insectile arm and blade were fused.

[Critical Hit]

The sickle spun off to embed in the dirt behind me. Sunlight trickled from the stump of the abomination's arm to sizzle in the dirt. Bizarre as this thing was, if it bled, we could kill it.

Spinning back into motion in a shimmer of sharp edges, the whole abomination moved off along the ridge, dancing out of reach. Apparently, it had taken notice of me at last.

Asher must have been up again because a bolt of lightning cracked through the air to hit the abomination square in the center of its mass. It was the same spell that had killed Orphia in one hit, and the abomination barely rocked on its bug legs.

There went the theory that it was scared of magic. Asher must have just been the only enemy in range of its sunbeam. Just like I was now.

The realization arrived just a moment before the fire. Just enough time for me to get the flat of my sword up.

The first hit of the beam sent me skidding along the ridge, both arms straining against the pressure being exerted against me, and the dull iron of my sword started to glow red at the edges.

The red turned to white, and the metal lit up as the blade seemed to waver in the heat. Sword or no sword, I was burning up.

My skidding heel hit a chunk of buried stone, and I managed to brace myself, twisting my body to turn the flat of the sword. Instead of directly opposing the solar beam, I was now redirecting it, bouncing it off to ignite first a thick strip of grass, then up into the Svart archers that were still fool enough to take potshots at me. They collapsed in on themselves like they were made of wax.

My hands were scorched, and molten metal was searing through my skin, spattering in great dollops across my arms and eating into my flesh. I was not dying like this.

Setting my feet, I pushed back against the molten blade, fingers sinking into the softening metal as I took step after agonizing step back towards the enemy.

I tumbled forward onto my hands and knees when the beam was suddenly gone and the pressure relieved. Damn, I was tired. It took a real effort to lift up my head.

The abomination had been knocked over, and the beam that had been cooking me was now pointed up into the sky, like a pillar of light from the heavens. As I watched, it tried its damnedest to regain its feet, but something was pinning it to the floor.

Over by the pyre that had been the observatory, the other two Eternals were hard at work. Mercy stood guard over the Inyoka, firing off shots at the last few living Svart as Asher's claws were upraised and shaking with effort. His eyes were burning so bright it was almost blinding.

The strain came through when he spoke. He was usually so calm his voice was near monotone, but now every word wavered. "You wished to know what skills we unlocked? I have selected the pillar of Cosmos and the Gravity Snare ability."

Staggering to my feet, I called back, "That is unbelievably cool."

I tapped into my own Divine Pillar to fuse the metal scraps that had been my sword back together, then I charged.

Asher's snare couldn't hold forever. Stoicism aside, I could tell that he was almost tapped out already. This had to end. As I got closer to the gravity snare, it became easier to run, like I was going downhill. By the time I was within spitting distance of the abomination's flailing claws, it was less like running and more like falling.

I kicked off from the ground with all my strength, raised my re-forged sword above my head, and let the irresistible pull of gravity carry me the rest of the way, slamming my sword down into the abomination with all the strength I had left.

It bucked and rocked beneath me, trying to throw me clear or bring one of its blade-arms to bear, but the snare still held. Fighting gravity and the immense weight of my own sword, I hauled the weapon up and hammered it down again.

[18 Damage]

And again.

[19 Damage]

This wasn't a glorious battle. It wasn't even a fight. The abomination was meant to be carved, and I was the butcher.

[18 Damage]

Sunlight was pouring out of the abomination now, bubbling out of every hole and coating my arms, stinging my eyes, and soaking its way down my legs to drip down the sides. I struck again.

The shell that had kept all this juicy mess inside was shattered to pieces as the spongy flesh fell away. I could see the dying flickering light in the heart of the abomination now, and I wanted it blotted out. The sword fell from my flame-deadened fingers, and I plunged my numb hands into the cavity, digging around inside the light until I felt the heart of light trapped deep inside it.

My fingers closed around that pulsing life inside it, and I ripped it out.

[Critical Hit]

All the light left the abomination in an instant, and it became nothing more and nothing less than flesh. Just like my fellow Eternals, it began to melt away to nothing, decomposing beneath me before I could clamber free. The beating heart turned to ashes in my hand. When I felt solid ground beneath my feet again, I finally believed that it was over.

Legendary Foe Defeated!
Potency increased to 24
Combat: 10/10

Sword: Rank 2/10
Acrobatics: Rank 2/10
448 Experience Gained
400 Glory Gained
Tier of Glory Ascended!

Sweet.

CHAPTER 8

Asher was slumped down in a heap in front of the blazing observatory, not dying from his burns but looking miserable enough that he probably wished he were. "Why the long face? We won!"

Mercy didn't even smirk at my Inyoka-snout humor. "Ugh, gross! I can see your burnt-up hand bones!" Guess misery was infectious.

"Come on, guys, we've been here one day, and we are already Tier Two. We killed that…whatever it was before it could kill us. I'd call that a win."

"The flesh-forged were weapons in the Revelation. A living arms-race," Asher moaned. "Grotesque corruptions of the Primal Divine Pillar by both mortals and the servants of the Void God."

"You got that from the prophet's old papers?"

"They contained a wealth of knowledge about this world," Asher answered as he flopped onto his back. "A bountiful cornucopia of knowledge that is now nothing but kindling."

The roof of the observatory was made of paper, so it burned up faster than you could say "Fire hazard." It was enough to make me take a step back and really take in the damage. There was no real way to tell when the place caught fire—whether it was Asher's lightning bolts or a glancing zap from the abomination's sun-ray—the only thing that was certain was that nothing inside was going to be usable, ever again.

I plopped myself down beside Asher with a grunt. Now that the fight was done, I could really feel the pain. I tried not to look at my hands. Mercy was right. It was enough to make you sick to your stomach.

The heat on our backs was far from pleasant, but I couldn't rustle up the energy to move. I needed to do something about the state of myself. I couldn't go on with a fraction of my health left forever. Not fighting the way that I did.

Turning my attention inwards, I was immediately confronted with the Pillar of *Artifice* already glowing brightly in my mind. Maybe armor would keep me from ending up in this state again, but right now I needed something more immediate. I turned away to consider *Ascension*. This was the self-improvement pillar, the one that would let me super-charge this new body of mine. Could I use it to give myself some sort of health regeneration? Even if I did, it wouldn't help Asher. I needed to be able to heal other people too, and that meant *Primal, the creation of life*.

I poured my glory into the Primal Pillar and flinched as it blazed to life. This time around, I didn't linger. Staring at the pretty light show, I leapt right into the divine skills that had been unlocked.

> **Primal 1:** *Restoration*
> *Restores 45% of an injured creature's health.*
> **Primal 1:** *Origination*
> *Allows for the creation of new life; Limited by an Eternal's knowledge of lifeforms.*
> **Primal 1:** *Primal Infusion*
> *Infuses weapons and spells with the primal properties of venom and disease; Limited by an Eternal's knowledge of venoms and diseases.*
> **Primal Passive:** *Lifesense*
> *Detects all living creatures within an Eternal's Sphere of Influence.*

Restoration was the one I wanted, but I took a glance at the others too. All the fighting had given me 541 experience points to invest in new skills, so maybe I could splash out.

Origination let me create life, but I wasn't anywhere near ready to be a daddy just yet.

Primal Infusion let me push venoms and diseases into my attacks and spells. As Mercy would say, yuck.

Even *Lifesense*, which let me detect whether something I was touching was alive or dead seemed to be only circumstantially useful at best. At least nobody could play possum and get away with it as long as I was prodding all the corpses I found.

After I'd invested 300 experience in *Restoration,* I felt the breath of Chernghast on the back of my neck, so I turned my attention back to the breakdown of all my abilities. There, next to the words, *Acolyte of Chernghast,* I saw *Tier 2.* A new blessing from dog. God. God-dog.

Maulkin – Chagnar Faun of the Lunar Court – 2nd Tier of Glory
Statistics:
  HP: 65/440
  Devotion: 240/240
  Glory: 0
Attributes:
  Potency: 24
  Celerity: 17
  Vitality: 11
  Piety: 4
Skills:
  Combat: Rank 10/10
  Sword: Rank 2/10
  Acrobatics: Rank 2/10
  Bestiary: Rank 1/10
  Dungeoneering: Rank 2/10
  Ancient History: Rank 1/10
Traits:
  Relentless: *The Faun are the greatest hunters on Amaranth, known for*

pursuing prey for days or even weeks at a time before closing in to strike.

Effect: Faun are immune to fatigue, their Attributes do not degrade over time without rest.

Acolyte of Chernghast: *Chosen by the wolf that waits, you bear his invisible mark and walk the path that will someday make you the personification of inevitable death.*

Effect: The presence of the dead reinvigorates you. For every corpse within your Sphere of Influence, all of your attributes are increased by 1.

Bloodthirst: *Your continued devotion to Chernghast has granted a fresh boon.*

Effect: The coming of death fills you with grim vitality. Each injury that you deal restores a portion of your own life. 3% of Damage Dealt.

Bloodthirst was sweet. When I dealt damage to an enemy, I would be healed by 3% of the damage done. That wasn't much, but if I kept whaling on big gangs of weak monsters like svarts, it was going to add up. I could have used that earlier. Thanks a bunch, Chernghast.

Opening up my eyes, I realized that Asher and Mercy were staring down at me, or rather, level with me, since I was still the same height as them standing when I was sitting. "Uh, hi?"

Mercy kicked me in the foot. "We were talking to you, and you didn't say anything. Then you started glowing. What the hell?"

"I was spending my Glory. And now I can do this!"

I held up my withered and flaking hands, then concentrated on the place in my mind that felt like *Restoration*. Almost immediately, my injuries began to ooze clear fluid. Mercy gagged and turned away, but Asher was fascinated as the flesh grew back into the places where it had been burned away, and my skin crawled back up my forearms to seal over the top.

[215/440 Health]

I wasn't quite back to normal, but *Restoration* didn't seem to have anything else to give at the moment—at least, not for me. I held out my hand to Asher, and he took it. Through my *Lifesense*, I could tell that he had 286 health left. Maybe that ability wasn't going to be completely useless after all. *Restoration* flickered back to life when I touched him. I guess I could only heal any one person by so much at a time. I had to grab on so that Asher didn't pull his hand away when the Primal energy started flowing through me and into him.

The blackened scales on his chest, charred by the sun-beam and exposed by his incinerated robes, returned to their old blue-green luster, and he was left with 336 health when I was done. 50 points a pop wasn't bad. I wouldn't be saving us from certain death any time soon, but I could get us back into action after a minor tussle or two.

"Mercy, do you need healing up?"

She still wasn't looking our way. "Nope. I'm fine. Totally fine. Please keep your nasty oozy hands away from me."

The weird plasma had vanished once my injuries were gone, but there was no reason to tell her that. I clambered to my feet and immediately rubbed my hand through her hair. "Free gel!"

She spun on her heel, eyes narrowed, jaw set, and fist pulled back. "I will end you."

"Bickering children"—Asher saved me from the inevitable but fair bruise I was about to receive—"we need to move on."

Mercy touched her hair, realized I was just messing with her, and let her rage simmer down. "How do you figure? Aren't you meant to stay put when you are lost?"

"This fire is sending up a tower of smoke. Smoke that can be seen for miles." Asher's tail lashed. "It is a beacon to any who might wish us harm."

"And since everybody in this world has been trying to kill us since we arrived, that's bad news," I said and groaned.

Mercy was already in motion, grabbing what she could from the svart corpses. "But where do we go?"

The svart didn't have any money. In fact, they didn't have anything of value at all beyond their weapons, and those were pretty crappy even compared to the stuff that I'd knocked together out of prison bars. Mercy had as many arrows as she could carry within a minute or two, and then I turned to Asher. "Any bright ideas? Did you find any hints about where we should be headed in all the notes?"

"The Prophet felt certain that there was a shard nearby, that our arrival here was indicative of its presence."

"That's vague," Mercy chipped in as she passed.

"And it doesn't really point us in a direction…"

I walked around the burning building in a slow circle, coming back to where I started with my finger already pointing. "Let's go that way."

Mercy was finally done raiding all the corpses. "Why?"

Asher sighed. "Any direction is as good as another."

"Because there are hills over there. We'll be able to see farther from up high. We can then work out where we are going."

Mercy's mouth fell open. "That… is actually a smart idea."

"I'm not just a pretty face." I grinned down at her.

"We really need to find you a mirror before you embarrass yourself by saying stuff like that."

We headed for the hills as fast as our newly healed legs would carry us for the first mile. Then when an army of svart didn't come pouring out of the woodwork to slaughter us, we slowed down a little and started to chat. "So all those notes and we don't know where a single shard is?"

Asher seemed to be moving faster now that we were out in the sun, finding his stride. Maybe it was a cold-blooded thing, or maybe

Restoration had made up for the night's sleep he had skipped. "The provenance of the human shard was simple enough to trace. It has never been hidden. Rather, it has been publicly displayed at every opportunity."

"So we go get that one?" Mercy asked.

"Were we natives to this world, well versed in the geography, that would most likely be simple, but I for one do not know where the Shattered Bastion lies."

I perked up. "Shattered Bastion? Oh yeah, that is just on the other side of this hill."

He glanced my way. "Indeed?"

Mercy rolled her eyes.

"No, man, I don't know my ass from my elbow here."

Asher's tail lashed as he strode on ahead, but he didn't deign to respond to that. Fair.

Now that we were getting farther from the observatory ruins, the grass was growing lush and green, run through with wildflowers. Now and again, a petal would drift by on the wind—not the pale pink of cherry blossom, but rather rich and red like a rose's. Following a stream down into a dip soon revealed their source. There was a copse of trees lying between us and the hills, blossoming blood red and showering the whole area in their cast-off petals. Mercy stopped to take them in. "Five bucks they are evil vampire trees."

"You've got money?"

She patted her non-existent pockets. "Figurative five bucks."

We'd all stopped by now. Going around the mini-forest probably wouldn't take that long compared to wading through. An extra hour's hiking maybe. "I don't know…we had some pretty wild colored trees back where we came from without them needing to drink human blood."

"Hey, I'm just going along with the theme of everything here trying to kill us."

Asher glanced back at us. "The Prophet did not try to kill us."

"Didn't he though?" I might not have wanted to have this argument again, but Mercy had no inhibitions about it.

"The Prophet provided us with everything that we needed to pursue our fate."

Mercy held up her hands. "Or maybe he was just a nutcase that dropped us in a dungeon to die, and two of us did."

I didn't want Asher to feel like we were ganging up on him. "I don't think we can blame him for Orphia being a psychopath."

Mercy turned her scowl on me. "If he could see the future, how come he didn't predict that? I say we blame him for everything that happens from now on since he knew it was going to happen and didn't warn us."

"Not sure it works that way."

She sneered. "What you do know for sure could be written on the back of a stamp."

"None of us know what is going on here." I was trying to keep my own temper under control. I'd dealt with worse abuse than this working in a fast-food joint and kept on smiling. "Getting bitchy about not knowing isn't going to help us find out."

Her hand drifted up to her quiver, and her eyes widened. "Did you just call me a bitch?"

"If the collar fits?"

She was pulling an arrow and I was bringing my sword around when Asher's *Gravity Snare* knocked us both off our feet, sending us tripping and tumbling sideways until we ended up pressed together next to the tiny black hole he'd just conjured up. "Civility among Eternals, if you would."

Mercy hissed. "Tell that to beef boy!"

"Beef boy?!"

I "accidentally" nudged her with my elbow as I tried to pull away from the snare, but I didn't say anything. Now that the initial flush of irritation had passed, I could see that Asher was right. We were acting like brats.

"Beef Boy is definitely my rap name." I grinned at Mercy even as she tried to pry us apart by kicking off my ribcage, and whatever tantrum she was having ended in a snort of laughter.

She called out. "Alright, *Dad*, we'll behave ourselves."

The snare blinked out of existence, and we tumbled apart. Asher was shaking his head at us, but if he'd really been mad he could have left us pinned to our get-along event horizon. "Shall we proceed to test your theory of sinister vegetation?"

Mercy was gathering up her scattered hoard of arrows, but she stopped long enough to call out, "Team vampire trees!"

As it turned out, the trees were not trying to kill us. The undergrowth and the rabbit trail alongside the stream we followed into the dense wood were carpeted in their petals, so you might have turned an ankle if you were rushing, but I didn't consider that to be a sign of evil, exactly. "Guess you owe me five bucks."

"There is still time for this to go bad." For all that Mercy was probably joking, she did have an arrow nocked the whole time we were creeping under the canopy. We traveled through the woods bunched together, waiting for an ambush, and when it didn't arrive, there was an almost palpable sense of disappointment.

The trees aside, it was hard to feel like everything else in the forest didn't have at least a little bit of bloodlust to it. Tiny black birds with feathers that shimmered like an oil slick swooped at Mercy without cause or reason, and the path that seemed so solid one moment slipped away from beneath our feet the next.

There was no wind beneath the trees; it was almost unnaturally still and silent. I could hear my own breath, and I could hear my own heart. When one of us took too heavy a step, you could almost feel it vibrating to you through the roots.

None of us were speaking; it felt irreverent to chat while you walked through such utter stillness. It'd be like farting in a church. That silence was probably what let us hear the distant sound through the muffling effects of the woods. The rumble beneath our feet. The rhythmic heartbeat thump of something coming.

Mercy glanced my way with alarm apparent on her face, but we had to grab Asher by a sleeve and press a hand over his mouth before he was shaken out of his reverie. We scrambled up into the foliage. I was the ladder, and Mercy was the hoist to get our reptilian companion off the ground.

We stayed there longer than I liked to think about, just feeling the shaking coming up through the tree. I was ready to fight, of course—just because something was big enough to shake a whole forest, that didn't mean I didn't want a piece of it—but the way that the petals were bouncing on the ground made me want to see what I was up against at least.

We caught glimpses of them through the trees. White as death, they were surrounded by a cloud of the same birds that had swooped down on Mercy, again and again. They were too big to be animals. Too big to be anything that moved. The smell hit us a moment later. Rot.

When one of them finally came into sight, I didn't even know what I was looking at for the longest time. I'd assumed it was going to be something like the abomination that we fought before, but it was something else entirely. The bulk of its body was mountainous, and its shape wasn't far off that of a hill either—until you got down to the stem protruding from beneath the dangling cap of its fruiting body. Beneath the umbrella of its mass, there were three legs as thick around as the trunk of the tree we were hanging onto. It was devoid of any real shape but moving furiously.

The birds swooped at it, pecking tiny gobs of the giant moving mushroom's cap away and setting the stink of rot free. Green-tinted slime ran down from those little pecks, crusting onto the surface as it dried in the air. Where the creature hit a tree, it rebounded, blind, and set off rambling in another direction until it found some space that it could squeeze through. It was pure luck it didn't try to push past the one where we were hiding and crush us into just another stain on its surface.

One of these things would have been bizarre enough, but there were dozens of them roaming through the woods, running as fast as they could with no reason or drive, followed by a cloud of birds and spores that stained the red petals a dusty pink. We held onto our place in the tree until the soft tramping sounds of the stampede had passed us by, then we eased our way down to the ground.

Even now, we didn't speak. Asher and Mercy were both wide-eyed, and I probably looked a bit shell-shocked too. The air was thick with spores, and they clung to us as we moved through the woods. By the time that we found another river to wash off, some of them had already started spreading little spiderweb-thin tendrils out across our skin.

In case you were wondering, nothing helps with team-bonding like having to scrape fungus off one another. Try it some time.

After we'd all stopped fretting about mushroom growth, we went back to heading for the hills, but all the dazed sightseeing was done. We kept our heads down, our ears open, and our feet moving. When blue sky started to filter back through to us without a bloodstain to it, I let out a huff of held breath.

It was premature.

Just beyond the tree-line, another band of svart were swarming, heading away from us, uphill alongside the waterfall that fed the stream we'd followed out of the woods. At first, I couldn't make sense of what I was seeing ahead of them, flashes of color beyond the waving spear-heads, glimpses of people, not monsters. The svart hadn't noticed our arrival at all. We could have stood back and let them pass unscathed. Mercy parsed what she was seeing first. "They're attacking a caravan."

I hefted my sword and started forward. "Let's stop them then."

Asher's cold touch on my arm made me pause. "We are not recovered from our last conflict. To fight now will be a risk to our lives, and we have a greater purpose to fulfill than clashing with simple raiders. We must let our heads guide us, not our hearts."

"Those people can die. I can't." I brushed his hand off me. "Shove that logic up your ass."

The screaming up ahead had already started. The trilling shrieks of the svart. The pain of the Dvergar. I was running as fast as I could, and I still wasn't going to be quick enough. I made a clumsy swipe at the svart stragglers as I caught up to them.

Ichor spattered across the slope, tainting the stream, but I didn't slow. The clattering and shattering sounds of combat up ahead would not give me that luxury. The rear ranks of the svart were bunched up, trying to press in between the wooden wagons that the Dvergar had circled as makeshift barricades. Fish in a barrel. A proper swing lopped off a row of heads before the rest even noticed I was there.

Caught between the Dvergar shield wall and my fury, there was no way out for the svart. In that circle of wagons, they had two options, die or face me head-on. They were cowards enough that they seemed to waver between their choices long enough for me to take another wild swing, and I cut into some and bludgeoned others with the bodies of their kin.

The courage of the desperate seized the svart, and they came on at me. There were a dozen of them, stabbing and swinging their weapons, but mostly, they planned to bear me down with their weight of numbers alone. Like cornered rats, they'd turned vicious, and I was too busy trying to hack them up to defend myself.

They were driving me back by the mass of their bodies alone, and their crooked little faces were contorting as they pushed into wicked peg-toothed grins. They thought they were winning. They were right. My sword was pinned between their swarming bodies and mine, holding back the press of them while the others reached around it to stab and hack at me.

One clambered up over another's backs until it was level with my face. Stepping onto the back side of my blade for balance, it brought a pair of cruel hooked daggers up, ready to bring them down and stab the light out of my eyes.

Then an arrow took the svart through the throat, and it toppled back on top of the rest. From behind me, I could hear Mercy's battle cry echoing up the hill. "Beef boy!"

I couldn't help laughing, despite my wounds, and despite the snarling monsters just inches away. I knew that everything was going to be alright now.

A volley of arrows came down, peppering the ranks of the svart and setting them to wailing. With every one that fell away from the press of bodies, I took a step forward. Finally, there were only three svart left, trapped between me and the Dvergar, and I was able to break free of their grasping hands to hammer the blade of my sword down with both hands like a guillotine blade, straight into their chests.

Ichor bubbled up, and their death rattles warbled out, but the fight was over. We had won again.

Victory!
Potency increased to 25
Sword: Rank 3/10
125 Experience Gained

For a moment there was blissful silence, then the shield wall fell away, the half-dozen Dvergar backing away from me amidst a cloud of whispers. I could understand their language thanks to my Eternal gift of speaking in tongues, but all that they seemed to be whispering was that one word, back and forth to each other. "Eternals."

Behind the line, I saw the bodies on the ground. The Dvergar who'd taken up arms or stood sentry before the coming of the svart. One was torn clear in half, and another was missing his head entirely. The last, beardless, and presumably female, was full of holes, punched through with enough spear thrusts that she looked like a particularly meaty swiss cheese. Yet something made me reach out and touch her—the same sense that let me know that she was still alive against all evidence to the contrary.

With a pulse of divine power, I let *Restoration* flow into her, and the woman jerked and heaved beneath my hands. That same sticky fluid bubbled up in every one of her wounds. One of the other Dvergar darted forward with an axe in hand, ready to stop my desecration of his friend's corpse, but that was when her eyes snapped open, and she gasped in a lungful of air. He scampered back.

Whatever font of life I was drawing on to heal wounds ran dry before her injuries could close, but they had gone from lethal impalement to surface punctures. She had a chance to survive now. Mercy was at my elbow by the time I was done, eyeing the other Dvergar cautiously. "Do you think you could get in one fight without nearly dying?"

I coughed up a little moon-tinted blood when I laughed. "Who wants an easy life anyway?"

Asher had arrived, lurking between the wagons with his tail lashing. Guess he was mad I'd saved these people. Well, that was just fine. I was mad at him too.

With an arm over Mercy's shoulders for a little assist back onto my feet, I turned to greet the Dvergar. The half-dead one propped herself up on her elbows, still oozing blood. "What be you wanting?"

Mercy scoffed. "You're welcome."

"Yes, my thanks to you." One of the other Dvergar moved in to help support her, and she shooed him away with a grunt. Guess she wore the pants around here. "What be you wanting for the help?"

That took the wind out of my sails. I was expecting gratitude, but that was about it. Being asked what reward I wanted made the whole thing seem less heroic and more sordid. Asher piped up from the back. "Where is this caravan headed?"

The Dvergar bristled at the sound of his voice, but after a moment, their leader called out to him. "Our next trading post be Khag Mhor."

Asher came forward until he was almost level with us. I didn't turn to see him. "May we accompany you?"

The Dvergar licked her lips, gaze flicking between us. "That is all you're wanting?"

"This is new territory for us." Mercy picked up the conversation. "Some sort of settlement where we can find our footing is probably just what we need."

One of the other Dvergar butted in. He had a ginger beard dangling in a braid beneath his bucket helm. "They won't be letting outsiders in. They're barely tolerating us, and we're blood-kin."

Despite murmured protests from her people, the Dvergar leader climbed to her feet. "They'll be welcoming Eternals. Everyone's got a problem needs fixing these days. Three Eternals is a lot of fixing."

This was more familiar territory. I smiled down at the Dvergar. "Happy to help."

That drew another scowl out of her, but she stepped forward nonetheless, her hand held out in a fist. I bumped it with my own. "I be Gunhild. These are my boys."

"I'm Maulkin. This is Mercy. That's Asher."

With introductions made, the Dvergar seemed to relax—which for Dvergar looked like getting busy. Beyond Gunhild's odd outfit, all were armored up from heel to head in squared-off mail, bound in leather straps that made no sense at first glance since they kept their weapons and gear stowed on the sides of the wagons instead of on their person. They set about the business of getting their dead buried beneath cairns of gathered stones and getting the caravan rolling again. It took only a few minutes. This was a well-oiled machine, and these weren't the first dead they'd had to bury.

Gunhild herself had some combination of dark riding leathers and heavy silk veils draped about her. There seemed to be no logic or pattern to them, hiding odd strips of skin from sight and holding down some hair, but letting the rest of it hang in thick dark braids elsewhere.

It took two of them to hoist Gunhild up onto the footplate of the closest wagon, but then the bondage gear they were wearing over their armor started to make sense. They clicked into place at the front of each of the wagons perfectly. Leather, metal hoops, and the wooden struts all fitting together perfectly. They had no horses to haul these things around, only themselves. I suppose that made sense for folk that lived underground. Caves probably weren't the best place to keep a pony ranch.

Some of the wagons lacked drivers now, but they'd never needed them except to serve as lookouts. "We'll be running hard for Khag Mhor to be beating sundown. Will you be keeping up?"

Mercy gave a terse nod. "We'll manage."

Gunhild gave the first thing we'd seen resembling a smile. Her teeth were grey. "Won't be waiting for you."

I laughed, letting *Restoration* close my wounds while she watched. "Won't be needing to."

[224/440 Health]

Asher didn't even try to walk alongside me and Mercy, crossing over to the opposite side of the caravan to serve as a lookout on the upper slope as we followed around its curve. Either he knew he'd screwed up, or he was seething because he still thought I had. It didn't matter which. I'd deal with him later.

Gunhild's wagon took point, so that was the one Mercy and I stuck close to. The rest of them weren't too chatty, and more than anything else, we needed information right now.

Mercy took point on that. I had all the social graces of a sledge-hammer. "So what is Khag Mhor like?"

"What do any place be like?" Gunhild shrugged. Good to know that was a universal gesture. "Old city. Dvergar city. Half lost to svart from the mines now."

"Anything else around here worth knowing about?"

Gunhild's eyes narrowed. "That'd be depending what you're wanting to be knowing about. Got bloodwoods. Got the old khag. Good iron be in the hills. Sea is splashing to the east."

She was suspicious, but Mercy went on trying to play it cool. "Any old ruins? Any interesting history?"

"What do three Eternals be looking for exactly?"

Mercy was shaking her head, but I asked anyway. "The Rusted Blade."

Gunhild laughed in my face until she started coughing. "You're joking? Do you be babes believing cradle stories? There be no Rusted Blade. Nothing but an old story."

"Hold on now." Mercy was the one scowling now. "There is a warlord in the Shattered Bastion who has a shard right now."

"A little man be saying he has a shard. Scaring all the other little men. Making them be bowing down to him. I can be saying things too. Doesn't be making them true."

If Asher was close enough to join in, he probably would have been in hysterics about destiny and the like by now, but he wasn't. Instead, there was just three sort of sane people talking about whether or not some pasty Inyoka hiding out in the middle of nowhere was lying about a magic sword.

The conversation lulled for a while as Mercy and I chewed that over. Enough time passed for the path to tip from flat to steep. There were a few animals hopping around up here that looked kind of like long-horned goats with mossy green fur, but I guess they weren't my distant cousins from the way they ran from me on sight.

Eventually, Mercy's patience boiled over. "So the Dvergar weren't given a shard?"

"Never seen it; never heard of it." Gunhild chuckled. "Whatever Dver be having it never told anyone about it. If it be real. Which it be not."

I recognized a dead-end when I saw it, but just because our train of thought was derailed, it didn't mean we had to stop rolling. "So where did you guys come from?"

"We started out from Khag Elock. Far south." Her eyes stayed fixed on the horizon. Always looking ahead. "City be falling to void spawn. Too few defenders left after raids. It be empty now, 'less you be wanting to do trade with monsters."

"Sorry to hear that." Great, another touchy subject. "Khag Elock? You must have passed through some interesting places on your way up here."

"More of my boys be dead from the road than from the siege." Her already grim expression grew ever stonier. "If it don't be monsters, it be bandits. If it don't be bandits, it be void spawn. If it don't be void spawn, stone storms be pitching us off the roads. Amaranth be trying to shrug us off. Pretend the Dver never exist. We be a cursed folk."

With that charming little show-stopper, the conversation fizzled and died again. By the time that the sun dipped behind the mountain's zenith, I was silently praying for some monsters to attack us just to break up the awkward silence.

Unfortunately, they didn't oblige me.

CHAPTER 9

The bloodwood trees became more and more sparse the higher we climbed, and soon they gave away entirely to a scattering of standing stones, worked not with the whorls and swirls we'd seen in the observatory basement but a set of rigid, angular designs that looked about a sneeze away from being runes instead of abstracts. It wasn't hard to make the connection between the blocky designs on the wagons and the shapes on the stones. Old Dvergar road markers guided us up to what I should have been able to describe as a cave but couldn't quite manage to. Every line of the opening in the cliff wall was pristine and perfect—almost too perfect to believe that it had been shaped with simple tools. Maybe it wasn't. Maybe we were off to see the wizard who'd carved it out.

Even if we'd somehow overlooked the simple perfection of the entrance, there was no mistaking what came after. A set of bronze gates were set into the stone, patterned with the same designs as the stones, and they were so perfectly fitted to the tunnel that I'd wager they were watertight. They were big and shiny and caught your eye the moment you stepped in out of the dimming light. That was deliberate. I probably would have overlooked all the rest of the cunning masonry if it weren't for my *Dungeoneering knowledge* dragging my eyes away from the bright and beautiful to take in all the things meant to kill me.

A row of tiny squares was cut out of the floor just a short distance into the cave for the portcullis to lock into when it was dropped from the darkness above. A glance up showed me not only the line of shadow drawn across the roof where it would emerge from but also an array of perfect square cut holes covering the whole ceiling—holes that my new skill was whispering could be used to dump scalding oil down onto anyone trapped in this killing zone. High on the walls, there were even smaller squares where archers could fire out. It seemed that the Dvergar took their security pretty seriously. That was fine by me. I didn't really fancy the idea of waking up to an army of invading monsters either.

Gunhild didn't give any of this impressive design work a second glance—I guess it was just normal for her. She rode her wagon all the way up to the gates and then her lead "horses" reached up to hammer on the metal with the flat of their hands.

"Who be seeking entrance to Khag Mhor?" a voice boomed out from all around us. More clever engineering at work.

"Gunhild, Matriarch of Remnant Elock, be seeking to trade and share in Mhor hospitality." Gunhild wasn't to be outdone, she'd stood up on the bench and was bellowing right back.

Standing there under the oil holes, with who knew how many arrows trained on us and no hope in hell of getting back out of this cave before we were full of holes, may have warped my perception of time a bit. When there was a long pause, it felt like a full year had passed.

When the voice boomed out again, I literally jumped. My feet left the ground. "Khag Mhor welcomes the Remnant Elock, but who be they longshanks with you, Gunhild?"

Of course, we were the source of the problem. Of course. I stepped forward and opened my mouth only for Gunhild to silence me with a glare. She definitely earned that Matriarch title, that was a distinctly mom-flavored glare.

"They be servants. Guardians of my train."

Mercy made a grunt of exasperation, her mouth flying open. I had to pick her up by the head, wrapping a hand around her mouth before she could interrupt.

"Longshanks don't be welcome here, Gunhild. Specially not them with firedamp eyes. Send them outside and the gate be swinging open."

Mercy did her best to kick me, but I was so used to it by this point that I didn't even fuss. When she licked my hand, I figured her tantrum had passed, so I dropped her by my side once more, smearing her own spittle up her face and drying my palm on her hair.

"They be more than servants." Gunhild glanced down at the two of us as I held Mercy and her wildly swinging fists away from me at arm's length. "Saved my life. Saved my train."

"You be claiming them as kin?"

Taking hold of Mercy's head, I twisted her around to face Gunhild's distressed expression as the Matriarch sighed, "I do that. I do."

With gates that big, I expected a creak that shook the mountain when they split down the middle and swung open, but in this, as in everything, the Dvergar craftsmanship won out over the dramatic. They opened without a peep, swinging open to reveal a glowing world of wonders beneath the surface of the earth.

The carved stone continued, but on the floor and up the walls it was inlaid with the same brass as the gates. Up by the ceiling, crystals protruded through the upper corners every few feet, not like they'd been placed there, but like they'd grown out of the stone. Each cluster was identical in shape but not in color. Dim light shone within each crystal cluster, filtering out to fill the chamber with a stained-glass dappling that stretched across the width of the broad corridor and the breadth of the rainbow.

There were no new Dvergar to meet and greet as we marched in, but I didn't think too much about it. Maybe things were done differently among Dvergar. Maybe they just didn't like the rainbow room. As long as Gunhild didn't fuss, I wasn't worrying either. The gates closed silently once the last of the Dvergar drawn wagons was inside, and it was only when I was glancing back when the air pressure changed that I spotted Asher. Instead of taking in the sights, his eyes were fixed on the ground. His tail was even dragging along behind him.

A pang of sympathy for the miserable lizard man distracted me from the memory of what he'd said. If it were up to him, every one of Gunhild's little family would be dead and gone, just because it wasn't convenient to save them. I wasn't totally on board with the whole hero plan myself—it felt like it was a recipe for disaster to rely on me to save anybody—but at least I wasn't willing to stand aside and let bad things happen. Asher was smarter than me, but that didn't mean he was right, it just meant he could come up with better reasons to be an asshole.

Still, if it weren't for him, we'd all be dead down in the basement of the observatory, and then dead again when the svart attacked. Or if not that, then still standing around up on the top of this hill, trying to work out what reward we wanted from the Dvergar we'd saved. I couldn't remember having siblings in my old life, but I figured that Asher was as close as I was going to get to a brother in this world, and you didn't throw away family just because you disagreed with them. You still invited the racist old auntie around to dinner once a year to listen to her ranting about how mobile phones were mind control devices invented by China. That was just polite.

If I could forgive and forget for the racist conspiracy-theory auntie, I was pretty sure I could welcome Asher back into the fold. He was at least sane enough to be reasoned with. Maybe he wasn't a natural to the hero gig like me, but even he could see the advantages we'd won by saving these people, and next time around he'd probably be the first to jump in. It didn't matter if he was doing it for the rewards, or because it was the right thing to do. All that mattered was that he did it.

I crossed over to the other side of the corridor, nipping in front of the next wagon just ahead of the Dvergar pulling it. Asher didn't even look up until he'd almost crashed into me. Then he suddenly seemed to spring back to life, tail lashing from side to side and mouth falling open.

"I regret what—"

"I'm sorry."

We had both spoken over each other, but the message was clear. He fell silent, shame still hanging over him, so I pushed on. "We aren't one person. We aren't always going to agree on everything, and that's alright. Sometimes you're going to want to do things differently from me, and that's alright too. I think that not wanting to save people that need saving is a weird hill to die on, but that doesn't mean we aren't still on the same side."

"I regret what I said. I…you made the correct decision. My judgment was clouded. Selfish. I cared more for your safety than that of the Dvergar."

I did a double-take. "My safety?"

"Your injuries since we arrived here have been severe. I feared that another conflict would be your last." His shoulders slumped. "I should have trusted in your own assessment of your abilities."

I let out a startled little laugh that turned the head of the passing Dvergar. "Oh, man, no. Never do that. I was an idiot. I totally could have died back there."

He cocked his head to the side. "Indeed?"

"Oh yeah, those little svarts were kicking my ass until Mercy showed up. But the thing is, even if I knew I was going to die, I still would have done it. Even if dying was permanent for us, I'd like to think I'd still have done it."

His tongue flicked out like he was trying to taste lies in the air. "You would die so readily for strangers?"

"People are people."

He stared at me for a moment, then began walking again so we weren't left behind, pausing for me to fall in step beside him. "You are an unusual person, Maulkin."

I wrapped an arm around his narrow shoulders and gave him a

squeeze. "I'm going to pretend that was a compliment."

Up ahead, another set of gates were swinging open, so I jogged forward to catch my first glimpse of a Dvergar city. It did not disappoint. The stone had been carved out in every direction. It was like somebody had built a toy city inside their empty room, except we were toy-sized.

The walls curved at the tops creating a perfect arch nearly a mile high, running along the length of the colossal cavern. More of the same glowing crystal formations filled up that ridge, illuminating the whole place with an ambient glow that probably wouldn't have been enough for humans but provided our new eyes with just enough to comfortably navigate without seeing too far. It was impossible to tell how far back the cavern went because buildings sprang up in carefully ordered lines just beyond the open square near the entrance, where Gunhild's boys were already unloading their wares. The squat one-story houses were squared off at the top, identical in every way, barring the mark inscribed above their open door-frames. Guess the Dvergar weren't big on privacy.

Cleanliness didn't seem to be a top priority either. The crisp lines where the streets and buildings met were clotted with dust and thick banks of soot. It lay over the whole city now that I looked, staining the stonework and obscuring the carvings that had once served as a means to navigate the endless blocks of buildings. It wasn't exactly a beautiful place, or a comfortable one, but you had to admire the craftsmanship required to get everything so identical.

There was only the one Dvergar that hadn't come in with us in sight, and he was doing that little fist bump greeting with first Gunhild, then every one of her boys according to the pecking order. Time to say hello. "Hello!"

Oops, I didn't mean to shout. The Dvergar greeter manfully resisted the urge to duck when I strode over, but he definitely did flinch. There was a beard hanging down one side of his chest in a braided loop, so I assumed I was dealing with a dude, but he was robed up in even more silk than Gunhild, with half of his face obscured behind one scarf and the majority of his body squared away inside armor. Cautiously, he raised a fist, and I gave it a nudge with my own. "We be welcoming you to Khag Mhor."

"We?" Mercy caught up with me. "I can only see one of you."

"I be speaking for the elders of Mhor." He held up a begrudging fist for her to bump. "I be one, but they be many."

Asher had closed the distance without me noticing. Again. His stealth skill must have started at one hundred. "Greetings to you and your elders." He held out his fist, which the Dvergar bumped with entirely more force than was necessary.

"What be bringing sky-born to the khag?"

Before we could answer, Gunhild spoke over us. "Your svart problem be spilling out on the hills, that's what. Weren't for these long-shanks, me and my boys would be roasting over the deep-fires now."

There was a moment of silence, that I fully expected to be followed up with a lot of shouting, and probably our prompt eviction, but instead, the ambassador was staring off into space. "Half the khag be svart now. Mine-side be theirs now. Took the spinner-worms three moons back. No more silk to trade. They be pushing for the farm-rooms now. Starve us out. Just time until the khag's theirs."

Gunhild growled. "No fight be left in you?"

"Too many barricades to man. Too many Dver gone to the stone." I was starting to get pissed off on this poor guy's behalf.

I stepped up. "Good thing we're here to help you then."

Gunhild, the other Dvergar, and Mercy looked at me with varying degrees of shock and horror. Mercy hissed, "You want to fight a whole city of monsters?"

I smirked at her. "It's free experience?"

"I do not wish to return to our previous dispute, but this does not seem to lead us closer to our goals." Asher, being as political as always.

"Come on, guys, it is a few svart, how hard could it be?"

Gunhild looked from me to the other Dvergar, and then they both burst out laughing. It continued for a solid minute, while I stood there looking sheepish. Through her tears, Gunhild managed to sputter out, "A few svart!" which just seemed to set them off all over again.

More Dvergar had begun to emerge from the silent city. Some were strolling down the street like it was an average day, others hobbled and limped, dragging a leg or arm along like it was a dead weight. It was just enough like a zombie movie to make me uncomfortable, but since Gunhild was still cracking up while giving them greeting fist-bumps, I guessed it was business as usual. Maybe the svart attacks were really kicking everyone's ass.

The Dvergar caravan we'd rolled in with sprung into well-oiled motion as the town woke up, stowing away their helmets and setting out their wares, using the ridged sides of the wagons as shelving. By the time the first of the locals had arrived, they'd plucked off their helmets and were chatting away like it was a normal day at the market. I guess for the Dvergar, it was.

There was even more silk on display now that the helmets were off, patterned and pretty in a way you would never have guessed was hiding under the blank metal faceplates. Almost every one of them had a silk scarf or two wrapped over their whole heads, though a few still proudly displayed braids and beards. No cash was changing hands, but there was a murmur of promises being traded back and forth. Barter at its finest. Maybe Amaranth just didn't have money. That would be nice. That would mean I wasn't broke.

Now that Gunhild had stopped pissing herself laughing in my face, she decided to give me a bit more to go on. "You'll be thinking the svart down here are like the stragglers that nearly did for me up on the hill."

"You'll be thinking Khag Mhor is feeble that it can't beat them back." The ambassador rolled his eyes at me. "Hundreds of them rush out the tunnels like floodwater. They be washing over everything. No stopping them. No fighting them. Just bodies."

I shrugged my giant shoulders, making the dead weight of the sword resting across them bounce. "Hundreds die as easily as dozens. I don't see the difference."

"The difference be the beasts." The ambassador's good humor faltered. "Down in the mines, the svart be digging out the flesh-forges of old. They be rekindling them. They be coming with void-spawn in chains. More than even you longshanks could be facing."

Mercy got in before me. "The abominations? We wasted one of those on our second day in Amaranth."

That took the last mirth out of Gunhild too. "Do she be speaking truly?"

"We killed one. It wasn't easy, but... yeah."

"Could you be doing it again?" Her eyes were practically sparkling, and I've never been good at saying no to girls. Especially not girls that only came up to mid-thigh. "Could you be helping these folk?"

I bent down to clap her on the shoulder. "Isn't that what Eternals are for?"

She and the ambassador exchanged some looks that told me that probably wasn't what Eternals were for, but I didn't let it dent my confidence. That was what Eternals were going to be for from then on. Eventually, the ambassador let out a sigh. "They'll need to be meeting the elders. It'll be them who decide it. Prepare them best you can, then bring them on in."

He headed off into the city, but when I stepped up to follow him, Gunhild had a hold of my rope belt. "There be some things you're needing to know first. Let's take us a walk."

While it seemed like a straight shot to wherever the ambassador was headed, Gunhild led us off to one side until I could make out the looming wall of the cavern curving up towards us. The stone above us started to feel oppressive like we had the weight of the world pressing down on us. I didn't know how the Dvergar lived like this.

The narrow grid of the streets angled out once we were away from the gate, assuming new straight paths for us to follow along. Some fired off towards the walls like the one we followed, and the others spread out wider and led deeper into the warren of the city. I was starting to understand why barricading parts of the town off was so difficult to manage. There must have been a hundred paths to stopper, and while the buildings climbed a little higher towards the roof farther in, all the outlying concentric squares were only a little taller than me. A run and a jump would have had me on top of any one of them, and what the svart lacked in height, they probably made up for in willingness to clamber on top of each other.

By the wall, the buildings fell away into broad open squares. Cultivated earth was sunk into the channels that had been carved in the same broad patterns as decorated everything here, and mushrooms sprang up out of the patterns, glowing in as many colors as the crystals above. The Dvergar really seemed to love their rainbows.

I could tell that Mercy had been simmering the whole way, but just before we cleared the last line of buildings, she socked me in the arm as hard as she could. "What do you think you're doing signing me up to fight a mine full of those monsters? One of them nearly messed us all up earlier. One of them. Not a mine full. One."

"What, you don't want to?"

Asher was quick to intervene, catching her by the arm before she hit me again. "Once more, I question how this path leads us closer to our goals."

"This place is the only thing anywhere near the observatory." I shrugged. "I figure if the shard is anywhere, it is probably down in the mines where all the monsters come from. Video game logic, you know?"

Asher opened and closed his mouth, falling silent. Mercy's clenched fist turned into an accusatory finger, then her hands fell to her side. "How can you be so obviously stupid and still keep saying things that make sense?"

"My blessing"—I pressed the back of my hand to my forehead and dipped back—"and my curse."

Gunhild watched all of this play out with mounting puzzlement on her face, but as she slumped down onto one of the benches, she pushed that confusion away. "There be an old story among the Dvergar to explain the things you need to know, but I know you be over-fond of cradle-tales so I'll be telling you this now. It be a story, not the truth."

Asher and Mercy sat themselves down beside her on the bench, and I parked my backside on the path, leaning back on one of the bigger mushrooms and hoping it wasn't a hallucinogen. Or if it was, it was the fun kind.

"You be knowing the void god story. We dug him out. Dver are taught shame for it at the teat. Our wanting for gods brought doom on the world."

"Yeah, you all suck." Mercy was a big believer in audience participation. "We know. Get to the point."

It was enough to break Gunhild's maudlin streak and draw out her grin. "Cheek on this one. Could be a Dvergar herself.

"There was a war, void god lost, void god died. None of it matters. What matters be the oath. The Dver swore themselves to the dark one when he first rose up. Dvergar oaths don't be like the spit in the wind men and faun make. They be writ in our heart. Unbreakable. But here was one we had to break. We didn't see Araphel for what he be at first. When we swore, we didn't know what he'd become. So we did what we be needing to—no matter how it cost us." Her voice trailed off into silence, and she seemed to be girding herself for the next part.

Asher cocked his head to the side. "What was the cost, Gunhild?"

She jumped when she realized that Asher was so close to her, but when she heard his tone, all the lines washed from what I could see of her face. She put her hand down on top of his upturned palm and didn't even flinch when the claws closed over her glove. "They be calling it the curse of stone. When we betrayed Araphel, he said to us, 'If you be loving a life surrounded by stone over the world I'd give you, then let the stone be taking you.' It's all just a story, but there be a truth in it. Truth of a blight."

With the hand that wasn't clinging to Asher for all she was worth, Gunhild reached up to draw one of the silk strips banded around her forehead up, revealing the grey-toned flesh underneath. "You needn't be flinching away. Only Dvergar can catch it, whatever it be."

Asher's voice was as soft as a whisper. "The curse of stone."

"Aye, that it be. We're born to stone and die to it too. Every Dvergar babe is born with the mark upon them, and as the years be passing, the stone be spreading. That's why I'm telling you all this now so that when you be seeing the elders, you don't go thinking there is some trick being played. It isn't a secret longshanks get to hear, and if I didn't be claiming you as kin, you'd never have heard it for all the time you walked Amaranth."

Mercy reached out to take Gunhild's other hand. "Thank you for trusting us."

"Trust? Do you be seeing trust?" Gunhild let out a snort. "You'd still know naught if that bumbling fool over there hadn't set you to the task of fighting all the monsters in the mountain."

"Glad I did then." I smiled back at her. "Your people shouldn't have to carry this weight alone."

Mercy rolled her eyes at me trying to be sincere, but Asher nodded along with me. I guess his change of heart earlier wasn't just for show.

"Come along then." Gunhild hauled herself to her feet, leading Mercy and Asher up in a daisy chain. "My boys will be handling all the trading, let's get you to the elders of Mhor and be seeing what use they can find for you."

CHAPTER 10

The deeper into the city we delved, the more apparent the state of ruin it was sinking into became. The solid stone that the buildings had been carved from was war-marked and flame-scarred. Chunks were missing here and there, and there were signs of collapse everywhere that I looked. The buildings that had lost their integrity were bad enough, but when we had to detour around a glowing crystal cluster that had fallen from the ceiling, I started to get genuinely concerned. Getting crushed to death under a giant pile of rocks sounded almost as bad as being dissolved by spider god venom.

My brother and sister in glowing eyes didn't seem too concerned about it, and I wasn't going to be the first one to wimp out, but I still kept catching my eyes drifting upwards. Maybe it was my *Dungeoneering* setting alarm bells ringing. Mercy caught me at it, gawking up at the ceiling herself. "What is it? Giant spiders?"

"It's nothing." I dragged my eyes back down. "Just... wondering if the whole thing is going to fall down."

Gunhild didn't look back, but I could hear her chortle. "Don't be letting the elders hear you talking like that. It be an insult to the ancestors to suggest a khag don't be sturdy enough to last out all of time, and half of the elders almost be ancestors themselves."

More of the plazas with glowing mushrooms were dotted through the city, and this far in, buildings had a couple of stories or more going for them, although I was interested to notice that ramps ran up around the outsides of them instead of there being stairs inside. Why was that interesting? Was I an architect in some other past life that I couldn't remember? That did not sound like the kind of rock and roll lifestyle that I wanted for my imaginary previous self. If I was an architect, I hoped it was the kind that built giant mirrored skyscrapers with a curve that accidentally set adjacent buildings on fire. Maybe it was just that *Dungeoneering* was this world's version of architecture, with all the students studying up and hoping to land a gig building a dungeon of their own someday.

The barricades reared up almost unexpectedly when we rounded a corner. There were as many Dvergar manning them as I'd seen in all the rest of the city, firing crossbow bolts over the top of the heaped furniture and cobbled together walkways that were holding back the monsters on their doorstep.

We followed alongside the barricades, taking in all the sights and sounds of a war being ever so slowly lost. The odd crystal-tipped arrow made it over the top of the palisades, but they never reached us. The svart didn't even seem to be aiming, just shooting something off in the general direction of the Dvergar to make them duck.

I doubted that the svart were smart enough for psychological warfare, but even if it wasn't deliberate, the bombardment still had the same effect. Every one of the Dvergar manning that barricade seemed to be at their wit's end.

We followed along the ragged line that the barricade had formed between Dvergar and svart territory, all the way to the far wall of the city. When we got to the elaborate entrance to the elder's chambers—as big and impressive in their own way as the entrance to the city itself, albeit a little more ornate and less functional—you could still hear the baying of the monsters from a few streets away. The barbarians at the gates were in spitting distance of their seat of power. No wonder they were all so bummed out.

After passing beneath an arch of shiny brass-work that my *Dungeoneering* knowledge kept insisting was some sort of trap, we were shuffled through a few corridors into a waiting room and more of the same stone benches that we'd seen outside, rendered even more uncomfortable by the fancier engravings digging into my ass. The place was serious and solemn enough that I felt like a dick for trying to kick off a conversation, so I turned my attention back to the heap of experience points I still hadn't divvied out. If I was about to go and fight a whole town of monsters, I wanted to make sure that I didn't have much to lose.

366 experience was enough to buy three ranks of anything or one divine skill. Since my sword was still looking rough as hell, I figured that I'd toss the extra experience into upgrading *Rough Hewn Weapons*, but it was a no-go. I needed to rank up the pillar first. *Rough Hewn Armor* seemed like a good alternate option. Down here in what was essentially an oversized mine, I could already feel all the materials that were available to work with. Sure I'd be stripping the décor if I did it here, but surely nobody would mind if I borrowed a bit from inside enemy territory. I poured experience into the skill and felt the moonlight fill me up with knowledge.

When I opened my eyes again, everyone was still sitting silently, even though Gunhild kept giving me serious side-eye. I wondered if I'd been glowing again. We were there a long time before one of the local Dvergar—wrapped up in so much silk they were barely recognizable—popped in to tell us they were ready for us.

Short-stack mummy led us back and forth through what I could swear were the same corridors, dipping up and down between different levels until I was so turned around I didn't have a hope of finding my way out. The svart might have been right at the door, but if they didn't know their way through this maze then it would have taken them months to find the right way through. These Dvergar were smarter than they looked.

Finally and abruptly, the chamber opened out into something more closely resembling a cave than any of the fine and beautiful masonry we had seen before, and a single cast-iron brazier burned green at the center of the room, casting long shadows up the rough walls and revealing shapes that your eyes could convince you were faces staring back at you out of the dark—faces that seemed to scowl down at us as the wind made the fire flicker. Looked like we were expected to wait here too. I hefted the sword off my shoulder and set its tip down with a clang. Strong or not, that thing was huge.

It echoed up the walls and was answered with a low grumbling sound that resolved into something like throat singing—deep and reverberating. It took me longer than it should have to realize that there were words in the groan as a long litany of Dvergar names—stretching back through the depths of history all the way down to our very own Gunhild, daughter of Gundar the Son of Gungridr—poured forth. She didn't even try to match them in groaning tone or in the length of their memory, but she still shouted out to each elder in turn. "Elder Krannog, I be greeting you. Elder Rodar, I be greeting you. Elder Kalga, I be greeting you. Elder Jormun, I be greeting you…"

It went on and on until she'd rattled off a dozen names or more. The same groaning chorus came down to us, and I wondered if this was some other feat of Dvergar engineering, throwing their voices into an empty chamber to impress the local yahoos. My eyes struggled in the half-light of the fire. If it had been pitch black, my internal glow would have lit things up, or if the fire had been stoked higher, I would have made it out sooner. That is my excuse anyway. In honesty, I think I just didn't want to accept what I was seeing.

The elders weren't just in the room, they were the room. The curse of stone had spread across every surface of their skin and hair, but that had not been enough. It had pushed beyond that limit, spreading out from the Dvergar themselves to encrust their bodies against the wall, embedding them in stone, and growing thicker and thicker. I didn't know how they were being kept alive. If some poor Dvergar had to climb a ladder to pour food in their mouths and shovel out the shit or if the magic of the curse preserved them as these living statues, crudely cut into the walls and sinking back into the rock that birthed them.

Now that I knew what I was looking at, I could tell when each one was speaking. "Why do you be bringing sky-born to witness our shame? Why do you dare to be bringing any outsider to the fire-damp tomb?" I could see their lips straining to move against the weight of rock trying to hold them slack-jawed.

Gunhild wet her lips and took a deep breath. "These be Eternals, come to aid your khag."

There was a sound like grinding stone as the Elders tried to crane their necks and get a better look at us. Flecks of stone rained down all around us like the cave had dandruff, and opinions started raining down about the same time.

"Eternals, be they? I don't be seeing it..."

"Can't be trusting longshanks. Never met a longshanks you could look in the eye..."

"Never be needing Eternals before..."

"No good be coming of the gods or their spawn. In my day..."

"We be needing no aid. All be well in Khag Mhor..."

What had been a harmony before now rumbled around us discordant with every one of the elders rambling off in their own direction. Gunhild was just standing there, letting them blather on, but I had better things to be doing with my eternity. "You can smell the Svart from here. We might be outsiders, or tall, or whatever else you hate, but you can't deny that this place needs help."

There were a lot of grumbling noises echoing around us. They might not have agreed on much, but none of the elders liked being interrupted.

"You be shutting your shouting-hole."

"Disrespect like I've never been seeing..."

"Never been needing Eternals before…"

"Who be you to speak such to the Elders of Mhor?"

I jumped in on that last one. "I'm Maulkin. This is Mercy, and that's Asher. We fought your svart problem above ground, and we killed one of the flesh-forged. So maybe you should show us a bit of respect. We've earned it."

The bitching and moaning continued all around us, but there was a rumbling undercurrent now.

"Never in all my days."

"Never been needing Eternals before…"

It took me a moment to realize that the rumble was a laugh, a laugh so rough and raucous that it soon drowned out all of the other elders until only the laughing Dvergar remained. "Got some stones on you!"

A sideways glance to Gunhild didn't help me work that one out any better. "Thanks?"

"Let's say you be right. Let's say there be trouble in this khag." I finally spotted the one Dvergar that was still talking. He was embedded in the wall above the entryway we'd come through, and his beard hung down in jagged stalactites. "What might you be offering to do about it?"

"We're here to help however we can." I turned to face the one reasonable person in the wall. "If you want us to fight, we can fight. If you want us to talk to them, we'll try. Hell, if you want us to water the mushrooms we'll do that. Whatever it takes."

The rest of the room was rumbling all over again—loud enough that I genuinely started to wonder just how many Elders this place had. How many Dvergar had been brought in here to hang? Eventually, one creaking voice called out, "The worms. Win us back the worms, then we'll be talking to you. Not before."

I turned back to Mr. Stabby Beard and winced as he tried to nod. "Aye, the spinner-worm farms be fallen to the svart. If you be winning them back, then we'll be accepting your help."

I opened my mouth to tell them where they could shove it, but Asher cut me off. "We gratefully accept your quest and hope that our efforts prove fruitful in earning your trust."

My little posse all started heading for the door, hooking into my elbows and dragging me along with them as I tried to work out the right words to convey exactly what I thought of the Elders demanding that we work for the right to help them out. Most of the words I was coming up with only had four letters.

When I actually got my mouth to open, Mercy slugged me in the arm before I could say anything. I looked down at her. "If I ever feel you hitting me, you're going to be in real trouble."

She snorted but loosened her grip on my arm so that I could turn around and walk alongside them instead of being hauled out into the hallway where our mummified guide was waiting to lead us out again. Whatever they'd thought of the exchange inside, I couldn't make out an expression beneath all the wrappings.

This time, I paid extra attention to all of the twists and turns, but I was still surprised when we came back out into the main chamber of the khag. According to my recollections, we should have just come back out in the firedamp chamber where all the elders liked to hang. Guess I needed a higher *Dungeoneering* skill to make sense of it.

The ambassador was waiting to greet us with a skeptical look on his face. Gunhild gave him another knuckle-bump then turned to face us. "They'll be taking the worm-farms back from the svart."

"You'll be doing that, will you?"

Mercy scowled up at me. "That's the plan."

I mock scowled back at her. "That is the plan."

Asher had his hands pressed over his eyes so he didn't have to see the two of us. "Might you furnish us with more details?"

The ambassador's name was Gorm, and his half-masked expression was incredulous as he talked us through the layout of the city and what we'd have to do to drive the svart back. The worm-farms were another side chamber off from the main city—vast humid cuboids hacked out of the stone and crisscrossed with ropes that the silkworms dangled from, doing their silkwormy business.

That bit was easy enough. It was the battle-planning that took some effort to get my head around. The svart were too dumb to fight like an army, according to Gorm. A normal army took enough losses in one area and it would retreat from that area to regroup, but that required a level of communication and awareness that was beyond the little pasty bastards' capabilities. They would just keep on coming, draining every other front of the conflict to flood into any space where they thought that there was action. So if we went charging in, all that was going to happen was that we would be drowned in svart. The end goal might have been to wipe out all the svart eventually, but not all in one go. Even I wasn't that confident in our abilities.

There were no maps of Khag Mhor. Gorm and Gunhild looked taken aback when I suggested it like they couldn't understand the concept. Every Dvergar that lived in the khag knew its layout like the back of their hand, and since that layout was literally set in stone, they never had to relearn it. This was great for them but didn't help us with our planning all that much. Eventually, I kicked a big heap of ash out from a corner, and they started sketching the place out. We brave immortals stood around twiddling our thumbs for a bit until Mercy let out a cry of dismay. "Oh, come on."

I followed her glower to the little map, where Gorm was diligently doodling out every single building and street in the city, starting from the gates and working back. When I sighed, it came out like a guttural grumble. Would I ever get used to this new voice?

Getting down on my haunches, I dragged my thick finger along in a wobbly line at about the right distance in. "Here's the barricade.

Where's the farm?"

Both the Dvergar were looking at the mess I'd made of their dust pile with unabashed horror, but Gunhild managed to get her mouth to snap shut first, and she scribbled in the outer wall and the farm caves, though it seemed to physically pain her to do it.

It was a fair distance beyond the barricade. More than I'd trust myself to successfully sneak. Not that I'd know what to do even if I did sneak in. Mercy and Asher knelt down to study the ever more expansive map as it was sketched out. Asher let out a distressed hiss. "This is all beyond the range of my knowledge."

Mercy snorted. "You never waged an underground war on a bunch of evil gnomes before?"

"He lived a sheltered life." I grinned.

Asher did not seem amused. "Have either of you any experience with this sort of planning?"

"I played a lot of video games?"

Mercy snorted. It was not ladylike. "Of course you did."

"What is a video game?" Asher tilted his head to one side.

"You poor, deprived little Inyoka." A tear welled up in my eye. "Video games are what makes life worth living."

I was so distracted by the usual snide jabs that I didn't even notice Gorm taking a hold of my wrist until he started dragging my thumb across the map again. Dipping in and out amongst the fine-lined buildings that he'd sketched out. Mercy's eyebrow crept up. "What are you... what is that?"

"That be the old barricade we had to abandon."

Asher's head cocked to one side. "The structure stands?"

"Svart be thick as moles in the middens." Gunhild scoffed.

Gorm elaborated, "They'd never be thinking to do it. Once they're unmanned, the svart just be clambering over, back and forth. Svart don't be building. Svart don't be changing things to make their lives easy."

I tapped the area on one side of the barricade, adding an unexpected blob to the map. "So if we got all the svart in here pushed back, you could take those barricades back and hold them?"

"If your lot be up to the task of clearing them." He stroked his beard. "Aye. We could be doing that."

Putting an arm over both my comrades' shoulders, I said, "Alright, kids. Here's the plan…"

Stealth was never going to be my thing. I acknowledge that. Sneaking around is not in my nature. We've all got our faults. Mercy took to sneaking around like a sneaky fish to sneaky water. That was why she was as far away from me as she could possibly get. Even if I didn't actively ruin her sneaking by yelling nonsense at her when it seemed funny, the sound of my stomping around would have drawn in all the svart from miles around.

As for Asher, there was no denying that he moved around in a deathly silence that made all of his friends crap themselves when he suddenly appeared next to them—I was giving serious consideration to tying a bell around his neck—but his magic was big, bright, and flashy. He wouldn't have been able to defend himself without all eyes and floppy ears turning his way, so he got lumped into working with me.

I jumped down from the barricade onto a nice squishy pile of svart.

The ones directly beneath me died in an instant, but they were just a tiny fraction of the gathered monsters. I hefted my sword up over my head and roared defiance in their blank, pallid faces. A few svart had the sense to stagger back, but most of them didn't. They came charging in at me, with all their cobbled-together weapons held high, ready to butcher me the way they had the few defending Dvergar I could see lying around my feet, their bones well gnawed.

I closed my eyes and let my *Sphere of Influence* expand out as time slowed to a crawl. The scrap metal in the dead svart's weapons, the armor of the dead Dvergar, the bones themselves… all of it resonated, and with a pull of will, every part of it came apart.

The fine worked metal of the weapons on the ground, the cunning craftsmanship, it all twisted into slag as I exerted my will. I couldn't work with fine metals yet, but hidden inside the best and the brightest were still the base components that I *could* use. Iron was woven into steel, and leather strips stitched neatly into jerkins and straps could tear apart at the seams. With one great heave, they all came up into orbit around me. The svart's weapons resisted my pull, with only the most poorly tied axe-heads snapping free. It was a trick I could never pull on enemies with properly forged gear, but here and now. It worked.

Even with time running slow, the svart would have been on me by now if they hadn't all frozen in terror, watching as I forged myself a new set of armor out of the fragments that surrounded me. It wasn't pretty, and it didn't cover as much as I would have liked—I was going to catch a nasty draft through some of those open panels—but it was armor, and it was mine.

It hissed and clicked as it cooled into place around my body, rough and ready for action with an *Armor Rating* of 64. Whatever that meant.

I stretched my arms out to get used to the new weight, then readied myself for their charge again, grin fixed firmly in place.

"Come get some."

CHAPTER 11

They did come and get some, but not from the direction that I was hoping. The startled ones up ahead of me were still riveted in place by the sight of me pulling a suit of slightly-ratty armor out of thin air. However, the ones just arriving to see what all the commotion was about didn't hesitate, bursting out in a tidal wave of bodies, washing out from between the perfectly ordered buildings like a dam had burst.

I spun my sword down to meet them in a great arc, neatly nipping the head off the first in the row, carving a gouge out of the chest of the second, and lodging in the pelvis of the next. Momentum didn't let me stop, so I bludgeoned the next one along with the body of his buddy, and the one after that with the both of them, like svart dominos.

If it had just been that one swarming wave of bodies, I would have won the whole war in a swing, but the next ones were leaping off the top of the corpses of their compatriots before I had time to blink. Good thing I didn't come alone.

Asher's *Gravity Snare* burst into life above them, back over their own lines where the swarms of bodies had just started converging into the overwhelming mass I now faced. It looked like a tiny spot of darkness, then everything started dragging in towards it. Even the air and the light twisted in towards it with a roar.

The leaping svart snapped backward as though they'd reached the end of their collective leash. The ones that weren't impaled on the weapons of the rank behind them still managed to knock the whole row down. The charging svart behind them tripped over their fallen friends or tried to jump over and got caught in the gravity snare's effect, tossing them up and over to knock more svart farther back down.

It was a chaotic mess, and I loved every second of it.

I charged into the mass of puzzled svart that I'd originally faced off with and started hacking at them wildly—quick brutal chops that were less about killing and more about inciting more of that handy fear that had been keeping them all at bay.

They started to scatter and run. Without functional weapons, they'd lost all of their courage. The few that had the crystal-tipped spears and knives were washed away in the turning tide of bodies before they had a chance. This was all going to plan. They were running away to hide and lick their wounds, but they left a vacuum behind to draw in more svart.

Even as the gravity snare sputtered and died, the svart that had been in the shadow of that dark star found their courage faltering. With a roar, I bore down on them, and the few that were back on their feet turned and fled, leaving their wounded or confused to be trampled underfoot or hacked apart by the guillotine fall of my blade.

Both ends of the sword were in my hands. In this close, there was no need to swing it wide. Speed mattered more. Legs and arms fell away in a spatter of black ichor, and faces, twisted in fear, were split down the middle. I was slick with their blood, and the perfect cobblestones were lined in symmetrical gore.

With his big trump card already played from atop the barricade, I could feel rather than see Asher working his magic. I'd only grown a little stubble in the couple of days I'd been alive, but every one of those tiny hairs tried to stand on end as he summoned up a crackling orb of electricity between his hands. I was glad he was on my side.

More of them came on. More and more svart pouring in from everywhere that I looked, scrambling over rooftops when they couldn't squeeze through the alleyways, and climbing the heaped corpses of their kin to come and meet the same fate. My back was to the barricade, but on all other sides, there were enemies.

Static crackled amongst us, and then the whole crowd was lined in sparks. Asher's work went unnoticed.

I turned the first brave svart's blade aside with the flat of mine, but I couldn't press my attack and punish him for his hubris without abandoning the wall at my back. There were just so many of them. It didn't matter how powerful I was. The fight on the hillside had proven that; if you got enough of these little horrors together, they'd win by weight of numbers, like crows mobbing a hawk.

An arrow arched past the cowed front lines to trace a bloody line across my exposed shoulder. At the sight of some red blood flowing at last, the whole crowd seemed to go into a frenzy. Svart had no language of their own, but in amongst the snarls and barking, I could swear that I heard fragments of some other speech.

"Kill!" featured prominently.

Normally I don't take requests, but this was a private party, so I wasn't going to let them down. As they charged across the slippery stonework, I met them partway, dropping to one knee as my sword whipped around in a lethal arc.

Arrows flew through the air where I should have been standing, and the front runners' guts exploded out along the length of my blade on my left.

The legs toppled out from under the ones on my right, leaving a heap of them wailing, a mostly-living, shrieking defensive wall on my flank.

Worrying about my flank was pointless when every one of them charged at me head-on. I tried to whip my sword around—as much as you can whip something that weighs the same as a vending machine—to catch the next wave as they charged, but there was no solid wave to meet head-on, just scrambling stragglers.

I turned a pair of descending axe-heads away with the notched edge of my blade, and another couple of over-enthusiastic jumpers caught the flat of my sword in their guts when they landed on me. It wasn't nearly enough. There were so many.

Swords, knives, clubs, shivs, and spears with wiggly hafts too thin to support the rock heads mounted on them. I couldn't even see the damned svart anymore. Just sharp edges. The weight of bodies pushed my own sword back down towards me, and their blows rained down on my body.

Except this time my body wasn't completely unprotected anymore. The nicks and scratches on my bare skin hurt, but the lethal blows being thrust into my torso felt more like rapid-fire punches. The armor I'd conjured up was turning their blades.

Straining with all my strength, I drew my knee off the floor and got both my feet under me as more and more svart were piling on top, flailing uselessly at me with their tiny little arms and tiny little weapons. I could feel the weight of them bearing down on me, threatening to take my feet out from under me.

Drawing in a lungful of their sour-milk breath, I rose. It was the squat of a lifetime. All the *Potency* this body had been born with and acquired through my efforts converted into pure upward thrust. There was no black hole to whip them into the air and scatter them this time. Only me. Anything Asher's magic could do, I could do better.

The svart flew back into their own ranks once more, bowling over their own army. The front rank who hadn't tried piling on top didn't fly, they were merely knocked on their asses—in perfect position for me to bring my newly hefted blade hammering back down. It was a nice change of pace to have gravity on my side.

I staggered a little when I reared back up, but that was alright. None of the svart could see me over the wall of dead svart. I could still hear them though. Everywhere around me, their screams and baying for blood echoed up off the ceiling, drawing svart in from all over their half of the city. I looked up to Asher. He was the man with the view out over the town, and so he'd be the one to judge whether the plan was working or not. "Are we winning, son?"

Once more, I felt the impact of thunder rippling out as he tore his claws apart, and lightning leapt past my wall of corpses. Shouts turned to screams, and the putrid stench of the svart was replaced with the oily scent of deep-fried meat. Crackling spread out from where Asher's bolt had struck, rippling out through the mass of bodies.

"We have no familial relationship"—Asher rocked a little on his feet after his exertions—"but it does appear that your plan has been successful."

That was all I needed to hear. I ran for the barricade, even as crispy critters clambered over the top of their dead to hound me. Lobbing my sword up over the rim, making Asher duck for cover, I threw myself against the tangled mass of furniture, pseudo-industrial equipment, and twisted metal. Hand over hand, I dragged myself up. Sharp edges scraped over my armor and hooked into me in unexpected places. Odds were I could have powered through if it weren't for the svart.

I was halfway up and going strong by the time that the arrows started to fly. It was only another length of my body before I was over the top and free. Even if the arrows stuck me, I wasn't going to stop. Which all would have been fine if it hadn't been for the svart leaping up to grab onto my legs.

Blades pricked at me as they jammed their shivs and picks into my heels and calves, trying to get purchase through the armor.

One svart dangled from each of my legs, but they weighed practically nothing, and I probably could have kept on climbing with them attached if more hadn't latched onto them in a big svart ladder of wailing misery trying to drag me back. Still, I edged up, closer and closer to the walkway.

Feeling more than a little like an elastic band being stretched, I saw Asher reach down a hand to help me up, but between my weight and the weight of the svart beneath me, I was only ever going to drag him down too. Even kicking my feet wasn't doing much to dislodge my svart limpets, so I did the only thing I could and kept on climbing.

The straps that held my shin-guard in place snapped, and the rough metal fell away to smack one of the svart in the face. The chain of svart that had been held up by the dagger wedged under that strap toppled away too. Some of the left leg crew then tried to make the jump to my other side and missed, tumbling down to land on their dead and injured. Some didn't try to cross but instead flung themselves up. One caught on my belt. Jabbing into my kidneys with a ragged little dagger.

[320/440 Health]

The armor that had been keeping me alive until now became a dead weight with all the svart dangling off it. What had saved me before was about to kill me. So I did what I had to do. I let it go.

Closing my eyes and letting my consciousness slip out into my *Sphere of Influence* again, I didn't even wait for time to slow. The armor was of my own making. I knew every haphazard detail of it like the pattern had been burned into my mind, and I knew how to undo it with a single push of will.

As the plates of iron fell away from me, so too did the svart, until finally it was just me, bare-assed and scrambling over the top with a single svart still standing in the small of my back when I flopped over.

Maybe Asher played little league back when he was a little baby lizard librarian, or maybe not, but the hunk of chair-leg that he swung into the svart's face looked like a home run to me. It flew back to join all of its little friends, and I stumbled to my feet. "Thanks, Asher."

He sighed. "Please express your thanks through the wearing of trousers."

Sadly there was no time to wiggle at him until he cried. The svart were making good progress up the barricade now that I'd riled them up, and all this stretch's defenders had been relocated. I retrieved my sword and got to work.

[34 Damage]

"This is just like whack-a-mole!"

As the svart rose up, I smacked them right back down again, splitting heads and showering us both with black ichor. At least, it was less obvious I was naked now.

"Did you ever play whack-a-mole?"

I turned from the swarming monsters to glance over at Asher. "Oh, you're casting.

"So whack-a-mole was this game you got in arcades…

"Where little critters popped their heads up out of holes…"

I swept my blade along the very ledge of the barricade, sending up a shower of sparks and nicking off a few fingers.

"And you hit them with a little padded mallet."

Asher unleashed another thunderclap, coating the rising Svart in their own personal crackling ion clouds. With no small amount of exasperation now that he'd caught his breath, he shouted back, "I am familiar with the game in concept!"

I grinned at him and kicked a svart in the face.

"Why didn't you say so?"

Asher's eyes narrowed. "Some of us perform tasks that require concentration."

I flicked my sword in a figure of eight around my body, slapping the faces off two svart as they poked them over the precipice.

"Hey! Just because I make it look easy doesn't mean it is."

He rolled his eyes and focused back in on the storm he had brewing between his palms. I wished Mercy were here, she'd talk about whack-a-mole with me while we slaughtered svart, for sure.

"So have you got any spells that don't take half an hour to cast?"

He ducked behind me as the next wave came. "I believe that I have an instant cantrip for the lighting of candles."

"Well, that's super useful."

The steady flow of svart began to slow. They might not have been completely mindless, but without the immediate excitement of an enemy in their line of sight, boredom seemed to have set in. When we peered down over the edge of the barricade, there was a mass grave of svart and few of the living still lingering around.

A couple of the surviving svart were already picking over their companions like they were a buffet, though how anyone could stomach that grey-looking meat I had no idea. Even the little splashes of svart blood that I'd gotten in my mouth during the fighting had been enough to put me off the idea of trying Amaranthian food for another day.

My *Sphere of Influence* didn't stretch all the way down to the ground, but they were heaped up high enough that I was able to strip the leathers and metals from the top of the heap to toss together a light suit of armor that left even less to the imagination than last time. I could swear I had a whole ass-cheek hanging out. The *Armor Rating* this time around was only 41, but it would protect Asher's sense of propriety, and at the end of the day, I didn't want to accidentally club any Dvergar in the face by turning around too fast.

With a nod from Asher, we made our way along the top of the barricades, taking in the chaos that we'd wrought. As predicted, every svart in svart town had come running over to join the party—including all of the dumb-asses in the section surrounding the worm-farm. When we moved by the old barricades that had been overrun, we could see Dvergar stationed along them now, quietly assuming their positions as though this whole part of the city had never been taken from them—as quietly as they could in clanking armor, anyway. Thankfully, we'd been making even more noise than them.

Obviously, we weren't going to draw all of the svart out, there was no way that we were going to get that lucky, but that was what Mercy and her Dvergar ninjas were for. Maybe they weren't actual ninjas, but between all the silk wrap around masks and their almost comical attempts at sneaking, that was the name I was sticking with.

Mercy's job was to do the opposite of us. While we made as much noise as possible and dragged all the svart out of bed, she had to move through the newly abandoned worm zone and snipe any stragglers without drawing attention to herself.

Judging by the echoing silence, she had done one hell of a job. We made it along to the wall before we dropped down and made our own attempt at stealth. The longer that the svart didn't notice that this section had been retaken, the longer the Dvergar had to get their barricades repaired and manned properly. So long as we didn't bang into any svart, I felt pretty certain that we'd manage to keep the volume down.

We rounded a corner and came face to face with three svart, sitting around some sort of campfire, cooking what looked like a big grub on a stick.

They looked at us. We looked at them. They opened their mouths to scream.

Mercy's arrow took the closest one in the throat before it could make a sound. There was no way I'd clear the distance to the other two in time to keep them quiet, so I did the only thing I could think of. I threw my sword.

It hit the svart in their ugly little heads, the flat side making a nice clunking sound as it bowled them over, then the sheer weight of metal pinned them both to the ground until one of Mercy's ninjas rushed out to slit their throats. The clatter of my sword and their gurgles were the loudest noises that they made.

Victory!
Potency increased to 28
Sword: Rank 6/10
Acrobatics: Rank 5/10
532 Experience Gained

Mercy dropped down from the top of one of the buildings on our side of the square, then pressed a finger to her lips when she saw me smiling at her. I settled for waving.

A ninja Dvergar tried to pick up my sword and return it to me but only just managed to lever it up off the mashed face of the svart. I crept over, patted him on the head, grinned, and hefted the sword easily onto my shoulder. You might have expected awe in the eyes of the little fella when I did that, but no, just narrowed eyes and grumbles.

The Dvergar twisted and contorted his hands, and Mercy, watching them, gave a soft huff of laughter before signing back, "You get used to him."

Apparently, I could understand Dvergar sign language too. The gods really gave us the full package when it came to the speaking in tongues thing. My own hand gesture to the two of them was less intricate, but I think it carried my point over well.

We followed Mercy back through the streets towards the outer wall of the city-cavern, picking up the rest of her little team as we went. Block by block, house by house, they had been clearing out the svart. The Dvergar were nothing if not methodical. They'd swept the whole place by the time that we arrived, and now they had doubled back on themselves to make sure that nothing had been missed. The only place that they hadn't cleared out was the worm-farm itself.

Mercy signed to us both, "Something big. Moving inside."

I had my fingers crossed that whatever was in there was another abomination. Sure, they were terrifying and weird and liable to mangle us, but I was still 800 glory shy of my next Tier and unlocking some new powers. I wanted those new powers. I wanted them bad.

The refined looks of the rest of the buildings seemed to give way to a more rustic style here. Instead of the huge doorway into the farms being perfectly rectangular, it was a natural ragged shape, with the oiled wooden boards of the door cut to slot into the space, instead of the other way around—those doors hang ever so slightly ajar. They'd been haphazardly held shut with a length of ratty looking rope strung between two hooks that were clearly meant for a cross-bar, and mist was leaking out of the gap, turning all the nearby ash on the ground into a thick grey paste that showed the dozen crisscrossing paths of the svart running back and forth. One of the Dvergar was pointing to a perfectly formed little side-door, so rather than barging in, we ducked through there instead. Things were more uniform and familiar in that little tunnel, but yet more of the wood used on the door had been knocked into shape for each of the little doors hanging open here.

Wood couldn't have been easy to come by down here. It would have had to have been hauled down from the surface or traded for. It seemed like an odd choice to use it when they'd made every other fixture out of metal. A wave of *Dungeoneering knowledge* whispered something in the back of my head about wood contracting and expanding with moisture and heat. I supposed that made a certain kind of sense. It was getting hotter the farther in that we went.

The whole farm chamber was obscured by mist, and it was only when I nearly splashed into a little pool that I worked out what was happening. It was some sort of volcanic cave, with water heating up underground and being forced out here to bubble. The worms must have liked the heat. Not that I could see any of them at the moment. Steam blossomed up all around us as we crept forward, and while it kept us hidden from whatever was in here, it kept whatever was in here hidden from us too. There could have been a gigantic monster three feet in front of me and I wouldn't know until I stepped on its toes.

Our eyes might have been useless, but my other senses were working overtime. Beyond the hiss of the hot springs and muffled sounds of our own steps, there was something moving in the room. It didn't sound like the capering of svart or the stomping of the huge crab-legged thing we fought back at the observatory.

My horns got tangled in what I thought was a giant cobweb, and Mercy reached up to pluck off the coiled silk and toss it aside. The fog was thinner farther up, and I could make out ropes strung every which way above us, knotted together at odd angles, completely contrary to the Dvergar's usual devotion to perfect order. It was only when I realized that the lines were secured to stalactites that it started to make sense. Just like the wooden doors were adapted to the natural shape of the cave, so too were the rope lines. More of the gigantic grubs we saw being grilled by the svart earlier were dangling from the strings, bowing them down with their prodigious weight but not quite breaking them.

It was a good thing that we were looking up or we never would have seen it coming.

CHAPTER 12

This abomination had really earned its name. The weird geometric shape of the last one was still present but divided up. Instead of the whole creature being centered around one glowing orb, there was a run of three of them spaced out along the length of the thing, bright as day down here in the dark of the cave and cutting through the fog like the beam of a lighthouse.

The body surrounding those orbs was segmented—with visible gaps between each of the pale marble pieces and only the gravity of those tiny suns holding the whole thing together. It had a head at each end, vaguely pyramid-shaped, ending abruptly before a point with a flexing lamprey mouth set inside. It clung to the stalactites above us with a pincer pair of legs on each segment, impossibly agile for something so huge, and dangling as though it was weightless.

Chains trailed down from it like the silkworms' excretions, but the svart that had once clung to them were long gone, and the golden metal at the ends of each chain was twisted and melted out of shape. It had no eyes, but I had no doubt that it saw us. I could feel the weight of the monster's attention, dizzying in its intensity.

Sneak time was over. I bellowed, "Look up!"

Everyone looked up just as the abomination let go of its grip. With something that big, it didn't need to be smart or subtle. Weight would be enough to kill us all. The other two took a dive in opposite directions as the monster turned end over end in the air, snapping through strings as if they weren't there until its sooty underbelly came into sight, coming down on me like the cave-in that my *Dungeoneering* had been warning me about since the moment I first arrived.

I didn't have time to dodge, but I had enough time to swing, and the abomination fell on the edge of my sword.

[Critical Hit]
[66 Damage]

My whoop of victory was swallowed up as the bulk of the falling abomination landed full on top of me.

[81/440 Health]

I'd been hurt more than a few times since I landed on this new world, but this was the first blow that had taken the wind out of me. I should have dodged. I should have moved. I should have done literally anything other than what I just did. When I could feel my hands again, the sword was missing from my grip. When I tried to draw breath to replace the air that had been crushed out of me, I couldn't. I was being smothered.

Yet I wasn't lying flat on my back. Now that the shock had passed, I realized that I was still oriented the same direction as I'd started out, my head was still held up, my feet were still on the uneven stone. I nearly threw up when I realized what had happened. The abomination had slammed the open wound that I'd just opened up down on top of me. I was inside it.

In the belly of the beast, I was choking on the glowing slime oozing all around me. The abomination didn't even seem to notice I was in here. If it flinched, then I never felt it. All that I knew was one moment I was standing there, taking in my gross new surroundings, and the next the ground was ripped out from under me, and the monster was on the move.

Sound was muffled in here, so I couldn't hear the others fight or shout. When the orbs on the abomination lit up and fired out the lethal scorching beams, I could feel the whole beast vibrate, but I didn't hear a sound. I was trapped in place by the slick flesh around me, all my senses defeated.

Well, all my old senses defeated.

I reached out with my *Sphere of Influence* and found my sword still wedged alongside me, just out of reach. I twisted inside the wound, flexing the raw power of my shoulders against the crushing weight that surrounded me. I felt the handle of my sword brush my fingertips, and with one last heave, I caught hold and yanked on it for all that I was worth.

The blade was blunt by anyone's standards, but this was not the armored hide of the abomination that I was slicing into. I had slipped past its defenses. Inch by painful inch, I drew my sword up through the monster's flesh.

More of the glowing blood of the abomination eked out of the fresh wounds that I was carving. My hands were drenched in it, and the sunlight stung my skin.

Abominations might not feel pain, they might not have any senses at all, but this one flexed and twisted to try and reject me. The wound beneath my feet opened up, and a gust of fresh air rushed in, washing over my face and stirring me from my stupor. As I began to fall, I spread my legs apart, so that one foot landed on either side of the cut, braced on this inside of its rocky hide. I had room to breathe. I had room to move.

Aiming straight up, I swung my sword awkwardly.

Another arterial spray of golden light drenched down over me, showering out of the beast and making my toeholds even more slippery and slick. I was going to fall out of this thing. The fall might not kill me, but all that the big sparkly-centipede had to do was let go of its grip again and I'd be dead.

No point crying over spilt blood. I didn't wait to be forcefully ex-pelled, so I tightened my grip on my sword and tucked my knees up to my chest, cannonballing out of the abomination and into the open air.

A moment later I hit a rope, caught hold, and took in all the fun I'd missed.

The abomination was up on the ceiling, trying to keep out of range of Mercy's bow. It was smarter than it looked. The sunbeams had burned away more than a few of the worm-strings and turned a good portion of the groundwater into steam that was now billowing up around it, giving it even more cover. Clever or lucky.

I yelled down, "It's on the roof!"

"We know!" Mercy's voice echoed up from one side of the chamber. "Where are you?"

I glanced around, trying to come up with any useful landmarks. "I'm on a rope!"

There was a pause, then Asher called out, "Why?"

I opened and shut my mouth, but thankfully the giant monster decided to attack again before I could formulate an answer.

The abomination had twisted around to show its back to us again after humping and jerking around to get me out. We could see the three lights shining down again, getting brighter and brighter within the cloud of steam.

Before it could blast me, I dropped down to hang from the rope by one hand. The line bounced as I shifted my weight, and as it sprung back up again, I let go. Momentum flung me up in the air, and I had a moment to do some twisting myself before gravity caught me, and I fell to the next line down.

This one snapped away at one end. Rotten in the wet room, but the far end held. The triple beam of light burned down in parallel lines, chasing me through the room as I swung, tearing up another great cloud of steam from beneath us. I vanished into the fog, sweeping right towards a pillar. I kicked off as I passed, adding spin as I gained height. The pillars of light still chased me, blinking out for only a moment when the angle was wrong and they had to burrow through the solid stone before burning after me some more.

When I reached the ceiling of the chamber, I wrapped an arm around a stalactite and held on for dear life as my rope fell away and was disintegrated by the blasts that had been tracing after me.

Suddenly, the light was blocked out. There was a whole cavern's worth of dangling stones to deflect it. All that solid mass to burrow through before it could hit me. The steam cloud was gathered up around me now, and I couldn't see a damned thing except for the distant glow of the monster trying to kill me.

If it didn't kill me then the fall might, so I turned *Restoration* on myself, letting life pulse back through me.

[236/440 Health]

I had forgotten all about my *Lifesense* until I started manipulating that *Primal* energy within myself. Then suddenly, I could feel the abomination right there at the edge of my senses. With a touch, I'd be able to tell how much health it had exactly. Didn't really feel like petting it though. Down below, Asher and Mercy were darting about, and I could feel them too, their life fluttering like the heartbeats of rabbits at the edge of my perception.

Without the safety of my rope, I probably should have been trying to work out how to get down without dying, but there was an enemy right there, just begging for a good slap with the business end of my sword. I was just working out how to get close enough for that slapping when the frigging lasers cut out.

For a moment all was silent, then I heard an awful scraping sound like giant fingernails on a giant chalkboard, followed by a thunderous impact down below. Bug boy had dropped down again. Displaced air from the abomination's passage swept all the fog away, giving me a tunnel down through the clouded dark, right to its back.

I wasn't going to turn that down. Letting go and falling was the easiest thing that I'd done all day. With both hands tightened on the sword's grip, all the muscles of my back and arms sang with tension as I fell until finally, I hammered the blade home.

[Critical Hit]
[64 Damage]

There was no precision or control to my strike. I wasn't picking a soft spot or trying for a weakness. Pure luck brought my blow down on the central star.

It didn't actually make a sound when it made contact, but there was plenty of noise to follow. To me, at the other end of the blade, it sounded like 'Woof.'

The explosion flung me back through the air, and I would have hit the far wall if it hadn't been for all those handy dandy silkworms in the way. The ones above had silk trailing down that caught and cushioned me. The ropes on the same level as me snapped one by one, halting me just before I hit rock. Lucky again.

A spin of my sword cut me loose of the silk and strings, then I landed in a knee-deep puddle that was about the same temperature as a cup of coffee. The kind of coffee that ended in fast food joints getting sued.

"Hot, hot, hot!" I shouted as I scrambled out of the water as fast as my toasted toes would carry me.

Mercy dashed past without a word, still firing off arrow after arrow into the abomination as she moved. I had no idea if they were doing anything other than irritating it, but I wasn't about to spoil her good mood.

I couldn't believe how fast she was moving. She was almost a blur. I'd been wondering where her glory was being spent—apparently, it was on going fast. The Pillar of Ascension and I really needed to spend some time getting to know each other.

Asher was somewhere else, out there in the fog, alone and defenseless, except for his lethal magical powers. Maybe I shouldn't have been worrying about him so much, but he just seemed so squishy. Like a scaly balloon full of pudding.

The only one I could place for certain was the big buff bug boy, still glowing bright as day in the otherwise dim cavern. Guess it was time for both of us to go into the light.

I charged, roaring with that resonant new voice of mine echoing off all the walls. I wanted the abomination to know that I was coming. I wanted it focused completely on me so that it wasn't trying to blast, gobble, or otherwise maim the other two.

The abomination obliged me.

It loped across the room to meet me with an almost casual disinterest in the giant sword I was holding above my head. Maybe they didn't know about mortality either? I mean, it looked like it had been stitched together with the same glowing goop that made Eternals work; maybe it thought it was immortal too. I was going to shatter its illusions while I shattered its face.

At the last moment, I let my feet slip out from under me on the drenched stone. Whirring teeth passed in front of my face as it tried to snap at me and failed, and then my sword swung up into the leg on my right, snipping clean through it at the joint.

Momentum carried us both forward, me along the underside of the abomination, and the abomination nose-first into the rocks where I'd been standing a moment before.

I'd forgotten about the mouth on the other end until it was dipping down towards me. The whole abomination had come to a crunching halt, and its ass end had been bucked up in the air above me when I came to my own stop. It came down, buzzing through my new armor as if it weren't there, and burrowing into my guts.

Blood sprayed up. My blood. Everywhere that I looked was red. Still, those teeth bore down into me, trying to dig right through guts, bones, and all to reach stone on the other side. They shrieked when they hit bone. They rattled my whole skeleton as they tried to chew through, tossing gobs of vital organs aside like so much offal.

I brought my sword up one-handed to smack it in the side of the head, but all of my strength seemed to be leaving me.

[181/440 Health]

Why did I think that I could do this? Why did I think I could be a hero. The most heroic thing I'd ever done in my whole life before had killed me, and now I was about to die all over again for nothing.

Desperation took hold, and adrenaline flooded through me. I brought up my sword and hacked at the smooth white expanse that might have been called the abomination's neck—if you were feeling charitable or confused by its impossible anatomy.

The hardened hide turned my blade aside with little more than a scratch and a spritz of golden light raining out. My aching arm fell back, and my sword sang against the stones.

I was not going to die like this.

Taking hold of both sides of the conical ass-mouth, I pushed. I may as well have been trying to move the mountain.

My arms creaked, and my shoulders felt like they were about to pop. The ragged stone dug deeper and deeper into my back as I strained, and the head moved.

A fresh wash of blood bubbled up out of the hole in my torso as the gnawing sphincter lost contact. If I hadn't been clenching my teeth, I would have bitten through my tongue from the pain. But it was moving. Inch by inch, I hauled it up out of me.

Finally, it was at arm's length, held above me but still trying to bear down with all its weight. Inside the rows of teeth flexed and pulsed, trying to snare me and draw me in deeper. This close, it was so obvious that the monster was artificial. The teeth were like a shark's—perfectly triangular with only a blood groove etched up their center.

My arms shook with the strain, or maybe all the blood-loss, and looking down was definitely not in the cards until my *Restoration* ticked off whatever cooldown it was on. Knowing yourself is great and all, but knowing what my own mushed up intestines look like is something I could live without.

Letting go was madness. The whole thing would come right back down into me again. I'd have to be insane to let all the strain go onto one shaking arm, reach down, grab my sword, and angle it up so that the abomination impaled itself when my arm gave out and it started trying to chew on me again. I'd have to be crazy.

The sword danced around inside the mouth of the beast like a spoon in a garbage disposal with about the same sound. The pommel was wedged into the ground by my side, braced against the force being hammered down against it.

There was a moment's reprieve when the abomination realized what was happening, then I got my hands on it again and started to pull.

The grinding, wailing sounds coming from inside the monster's mouth grew louder and louder as I hauled it down, and the blade dug in deeper. It tried to pull away, but I was ready for it now, bringing all my strength and weight to bear. Dragging it down as I roared, "Eat it!"

The abomination did eat it. I had to twist to get out of the way. Stumbling to my feet, I braced my shoulder against its side to stop it from escaping laterally, but I managed every step in one fluid motion, never letting it buck free.

Golden blood rained down out of the pulsating pyramid head. The sword was still battering around inside it, spun in a whirlwind dervish of teeth and gore.

"Kiss!" My shoulders screamed as I bore down on the beast.

"The!" It bucked and rocked, trying to pull away from the cutting edge.

"Stone!" With a jump and my full weight carrying us, I slammed the pyramid head down.

The abomination slipped down another foot, and the tip of my sword burst out the side of its head.

It went on writhing in my arms for a moment longer, but this end of the abomination seemed to be well and truly wrecked. When I let the head go, it flopped limply to the side, and a shower of teeth fell out the now-ragged-edged hole at the end. When I pulled out my sword, it was coated in the same fluid as before, but now the light was dying down it looked more like molten gold than sunshine.

I wished that my own flopping innards looked nearly as appealing, and then I did it. I did the stupid thing. I looked down. Things that were meant to be on the inside were poking outside. *Restoration* still wasn't ready. This whole situation was gross.

The rest of the abomination didn't seem to realize that this ass was dead. The other head-ass had been chasing Mercy back and forth as she peppered it with arrows, and there was still no sign of Asher in the clouds of steam. The dead head lay limp on the ground, coiling up towards the glowing orbs spaced out along its back like a ramp.

Moisture clung all over the thing, making my feet slip out from under me as I climbed. It really was like marble on the outside, with all the underfoot grip that marble gave you. I made it to the end of the segment without smashing my face on the thing, so I was calling it a win.

After slipping and sliding all over the place, I didn't have much momentum, but I could still swing.

Light trailed from the back end of my cut, and an arc of light flared out of the orb like a solar flare. It was only when that ribbon of light snapped back into the orb that the concussion hit me.

The explosion itself did the damage. I was blasted off my feet, but I ended up with a rope wedged up in my crotch somewhere amidst the flips I did through the air, stopping me before I hit anything solid. Good thing I'd taken all those ranks in testicular fortitude. No, wait, that wasn't a thing. Ow.

From somewhere in the shadows, Asher's spell fired off, but something had gone wrong. The static charge that usually surrounded our enemies enveloped me too. Electricity rippled across my skin, sparking between my fingers, sparking like stitches over my open wounds.

Mercy yelped, "Asher, you got me too!"

I managed to untangle my legs and drop down onto my back in another scorching puddle. "Me three!"

The pyramid head that was still active had frozen in place, and now it cocked from side to side like it was sniffing the air. It had no eyes. It had no nose. What was it sensing? Like it had locked on to a target, the pointed head tracked over to one deep patch of shadows near the tied-up entrance. Asher.

With the dead weight of its dead-ass, the abomination couldn't go bounding over to him, but that didn't mean that he was out of reach. The three orbs on the abominations back grew in intensity. There was no way I could cross the room to Asher before they fired off.

I swung for the nearest leg. Aiming low.

Those claws were armored to hell and back, but the goal wasn't to breakthrough, it was to knock it off-balance. With a front leg missing and the ass fast asleep, the abomination had lost its equilibrium.

Knocking this middle leg sideways set the whole thing to topple back towards me.

Sunbeams burst out of the orbs, triangulating in on Asher's position, but they bucked up before they could make contact, burning clean through the wooden door and lancing up to blacken the roof of the city outside.

Given the choice of retreating or diving under the falling abomination, I did the stupid thing, as usual, rolling on one shoulder and coming up face to face with its blackened belly, right by the slit I'd put in it when the fighting began.

I was not going back in there, but my sword could if it wanted.

With a flare of moonlight, Sword Skill was carved into my mind and the number alongside it vanished.

There was a fresh mark carved across the hide of the abomination, crossing the broader cut midway. It was just a scratch, but it was all I had time for before it rolled back onto its feet, and I had to haul ass out of the way.

With the door burning and the lights sweeping down again, I could see Asher clearly, pinned in place by a spell still trapped between his hands. "Blast it!"

He struggled to speak in stuttering breaths between the chant of his spell. "I. Cannot."

The beams were splaying out, scorching the walls all around us. The abomination was flailing. "Why?"

I'd placed myself between Asher and the abomination without really thinking about it. But with my health in its current state, I wasn't liable to survive a blast. Asher huffed out, "You. Are. *Saturated.* And *Charged.*"

"Because we're wet it will hit us too?"

Even through his mumbling spell-work, he sounded bemused with me. "Indeed."

I could fix this. I could fix this by shouting, "Hey, Mercy! Get hit!"

She was somewhere at the far end of the cave. Still running, still moving. "What?"

"Jump in a beam." I was already jogging to the side, trying to keep my insides inside. Heading for the closest floodlight of death, sweeping across and frazzling every rope and silkworm in its way.

She bellowed back. "You jump in a beam!"

"I'm trying!"

I barely heard her shout "What?" before I made my jump.

When I hit the beam, it hurt like hell.

When I came out the other side half-blind, I had to dive to avoid the next beam heading right for me and roll to my feet on the far side. It was a lot more exercise than I should have been doing with a massive hole in my middle or burns all over my damn body. There was no trace of water or electricity left on me when I staggered to a halt and looked down. "I'm clear!"

There was this old parenting thing about peer pressure, where you'd get asked "if your friends jumped off a bridge, would you do it too?"

Turns out, Mercy would.

She came bursting out of the beam I'd just ducked and rolled to a halt beside me. "Why did I do that?"

"Watch!"

We couldn't see Asher from here, but there was no mistaking the boom as his spell fired off. Mercy and I might have been dry, but the abomination was still wrapped in steam, drenched with glowing blood, water, and most importantly, it was punched full of enough holes that the tough hide wasn't going to save it this time.

The lightning didn't shoot out towards the monster. Instead, it spread through the mist until it was a great expansive wall of raw destruction. It swept over the abomination like a wave, not striking but swallowing it whole.

It shook as the lightning swept over it. It shuddered soundlessly, except for the splashing its twitching legs made in the puddles. Mercy had a fresh arrow strung and ready to go, and I reluctantly hefted my sword for round two…or was it three. Might have been four. I was feeling punch-drunk.

We shouldn't have bothered. What was left of the abomination's legs gave out beneath it, and the stars along its back flickered and died. The room then was plunged into darkness. I still didn't trust it until the gods tacitly confirmed that we'd won.

Legendary Foe Defeated!
Potency increased to 32
Sword: Rank 10/10
Acrobatics: Rank 6/10
263 Experience Gained
400 Glory Gained

I turned to Mercy. "Am I allowed to make noise now?"

"Damage is done."

I threw back my head and whooped. "We kicked its ass-faces!"

CHAPTER 13

The silkworm farm had seen better days, but as the Dvergar ninja squad came creeping in, they didn't seem too mad about it. I caught scraps of conversation, and it sounded like they had been expecting a lot worse. There were enough worms left to get things going again, and they were still in good shape despite all the time they'd been left dangling untended. I was calling it a win.

I put an arm around my companions 'shoulders out of camaraderie, and definitely not because my guts were dangling out, and I felt like falling over. "Mission accomplished, guys. And you were worried about a few svart."

Asher hissed. "A few svart?"

"Isn't that your liver on the floor over there?" Mercy was less subtle in her reproach.

I had to admit, it did look like a liver. "Eh, that could be anyone's."

Now that the rope had been burned away, the wooden doors of the worm-farm hung open, and we could stroll right out into the city again. The silence that we'd worked so hard to maintain was over, and more Dvergar than I'd seen since we arrived here were hard at work, rushing from house to house, reclaiming all that had been left behind when the svart broke through—anything that they hadn't broken, eaten, or smeared with feces anyway.

Industrious sounds had kicked off back at the barricade as the Dvergar worked to break down the barrier there and relocate it. I'd expected them to reinforce the line that we'd already reclaimed, but they seemed to be building yet another barricade running parallel to the wall, sectioning off a clean run to the worm-farm without having to hold a huge area of the city. It was probably smart, but it still felt like they were giving up the land we'd just bled to reclaim for them. Okay, I did most of the bleeding, but still.

We had made it almost as far as the barricade that we'd originally had to hop when *Restoration* finally flared back to life, and I immediately used it.

So much had been torn down and moved already, we were able to stroll right through. The echoes of industry seemed to have brought out all the Dvergar in the city. There were still barely any creeping out from wherever they'd been hiding, but compared to when we first arrived, it felt like the place was bustling.

The regular everyday Dvergar were starkly different to Mercy's ninjas and the political position people that we'd crossed paths with earlier. Where the fighters like Gunhild and her posse were bound up tight in leather so they could move around easily, these Dvergar wore flowing robes of silk, with leather draped over in pinafore aprons to protect that silk from whatever they encountered. The big thing that surprised me was the veils. Every one of them had a diaphanous cloth hung over their face from a little bronze filigreed headband. Some had braided beards dangling out from beneath the veil, and others didn't, but you couldn't see a single face regardless. The effect was a little unsettling—particularly combined with their total refusal to actually speak to us.

I mean, a giant horny dude like me stomping around might be a little intimidating sure, I get that, but Mercy? She was as cute as a button. There was no excuse for all of us to be ignored.

Our old buddy, Gorm, spotted us as we emerged into one of the glowing mushroom squares, and he bustled over with a few more of the more dressed up Dvergar to greet us. He held up both his fists for us to bump them in turn, so I guess we were now all on double fist-bumping terms. "If I hadn't been seeing it with my own eyes, I'd never be believing it. You did it. You really do be here to help us."

I was halfway through an 'I told you so' when Mercy hit me in the fresh scar that had previously been the hole in my gut. She cut in. "We were happy to help."

"The elders will be wanting to see you again"—Gorm's partially hidden face contorted into a grimace that it took me a minute to recognize as a grin—"but they aren't going anywhere. This be a cause for celebrating. One like we haven't been having in many a turn."

Finally, the Dvergar around us piped up, not in the cheer I was expecting, but in a long, warbling hoot that set my teeth on edge. I really needed to get over the idea that this was a world I knew. They might have looked like something out of Tolkien, but these were a whole new species I'd never met before. This was like first contact with an alien race or something.

Barrels were rolled out, and some terrifyingly clear liquor came pouring out of the taps hammered into them marginally faster than molasses. All my senses were sharper as a Chagnar Faun, and that included the sense of smell that was currently screaming at me to run for my life. Instead, I took the proffered pewter flagon and knocked the whole thing back.

New Skill Discovered! [Poison Resistance]
Poison Resistance: Rank 1/10

All around me the Dvergar were sipping their drinks, and Mercy was pretending to drink hers, with her eyes watering every time she lifted the flagon to her face. Asher had simply handed his cup back after peering into it, and the Dvergar didn't know enough about Inyoka to know whether they should be offended or not.

Gorm pressed another drink into my hand. "We've all been waiting so long."

"Waiting for what?" I knocked back the liquor. It tasted vaguely... meaty. "Us?"

The Dvergar scoffed. "For death. There don't be anything else for us Dver. Svart take our mine. Stone takes our flesh. Void takes our souls. We've been waiting here, dying by inches, counting our losses."

Oh great, Dvergar were the maudlin kind of drunks. Mercy stepped up and slapped Gorm on the back. "That's all over now."

The ululating sound was back, but now it was creeping up and down in some sort of song. Someone had hauled out drums too. Ain't no party like a Dvergar party. There were then a few rounds of drinks and some speeches from the Dvergar who were important enough that they felt the need to have their faces on display.

The Dvergar started dancing with lots of foot-stomping to the drums and spinning so their robes swished around. I said some stuff about how great they were, and everyone cheered. I tried to dance, but I stepped on one of the Dvergar, and he got mad even though I said sorry, so I went and leaned on a wall and tried to remember what I was here for.

Another cup was in my hand, but I couldn't remember picking it up, and Gunhild was here now. That was great.

"Hey, Gunhild is here now. That is great!"

She looked taken aback by my bellow but accepted the lopsided hug in good humor, even though I kind of mashed her into Asher, who was tucked under my other arm and trying to steer me away from the crowd.

Mercy was off chatting to some other Dvergar over by the thingy, the wall thing that they built to keep the little svart dudes out. She was scowling at me. Was she mad at me? Was she really mad or funny mad like normal? Where was I going?

Asher and Gunhild had steered me into one of the houses. My horns scraped along the ceiling, the vibrations ran down into my bones, and I felt kind of sick. I needed to lie down. They had made a bed for me. "I need sleep now."

Asher was nodding and trying to gently lower me to the ground. Gunhild had left. "You're my best friend, Asher. You're the best. Best friend in this whole world."

It was really important that he knew that, especially after us arguing earlier. He cocked his head to the side when I spoke but didn't say anything back.

The roof had lines on it. Wobbly lines. Two wobbly lines scraped in the solid stone. Oh, that was me. That was my horns. I was sleepy. I needed to sleep now. Nap time.

Sleep on Amaranth was just the same as sleep back home. Everything was dark. Everything was peaceful.

Pain was waiting for me when I woke up. Pain and confusion. My head was throbbing, and I couldn't remember much of anything after we killed the abomination in the worm-farm. It was a bad time to be me.

Poison Resistance: Rank 9/10

Oh gods.

I was never drinking again. At the very least, I was never drinking whatever the hell the Dvergar were serving. My mouth tasted like I'd licked a decaying badger, and I wasn't even sure if they had badgers here. Had they imported a dead badger across dimensions? When I tried to sit up, I immediately regretted it. It was like the hangover was just hanging above the floor like a fog, and I'd just slammed my face right into it.

Oh, that was bad. My only consolation was that I didn't have internet shopping here on Amaranth, so I wasn't going to be getting any nasty surprises in the mail over the next few days. At least, that was what I thought until an obscure fact about the feeding habits of dholes popped into my head. Apparently, dholes were giant death worms that popped up under the feet of anyone dumb enough to walk over the ash wastes. Good to know. How did I know it?

Turning my attention inward, I discovered how I knew. I'd been drunk shopping for skills.

In addition to upping *Bestiary* by two ranks, I'd purchased the Divine Skill of *Rough Hewn Architecture* for some reason. What was left in my experience pool had been gobbled up by three ranks of *Brutality*—which seemed to be one of the follow-on options from *Sword Skill*. My *Potency* had hopped up a few points as a result of that last one, so I wasn't really mad about it, but I did wonder why I thought spontaneously creating architecture was something I desperately needed. "What the hell, drunk Maulkin?"

Skills:
　Combat: Rank 10/10
　Sword: Rank 10/10
　Brutality: Rank 3/10
　Acrobatics: Rank 6/10
　Bestiary: Rank 3/10
　Dungeoneering: Rank 2/10
　Ancient History: Rank 1/10

I nearly tripped over Asher as I lumbered towards the door. He'd settled himself down to watch over me with his back to the wall and his tail coiled around onto his lap. He'd been busy since we got to Amaranth, so I decided that I'd let him rest a bit longer.

Outside the open doorway, Gunhild and Gorm were waiting. They didn't look impressed. What did I do that I couldn't remember?

"Is there going to be a shotgun wedding?"

Both Dvergar echoed back, "What?"

I glanced from face to face. "Did I get someone pregnant?"

"What?!" The Dvergar response was getting louder and madder each time I asked a question.

"Okay, let's start over. Good morning."

Gorm nodded slowly. "If it be morning, then I'd hope it be a good one."

That was cryptic.

"So… what's up, guys?"

"You and your shine-eye'd kin made us some promises," Gunhild piped up. "Said you'd drive out the svart. Take back the khag."

I started nodding and immediately regretted it. I should not have been drinking on an empty stomach. "Yup that is the plan."

Gorm pressed his knuckles together. "We be here to see you do it."

It took me a few blinks until my brain spun up to speed, and I understood what they were saying. "What, did you think we were going to sneak out?"

"Dvergar be oathbound folk, but we know them that walk under the sky don't be holding much weight to words," Gunhild said. Every time I turned from one to the other, another wave of nausea swept over me.

"Did I say something when I was drunk?"

"You didn't be saying nothing," Gorm started, but Gunhild butted in to correct him almost immediately.

"Well, you be saying a lot actually, not much of it making sense, but nothing about leaving us to rot."

I took a deep breath, wishing I couldn't smell my own sweat. "So this is just run of the mill regular distrust instead of something I did?"

"That be the size of it. Aye." Gunhild shrugged.

I let my shoulders slump. "Oh thank the gods. I thought I'd screwed everything up, but you guys are just being dicks."

There was only enough time for the two Dvergar to look moderately outraged before Mercy strolled around the corner with a couple of her ninjas in tow. "I really can't leave you alone for a minute can I?"

"Mercy!" Finally, there was an adult to help. "Tell them we aren't going to run away."

Mercy laughed out loud. "Oh they know. They're just being dicks."

Neither Gorm nor Gunhild smiled at that, but they weren't exactly denying it either. Dicks. A whole cave of dicks. My head hurt.

"So what's next?" I clapped my hands and immediately regretted it. "More drinking?"

Mercy was frowning again. Great. "You're banned from even thinking about alcohol ever again, you complete train-wreck. While you were sleeping it off, I went and spoke to the Elders. We're honorary Khag Mhor citizens now."

"So they're happy?"

"I don't know if happy is the right word." Mercy had come closer, and now she was talking really loudly. Like she thought I couldn't hear her right. Every word made my horns ring. "They believe we're here to help now. Can't really blame them for doubting us when nobody has tried to help each other out around here for a few thousand years."

"I don't get that. Why didn't they ask for help? There have to be other Dvergar out there, even if they don't trust anyone else."

"Some of it was pride, but most of it… you've got to understand this place is screwed. Not just Khag Mhor, but the whole planet, plane…whatever it is." She was so damn loud, I had to sit down on the ground. "The bits that aren't at war with each other over old grudges are overrun with monsters from the Void War, or just general…monsters. Everyone is trying to look after their own people first, or if not, just themselves."

Her words buzzed around my head for a while before they came in to roost. "What about the Eternals?"

Mercy crouched down so our faces were level and she could keep on yelling directly into my ear. "What about them?"

"I mean, we were sent down here by the gods to get the place right. How come the rest of the Eternals aren't out there doing that already?"

"From what I've heard, most of the Eternals are either mad, buried, or…just gone. A few of them used all their powers to make themselves kings of little kingdoms. Nobody holds onto a grudge like somebody who can't die."

I hadn't been holding out much hope that super-powered mega-Eternals from the dawn of time were going to show up and save the day, but it was a nice fantasy. "So we're on our own?"

Mercy flopped onto her ass with a sigh. "Did you ever doubt it?"

"Do you be planning on doing anything but flapping your face-holes and blocking our streets this day?" Gunhild was such a charmer. I was starting to see why nobody had come rushing to the Dvergar's aid if this was how they treated people.

Asher was standing over us, quiet and composed as always. That was it. I was buying a bell and tying it around his neck. When he spoke, I jumped. "So once more the question becomes, what do we do next?"

"The Elders figure all the Svart are coming up from the mine. Maybe there was a collapse that joined up their old shafts to the svart den or something." She paused for me to snort at the word shafts and rolled her eyes. "Anyway, until that is sealed off, more svart are just going to keep on coming. They want us to cut them off at the source."

Asher nodded. "Nip it in the bud."

"Strike at the heart," added Gunhild.

"If you be collapsing the connection," Gorm interjected, "you'll cut off their reinforcements."

Now that I was this close, I noticed that Mercy had a new bow, new arrows, and even some pieces of armor strapped on. I didn't get any prizes. Why did she get prizes? "How are we meant to collapse a tunnel?"

The Dvergar began furiously debating this amongst themselves. I could hear something about redirecting explosive gasses, a sapper team, and ten brave Dvergar miners who would willingly die in the tunnels to put an end to the svart blight. Mercy waded in, "You don't have enough people to be throwing them away."

That set off another round of shouting from the shorter contingent of the group. "Dver be knowing their lives' worth."

"You dare to tell us how to be working stone?!"

Mercy had her hands up, but her shouting did not seem quite as conciliatory. "If any more Dvergar die, the whole khag is done. You can barely keep things going as it is."

"Don't be thinking to tell us how to die, longshanks."

I held up my hand. "Uh, I can do it."

There was a resounding moment of silence, then scoffing.

"What, you're going to punch the rock real hard?" If Mercy kept rolling her eyes like that, eventually she was going to strain something.

"I've got *Divine Architecture* and *Dungeoneering*. I could probably pull down this whole city."

That put a longer stop to the short-lived shouting match. Even Asher was stunned into silence.

Eventually, Gorm coughed and said, "Please don't be doing that."

There was a lot more debate that I kind of missed out on because I was trying not to throw up. At some point, everyone sat down in the dirt, and the Dvergar started sketching out another map, which meant we probably had plenty of time before anything useful could be decided. I almost laughed when Gorm took a hold of my hand and used my thumb to sketch out the barricade lines, but he was so earnest I couldn't let the chuckle slip free. The map wasn't as clean-cut as the Dvergar wanted it to be because Mercy kept stabbing her finger into it, pointing out landmarks she'd seen while exploring her own little corner of heaven yesterday.

Half of the city was still what Mercy was affectionately calling "Svart Town" despite all our best efforts the day before. While we'd been drinking, carousing, and whatever Mercy had been up to, the old barricades had fallen to the svart hordes. All the ground we'd gained had fallen into their grabby little hands without contest. They'd rammed into the new barricades, but the defenders had held, so at least the worm-farm was still under Dvergar control.

The entrance to the mine was directly opposite the entrance to the city, and from the way that the Dvergar described it, it had about as much cultural significance and defensive capability built into it. Traps, tricks, and big old doors. The Dvergar had learned their lessons well about beasties crawling up out of the deeps. Unfortunately, all those things were now in the hands of the svart.

Now that the liquor was out of my system, I'd lost a little bit of confidence in my ability to do this. None of us had ever taken a city before, and yesterday's plan had only worked because it was pretty limited in scope, and we had the barricades to fall back to.

In theory, we could try Mercy's sneaky ninja tactics to get across to the mine entrance, then head down to find where the Svart were coming from deeper in. The Dvergar were extremely insistent that we didn't just collapse the whole mine. Crazy insistent. They seemed to care more about keeping the mine open than they cared about us surviving—by a long shot. Mercy leaned in close and muttered something to me about the mine being the heart of Dvergar trade culture or something, but Asher and Gorm were in the middle of trying to loudly out-polite each other, so I missed everything but the gist.

The thumping in my head got louder with every passing moment. There were at least seven distinct arguments going on around me despite there only being four other people. I stared down at the map in the dust as if there was some hidden answer in there. Svart Town was vast. More than half the cavern-city belonged to them. Every inch of it was liable to be crawling with them. What we needed was a clear path through. I wriggled up onto my knees to lean over the map.

There was a straight run of streets from the middle of the barricade all the way to the mine. A thoroughfare from the entrance gate. I took my first two fingers and drew them down either side of the street, sketching out a barricade along every alleyway and cross-road. "There."

Mercy looked from the map to me and back. "You do understand how maps work? You get that drawing on the map doesn't make something happen in real life."

"I keep forgetting how funny you are until you open your mouth, and then I remember how funny you are: not funny." I turned from her stuck-out tongue to the Dvergar. "Is there anything blocking the main road, or would we get a clear run along it?"

"You'd be getting overrun from the side streets before you've gone ten steps, no matter how fast you be moving." Gunhild also thought I was a moron, apparently.

"That wasn't my question," I interrupted before she could dive back into the argument at hand. "The road. Is the road clear?"

Gorm answered me with a speculative look in his eyes. "Aye, the road be clear."

I flopped back onto my ass with a satisfied groan. "Then we're good to go."

Asher really was remarkably polite. He barely raised his voice when he snapped, "We most certainly are not."

"Well, we'll need to stock up on some basic supplies, check over our gear, and say bye-bye to all the little ninja buddies some of us made, but apart from that, I'm ready to start the quest."

Mercy snorted. "Did you seriously just call this a quest?"

"In what world is venturing into dark tunnels to find the source of the evil monsters plaguing a land not a quest?"

"Any sane world?"

"Welcome to Amaranth." I grinned at her. "Population: us, and a whole load of quests."

She was really staring at me now. Like I was something she'd never seen before. "You're really enjoying all this aren't you?"

"What's not to like? Monsters bad. Hit monsters good." It took a few attempts, but I got myself back onto my feet. "I wish every day could be this easy."

She got to her feet just so the height difference was less obvious. "You're a real character, you know that?"

"Thanks."

She wasn't smiling. "Not a compliment."

The rest of what I assumed was the morning was spent on the crafting and organization stuff video games tended to gloss over. I rebuilt a solid set of armor for myself out of the Dvergar's fairly massive scrap heap and patched up the damage to my sword.

The weapons that the Dvergar made were vastly superior to what my divine powers could conjure up, but I refused to swap out my sword and armor for the fancy stuff that Mercy had dressed herself in. Sure her new silk-strung bow might do more damage, and the studded blackened leathers she was wearing might tank more hits than the rags I could stick together, but I was sticking with the stuff I knew I could change on the run. More damage was great. Being able to repair a broken sword by blinking was better. I graciously accepted some clothes to wear under my armor, just to stop Asher from bleating every time I swung my magnum faun dong around, but I was certain that I was better off not ending up in a sticky situation—covered in sticky-fingered little svart—with armor I couldn't flick off.

Once I'd explained the plan to Gunhild and she'd double-checked with the other two that I wasn't insane and that it was actually possible, she set off with Gorm to make plans of her own. While we stoppered up the Svart at their source, the rest of the city was going to start laying plans of their own. Their fight would be slow and methodical, but the Svart were too stupid to organize against them. As long as we succeeded, the whole of Svart Town might be cleared out by the end of the week.

It took me a while to understand what I was seeing in the city. The Dvergar who'd been in hiding up until now were out and about, bumping fists and scurrying around the streets at such a speed that I genuinely worried about stepping on them. They'd been hidden, invisible, or buried in their work when we arrived, but now they were everywhere. Asher was at my shoulder. "They have hope again."

It was weird when he said it like that, but he wasn't wrong. The Dvergar had been waiting for death. Now they weren't. They were still waiting, watching, and shuffling out of our way like we were unwelcome guests, but inevitable death was no longer on the menu. Hopefully, Chernghast wasn't going to be too mad at me for messing with his domain. Although, given that the gods weren't allowed to directly interfere with what was going on in Amaranth, I guess that if he was angry then he would just have to suck it up. I was the only horse that the Lunar Court had in this race, so they weren't going to knee-cap me just because I happened to trample over their existing plans. Horse metaphors always seem to get away from me.

Mercy was with us now that she had her gear, still muttering about how I was going to get us all killed at a volume just low enough that I could pretend not to hear her. She was getting really negative. It was almost like she didn't trust in the bright idea that I half-remembered from when I was blackout drunk.

Beyond Mercy's gear and a bit of food in case we were exploring down the mine for a day or more, the only thing we really wanted was rope and some pins, just in case our exploration went vertical on us. While Mercy and I were debating how much we needed, and I was reminding her that I could personally carry the whole khag's supply of rope, so worrying about the weight was a bit pointless, Asher slipped away sometime in the middle. By the time that the debate was over, he came slinking back to join us in some silky new robes bound in tight around his torso with leather straps. "Kinky."

He cocked his head to one side as though he didn't understand what I was saying, but I knew he understood me just fine, he just didn't want to admit it.

With that done, we were ready. We headed for the barricade amidst the complete lack of cheering and applause that I'd kind of been secretly hoping for. It was fine. There'd be plenty of time for them to cheer when we came back…victorious. They could have a parade, or more of that mushroom booze, or a parade with more of that mushroom booze.

I gave the other two a boost up onto the barricade's walkway so we could look out at the road to the mines. There were Svart as far as the eye could see, screeching at each other and scampering around like a big old barrel of monkeys. Not as many as we saw yesterday—I guess some of them were sleeping off the excitement—but enough to make me think that just making a run for it was going to end in us getting royally chewed.

The only real charity I'd taken from the Dvergar was a slightly complicated baldric and metal clips arrangement that they'd made to hold my sword on my back when I needed my hands free. I clicked and snapped that hefty cleaver of mine into it now, held up my arms, and closed my eyes.

It was time to see if this plan of mine was going to work or not.

CHAPTER 14

With my eyes closed, it was easier to feel the extent of my *Sphere of Influence*. It wasn't huge. Every Divine Skill from the Pillar of Artifice that I'd bought had extended it a little farther, so with Weapons, Armor, and Architecture, I could now reach out with my mind and brush over the façades of the buildings on either side of the road. Turns out that leveling up my *Dungeoneering* knowledge had also taught me what a façade was. Every day in Amaranth was an education.

It was hard to move when I was using the Divine Pillars but not impossible. I couldn't feel my body, so that made it harder to steer, but from my exterior view, I watched the grey bulk of my new body leaping off the barricade like it was moving through molasses. It looked almost graceful from the outside.

My consciousness got dragged along with my body, the sphere still centered on that big hunk of meat. *Rough Hewn Architecture* had added a lot of new materials to my awareness—the cobbled stone beneath our feet, the half-rotten wood of the doors, and the brass inlaid along the sides of the street to demarcate this as a main thoroughfare. Combined with all of the trash and scraps that could have been made into weapons and armor, the balance of signal to noise was getting skewed. It took real concentration to find what I was looking for.

As my feet hit the ground, the earth beneath us gave way. The whole street sank down as the stone below it flowed out. Like a wave hitting rocks, the stone hit the limits of my sphere and splashed up. Shooting out just beyond the brass strip into a six-foot wall of solid stone on either side of the road.

Snapping back to my body, I fell onto my hands and knees. That took a lot more out of me than I'd been anticipating, but there was no going back now. My only comfort was that I didn't have to wall up the whole thing. Most of the work had already been done for me by the original builders of the khag. A wall every so often to block the gap between buildings was a lot easier than me hauling a barricade up the whole length of the way.

The only downside of moving several tons of stone by force of will was that it wasn't exactly quiet. First, there was a rumble, then a smashing noise as the stone broke the surface, and then an ongoing grating sound like a wolverine having a slap-fight with a chalkboard as the rock grew up. Every svart in Svart Town came running. This was going to be awesome.

Mercy's arrows started to fly the moment a Svart stuck its head out of a doorway, but I didn't reach for my sword yet. Instead, I took a few lumbering steps forward as I tried to remember how things like muscles and bones worked. We reached the next intersection, and I slipped back out of my body again.

Another rumble, another crack, and another shriek of stone on stone. More screaming and charging Svart—now too close for me to ignore them.

The sword unclipped from my back smoothly, just as I dropped back into my body. Again, I took a stumbling step forward, but this time I was expecting it. That momentum turned into an overhead swing.

The other svart seemed to realize their mistake in charging at me head-on when the leader of the pack fell neatly into two halves. Unfortunately for the front-runners, there was a wave of bodies right behind them, tripping and trampling over any svart that weren't happy to charge directly into my blade.

Mercy's arrows popped up out of Svart eyes like they were weird jack-in-the-box toys, but even in the cul-de-sac I'd been building there

was too much space for the svart to wash around me. I took a horizontal swing with my sword as they dashed by, right at my waist-height.

My waist height was their head-height, and six heads sprang clean
off svart shoulders to tumble along the road. The bodies hit the stone,
throwing up puffs of ash and dirt.

"Come get some!"

Weirdly, they didn't take me up on it. The tide parted around me,
and they ran for Mercy and Asher. Nice soft targets in easy grabbing
range. To hell with that. With my eyes closed, I reached down into
the earth again. It was so much easier this time to push a ditch down
into the ground and haul a wall up on the other side at the same time.

The svart charge broke on the solid stone wall, and I snapped
back to my body just in time to catch a crystal dagger right in the
armor-free back of my knee.

I dropped, hammering my horned head into the svart that took
the sucker punch while I was distracted with building.

With a growl of pain, I yanked the jagged crystal shank back
out of my leg and tossed it aside, using my sword as a crutch to haul
myself back to my feet.

"Hey, genius!" Mercy bellowed to be heard over the baying of the
svart. "You can't fight them all alone!"

The svart that had slowed enough not to smash into the stone
and their less fortunate predecessors turned on their heel and charged
back towards me. Putting weight on my stabbed leg hurt like hell, but
it held. I hefted my sword and got ready to swing. In the moment of
silence before the swarm hit me, I shouted back, "Hey, genius, climb
on top of the wall!"

I pulled back with my sword, ready for another broad swipe, and
something poked me in the back of the neck. A glance back told me
that my back was peppered with arrows. My armor had stopped some
from digging into me, but others were just jutting out of me, unnoticed

until now. When I was using *Artifice* I couldn't feel anything that was happening to my body. Not helpful.

Getting distracted while you're facing down a charge wasn't helpful either. The svart swarmed inside my reach before I had the chance to swipe them all away.

The closest ones got the side of my arms instead of the edge of my blade. Enough to knock them aside, but not enough to bisect them like their little buddies.

Any svart my blade touched died. The one that caught my elbow to the chest burst like an overripe watermelon, and the two that caught the flat of my arm instead hit the ground in one piece and tumbled to hit the fresh-made wall. None would be getting up again.

Arrows started raining down again, signaling that Mercy had gotten her act together. Whatever Asher was working up to would take all day, as usual, but there had to be ways I could help out. *Dungeoneering* was whispering in the hindquarters of my brain. Something about lightning and copper. *Conductors!*

There was then a moment's reprieve from svart attacks. They were regrouping, getting peppered with arrows, and gawking at the bits of their buddies that I'd scattered across the road.

Slipping back into god-mode, I reached out to the brass stripes and pulled. At first nothing happened, then I flexed my will a little harder. The metal creaked, and the stone around it cracked. I pulled harder. The metal was worked, refined, and perfected by real craftsmen.

It was beyond the limits of my Divine Skill to work with it, yet still, I could feel it in my Sphere. I could still feel the raw copper ore deep down inside it. With one last grunting pull, the veneer of perfection fell apart, and the bronze strips burst apart. Only the copper came. Fragments and tangled wire-widths of metal exploded out in every direction, out of all control. I snapped back to my body just in time to dive beneath the shower of sparks and metal. That was a mistake.

Blood started seeping out of my eyes to patter in the dust beneath me. I'd pushed too hard at something I didn't even vaguely understand. I could taste copper in my mouth, and I didn't know if it was dust or my own blood. Definitely a mistake.

More blood oozed up out of the hole in my leg and the wounds on my back, and it trickled down from my nose. I got the message, body. Don't do it again. Inch by inch, I started to scramble back towards the Mercy-topped wall, dragging my half-numb leg behind me and hoping that the contortions of unspooling bronze didn't come my way.

I was so dazed that I didn't even realize I was there until I felt the thump. I got my shoulder to the wall and tried to push myself up onto my feet. Mercy roared, "What the hell did you do?"

"Copper. Conductor." I spat blood against the wall. "Mistakes were made."

My insides may have been trying to become my outsides, but there was no denying that the tangled briar of metal that I'd thrown up was slowing the tide of the Svart to a trickle that even Mercy's arrows were sufficient to deal with.

Beyond the walls on either side of the street, the monstrous baying rose up, discordant but somehow musical all the same. Svart voices sounded like a live chicken being fed through a blender, but all together there was no denying that there was some sort of communication going on. "Kill. Kill. Kill," was all that our ability to speak in tongues could translate, but it was the main thrust of the conversation.

When exhaustion dipped me down and my eyes slipped closed, I could see the pillars of divinity within me. I could see the cracks running through the once sleek form of the Pillar of Artifice. Reading you loud and clear, gods. Don't push the powers. Still, at least the glowing spindle of Primal was still standing undamaged.

Restoration set that pillar blazing with moonlight, and when my eyes slipped open, the flow of blood from all my holes slowed to a trickle.

[102/440 Health]

Yikes. I'd really been on my last legs without even knowing it. God mode was cool and all, but losing contact with my body was a good way to get it trashed before I got home.

Almost as soon as my vision cleared up, Asher's spell fired off. The copper bramble I'd made did exactly what I'd hoped, conducting the bolt of lightning that he launched. Dozens of svart were in the midst of clambering through the mess of metalwork to reach us when his spell hit, and they were crispy-fried in an instant. It smelled like fast food. I was going to miss fast food.

With a grunt of effort, I pushed myself back to my feet. It didn't matter that I'd screwed up with the metalwork, we still needed to keep pushing forward or this whole thing was going to come down around our ears.

"Hey, dumbass. Still alive?" Mercy always knew just what to say.

I let out a chuckle that rumbled in my chest. Turning my words into a growl. "Mostly."

Dropping the wall that they were standing on top of was surprisingly easy. Like gravity was helping the stone back down into its natural position beneath our feet. Mercy stumbled when they hit my level, making me grin. Asher remained as cool as a cucumber, as usual. Maybe the tail helped with balance.

Mercy gave me a shove as she passed, but it wasn't very hard, so she must have really been worried about me. "Great, now we get to wade through svart bits. Thanks."

"Wouldn't want you to miss out on the fun."

I couldn't do anything more with the mass of tangled metal up ahead of us—I wasn't dumb enough to try using Artifice on it a second time—but I could still work the stone. Stomping forward and raising my arms, I touched the fractured pillar of Artifice within me and raised the next set of walls.

As the stone flowed up, it pushed the nest of copper above us like a grand thatched roof. I was only raising walls where there had been none before, so the thicket of metal only lifted here and there, but there was definitely a clear route through beneath it, even if I'd have to duck.

Roasted svart corpses started plopping down out of the tangle of metal like overripe fruit before we'd made it a step. Asher really did a number on them.

Beyond the dubious shelter of the wire wool, the svart were waiting, too scared to come closer but too dumb to run. They had flowed in to fill up the road where I'd blocked it from the sides. Wall to wall svart, screeching and crawling over each other to be on the front-line. Like dying first was some big honor.

I rolled my shoulders and hefted my sword. "Ready?"

"As I shall ever be," Asher hissed.

Mercy opened her mouth to respond, but I missed whatever comment she just had to make as I charged in with a roar that literally made some of the svart trip over themselves.

I didn't have to kill them all, I just had to keep all their beady little black bug eyes on me. Every arrow that Mercy loosed killed one. As soon as Asher's spells were ready, he'd be able to wipe out the remnants. We'd fallen into a perfect rhythm already, and we'd only been alive a couple of days. If we had all eternity to work together, it could only keep getting better.

The svart scattered back from the bloodied edge of my blade, baying for my life and screeching at each other. The closest Svart turned to its buddy and screamed, "Kill!"

Svart two looked incredulous, "Kill?"

One in the back rows cried out, "Kill!"

Back row would have to wait, but the first two arguers caught the backswing of my sword.

Mercy's arrows were raining down onto the back rows to avoid getting too close to me, which I appreciated, but it also meant that the front rows had a moment to think. When you've only got two settings, dick around or kill things, a moment was all it took to switch.

Svart ichor had splattered all across the smoothed stones of the street, and I could feel my feet slipping as I spun on the spot, bringing my sword around in another arcing swipe to catch the first ones with the guts to jump for me.

Those guts tumbled out of them, dangling all over me like silly string as I waded farther into the press of bodies. I could feel blades scraping over my armor, but nothing was finding much purchase yet. The armor rating of this latest set was somewhere in the 70s. I couldn't remember exact numbers—I'd made the armor sometime when I was drunk. You could still see part of a blackened cooking pot mangled into the pauldron. *A cauldron pauldron?* A crystal-tipped arrow plinked off it.

"Come on!" I felt like my throat was trying to choke me as I worked through the sounds of the svart's mangled language, but I made it. "KILL!"

The sound of their own language on my lips seemed to give the svart more pause than all the blood and guts I was drenched in. They stopped and stared, and I took advantage of the lull to hack them apart.

Bones splintered like twigs, and flesh tore apart like red clouds. With my sword in my hand, it was like they weren't even real. Like they were paper dolls made for me to tear through.

Behind me, I heard a yelp. Mercy was surrounded by the few svart that had skirted around me, and the circle was closing around her. With a push of will, the floor beneath her erupted, lifting her up on a pedestal, out of the svart's reach.

Even with time still slowed as I concentrated on my *Sphere of Influence*, I could already tell that I'd be too late to save Asher the same way. He had a duo of svart hanging off his sleeves and another riding his tail while stabbing down into it with a dagger in each hand. Concentration faltering, the electricity trapped between his claws sputtered once or twice, then blinked out entirely.

I wasn't going to have time to save him. Even if I lifted him up, the svart would go with him. There was no way I could cross the distance before he was dead. He was going to die because I'd been too busy playing whack-a-svart to notice what was happening right behind me.

Back in my body, I couldn't help myself, and I turned to run back to him. Even if I was going to be too late, I couldn't just leave him to die alone.

Turns out, he could take care of himself. His gravity snare burst to life above him, and while he was dragged up along with the svart clinging to him, he was expecting it. They lost their grip and tumbled up into the orbit of the little black hole while his weight kept him suspended between the two forces exerting their pull on him. Pinned in place between the darkness and the floor, he returned to casting his spell without flinching. The man was cold-blooded in more ways than one.

Tearing my attention away from Asher and his soon to be crispy pests, I turned back to the small army that I was meant to be fighting, only to realize that they'd regrouped while I was distracted. There was a solid wall of Svart at the front waving short blades, a second rank with spears, and then the mass behind that all seemed to have either the janky little bows of theirs or rocks to throw. That wasn't the random work of animal intelligence; that was tactical. Individually, every svart seemed to be a moron, but all together, there was something more to them. The plural of svart was smart.

Of course, I responded to this cunning tactical display with all the delicacy you could have expected. When all you have is a hammer, every problem looks like a nail. When all you have is a giant sword, every problem looks like a small army of svart just waiting to be cleaved. Cloven? Chopped.

Rushing in under a rain of arrows and rocks, the first swing of my sword knocked the spearheads aimed at my actual head aside. Momentum carried me crashing forward into their front lines, and their front rank shattered beneath my weight, tripping and falling back as I just kept on coming.

Nose to nose with the svart, I bellowed, "KILL!"

My foot slammed down onto a svart's face as I charged on, my sword dragged free of the morass of squealing svart all around me. I took another swing.

Bits and blood scattered everywhere, and I realized somewhere in the midst of it I'd started chanting "KILL, KILL, KILL," just like the svart all around me. With their one line of defense broken, the back ranks started to scamper for safety, but there wasn't a chance in hell that I was stopping now.

The routed svart started peeling off, heading for the gaps in the buildings on either side of me. Not happening. I closed my eyes and hauled up walls. The fleeing svart crashed right into the stone, and outside of my body, connected to the rock I was shaping, I felt each and every vibration as though they'd run into me.

I snapped back into my body and turned just in time to see Asher's spell rush out past me. Just when I was starting to get bored with his old static charge and lightning crackle, he whipped something new out of his bag of tricks. This time, he'd skipped the charge and just launched a ball of lightning that shot past me in pursuit of the svart line. Everything it touched died, and everything it missed got a cap from it, then was surrounded by a clinging electrical charge.

Mercy leapt down from her pedestal instead of waiting for me to lower it and dashed forward along the road, still peppering the hindquarters of the fleeing svart as she went. "Move it!"

She was right, not that I'd ever admit it. This was the kind of opportunity we'd been waiting for. Mercy shot the stragglers, and Asher's ball lightning chased along the road, dissuading any of the svart that weren't running for their life from coming out. As for me, I didn't even have to use my sword again. I slammed up walls as we passed by gaps in the buildings. I sealed up the open stone doors and windows of the houses, trapping fleeing svart inside. Before I even knew it, we were at the grand mine entrance, and the whole city's worth of svart had been sealed away.

Victory!
New Skill Discovered! [Brawling]
Potency increased to 40
Brutality: Rank 8/10
Brawling: Rank 2/10
270 Experience Gained

"If we stopped here and turned back, the Dvergar would still have their city returned to them. The svart are sealed off from reinforcement. This is the victory they sought." Asher chimed in, looking into the cavernous entrance to the mines.

"You guys don't get it. The mine is like...the *soul* of the khag. They'd never stop trying to take it back." Mercy was plucking arrows out of dead svarts and eying them to make sure they were still straight enough to fly true. "Even if it wasn't like a religious thing, the Dver need to mine for trade, their whole economy is digging stuff up, hitting it with hammers and selling. If we stopped here, they'd try to do it themselves, and they'd die over and over until there was none of them left."

I was nearly speechless. Nearly. "Hold up. Are you actually on board with the quest?"

She shrugged. "I'm here, ain't I?"

"Yeah, but you've been here all along, bitching and moaning every step of the way about me dragging you into this." I caught her by the shoulder and forced her to look at me. "This is different. You actually care about these people."

She still wouldn't meet my eyes. "Well, yeah. Asher told me what you said."

"You'll need to be more specific. I say a lot of stuff. All the time. I mean, I'm saying stuff right now. I can't seem to stop saying—"

She cut me off by slapping her hand over my mouth. "They're people. They look different, and they sound different, but they deserve better than this."

I licked her hand, and she jerked it away with a yelp.

"They do."

Asher nodded in agreement.

As one, we turned to face the entrance of the mine. I took back what I said about it earlier. It wasn't as big and impressive as the entrance to the khag.

It was bigger.

CHAPTER 15

There were fewer murder holes to creep under as we moved beneath these great brass arches, and the few that I could spot seemed to be unoccupied. After all the chaos of the running fight across the town, it was almost eerily quiet. There were traps set up here and there, but the majority had been triggered long ago. Huge pillars of stone had dropped down from the ceiling to crush capering svart and had never been reset. The bones still protruded from under them, gnawed clean of all flesh.

I kicked one of their deformed little skulls to smash on the wall. "Love what they've done with the place."

Mercy hissed. "Will you shut the hell up."

"You think they didn't hear us coming?" I laughed. "We just fought the whole damn town. If they didn't hear that, they aren't going to notice light conversation."

"You are correct," Asher chipped in, "but I believe that Mercy's approach is wiser, nonetheless."

"What are you two so scared of? We just beat the crap out of a whole town's worth of svart. There isn't going to be anything we can't handle."

Mercy had frozen in place, her head cocked to one side. "You really need to stop speaking."

The bones at my feet began to twitch, and the abomination's golden glow sprang to life on them like Saint Elmo's Fire.

I wet my lips. "I really need to stop speaking."

Mercy yelped as the bones around her feet started to chatter together and roll across the floor. I hadn't even noticed how many corpses littered svart town until they started moving, and now it seemed you couldn't turn your head without a rack of ribs popping up out of the ashes. Bits of Dvergar and svart, some still strung together with mummified strands of tendon all gathered together in a great heap between us and the mine. Heaving and glowing.

I wasn't waiting for it to explode or turn into some giant skeleton boss. I closed the distance in a heartbeat, sword held aloft. "Knock it off."

Fragments of bone scattered across the stone as I hammered my sword down.

Still, the heap continued to glow and gather boney bulk. "No, thank you."

"Not today."

The bones shuddered and dropped to the ground. Lifeless once more. "And stay down."

A little bit of the tension drained out of Mercy, and I caught a brief glimpse of her smile before she hid it behind the usual mask of sarcasm. "Did you just pick a fight with an inanimate object?"

"I just won a fight with an inanimate object, thank you very much."

Asher had crouched by the pile of bones, hand held out as though checking its temperature. "I sense no magic here."

I shrugged. "I don't remember seeing necromancy in the skill options anyway."

"You misunderstand me." He passed his hand back and forth over the bones. "If there is no arcane working animating these remains, then the cause for their attempted revival must be divine."

I shrugged. "So they were good religious corpses?"

"He is saying an Eternal did it, you boob." Mercy had her back turned, her eyes darting from shadow to shadow, searching for whatever enemy was out there waiting for us.

"Lady, if your boobs look like me, you might want to consult a doctor."

She snorted. "Dude, if my boob looked like you I'd cut it off."

"Amazon-style." I nodded. "I can respect that."

Asher's sigh came out like a hiss of steam. "This conversation is not constructive."

"The abominations have that glow too." I pointed at the bones, where the last of the light was flickering out. "I'd bet on one of them before I'd bet on an Eternal. At least we already know that they are here."

Asher rose and brushed the ash from the front of his robes. "The real question to my mind is why the abominations have the light of the divine within them."

"Maybe they ate an Eternal?"

Mercy's careful scouting was interrupted when she had to stop and pinch the bridge of her nose. "I'm not even going to acknowledge how stupid that sentence was."

I shrugged. "Maybe they're made out of Eternal parts?"

Mercy opened her mouth to dunk on me again, but Asher spoke up first, "This was my first thought."

Mercy and I both replied with the same tone of surprise. "Really?"

Maybe we were spending too much time together.

"There must be some reason that they contain the spark of the divine, and as Mercy explained to us earlier, the Eternals that came before us have now vanished from the world despite the longevity implied by their names. I do not believe it unreasonable to suppose that they were used in the making of these legendary creatures."

Mercy scoffed. "Maulkin was right?"

I kicked a skull at her, missing by a mile. "Eternals are being put through a meat-grinder to make burger-monsters, and me getting something right is the surprising bit?"

"Asher's right. That bit makes sense." She had given up in her hunt for monsters in the shadows, strolling over to smirk. "You getting something right though…that defies all logic."

"I should have left you to rot in that first dungeon."

"Oh, please"—she jumped up to tug on one of my horns—"you live for my abuse."

"Once more, this conversation has ceased to be constructive." Asher sighed. "Shall we press on?"

"If you're finished with the bone zone."

Mercy laughed. I heard her. She couldn't take it back.

Deep enough into the tunnel that I had a real sense of being past the point of no return, we came upon the gates to the mine.

When the monsters came, the copper door had been locked in place with a crossbar. That hadn't been enough. The Dvergar of the city had rushed in to brace the door against the charge. That hadn't been enough. The metal itself had been twisted by some unstoppable force from the other side. The Dvergar who had thrown the weight of their bodies against the door were now nothing but scattered bones and odd fragments of rock, like broken parts of statues strewn across the ground.

There were dead svart here too—more and more bones the closer that we got. The fight for the city had been lost here, but not without a terrible cost to the invaders. For every dead Dvergar, there were at least three dead svart, their bones gnawed just as clean as the enemy's. Hunger knew neither friend nor foe.

Mercy whistled. "I don't want to meet whatever busted that door open."

"No? I kind of do." I grinned. "I want to kick its ass."

Asher climbed up on the back of the dead to reach the gap in the doors. "No doubt we shall cross paths. If we haven't already."

He hopped down out of sight, and Mercy and I only had a moment to exchange a glance before we both jogged after him. Squishy magic users should not go wandering off on their own.

Luckily for us, there was no monster sitting with its mouth hanging open on the other side of the gates, just a whole lot more bones. We skidded down the slope of them, coming to a halt by the edge of the same brass track that had led all the way along the main thoroughfare, only now could I see its purpose. There were mine-carts rigged up to roll along the single brass rail, counterbalanced with a wheel to each side. Decorative, but also practical.

The rest of the mine entrance told two stories, overlaid in the same space. Beneath the dust and the filth, you could see the miner's tools, their armor, and their lanterns, most still hanging from pegs in the little cut-out rooms to the side of the main tunnel.

Over the top, you could see the new story. The svart's little encampment here in the dark away from the lights of the khag, where they could chew on the dead in peace. Everywhere was their toilet. Everywhere was their trash-heap. Whatever mind they had ticking and creaking behind those black eyes, it didn't hold the same sense that most rodents had to not crap where they ate. This side of the copper gates was scarred with the blows of their weapons, embedded with crystalline fragments, and streaked with ichor from where the svart had tried to pummel their way through solid metal with their bare hands.

Pieces of svart had been ground up and spread like a paste around the bent back metal. Whatever had come rushing through to break the gate hadn't given a damn about preserving the lives of its allies. If it was one of the chained abominations, as we were guessing, then it was hard to blame it for wanting to smash up as many of its captors as possible.

There was so much blood spilled that it still shifted under the dried surface crust. "Juicy."

"How?" Mercy wailed. "How did that one word make it so much grosser?"

Asher's head snapped to the side. "Heed your own advice, Mercy. Silence is our ally here."

When he turned back to look out into the dark, she wobbled her head from side to side mouthing, "Silence is our ally," to herself. I bit down a chuckle.

In the silence, all we could hear was the tumble of the bones we'd dislodged, clacking and clattering about behind us, and echoing back and forth across the width of the tunnel. The farther into the dark we walked, the brighter the light behind us seemed. Bright as sunlight. "Hold up."

The chattering bones grew louder and louder instead of dying away. I was reaching for my sword as I turned, but it was too late to nip this one in the bud.

It stood a head taller than me, shaped like a man made of sunlight but bound all around by a full suit of bone armor that was even more haphazard than mine. Skulls bulged out from the flat of the surface, and vertebrae were slung in strings to bind longer bones down. There was no question that this thing was an abomination like the rest, even if it lacked the marble bodies of the others we'd faced before.

I drew my sword and gave it a spin in my hands. "A-bone-ination?"

"Abominable Boner?" Mercy called back.

"If this abomination persists for more than four hours," I cackled, "please contact your physician or local necromancer."

Asher was getting tired of our nonsense. "Focus!"

Mercy's first arrow deflected off one of the skulls, and the next found a gap in the armor and burned away in the light within. That might be a problem.

The abomination took its first baby steps towards us, still clumsy in the new shape it had taken. It wasn't much of an advantage, but I'd take what I could get. With a whoop, I charged in.

Nothing as big as that abomination had any right to move as fast as it did. Before I could swing, it's leg jerked up to catch me in the gut and send me flying.

[88/440 Health]

Oh yeah, I'd already nearly killed myself. Probably should have remembered that before I charged in face-first.

When I reached for the Pillar of Primal, it gave me a little shudder to tell me *Restoration* wasn't up yet. I wasn't going to push it. I'd already cracked one pillar by pushing too hard, Primal was probably the only thing that was still propping me up.

I skidded to a halt before I hit a wall. So that was nice. Wish I could have said that I sprang back to my feet and charged back in, but I got up like an old man who'd broken his hip. All the damage was starting to take its toll. Eternals might not be able to die, but we could sure as hell wish that we had.

Using my sword as a crutch to haul myself to my feet, I took in the chaos unfolding before me. Asher had ducked into one of the side chambers, and Mercy was sprinting at full pelt to avoid the stone-shattering blows that the abomination was raining down.

She was trying to lead it away down the tunnel, to give the two of us time to recover. She was playing the hero. Fast as she was, the abomination kept pace, always right behind her. The arrows she had launched had deflected or burned away without leaving a mark.

I put one foot in front of the other. I crawled, then I walked, and then I ran. My bloodless arms hefted a sword bigger than my whole body had been in my last life like it had no weight at all. This close to death, I swear I felt that spark of eternity inside me burning brighter than it ever had before.

The abomination's last punch fell a breath short of Mercy, and I leapt past her, onto the wrist, then the arm, then the shoulder of the heaving mass of bone and daylight. The head turned to me as I came, a jagged tear across its face amidst the bones where real armor would have shown an eye-slit. With one last haphazard lunge from the slippery slope of loose bones, I swung my sword into the light.

The blade was molten when it came out the other side, trailing molten metal droplets that spattered across the bones as I tumbled back towards the ground, and I landed on my back with a crunch.

A glowing stump was all that was left of my sword as hot metal sprinkled down around me like confetti. I started to rise and then saw death bearing down on me. Anything else would have stopped after a slash across the eyes. Anything else would have paused. The abomination moved on like it was nothing. Its massive foot was coming down towards me so fast I didn't have time to think.

It was actually touching the tips of my horns, pinning my head between the stone floor and the sole of bones when it stopped. A moment later and I'd have been crushed. Instead, I was lying there, looking up into the mass of dead bodies, and wondering what the hell was going on.

Vibrations were coming down into my skull, the immense strain of the abomination trying to bring its foot down and kill me against whatever was restraining it. I closed my eyes and saw the pillar of Primal blazing bright once more.

[163/440 Health]

Restoration brought me back from the brink, and I opened my eyes to vision that was no longer going dark at the edges. Letting the ruined remnant of my sword fall from my hand, I set my palms on the ragged expanse of bone, and I pushed back.

In a straight fight, there was no way I could have shifted this thing. It didn't matter how high my Potency had climbed, it was definitely bigger and stronger. But this wasn't a straight fight. It was already pushing down as hard as it could to no avail. I had help.

Inch by inch, I rose up. I got a knee underneath me, and I pushed up some more. I got my feet beneath me, and my whole body flexed. Muscles that I don't even think that human beings have tightened up, burned, and screamed as I pushed with all my Faun might against the Abomination.

It fell.

As it toppled over, I finally got a glimpse of my salvation. Asher's gravity snare—black as night and twice as alluring. The abomination was heavy enough that it couldn't be hauled from the ground by the snare but not big enough to resist it entirely. Now that it was off-balance, the snare continued to drag at it.

I must have been half-mad with excitement when I yelled out, "Timber!"

When the abomination hit the ground, the impact set the brass rails singing—a low hum I felt in my teeth and horns. Reaching out into my *Sphere of Influence*, I could touch every part of my ruined sword, so I hauled it back together as I saw my body trundling forward with nobody at the steering wheel.

Every time I had used Artifice, it got easier to repeat. Making my sword was as natural as breathing now. The cracks in the pillar looked like they were almost gone now, whether it was time or use that had healed it, it didn't matter. What mattered was that I hadn't permanently broken myself.

With the comforting weight of metal back in my hands, I jumped up onto the chest of the abomination and set to beating my way past its crusty shell.

Nothing. Every time I knocked bones away, more scurried into the gap. Every time the bones shifted, I felt it like a tingle on my skin. It was the overlap of the abominations' *Sphere of Influence* with mine.

Its Artifice the same as my own.

Two could play at that game. I shut my eyes and yanked at the bones beneath me with my own Artifice. At first, nothing happened, then, when I strained, one long bone sprang up to smack me in the face like I'd stepped on a rake.

With a grumble, I caught hold of that big bone and yanked it out, only to see new plates of bone sliding smoothly into place to cover the gap it had left. I had no idea what this bone had come from—it seemed bigger than anything we'd seen in the svart or Dvergar. It was nearly as long as my torso. Great, there were giant monsters down here too. Not counting present company.

At least the bone gave me a good idea. I hefted it above my head with both hands, letting my sword fall aside. All it took was a pulse of Artifice to turn the metal of my weapon into slag, then another to mash it all together in one great dense lump around the top end of the bone. My arms creaked under the accumulating weight.

"Forget the bone zone. Welcome to pound town!"

With all my strength, I brought the makeshift sledgehammer down.

That was more like it. The bone armor shattered to dust beneath the hammer, and the ones around it cracked. The abomination tried to close the gap, but as it dragged bones around it was just opening up fresh gaps.

Asher's snare died, and without its interference with gravity, the abomination was getting back onto its feet all too easily. I had to jump to avoid being flung off.

"Get out the way!" I heard Mercy shout, and only a moment later, I realized what she was freaking out about. Asher was there, lighting up the whole tunnel in strobing white and blue with the massive ball of lightning he was holding between his claws.

The abomination's fist hammered down on either side of me, and it pushed up off the ground. "I'll do you one better! Take the shot, Asher!"

Without hesitation, Asher launched the ball of lightning. I saw it bounce once on the smooth straight stretch of stone between the rails, heading right for me, then I swung for the abomination's chest with all my might.

The damage I dealt didn't matter so much as the hole that I'd punched. The big glowing ball bounced one last time, and I flung myself aside. The lightning passed through the gap in the armor, and the bones slammed shut behind it. "Nothing but net!"

The abomination went on rising, but its movements stuttered as the ball of lightning pin-balled around inside of it. It took a step towards Asher, then its knee locked up, and it stumbled. Where the ball bounced, showers of sparks exploded out amongst the bones, and the golden glow died. Back and forth the lightning bounced and leapt.

I hefted my hammer, ready to knock bone-boy back the moment it took another step, but it never did. With one final crackle of lightning, the golden glow within the bones blinked out.

New Skill Discovered! [Mace]
Legendary Foe Defeated!
Potency increased to 41
Mace: Rank 1/10
48 Experience Gained
400 Glory Gained
Tier of Glory Ascended!

That was long overdue.

Time ground to a halt once more as my attention turned inwards. The Pillars of Divinity stood before me, still a little worse for wear.

It might not always be obvious that I'm thinking stuff through—because honestly, I'm not a lot of the time—but there was actually a brain inside of my horny head. I'd been thinking about my next chance to Tier Up since the last one.

Artifice was great, and Primal was the only thing that kept me alive most of the time, but neither one of them was actually making me any better at doing what I do. I needed to get better at hitting things with swords.

The Pillar of Ascension seemed to be the way to go. It was all about improving the bodies we'd been given, so I poured all my hard-won glory into it. All three pillars were blazing around me now, and I felt a bit more stable as a result. If I cracked one, at least the other two would keep me up. Not that I was planning on cracking any of them again. Honest.

I slipped straight over into the divine skills that Ascension had opened up for me. There was one for each of the basic stats, so I jumped right in and dumped my 300 experience right into *Potency Surge*. Ten seconds of double strength didn't seem like long, but in a fight, a second could last a long time. Even if I only got one hit in, that was still going to be a hell of a hit. That left me a little over 20 experience in change.

I snapped back to reality just in time to feel Mercy slap me across the face.

"Rude."

Mercy rolled her eyes. "Dude, you've got to stop doing that."

I rubbed my cheek. "Alright. I'll tell everybody when I'm leveling up if you stop hitting me."

Mercy fell into step beside me as we headed down into the mineshaft. "No deal. Sometimes you need a good slap in the face."

"Sometimes I need to level up."

Asher sighed behind us. "Sometimes I wonder if I would not have been better off traveling with Uthelred."

"Wasn't he basically a vegetable?" Mercy quipped back.

"The conversation would have been much more tolerable."

I smirked over at Mercy. "If he were in charge, he'd never lettuce do anything fun."

She groaned, then smirked back. "You know he was an Eternal with a lot of layers, like an—"

Asher cut her off. "While I am certain that you are both well versed in many different edible plants, might we turn our attention to the mine full of nightmarish monstrosities for now?"

We both mumbled, "Fine," then trudged on.

The tunnel narrowed and then branched the farther we went, but the two rails still ran on, and we kept on between them. Asher and Mercy had decided that the end of the line was probably the best place to start our search for whatever was farting out the svarts, and I didn't have any brighter ideas. Presumably, the rails would run down the central shaft as deep as it could go so that the side tunnels could get the most use out of it.

Far from the light of the khag, we came to rely exclusively on the glow that our own eyes cast. We were going down tunnels with tunnel vision a unique combination. As calm as Mercy looked striding along beside me, I could tell that she was nervous from the way that her golden eye-light strobed back and forth across the tunnel. She was twitchy. I suppose if all my attempts to shoot stuff completely failed, I'd get twitchy too.

The tunnels were uniform as only the Dvergar could make them, but again, there was a second story plastered over the top. Here and there, we could see signs of the svart. A pile of dung. A gnawed bone. A scratch on the stone. A primitive symbol carved into the few wooden supports that had been placed sparingly where they were needed the most. Tools had been dropped to the wayside as the miners fled ahead of the tide of svart. Some had been taken up by their pursuers, but most lay trampled down into the grit.

Mercy stiffened beside me, and I held up my hand to halt Asher. We all stood there in silence, straining to hear whatever had set her off. When I finally did, it made my skin crawl. Something was breathing in one of the side tunnels. Wheezing.

All three of us crept into the tunnel, inching towards the sound of wheezing until it seemed to be coming from all around us. It was only when it started to recede that any one of us thought to look up.

Bestiary was muttering away in my brain about this being ideal Hob territory, about them being ambush predators that used their uncanny ability to climb to get the literal drop on their prey. I pushed all of that aside and let my brain make sense of what it was seeing. Melded into the stone above us was one of the Dvergar. The Curse of Stone had blended his flesh with the rock around him. How he got stuck into the roof was anyone's guess, but from the smooth blend of stone, it was apparent he'd been there for as long as any one of the khag elders.

When our eyes lit him up, his wheezing went from labored to frantic, then on further into pained squeals, like we were tormenting him just by seeing him like this. Maybe this was torture for him. The Dvergar seemed to be pretty private about the whole curse situation. Seeing one of them like this was probably as embarrassing to them as a nurse walking in on me after I'd shit the nursing home bed would have been to me.

That is if I hadn't lived slow, died young, and left a half-chewed corpse behind instead.

Mercy was the only one to speak. "We should do something, right? We should... cut him down or something."

It just took a quick blink to explore my *Sphere of Influence*, then I came back empty-handed. "I can't tell what is stone and what is him. If we cut away all the stone... I don't know what would be left."

The whimpers and wheezes came out in a gust it took just as long to decipher. "Kill me."

Asher looked torn. "We must press on."

"The white ones. They be torturing us," the Dvergar's voice grated.

Asher paused. "Us?"

It made a horrible sort of sense. Where else would ashamed Dvergar retreat to when their bodies were hardening to stone but the great big hole that their whole town revolved around. If you went off into the mine and vanished, nobody would think much of it. People probably died down in the mine all the time. You could find some dark corner to hide yourself away and sink into the stone in peace.

I opened my mouth to try and offer some sort of comfort, though I had no idea what you're meant to say to somebody who'd fused into solid stone, then got prodded by little svart. Luckily, Mercy lived up to her name. Her arrow went right through the one living eye that still glimmered in the midst of dull stone.

Then with a final gasp that might have been a 'thank you', the labored breathing that had drawn us off into this tunnel stopped, and we resumed our journey.

CHAPTER 16

We were back in the main tunnel again, following the rails before Asher piped up. "It seems that we shall have some guidance through the mine after all."

Mercy looked like she was liable to spit. "Living signposts."

"If you can call that living." Asher sighed.

That stopped me short. "I'd call it living. Because they're living. Just because they can't move around doesn't make them any less than us."

"I could not abide to live on in such a state."

"Well, don't you go turning to stone then," I griped. "The way I see it, where we're from, somebody gets old and dies, and everything they know dies too. The Dvergar get old, and they turn into a statue you can still come and talk to."

"Seems to work for them"—Mercy shouldered past me—"when there aren't armies of svart coming up the pipes."

Asher's mouth kept on flapping. "I…meant no offense. I had not considered this perspective."

"People are people," Mercy said over her shoulder. "Remember?"

I called after her. "I'm going to start charging you royalties for that."

She gave me a hand signal that definitely was not Dvergar in origin. "Sue me."

"Do they even have lawyers in Amaranth?" I chuckled, but it was short-lived. Sure there were monsters here that would eat your face as soon as look at you, but a world without lawyers might have been worth the trade-off.

Asher piped up. Anxious to move the conversation along. "A legal system would first be required, and it seems that much of the machinations of civilization have crumbled here in the wake of the Revelation of Araphel."

"Hey, if he killed all the lawyers, maybe this Araphel guy wasn't all that bad." I waggled my eyebrows at them.

"I do not believe that the Revelation is a subject that should be made light of in earshot of anyone native to this world." I could barely hear Asher over the crunch of gravel beneath our feet. "It would be comparable to some of the most horrific events in our own respective histories."

"That's a shame, I was working out a whole stand-up routine." Mercy's grin shone in the dark. "I just flew here from another dimension to fight the Void God, and boy are my arms tired."

I shrugged. "You could still do it, just keep it classy."

"So what?" She was giggling as she went. "Revelation jokes are too soon?"

"Dvergar jokes are punching down?"

Asher sighed. "I should not have encouraged this."

Abruptly, the brass tracks came to their end. Not with some big bumper to stop them crashing into the wall at the end of the tunnel, but abruptly, with channels dug into the stone for them to continue but no more metal. The tunnel itself stretched on a little farther before exploding out into a dozen different directions. I took it all in, listening carefully to the *Dungeoneering* part of my brain to see if it had anything to share.

It did not.

I sighed at the blank spot in my mind. Maybe it was on strike after so much overwork, or maybe I just wasn't seeing any clue as to where we should be headed next.

Asher had crouched to examine the disturbed gravel beneath our feet. "Mercy, have you developed any skills in tracking?"

"Nope." Her eyes were still flickering between all the different entrances. "You?"

Asher shook his head. "Maulkin?"

"Uh…no."

There was an awkward moment with the three of us just standing there, then Mercy took off down one of the tunnels. Asher called after her, "What is it?"

She was already too far gone to reply. I jogged off after her, and with much rolling of eyes and lashing of tails, Asher followed.

When I caught up to her she was still going strong, striding along like this was a walk in the park. "Why this one?"

"We had to start somewhere, didn't we?" She wouldn't look at me, her eyes searching around—floor, walls, and roof—hunting for more Dvergar. "This one seemed fine."

"I mean, I guess?"

"Yeah, I guessed too." She stopped at a junction and then turned left after only one missed step. "It is all guessing until we find someone to help us work out where we're going."

Asher caught up behind us. "We have committed to a tunnel at random then?"

"Beats standing around." Mercy took another turn.

Asher was in the middle of saying, "I am not sure that is the case," when the tunnel opened out into a cul-de-sac walled with wailing faces.

"Kill us."

Hands strained against the crumbling stone that held them. Reaching for us. "Please, be ending our suffering."

"We be begging you, kill us!" came from a mouth speaking out of the solid stone, no eyes, no other features but a jutting rock that might have been a chin.

Mercy spun on her heel, smirking. "See!"

I wish that I couldn't see them. All the damage that I'd worried about doing to the Dvergar we'd met before had been dealt to these poor people. Stone chipped away until raw flesh was exposed underneath. Flesh chewed away until only the unbreakable stone that had fossilized over the bones had stopped the encroachment. There were more of them dead in this little cave than were alive, and the dead probably got off easy.

Asher piped up. "Which direction did the svart come from?"

"Please let us die! We be begging you. Let us die!"

This might not have been the productive conversation that the other two had been hoping for, but we could work with it. "I'll kill you. I'll kill you all!"

Mercy looked aghast, but there was a ring of cheers from the people in the walls. "We want to stop what has happened to you happening to anyone else. Do you know where the svart came from?"

"We know nothing. Nobody talks to us. Let us die."

Blood rained down out of the stone where my sword hung, wedged in the roof. I had to put my foot on the wall to yank it back out.

Mercy stepped up and shouted, "Hey!"

With my sword freed, I lined up my next swing. "They don't know anything."

"They're freaking out." She grabbed at my wrist, and I let her. Her tiny hands didn't even make it halfway around. "Just give them a minute, and they might remember."

The wailing all around us continued, and I couldn't hold back a shudder. "They're suffering."

"Everyone is suffering. I'm suffering. You're suffering. That's the human condition, or the Dvergar condition…whatever." She was putting her whole weight on my wrist, trying to push my sword arm down. Her feet lifted off the ground. "The point is, their suffering can get us closer to stopping all this. So just wait."

She picked out one of the Dvergar at about head-height that was somehow still living despite the stone all around him being streaked with rust stains. She cupped the raw flesh of his face in her hand, drawing out a long, slow moan. "You need to help us. You need to tell us where the svart are coming from or we can't stop them."

"Nooo." The Dvergar's voice cracked like the flakes of stone falling away from him. "Please."

"Tell us, and we can let you go, we can end all this."

"Please!" Blood smeared on her hands as he tried to turn away.

"Please!" she screamed back in his face, drowning out his wails. "Help us stop this."

"Shaft eighteen. They be finding a vein of some quartz they didn't know. That was the last I be hearing before the screaming started." This croaking voice came from the farthest corner of the room, down by our feet, where a pair of baleful eyes stared up at us from out of the gravel, rimmed with dust.

If I ever stop chuckling when somebody says "shaft" you'd better check me for a pulse.

Asher crossed the space and dropped to his knees. "Our thanks to you, friend. Do you require release?"

There was a long moment where the Dvergar in the floor gave it some serious deliberation, then she said. "The svart don't be seeing me down here, and somebody needs to remember all this for the young Dver. Leave me be."

"As you wish." Asher carefully pulled himself back up to his feet, painfully aware that he was standing on this poor Dvergar's grave.

Mercy nocked an arrow, and I hefted my sword. There were only six Dvergar left alive, but we made short work of them.

As we headed back along the main tunnel, searching for shaft eighteen, I found that my hands were shaking. All the monsters and mayhem, all the fighting and dying, it hadn't bothered me one bit. I assumed it was because this body had been custom made for killing by the gods, yet now I'd snuffed out three more lives, and I suddenly felt sick to the stomach.

Mercy was by my side as we strolled along. "You're quiet."

"Just thinking."

She nudged my arm. "Has that ever worked out for you?"

"Hah."

She plodded along beside me for a bit longer, waiting for a snappy reply, but I just couldn't muster anything up. Asher's tail was lashing around, so she picked up the pace to stand beside him. I could hear them muttering back and forth, but my head just wasn't in it. Something about there being the wrong number of tunnels maybe?

All the Dvergar that had come down here to the place that they thought was safest for their final rest would have been at the whims of the svart. It was no wonder Mercy called the mine the soul of the khag. This was where their ancestors lived and spoke to the liv—

The arrow caught me in the side of the face, punching right through my cheek and wedging between my teeth.

[160/520 Health]

What came out of my mouth was somewhere between a scream and a roar, deafening as it echoed back from the stone that enclosed us.

Mercy and Asher turned just in time to see the svart pouring out the side-tunnel towards me, and I turned just in time to catch them all on the flat of my sword.

Dozens of svart poured out, shrieking in their inhuman voices, indecipherable except for the word "Kill" chanted again and again. I managed to get turned, get my feet under me and brace, but more and more of them piled on the back of their kin, reaching over to swipe at me, tiny crystal daggers poking at my hands.

I wasn't succumbing to them this time. I wasn't being overrun. The old determination to survive had a fire of righteous fury lit under it now. I'd seen what they did to the Dvergar. They deserved nothing less than death. I Surged my Potency, and I pushed them back.

The look on their faces when I began to bulldoze them was worth the cost in experience. They went from mindless rage to confusion and over the precipice into horror when they realized that despite their numbers, I was still pushing them back. Some tried to break away, but the same entanglement of their gangly limbs that let them lock together and become a force to be reckoned with in our little shoving match also kept them trapped.

I ran them all the way back to the tunnel entrance before my surge gave out, and with momentum on my side, I was able to drive the tumbling, squealing heap of them all the way out of the main shaft before they could get it together enough to push.

Mercy's arrows flitted by my head as the pommel and flat tip of my sword made contact with the tunnel walls on either side of the svart pipe. Hair rose up on the back of my neck as Asher prepared a spell. In the tunnel, the svart were untangling themselves and regrouping, but they knew to fear my strength now—they weren't going to try to make another rush at us. One of their arrows shattered on the flat of my blade, showering me in crystal dust glitter, and another shot past me entirely. The few that had ranged weapons were shuffling around, trying to stay out of reach while still getting a clean shot at me.

The tunnel had been cut for Dvergar's comfort. It was barely more than a six-foot square, I'd have one hell of a crick in my neck if I had to walk down it for any length of time. Still, it gave me options.

Artifice was a hell of a drug. Every time I used it, I liked it a little better. My sword spread out into a flat sheet, the leather handle skittering across the back surface to land in the center, and I took ahold of my new door-sized shield and braced myself.

The arrows and spears being flung at the far side pattered off the metal without so much as a dent. Even as primitive as my big lump of metal was, it was still way ahead of their stone-age gear. With their first flurry failed, I could hear movement on the far side of the shield. They must have been readying a charge. Well, so was Asher. He gave me a nod, and I pulled the door open. The line of svart that had been rushing at us skidded to a halt with a wail as Asher's spell washed over them.

Before they could realize the crackling electricity that had enveloped them didn't actually do any damage, I slammed the door shut on them all again.

Mercy let out a bark of laughter. "We should fight like this all the time."

She'd managed to launch an arrow or two in the time the door was open, and now she had another ready. I was just working out how to pop a hole in the shield for her to shoot through when the svart hit the other side and rocked me where I stood.

I put my shoulder to the door, but the pressure continued to build up as more and more of them flung themselves at the sheet metal. "Little help!"

"Dude, you take shits bigger than me, what am I meant to do to help?" Despite her charming words, she still ran forward and put her shoulder to the metal. Asher didn't, but since we were relying on him to blast all the svart when they finally kicked this thing down, it felt fair.

My Potency Surge wasn't ready yet, and I wasn't sure it would help even if I used it. We'd hold out for ten seconds without any trouble, then we'd be right back here in the same situation all over again. I tried to slip out of my body and throw an actual wall up, but the moment I stopped concentrating on holding back the tide I saw the shield tilting out. I leapt back into my body just in time for Mercy to snarl. "Really not the time to be tuning out."

If she wasn't straining with the pressure, she would definitely have been kicking me. Thanks, svart.

I leaned all the way forward until my horns were pressing against the metal, screeching like nails on a chalkboard. Every massive muscle in my body was bulging with effort. It was good to be strong, but it sucked to be pushed to the limit of that strength every five minutes.

It was a good thing Mercy was paying attention at least. After a glance back to Asher, she had a wild grin on her face. "Let it drop."

She sprang away, leaving me to take the whole burden for just a moment before I yanked the shield to the side. This time they were ready for the surprise, and they reared back instead of falling through, weapons raised, ready to launch their counter-attack.

Asher's Ball Lightning blasted through their front rank, then pin-balled its way along the tunnel. I swear that every one of them got fired in that first roll of thunder, yet a moment later, others came crawling out of the corpse heap, their own pallid flesh stark against the charred black bodies they'd used as shields.

I hadn't been idle while all this was happening. My shield was back to being a sword, and it was up and ready as it ever would be. Before, killing these pasty little runts had been a necessary evil, and sometimes it had even graduated to being fun, but now I couldn't wait. Now I knew how much they deserved it.

They came scrambling forward despite it being obvious suicide. Mercy picked them off one by one as they broke free of the bodies until a single inky-eyed monster sprung for me, and I split it in half with a single cut.

Victory!
New Skill Discovered! [Phalanx]
Vitality increased to 12
Phalanx: Rank 1/10
64 Experience Gained

I gave each half a kick for good measure, then stowed my sword away. "This *is* number eighteen, right?"

Asher flapped for a moment, counting on his claws, then he sighed. "Possibly. If the Dvergar count shafts up on the right side and down on the other."

I chuckled again at "shafts", and Mercy let out a sigh of relief. "Glad you're getting back to normal."

Asher cocked his head to the side. "How did you decide that this was the correct tunnel?"

"They wouldn't fill it with monsters if you weren't meant to go that way."

Asher looked even more puzzled than before. "Who would not fill it?"

He looked so lost I couldn't help but laugh again. "It is video game logic! No point throwing a load of monsters in where nobody is ever going to see them." I turned to Mercy for support, but she was pretending not to notice. "Plus, we're looking for the place where all the svart are coming from, and they just came out of here. Seems like a safe bet?"

Asher tilted his head the other way and blinked. He had a vertically slit set of eyelids as well as the up and down ones. I wished I hadn't noticed that. "The latter part of your logic certainly seems to be sound."

"Thanks, I think?"

"So that is how you ended up this way." Mercy grinned. "You assumed that what people were saying to you were compliments."

"Every time you assume that you're smarter than me, you end up looking dumber, you realize that, right?"

"A broken clock is right twice a day."

"I'll break your clock," I grumbled.

That stopped her for a moment. I could see her mouthing it to herself. "I'll clean your clock?"

"Yeah, that."

Asher let out a rattling sigh. "Children. Might we please proceed?"

CHAPTER 17

Picking our way over the corpses of the fired svart was easy enough. The only real problem was the aroma. "And I thought they smelled bad on the outside."

Mercy rolled her eyes at me and Asher's tongue flicked out. "I understood that reference."

"You're getting there, buddy."

Mercy held up a hand at an intersection, and we stopped. She had taken point on the basis that I made more noise walking around than a full brass band, and Asher was essentially just some dude in a dress the minute that somebody got in melee range with him.

She started moving her fingers, and I was still kind of amazed that I could understand the complex hand signals she was wiggling at us meant. "More svart."

I reached for my sword, but she was already wiggling again. "Wait."

We all stood there, frozen like statues until she signaled the all-clear. I eased my hand back down with a sigh. Standing still for so long meant that I realized I was aching all over. Good thing I could magic it away.

[258/520 Health]

I loved *Restoration* so much. One of these days I was going to take *Restoration* out for a nice steak dinner. Give it a watch. Tell it in no uncertain terms that it was the MVP of my personal divine power selection.

"So we're just going to sneak all the way down?" I may have spoken too loudly as Mercy and Asher both flinched.

Mercy glared at me and signed back, "Yes."

"So what, you are allergic to experience points now?"

She fumbled through a few attempted signs before storming back over. "I'm allergic to being stabbed to death by a thousand little monsters. It's a serious allergy. It could kill me."

I leaned down so I could speak quieter. "Okay, but, uh…counterpoint. I'm bored."

"Are you kidding me?" Mercy was not doing as good a job at staying quiet.

Asher slipped in between us. "Maulkin, your hunger for slaughter shall be sated soon enough. Mercy, please keep your mind on the task at hand despite the…provocations."

She stalked back off down the corridor without a backward glance, even though Asher was giving me some heavy eye contact to make up for it. You could have even called it a glower.

The rest of the day was painfully slow. The main tunnel branched over and over, with all three of us stopping to examine the evidence to work out which way we figured the svart had been in longer. Their habit of crapping all over the place, smearing blood on the walls, and leaving their trash wherever they dropped it definitely helped. There were a few more Dvergar embedded in the walls as we went, but they'd been the first to start receiving the svart's torture sessions, and there wasn't much left of them except a few scraps of dried meat dangling from the jagged rocks.

Every time it looked like we might get a little bit of excitement, Mercy pulled us back or into some side tunnel. Every time there was a lone scout, she sniped them silently so they couldn't call for help, hogging all the kills.

This was the first time since we'd arrived on Amaranth that I didn't have something dramatic going on around me to hold my attention, and it sucked. If it went on much longer, I was going to start hearing my own thoughts, pondering my lot in life, wondering about what kind of sick universe would make me into a godling.

Being busy was better.

We kept an eye out for the crystal vein that our floor-friend had suggested would lead us to the svart-nest, but despite there being a whole variety of shimmering colors and cracks running through the stone all around us, there was no sign of a big lode of crystal.

Still, we were definitely on the right track. The smoothed stone passages that the Dvergar had been working for centuries was giving way to more rugged rock, and the filth that had been an unfortunate sign of the svart presence had started to smear its way up the walls.

The longer we went without a fight, the more I could feel the pressure building up. Maybe I was just tense. Maybe I was still mad about what the svart had been doing to the Dvergar down here. Maybe the gods had programmed me to be a murder machine, and now I wasn't getting to do any murdering. Who knew? We were now so far underground that I wondered if the pressure might be literal pressure, like when you went too deep in the sea, the weight of all that world above our heads pressing down.

It was a relief when Mercy shoed us back from the next bend in the tunnel and gave us the Dvergar sign for "Motherlode."

Finally.

I drew my sword and charged while Asher was still signing back an answer, and it was well worth it. There were about a dozen svart all milling around the crystal vein that our tour guide told us about, all of them distracted, staring into the pale blue glow within the crystal. It was the only light that we had seen in these tunnels since we arrived. It made them easy pickings.

One sweep sent them spinning into pieces. Ichor splattered across the crystal, blotting out some of the light, and only then did the remaining svart seem to notice that they weren't alone. As one they turned, and an arrow flitted by me to stick one in the eye, so close that I felt the feathers tickle past my arm. "Hey!"

"Stop."

Another arrow flew by my ear.

"Doing."

The next went between my legs to nail a svart in the gut.

"Stupid."

That arrow actually scratched over my cauldron pauldron, spinning off to jam into the back of a fleeing svart that saw where things were going.

"Things."

The final arrow would have hit me right in the area that my mother told me I shouldn't scratch in company if I hadn't jumped, and it hit a svart in the neck instead.

"Hey! Watch the merchandise."

She darted forward from cover, nocking another arrow. "Nobody wants to buy it!"

There were now only two svart left, sprinting away as fast as their little legs would carry them.

As it turned out, their legs couldn't carry them far when they were no longer attached to their bodies. A couple of execution-style shots followed from Mercy's bow to be sure and then silence fell over us again.

She turned on me with her bowstring drawn taut. "If you ever pull that shit again…"

"What?" I shrugged. "What could have gone better?"

She almost tripped over herself in her irritation. "You… You got lucky!"

I shrugged it off. "That's what people always say when you win."

"That is what people say when they have two brain cells to rub to-

gether and can see all the ways things could have gone horribly wrong."
She couldn't even look at me anymore. She put her hands over her
eyes. "What if there had been more of them waiting somewhere else?"

"I'd get more experience?"

"What if there had been an abomination?!"

"I'd get glory *and* experience?" I slipped my sword back into its
place on my back. "What is the point you're trying to make?"

"You're an idiot." She was shaking her head slowly. "You are an
actual idiot, and you're going to get us all killed. I thought you were
brave, charging in to help people that needed it, but you're just dumb
as all hell."

Once more Asher slunk in to console her. "Mercy."

She cut him off before he could get started. "No, don't try to
pretend that this is anything other than stupidity."

"Mercy, it is quite possible that both of your views are correct."
He tried again. "It is possible for both idiocy and heroism to exist
within the same man."

"Ouch."

"I am sorry, Maulkin, but that was a profoundly foolish thing to
do, regardless of the favorable outcome."

"That's it. Let's all pick on the horny guy."

There was a long moment of silence, then Mercy's rage crumpled
into a cackle of laughter. "The horny guy?"

I could feel my own face splitting into a grin, even as I tried to
fight it and stay angry. "I'm a guy, who has horns. So…"

Asher had his face in his hands once more. "If this conversation
degenerates into innuendos once more, I shall be forced to ask the
pair of you to secure private accommodations."

It was my turn to cock my head like some dumb animal. "Huh?"

"He's saying to get a room." Mercy's scowl was back. "Which is
gross. Because you're gross. And an idiot."

I shrugged it off. "I never claimed to be smart."

"At least you aren't a liar, then." Mercy was always way too quick with the quips. "Just do us all a favor, and before you do anything, just take a second to ask yourself if it might kill us."

There really wasn't much to argue with there, even if I was still holding onto some irritation. "Fine."

Mercy let out a breath of relief. "Okay."

"Wonderful. I am glad that is settled, now we can move on to the mystery of this crystalline structure glowing with such abundant arcane energy that it is confusing my other senses."

"Glowing with what now?"

As it turned out, neither Mercy nor I had taken any magical skills that might let us comprehend what Asher was talking about, but it was easy enough to believe anything he told you. He was so sincere and polite, he could have been telling me that the sky was green, and the grass was blue, and I would have believed him. Of course, here on Amaranth, blue grass might really be a thing, but we hadn't really discovered the country music scene of our new world yet.

According to Asher, this protruding hunk of crystal was absolutely pulsing with magical energy that it seemed to be drawing from somewhere else. A vein of the same crystal was visible, running across the floor of the cave to a partial collapse—the same place that our svart friends had been trying to run to when I cut them down. Dropping to my knees, I could just make out more light beyond the heap of rocks. "There's more glow through here."

"I would wager that the two things anomalous phenomena are related. This must be the svart's point of origin."

Looking the place over again with *Dungeoneering* on my mind, it was easier to work out what had happened here. Obviously, the whole place was trashed thanks to the ongoing svart presence, but you could still see some dropped tools amongst the filth on the floor. The

Dvergar had unearthed the crystal spire that the svart had been so hyped about, then tried to dig along the length of the vein to find its source. That was when they'd broken through into the cavern beyond, unleashing the svart.

Maybe the Dvergar were responsible for the partial collapse of that tunnel after they realized what they'd unleashed, or maybe it was just the natural outcome of it never being reinforced or refined. Either way, it seemed to have slowed the flow of little monsters, and it meant that I'd have to crawl if I wanted to make it through.

When I started to do just that, Mercy caught onto my foot. "Hey, where are you going?"

I wiggled around to face her. "I'm going to find out where the svart are coming from? Isn't that why we are down here?"

"Here. Obviously." She looked at me blankly. "They're coming from here. Let's block it up and go home."

"While I understand the impulse, I must ask, do we believe that the Svart, now knowing that there is a Dvergar settlement here, will not simply dig their way back through?" Asher had crouched down to peer through the gap, running his claws along the line of crystal. "Are we not merely postponing the inevitable if we close this tunnel and do nothing to the source itself?"

Mercy scoffed. "You really think they're smart enough for that?"

I turned all the way over and put my hands under my head as a pillow. "They're smart enough to make weapons?"

"Yeah, but so are you. That isn't a high standard."

Asher made a little sound that might have been a dry laugh, but he spoke over it quickly. "I believe that it is safe to assume the svart have object permanence. As such, there will be some aware of the khag beyond whatever obstacles we place in their way. The risk remains."

"Yeah, what he said." I nodded along. "Plus, I really want to see what is up with the magic glowing crystals."

Asher cocked his head. "I will admit to some curiosity about that matter also."

"So we're really just going to poke around because you want to see why stuff glows?" She did not seem enthusiastic.

"We have committed ourselves to considerably more dangerous tasks with less promise of satisfaction."

I piped up. "And worse comes to worst, we run back here, and I collapse the tunnel. Even if we can't find a better way to stop them, we can see what our options are."

She rubbed her temples. "For the record, I hate both of you."

"Was that a yes?"

She sighed. "Just go."

I grinned at her as I crawled back to the gap, then had to stop and roll over because my horns hit the overhanging stone with a clatter.

With my horns tucked down, I couldn't see much of anything but the vein of crystal beneath me, but I followed it forward through the gap. I don't claim any sort of expertise when it comes to rocks, but I was pretty sure that straight lines weren't a naturally occurring thing, and this glowing crystal was definitely running in a straight line.

On the other side of the stone, things opened out rapidly. My mouth fell open, and I made a noise like an ancient computer modem, if somebody had turned the bass right up. Eventually, I pulled it together enough to speak actual words. "Guys, you might want to see this."

First Asher, then Mercy emerged from the tunnel, and both of them were struck just as speechless as me at the sight of the city sprawled before us. We were so stunned that if the svart had come for us then, they probably could have had us without a fight.

The crystal that we had seen and followed was not some rare mineral vein, it was an outlying crenellation on this city's walls. The Dvergar might have decorated with shiny stones, but this whole structure was made from the glowing crystal, like some great ice-sculpture, all smooth arches and flying buttresses. If this place had been out in the open, it would have been blinding as it glimmered in the sunlight, but down here, the crystal itself was the only source of illumination. Even that light within it wasn't consistent. It pulsed and fluttered, and shadows chased each other under our feet.

Where the crystal met the stone outside the city there was no border. They merged smoothly into each other without any interruption at all. That was the first hint that something was subtly off about the whole underground city situation. The other big warning flag was that everything seemed to be set at an angle. The streets, the buildings, the spires, it was all tilted ever so slightly off-kilter. Maybe just a few degrees off flat, but it left you feeling like you were drunk, or that gravity was somehow lying to you about which way was down.

"Oh."

Asher's voice came out soft and reverent. "The svart did not build this."

Mercy clicked her tongue. "That's an understatement."

Not only had the svart not built this beautiful place, but they had also managed to avoid leaving their mark on it for the most part. Here and there you could see stains on the crystal, but considering the state the svart had left everything else in, this was practically sanitary.

If I were being honest, this city didn't look like anything I'd ever seen before in either of my lives. The Dvergar might have had the technical skill to carve something like this, but I don't think it would have ever occurred to them to do it. The only other buildings we'd seen were rustic-looking ruins. If you'd asked me what heaven looked like before it turned out to be this place, I'd probably have pictured something like this glowing city. It looked like it should have been floating up among fluffy clouds, not pinned down here in some cave, overrun by svart.

I said what we were all thinking. "They were coming from here?"

"They definitely were"—Mercy seemed to be trying to convince herself as much as us—"but this has to be just another place that they've invaded, right?"

Asher's eyes narrowed. His hands seemed to reach for the crystal without him meaning to. "We have no knowledge of the history of this place, nor how long it has languished down here with no populace. For all that we know, the svart have been here since antiquity stripped the builders of ownership."

I drew my sword and rolled my shoulders. "Or we're going to find some other hole down to an even deeper cave somewhere that they crawled out of before getting to this one. Then another and another, all the way down to whatever hell they actually come from."

Asher sighed. "Indeed."

"Better get started then."

CHAPTER 18

From the partially buried buttress we'd come in by, there was a smooth descent into the city proper. The transparency of the crystal actually made it hard to navigate. First, everything was slightly tilted, then we could see through the corners of everything. It made the whole thing feel pretty unsafe. The crystal wasn't as slippery as you might have thought, and crouching down to touch it I could feel the fine ridges cut into it, giving it texture. The light pulsed within the crystal—a little brighter here than where we'd first seen it. Looking out over what we could see of the city, that seemed to be the case all around. The farther in that we went, the brighter the light grew.

The way that I'm describing things, makes it seem like strolling in was easy, but for every wide-open shimmering thoroughfare, there were a dozen more that were blocked. Whatever had planted this city in the stone had done a pretty poor job of clearing the stone away. The roof of this cavern came down almost to the surface of the crystal in places. Elsewhere, where the city had intersected with stalagmites or stalactites they were just lying there in the street. We could still see the smooth plane where they'd been sheared off when we squeezed by them.

Given the density of the svart we'd seen upstairs, we crept forward with weapons and spells always at the ready, but the farther in that we got, the more obvious it was that we shouldn't have bothered.

There were more svart down here than we had seen in the past few days put together, yet all of the laser-focused aggression that they'd shown elsewhere seemed to have faded away in the glow of this crystal. The ones roaming the streets seemed to be in a daze, their black eyes so unfocused you could catch glimpses of the yellowed whites around the outside, their stumbling motions even more chaotic than usual. The wretched screeching that they'd only unleashed during their mindless charges came all too frequently now, a constant steady warble that echoed and set the walls vibrating and chiming. It was like they were having conversations, but if anything of the noises that they made had been a real word, our God-given talents would have translated them. They were like children play-acting at being adults, going through the motions without understanding the significance.

I followed carefully in Mercy's footsteps, moving slow and steady, as silently as I could. My armor definitely made a bit of noise as I went, but the svart didn't seem to notice. They had patterns that they followed here in the city. Not patrols exactly, but directions that they would walk until they seemed to lose track of what they were doing, and then they would backtrack.

It was like all the times I'd wandered into a room and forgotten what I'd come in for on a grand scale. A whole city of absent-minded idiots wondering if they'd forgotten to lock the door after they left the house. Asher signed, "What are they up to?"

The sign language stuff seemed like a lot of work when I could just respond with a shrug.

We pressed on deeper and deeper into the city. The main thoroughfares seemed to be blocked more often than not, and where the buildings rose up, the stone seemed to have been carved back, but in the open places, crags and rubble seemed to have rushed in to fill the gap. Sometimes the stone and buildings were melded right into each other, but for the most part, the crystal seemed to have won out and the rock had given away.

It was a miracle it took so long for us to hit a dead-end. We'd crept slowly towards the source of the ever-growing glowing, but eventually, we hit a street entirely blocked by a toppled crystal spire. Where it had hit the road, it had fragmented into massive, jagged shards. There was no chance we were getting through it without getting shredded to pieces. Since we had relative peace and quiet with the only ambling svart more than a street away, I thought I'd make us a way through. Closing my eyes, I reached out into my *Sphere of Influence* and realized that I couldn't touch a damn thing in this city. The worked crystal set my pillar of Artifice shaking the moment I touched it. It was almost as bad as when I'd tried to haul up the bronze rails, just from that brief touch. Like they were an order of magnitude more complex. I snapped back to my body and sighed. "We need another way."

While Mercy was the one doing all the scouting ahead, Asher served as our compass. Down in the buried city it was a maze, and if it weren't for his unerring sense of the direction where the most magic was built up, we'd probably have been lost a dozen times over. With a wave of his hand, he could always direct us to the center of the city, even if it didn't help us to actually find a route.

Confronted with the fallen tower, we finally did what we'd been putting off since we arrived in the city, and we went inside a building. Unlike the Dvergar city, there were doors everywhere you looked—tall elegant things that tapered up to a point and gave no real indication of what was behind them. Despite being carved from the same crystal as everything else, the doors and walls of the building seemed to have a degree of opacity to them, like somebody had painted them white on the inside. It looked to me like the building at the side of the road might extend past the end of the rubble blocking our way, so I went for it before pausing at the last moment to double-check. "Anyone want to yell at me for opening a door too quick?"

Mercy had an arrow aimed at the door, and its tip now wobbled over towards me instead. "Just open it."

Inside we could see a far more familiar version of svart life. There was a refuse heap in the corner full of droppings that had long since dried out, the walls were scratched up everywhere that you looked, and the creamy arches of wooden furniture that had once filled the place were now little more than splinters. All that remained of the svart within were bones, some of them ancient and chewed, and one fresher and unmarked, the last survivor of this little battlefield.

There were feathers scattered around a gutted mattress, and scraps of silk and fabrics I didn't even recognize. Whoever lived here before the svart got trapped inside had lived comfortably. Yet whoever they were, there was no indication of it now. No pictures, no treasured trinkets, nothing. When they left, they must have packed everything up.

We moved through the little villa by the roadside in perfect silence. The scratches on the walls interfered in our view of the outside, but whatever had rendered them opaque did not. You could see perfectly outside, like every surface of the house was a window.

"Oh, I would hate to live here." I broke the silence without meaning to. "Imagine seeing people walking by when you're trying to pee."

Mercy chuckled. "Really? You don't seem like a shy bladder kind of guy?"

"There's a difference between not being shy and wanting an audience for bodily functions."

"Do you mean to suggest that you have never expelled gas in company?" Asher was picking through the remains of the house, not really paying attention to us.

I put my shoulders back and proudly announced. "I could burp the alphabet."

"That's what I thought." Mercy scoffed. "So how is this different?"

"I don't know. It just is."

Beyond the shattered remains of chamber-pots and a claw-footed bath that looked like it had been carved from a single piece of pristine driftwood, we found the fragmented remains of some sort of dining room. Every trace of food was gone, but plates still lay obscenely in their place on a table that had somehow avoided the svart's delicate ministrations.

"This whole place is weird."

"I am forced to concur." Asher looked troubled. "I cannot determine what happened here. It is a puzzle."

Mercy waved us over. Looking out through the wall it was apparent that the shattered tower was only going to be the start of our problems. Whole sections of the road seemed to have given way after the tower fell, so deep that even the glowing discharges of light that leapt across the gap were insufficient to show us what was in the shadows.

The destruction was even more widespread farther in. Whole buildings had toppled in the direction of the tilt. Set loose from the crystal that served as their foundations, they had slid and shattered.

Through the far end wall of the house, we could see the next in the row. The front side had been caved in from some long-forgotten impact, but the rear was still mostly intact—a possible path forward if it weren't for all these walls in our way.

Mercy gave the wall a kick. "You can't use your god powers on this crystal stuff can you?"

"Nope." I slipped into the little trance of Artifice, scooping up pieces of wood and fabric from the floor in a little whirlwind of activity. My sword shifted shape, the metal compressing back down into a big dense block attached to the end of the new wooden haft I'd cobbled together. "But I can use a big hammer."

It was a bit noisy. The first blow left a great crack in the wall, but it also set the whole crystal structure ringing like a big glass of water with a giant wet finger rubbing around the rim.

Every hit after that intensified the noise until Mercy and Asher had their hands clamped to their heads and were screaming at me to stop.

Shame I couldn't hear them. The fifth hammer fall did the trick.

The wall exploded through into the next house. There was no

way that all that noise wasn't going to draw attention, so this time we stepped up the pace. We rushed through the abandoned house, this one untouched by svart but covered in a layer of crystal dust that would probably have turned our insides into some sort of salsa if we breathed it in. I kept a hand over my mouth and ran as fast as I could over the slippery surface. There would be no getting back onto the street through the ruined front of this building, but the next one along looked more promising. Both the front and back sides were still intact, and while it looked like the street wasn't clear, at least the rocks hanging down into it were probably passable.

I took a running jump and brought my hammer down.

This time the crystal blossomed out into cracks immediately. I might not have been doing more damage, but I was definitely placing it better. Asher and Mercy caught up to me just in time to move their hands from their mouths to their ears as another resonating gong set the whole place trembling.

With a spin on the spot, I brought all my strength to bear against the wall. A grunt of effort left me as a little roar.

The wall split. It didn't shatter like the last one, but a crack shot out from where I'd hit to the top of the wall, and there was a gap wide enough to fit my arm through. Setting the hammer down, I took a hold of both sides of that gap and pulled them apart. I strained and grunted and nothing happened except my fingers started to hurt. That was when I remembered I was more than just a big buff faun. I was a big buff faun with godly powers. I Surged my Potency, and the impossible task suddenly became possible. I pried the gap open and set the upper floor of this building and the next toppling back into the rocks beyond with one great tug.

Mercy's mouth was hanging open when I turned around to give her a grin. Eventually, she managed to say, "You're on jar opening duty from now on."

All the noise was starting to attract attention. The svart in the city might have been dazed and confused, but they were still svart. Beyond the fallen back wall we could see them coming, pouring out into the street in their hundreds. What we had seen beyond the city could not have prepared us for the sheer volume of bodies here. Upstairs they'd filled tunnels, but here they filled the grand avenues with the residents of a few of the villas alone. Trying to extrapolate out the number of svart that might be in the city from that little demonstration was giving me a headache, so I ignored it and hurried on.

The inadvertent blockade of the toppled tower and broken road gave us some protection from being swarmed on the front side of these buildings where there were doors in easy reach, but there was still a moment of hesitation before I shouldered the door of this last house open and burst out into the street. Spikes of rock jutted up out of the crack on the opposite side, where houses should have been there was a hole, and then something like stalagmites were growing up out of the remains. Growing into the gap that this city had left. How long had it been down here that rock was starting to grow back around it?

Stealth had run its course, so I took the lead as we ran deeper into the city. Maybe we could go back to sneaking once we had some distance from the noise I'd made, or maybe not. When we first started out I would have said that I hoped not, but seeing just how many svart were actually down here, I was starting to doubt my ability to hit them all. We rounded a smooth curve in the road, and suddenly, it went from ghost town to party city.

The svart had all gathered around some massive abstract sculpture made from the same crystal as everything else. It could have been a woman or a plant or just a tangle of smooth shapes, I wasn't an art expert. I didn't know, and we weren't going to get a chance to study it closer. The svart turned on us, all confusion gone and replaced with the same murderous intent we'd seen from their buddies above. Asher hissed. "Run."

We ran.

We ran straight at the svart for a few steps before Mercy spotted a side street spiraling off the main thoroughfare, then she dragged me bodily towards it. Slipping between the buildings was like entering a ravine in a glacier, shining white on either side of us, shimmering and shifting. The svart shrieks echoed up it behind us, setting off a terrible harmony with the crystal and drowning out Mercy as she repeated, "Go, go, go," nonstop.

The side-street was less of an alley and more of a ramp, spiraling up behind the next row of buildings before splitting out into an elaborate series of walkways that were now shattered, twisted, and interspersed with intruding stalactites. We ran as far in as we could before stone blocked our way, turning each time a barricade presented itself until we were thoroughly lost in the maze of walkways that once must have spanned over this whole side of the city.

The light grew dimmer as we ran farther and farther from the center of town, but we didn't have the time to worry about it. The screeching jabbering horde of svart were still hammering along behind us, setting the walkways ringing. When we rounded one particularly wide intrusion of stone and saw the walkway giving out in an abrupt horizon, Mercy let out a little yelp of despair and skidded to a halt. I didn't.

With both my arms flung wide, I caught Asher and Mercy around the waists and leapt. It was a straight drop down into a pitch-black pit where the walkway had fallen and taken out the lower level too, but beyond that, there was a wide courtyard. I landed just a few feet in from the edge with a crunch.

I blinked. "Crunch?"

The cracks began spreading out beneath my feet, and not even having a moment to drop the others, I ran for it. Piece by piece, the smooth crystal beneath us became fragmented and fell away. It was like the tile trap all over again, except this time I was going to outrun it.

Every time my feet slammed down, more cracks spiderwebbed out, but it didn't matter. If I had to keep running forever it didn't matter—there was no way the svart could follow us now, not with the whole road falling into the dark beneath us.

Asher was struggling in my grasp, so I let him drop and run himself. Almost instantly, the cracking beneath me stopped. Mercy called me an idiot so often that the word had kind of lost its meaning, but, man, I was really an idiot.

I dropped her off as I staggered to a halt. The crystal I'd already cracked was still tinkling down into the abyss, but the smooth courtyard we'd found was still holding out over at this end, terminating in the first solid-looking wall that we'd seen since we got here.

It was as smooth as the other walls but blackened instead of crystal clear, towering to two stories where all the elegant villas had sprawled out on one level to allow for the fluting walkways overhead. Whatever this place was, it was important enough to warrant disrupting the majesty of the city's decor to accommodate it.

Around the corner, the reason for the clash became more apparent. This might have been made by whoever built the city, but the design was Dvergar. The solid planes of stone had been replicated down here by whatever had built this place. Rounding the next corner, we could even see the runes carved into the surface of the crystal, running up the length of what I was forced to call a door for lack of a better word. It took up almost the entire side of the building, stretching almost all the way to the flat top of the structure.

Gone was all the pale wood and finery of the rest of the city, and instead, there was the blackened metal of industry. Interlocking pieces of it, too complex for the eye to follow, clear but bristling with more of the Dvergar runes. I had no idea how we could get inside this building, short of smashing through a wall, and the longer that we were there, the less sure I was that I'd even want to.

Asher had his palms spread against the surface of the dark crystal, and his head was cocked to the side like he was trying to hear it whispering. "There is a great power being channeled here."

Even without his sensitivity, it was obvious what he was talking about. The light flowing through the crystal beneath us had been dimming as we moved farther out of the city, but here the road beneath our feet was almost entirely unlit. A flicker of the light that flowed through the rest of the city would pulse into the area, only for the Dvergar-built structure to drink it all up thirstily. Pulse. Slurp. Pulse. Slurp.

"What is it?"

"What is anything down here?" Mercy turned her back on it and crossed her arms, scowling out into the shadows for any sign of our pursuers. "None of this makes any sense. Why are svart living here? Who built this place, and why were they obsessed with living in a giant chandelier? Why is there a Dvergar brick in the middle of it? Why is it guzzling power? Why are we wandering around down here instead of blocking off the tunnel and running like hell?"

We all jumped at the sudden scream. The interlinking metal was once well-oiled, but it had seen no maintenance for so long that when it started to move now every part of it ground against every other part. Every carefully-carved rune on every strut of metal seemed to have its own awful note to shriek as it scraped by. Asher leapt away clapping his hands to the side of his head, presumably where his ears lived. Mercy had an arrow strung and pointed before she'd even turned to face the sunlight pouring out of the…whatever the building was.

The light didn't come like a sunrise. Instead, it washed out like mist. The liquid light of the abomination's blood heated to a steam, and I was already grabbing for my sword before the first glint of porcelain white flesh appeared. Except I didn't have a sword, just a hammer. I grabbed that anyway.

The newborn abomination came out swinging.

Luck more than skill had my hammer's head in the way of its first attack. I hadn't even seen it coming. Even with the blow striking metal instead of flesh, the impact sent me sliding across the courtyard.

Emerging from the glowing mist, I was taken aback by the size of the thing. I'm a big guy, and the previous abominations were bigger than me, but this thing put them to shame. If it had had a head on top of its gorilla body, it wouldn't have fit out the door. As it was, it had to hunch right down. The big glowing orb that we all know and love was somewhere in the middle of that headless torso, floating in the gap where a neck might have started. Apart from being white as snow and smooth as the crystal around us, the gorilla thing was a pretty good match, except for the arms. It didn't have arms, it had big thick tentacles.

It had whipped one of them at me before it even got out the door, but now that it had emerged fully from the complex glow of machinery behind it, both could be brought to bear. I'd been flung out of reach, but the other two hadn't.

The left squid-bit lashed out at Mercy's legs, and she jumped it like she was playing with a skipping rope. The other tentacle shot right past Asher, boomeranging back around the other side of him and then wrapping up the length of his body in one coiling movement that would have made an anaconda applaud. He had enough time to say, "What?" before it yanked him off his feet and into the air.

As I ran back into the brawl, I slipped out of my body, reshaping the hammer into a great-sword once more but shifting it over into my left hand. The hammer haft that was left in my right hand was of finely graven wood, well beyond the ability of my Artifice to reshape, but I didn't need to reshape it. I just needed to leave enough metal where the hammerhead had been to form a spear-head.

Before I was in reach of the tentacles again, I snapped back to my body and threw my new javelin. I was aiming for the big glowing bullseye at the center of the abomination. The javelin flew from my fingers, soared through the air, and then clattered against the doorframe as the metalwork shrieked closed behind the abomination. This was why I didn't do sports.

Mercy sprinted past me, peppering the thing with arrows. Luckily, she wasn't too breathless to shout, "You suck!" as she passed.

When she took aim, she didn't miss. Every shot went right into the tentacle that had a grip on Asher and was currently swinging him around in the air.

Asher had started out blue, so I wasn't sure what color he'd turn if he succeeded in having all the air crushed out of him, but he certainly didn't look healthy. His head and tail flopped limply from side to side as he was flung left and right. Up and down.

The abomination had gone on lumbering forward, so I was in reach when it flicked its wiggly appendage out again. I had my sword up, but this time I wasn't lucky. The tip of the tentacle hit me right in the face.

[191/520 Health]

I blinked a couple of times until the cavern roof stopped spinning in front of my eyes. "Ow."

Asher came into sight above me, swinging down like a falling hammer. "Oh shit."

I had to roll to the side to avoid being bludgeoned with him, and the floor, and his head, took the brunt of the blow instead. When the tentacle reared up again, he had left a bloody impression of his face on the crystal.

Rolling on until I'd regained my feet, I was surprised to find my sword still in hand. Guess I'd clung to it like a safety blanket through my brief nap. The weight of Asher's limp body seemed to be slowing that tentacle down enough that I could see it coming at least.

No more blocking, no more dodging. If I was going down, I was going down swinging.

As the Asher flail swung my way, I took my best shot. A heavy overhand cut right into the tentacle that held him, and at the last moment, it tried to jerk Asher into my swing, but it was too late. I'd already committed.

Only the toughness of the abomination's hide saved Asher from being split in two. My cleaver blade bit through the tentacle that had wrapped around him but didn't quite make it all the way through.

There were still a few stringy remnants of abomination stretched thin around him when it yanked him back, but all the strength was gone from its grip, and Asher tumbled to the ground in a heap, tail sticking up in the air. My first instinct was to run to him, but instead, I had to comfort myself with the thought that if he were actually as dead as he looked, then he would have vanished.

Mercy was keeping her distance, raining arrows into the body of the abomination, chipping away at its health. Eventually, she'd be able to take it out, but it wasn't willing to sit still and let her.

Both of the abomination's tentacles were swinging above it now, though one of the tips was dangling loosely thanks to my handy hacking. They spiraled above us like a tornado, then lashed out together in one great sweeping attack.

I tried to jump over like Mercy had, and I cleared the first tentacle with a laugh that cut off abruptly when the second one hit me square in the gut.

Things were happening too fast to track. The hit folded me over, then the tentacle whipped around my waist before I could be flung away. I jerked in its grip, the tentacle stretching to its limit, and then it yanked me back like an elastic band. It spun me as I drew in closer, wrapping me tighter and tighter in layer after layer of strangely cool tentacle. I guess I was too dangerous to fling around like Asher. It wanted to crush me to death before I had a chance to chop us up any more abomination calamari.

Flexing every muscle in my big buff body still wasn't enough to stop the crushing pressure, and I could feel every loop of tentacle like a steel bar, crushing into my flesh. It was going to pop me like a zit.

With the last air in my lungs, I surged my potency and flexed. I was hoping for it to dramatically rip apart, but all I managed was to loosen its grip enough that I could crawl and scramble up the meat-tube it had me trapped in. The coiled tentacle snapped shut like a sphincter behind me as I was crapped onto the floor by its feet.

The surge would only last for a few more seconds, but those seconds were all I needed. I leapt into the air, hefted my sword over my head, and then slammed it down into the glowing orb with all of my buffed strength.

Now, I didn't have time to unpack all that right then and there. The abomination fell back from me, and the sword in my hands melted away to a stump of its former glory. With the still molten metal, I followed up my last attack with a stab into its thigh. The white-hot iron split the pallid flesh, and sunlight gushed out.

That was the end of my sword. The heat climbed up, and the leather straps I'd wrapped around the handle burst into flames when I reached to pick it up again.

Fair enough. I clenched my fists and started swinging.

The hide was thick enough to turn every blow, and the thing was too bulky for me to knock it off balance. There was no material around to make a new weapon, and I was all out of bright ideas. It was this or nothing.

A shower of arrows flitted overhead, melting away on contact with the glowing orb or rebounding off the smooth white expanse of perfectly sculpted musculature. One fell short and skittered across the crystal beneath our feet. That's when I saw my useless javelin still lying there.

I'd hoped I was inside the reach of the abomination, but it had lifted both tentacles up, and now it was slamming them down on me. I dove forward between its legs.

Behind it, I could see all the gruesome details that were hidden from the front. The pristine perfection of the abomination was missing back here. There were little lumps, like tumors all over its back, and tiny little tentacles the size of my fingers were stretching out from a good half of them, leaking liquid sunlight as they burst free in anemone clusters.

My fumbling fingers found the spear's haft, and I staggered to my feet. I thrust it into the thickest mass of lumps and was rewarded with nothing. The tentacles had caught hold of the spear before the tip could make contact, and now I couldn't even tug it free.

That spear was the only thing I had for a weapon, so I wasn't ready to give up on it yet. I rolled my shoulders and gave it another pull. Nothing. I was still hauling as hard as I could when the abomination turned around.

Attached as I was, it swung me around like I was on a carousel ride. Feet skidding over the smooth floor with no hope of traction. When it realized I wasn't behind it, it spun again. It stopped for a moment, Mercy's arrows still pattering off it, then its tentacles came around, feeling for me, groping across the sucking surface of its back until they were almost touching the spear haft.

I could work with this. Letting my frankly useless weapon go, I grabbed a handful of each tentacle and pulled hard.

A breath later, the abomination pulled back. I was yanked off my feet, slid along the length of the spear, and got both feet jammed directly into the sucking oozing mass on its back, which promptly grabbed onto me as tightly as it could.

Both tentacles flexed and whipped about in my grasp, but I wasn't letting go of them. Not now that I had it right where I wanted it. The half-hacked tentacle was still holding together, and even starting to heal back into shape. That wasn't fair. Only I was meant to be using *Restoration*. Yet as it tried to heal, it found my hand in the wound, holding tight despite the crackling and stinging of the golden glowing fluid seeping out. The other side was trickier. The length of the tentacle was unnaturally smooth, so it was only by wrapping it around and around that I could keep a grip on it. Inside my palm, it flexed and narrowed, but it was no good. I had it.

Without its tentacles to resort to, the abomination lumbered forward, heading straight for Mercy at the far side of the courtyard. I pulled with all my might to turn it, but there was something wrong with my reins, and it barreled straight at her without pause.

At the last moment, she rolled aside and saw me. "What the—"

I didn't catch the last word as the abomination spun us both around again. All I had to do was hold on. When *Potency Surge* was ready again, I was going to rip its flip flappers off, but until then, all I had to do was hold on.

It tried to stomp Mercy, but she was considerably quicker than it, rolling through its legs to come up on my side again. "What are you doing?!"

The abomination jerked from side to side as though it was looking for her, although it didn't really have eyes, so I wasn't clear on how that worked. I strained against it, almost fully extending my legs before it dragged me back into my hunch on its back. "Stopping it from octopus slapping you, obviously."

Mercy looked skeptical. "This was your plan?"

"I didn't have a lot of options!"

The abomination spun me away from her again before I could hear her incredibly helpful suggestions on what to do next. What a shame.

The orb at the center of the abomination started to flicker and brighten. With no other option, it looked like it was planning to burn the limpet off its back. I didn't think of that. I didn't have a lot of options as far as dodging went. This was going to hurt.

Surge Potency clicked back to life in my head, and I called on it immediately, hauling on the tentacles for all I was worth.

The beam sputtered to life, and thanks to my last-minute yank adjusting its aim, it was firing right into my face.

My whole world was white-hot pain, but my arms kept on moving all the same. Hauling the tentacles across my body, crisscrossing them in a haphazard shield against the burning light. The solar beam blazed and flared beyond my tentacular shield, and as I watched, they turned from pallid white to scorched black and then to ashes in my grasp.

With nothing to hold me up, I flopped down to bang my head on its calves. The beam tried to follow me, but the irregular surface of the abomination's own back protected me. One by one, the polyps on its rear side blackened and burst in a shower of goo, all the way down to the ones holding my feet.

Was the abomination as dumb as it looked or did it just take a while for it to stop the beam once it got it going? Either way, the searing energy sputtered and died at about the same moment that the anemone clusters holding my feet shriveled up and dropped me.

Disarmed in more ways than one, the abomination staggered back over me. Mercy was already there around its rear side, firing arrow after arrow into the slick blackened wound running down its back.

Shots that would have bounced off the thick white hide slid home into the broken flesh. Every arrow made the whole abomination jerk.

The tentacles had lost some of their length, and they were leaking sunlight from their blackened ends, but despite all that, they were still massive clubs, swinging down at me as hard as they could. I was only halfway to steady on my feet when they swept down. All I could do to defend myself was to try to catch them again with my bare hands.

The impact of the great blunt cudgels on my hands sent aching shocks up my arms. More pain. More exhaustion. More damage. The blinding glow of the abomination's orb was the only light left in my world. Everything else was fading to grey.

When I turned my head from side to side, I was surprised to see the tentacles still trapped in my hands, straining and writhing. I hadn't even realized that I'd caught them.

Even damaged, they were much stronger than me. I only had a moment before I either lost my grip or got flung across the room. I took one step backward, straining them to their limits, then I used that big slingshot to fire me, horns first, right into its chest.

My horns were sunk in deep enough that the stubble on my scalp was scraping over the abomination's skin. I put my hands against it and pushed, but I was firmly embedded. I dangled there like a rag doll as the abomination spun and chased after Mercy. I couldn't think through the grey static buzzing all around me. I couldn't think what to do.

"Maulkin!"

My hands dangled loosely at my sides, limp and useless, all these muscles gone to waste. I looked at my hands, slick with glowing blood, and then I reached up to touch at my own awful wounds.

"Maulkin, wake up!"

I blinked hard at the sound of my name. The light in my eyes kept flickering on and off like the battery had a bad connection. I needed to do something. I needed…*Restoration.*

[184/520 Health]

The light inside me sprang back to life, and the charcoal of my face softened back into flesh. All the aches and pains of the day were chased away.

With renewed vigor, I swung my legs up, folding myself in half, and braced them on the abomination's stomach. This time when I kicked off, every muscle up the length of my body strained, and my horns drew out, inch by dripping inch. It sounded like somebody stepping in a pot of macaroni and cheese.

The golden blood of the abomination flowed freely down over my boots, and the tentacles that it had raised up above its head to crush me flapped and quivered. It hurt, but I got my probably-broken hands under me and pushed myself up. I was almost to my feet when Mercy screamed, "Get down!"

I just let myself drop. I lay back and watched as the ball of lightning hit the abomination square in the orb. For one blinding bright moment, the two spheres existed in the same space, then the lightning orb carried on its arc, bouncing past my head and on to crash through the doors of the Dvergar-looking building. The solar orb was gone.

New Divinity Unlocked! [Ascendant Brutality]
Legendary Foe Defeated!
Potency increased to 43
Brutality: Rank 10/10
Brawling: Rank 4/10
Acrobatics Rank 7/10
186 Experience Gained
400 Glory Gained

"We won." I said it to convince myself more than anyone else. The hulking white body of the abomination, now robbed of its vital force, toppled towards me. In a blind panic, I tried to crab walk out of the way, but it was too late. With a thump, my legs were trapped beneath the oozing corpse.

I let my head fall back. "We won!"

CHAPTER 19

Mercy had an arm under Asher's shoulders and was half-dragging him across to me. He was a real mess. Despite that, he still had some snark to him. "If this is what winning looks like, I believe that losing may be preferable."

Mercy let him go when she got to me, and as he collapsed to his knees, I caught him by the wrist, and my *Restoration* flared back to life. Healing flowed through him, the mashed mess of his face reshaped itself, growing fresh scales, and his burst eyeball re-inflated. It was pretty gross.

The metalwork shrieked again.

Mercy's face had been so close to a smile before that sound. "Oh no."

"Pull me out." I didn't even have time to look. I had more practical concerns. "Pull me out!"

Asher grabbed an arm and started hauling for all he was worth, but he was weak, and there was no traction. "Mercy! Help."

She tore her eyes away from the monster factory and grabbed onto my other arm. With the two of them pulling and me flopping about like a beached whale, I managed to get out from under the abomination's corpse.

Almost immediately, I wished I'd gone the other way, camping out under the corpse and waiting for this next mess to pass us by. We had barely survived fighting the last abomination, and the next one looked so much worse.

Asher's bouncy ball had trashed the little output gate. The metal was twisted all out of shape, big hunks of it had fallen off, and whole pinions of metal were pinging off as it was being forced open.

The abomination looked wrong. I mean, they all looked fairly wrong, or we wouldn't be calling them abominations, but even by the standards of abominations, this one was a real mess. The pristine white of its porcelain hide was torn and hanging open, blackened and burnt. The golden glow within was clearly visible, but the color was ever so slightly off like somebody had spilled oil into the mix and it was still swirling around. The glowing orb at the center of its mass looked like it was on the fritz, and sparks showered down out of it constantly, turning to liquid when they hit the floor.

In terms of shape, I wasn't even sure what the hell I was looking at. One arm looked like a crab's claw, and the other like a human arm, but it terminated in a bleeding stump just below the elbow. It had the same four-legged set-up as the first one that we'd encountered, but it was as though three of those legs had been boiled for too long, and the one hardened claw-foot had to drag the rest of the dangling mess forward. A pair of scorpion-like tails tipped with wicked-looking scythe blades were rooted somewhere around the mid-section, but one of these was dangling limp and boneless too, lashing about like the death throes of the tentacles.

I closed my eyes against the sight of it and let my new senses roll out over the courtyard, seeking whatever was left of my sword so that I could fashion together something to work with. A knife maybe. Instead, I found all the shattered remnants of the ironwork scattered about my feet. "Oh yeah. That's more like it."

The shape of my sword was never going to change now, it was too ingrained in my mind, but with all of this raw metal to work with, I could make a version that had a bit more heft to it. It firmed up between my hands, hovering in the air as I tightened and planed it into shape, putting as much of an edge to it as my Artifice would allow.

I snapped back into my body to catch the tail end of Mercy saying, "…or do we run?"

"No." My voice came out soft. "We don't run."

"The odds do not seem to be in our favor in the current—"

"We don't run." I didn't mean to growl it, but the sound still rumbled up from my chest all the same. "We fight, and we win."

"I'm not ready to die just because you're too dumb to see that we can't beat this thing." Mercy reached for my arm and then stopped when she realized it was slick with blood. I hadn't even noticed that cut. "Look at you, you're falling apart."

"Forget me. Look at it. Asher messed up the machine. It wasn't ready to be born yet. It is never going to be weaker." The abomination was tearing at itself trying to break free of the jammed-up machinery. "If we give it time, it will heal, it will get stronger. But if we take it now, together, we can win."

Asher was looking at Mercy, and she gave him a helpless shrug. "Maybe?"

I took off running before they could try to stop me, charging right at the abomination as it burst free. "Asher, give me a boost!"

I leapt into the air, trusting in my serpentine brother in arms to deliver, and boy did he. The Gravity Snare sprang to life above me, turning my Olympic-level high jump into something cartoonish and impossible. I flew up to the level of the walkways all around us before plummeting right back down towards the abomination's blazing heart. Sword already swinging.

This new weapon had the mass to resist the heat. It came out the other side of the orb red and molten, but it was still in one piece. I managed to stay in place atop the abomination for only a moment before it's lopsided crawl across the courtyard bucked me off.

Still falling, I took a swipe at the scythe-tail as I passed.

The red-hot metal was quenched in the flesh of the abomination. A great rush of golden steam burst out where I'd split it open, and another one of its malformed parts fell out of use.

When I hit the ground the impact rolled up through my bones, waking up all the aches and pains I'd forced down with my Primal healing. The golden cloud I'd made started to drizzle tainted sunshine down on me as I lumbered back to my feet for round two.

With so many holes in its armored hide, Mercy was having the time of her life. Every gap that I could see had at least one arrow sticking out of it, and some were onto quarrel number three. Static clung to the thing as Asher's spell preparation moved ahead, discharging in little sparks to dance across my armor and my blade. It was all coming together. The one good claw leg gave out as one of Mercy's arrows thudded into it, and the whole abomination tipped sideways.

I'd already been sat on by enough abominations for one day. I braced my sword, and the glowing top slid right up into the side of it as it fell.

Another great wash of golden light turned liquid washed out over me. I must have been lit up from head to toe by now. The whole weight of the abomination was leaning against the hilt of my sword, and I had strength enough to bear it. Taking a step back from the downed beast, I managed to drag my sword clear, just in time for Asher's lightning bolt to tear through.

Every one of the abomination's broken and useless limbs flapped and fluttered as the current tore through it. Abominations made no sound, no cries or roars or anything else, but with so many holes in its hardened shell, this one let out a whistling sound as its innards fried.

When the last sparks had discharged to skitter across the crystal floor and set it vibrating beneath our feet, it was my turn again. With a guttural roar, I brought my sword down, double-handed, on the central stalk of the creature.

The metal had dulled back to black by the time I drew it back out of the abomination's meat, streaked and scored along its length by the heat and the blood of this newborn nightmare.

I lifted the sword again. There was no finesse here, no martial prowess or skill. There was just me and my butcher's blade faced with a thing I needed to stop moving.

Still, the half-born mess tried to rise up, even as I was raining blows down on it.

The strength seemed to be leaving it now. The already discolored glow beneath its skin flickering and dimming. It still wasn't enough.

"Will you just die!"

It did as it was told.

New Skill Discovered! [Airstrike]
Legendary Foe Defeated!
Celerity increased to 18
Vitality increased to 13
Airstrike: Rank 1/10
Phalanx: Rank 2/10
84 Experience Gained
400 Glory Gained

The tainted sunlight dulled to total darkness all around me and across my skin, and exhaustion swept over me. I had to lean on my sword. At least, the abomination maker was too trashed to churn out another one.

As I was catching my breath, Mercy came over to prod me with an end of her bow. "You look like you went swimming in a septic tank."

"Thanks."

"You smell like it too."

"Thank you so much, Mercy."

"Of course, that hasn't changed much…"

"Love you too, Mercy."

Asher approached in the midst of all this. He wasn't smiling, because he had no lips, but there was certainly a jovial note to his little head-bobs. "That was an impressive display."

"That was a team effort." I pulled myself up and clapped a hand on his shoulder.

Mercy was quick to rain on my parade. "That was luck. Pure luck. The thing came out all jacked up. If it had been a proper one you would have been toast."

"Good thing Asher destroyed the…uh…monster machine."

Mercy snorted. It was not ladylike. "Monster machine?"

I did my best mad scientist voice, "Abomination-inator?"

"My dear friends, the device before us is a Flesh-Forge."

Mercy said, "Ew."

"What's that now?"

"The Dvergar spoke of them, as did the gods." He ran a reverential hand across the dulled surface of the crystal block. "These were tools used during the Revelation War to create great biological weapons to fight back against the Void God's legions."

Mercy didn't look impressed. "So…monster machines."

Asher dipped his head in agreement. "Indeed, but capable of so much more than mere monsters. Imagine an arcane apparatus designed to replicate our divine power of origination. Whole races could be created. New genus. The only limit our imagination."

I shrugged to Mercy when she looked askance at me. "At least that explains where all the weird and wonderful critters on this world came from."

Asher pressed his face to the forge like he was trying to hear what was being said inside. "Would that I could learn how they operated."

Mercy's eyes were going to roll right out of her head if she kept spinning them like that. "If we meet anybody that isn't trying to kill us we can stop and ask, okay?"

Mercy had somehow made it through both fights unscathed, and my *Restoration* dimmed when I touched Asher, so I supposed that I could only use it on myself at the moment.

[296/520 Health]

Between Bloodthirst and *Restoration*, I was feeling better than I had in days. If I could just find some more useless crippled monsters to pound on, I'd be back to full health in no time.

It took a little convincing to make Asher give up his examination of the Forge, but at the end of the day, it was a wrecked thing now. Even if he could peer in through the broken gate and make out some of the needle-tipped assembly inside, it told him nothing of how the device worked.

We were far from the place where we'd started out now, but our destination was still the same—still signposted just as clearly by the glow building beneath our feet and in the walls as we crept on. Mercy was back in the lead, padding silently ahead while Asher and I did our best not to make a noise and failed repeatedly.

I turned my attention inwards since we had a quiet moment. One thousand four hundred glory was needed to hit the next Tier, and we'd acquired eight hundred in the last fight alone. That was nine hundred total. Two more abominations and I was up to the next tier.

I had three hundred and sixty-five experience in the bank—enough to unlock a new divine skill if I wanted. It was tempting. The abomination fights had just shown how squishy I was under my armor. Being able to Surge Celerity to get the hell out of the way or Vitality so I could tank the bigger hits were both sorely tempting, but I decided to hold off for now. Given how many abominations we were banging into down here, I couldn't help but think I was going to be hitting the next Tier soon. With a new Tier, new abilities would unlock. That was worth waiting for, probably.

After taking inventory of myself, I turned my attention outwards. Here and there as we walked I found skeletal remains, scrap metal, and broken furniture. All the remains of a city ground down until it was little more than dust. I gathered all that I could with *Artifice* and set about replacing the arrows that Mercy had used up. If she noticed them plopping into the quiver on her back, she didn't mention it. That was fine, I didn't need a round of applause, I just needed her to keep shooting the stuff that was trying to eat me.

Amusing myself with making arrows out of all the least pleasant things I could find kept me distracted enough that I nearly walked right into the back of Mercy where she'd stopped in the alleyway between two of the low-slung houses. She signed back to us, "Twenty little ones."

The sign language didn't have a word for svart, but little ones was pretty clear.

My thick fingers seemed to fumble every time I tried to sign, but she seemed to get the gist of "What we do?"

Her shrug was pretty universal. I glanced to Asher, who signed, "Is there another way?"

Another shrug. Great. Real helpful.

This time I took my time and got my fingers wiggling right. "Push through?"

After another painfully long moment of indecision, she nodded.

I cupped my hands together in front of my crotch, then unlaced them for a moment to sign. "Up."

Her face twisted into a look of absolute disgust before she realized I was offering her a boost. With both of them safely placed on the roof of the villa beside us, I walked out into the street without a care in the world.

The svart were swarming around like flocking birds, every one of them a fixed distance from the others, and every one of them turning in time. It was like they were dancing a waltz in time to the pulsing of the light through the street beneath them. They were so lost in their own movements that they didn't even notice when Asher's static charge gathered around them or when I walked right up to the closest one and took a swing.

I'd heard that if you cut a worm in half, the two separate bits could go on living. It doesn't work like that for svart.

The next one had at least turned to face me before I cut it down.

I felt less guilty about it when they saw it coming. Although I suppose I shouldn't have. They're just out there doing their happy dance and *wham*, sword to the face. Maybe not knowing would have been better. It didn't matter. They were all looking my way now, scrambling for the weapons that they'd dropped in their dance trance.

Mercy's arrows started to rain down now, precision shots to the heads and necks of the svart. She'd waited until I'd lost the element of surprise to start shooting—what a pro.

With so few svart working together, and so few of them putting up a competent defense, it really showed just how frail our enemy was. As I swept my sword around in an arc that divided another three, I started to feel pangs of sympathy for these twisted little creatures.

Maybe they were too dumb to know any better? Maybe we really should have just sealed up the tunnel and let them go on their merry way. They'd obviously found some way to survive down here. Maybe it was time to live and let live.

Then I remembered the Dvergar in the tunnels, picked to pieces for the svart's amusement. Hesitation left me. My blade came down.

"Back it up!"

I leapt back from the svart as they started to form a clumsy battle-line, just in time for a bolt of lightning to leap from Asher's hands and tear through them all. I was close enough to smell the ozone and the scorched flesh.

Just like that, twenty svart became none, and I wandered back to help the others down. Mercy sprang past me, unaided, but Asher had the good sense to jump into my arms. I placed him down carefully, then gave him a little bow. "My lady."

He blinked but said nothing more about it.

Mercy was already across the road and seeking out our next alleyway. Even I had to admit to feeling a bit exposed in these big open spaces. If the svart came upon us en masse out here they'd be able to bring their advantage in numbers to bear properly. I didn't fancy being on the receiving end of that.

Mercy waved us forward, and we started out again. Through street after empty street, we weaved around the ruins and rocky outcroppings where they'd made it into the city. Deeper and deeper we headed towards the source of the light until finally, we came out from a tunnel formed by two buildings collapsing into each other, and we saw it for the first time.

It was a pyramid, right at the center of the city, shorter than the two-story buildings that had birthed spires around it, and hidden from our sight up until now by them. It was gilded around the edges in silver, but within that silhouetted metal there was the purest white light that I'd ever seen. I had to hold up a hand or risk blinding myself. Asher couldn't look away. "A great magical battery, powering the entire city."

"Asher."

"Can you imagine the impossible arcane power that it contains?"

"Asher!"

He still couldn't tear his eyes away, "What?"

"Blink!"

Startled out of his staring contest with the giant glowing pyramid, he did blink, then reached up to rub at his eyes. "Ah. My apologies, that was foolish."

Mercy patted him on the back. "Don't worry about it. If we needed apologies every time somebody did something dumb, Maulkin would never stop apologizing."

I growled. "Your face would never stop apologizing."

"That doesn't even make sense."

"Your face doesn't even make sense."

She opened and shut her mouth a couple of times before shaking her head. "So remind me why we're going there?"

"Whatever may be happening in this city, that will be the focal point. With all that power, we might stop the svart in their tracks or pull the mountain down upon them. I cannot believe that nobody else has sensed such a potent source of power in all the time that it has been down here."

Mercy looked towards me skeptically. "So what then? We're just going full moths-to-the-flame on this one?"

I nodded. "If the svart ever realize how much power they are sitting atop, do you think that they'll let it lie, or would they try—and maybe fail—to wield it safely, destroying themselves and everything around them in the aftermath? They're clearly sensitive to magic—it's my bet what drew them to this place and we've all seen them swaying and dancing to the rhythm of the power within the crystal. They are like primates armed with revolvers. The danger is not that they are expert marksmen, the danger is that they have no idea what they are wielding."

"You really think the svart are smart enough to use it? Whatever it is."

Asher bowed his head and nodded beside me. "I think they are foolish enough to try."

"Great! Then we all agree." I said as I clapped my hands together, making them both jump. "The new plan is to then disarm the giant magic bomb, then get away before the svart realize we've stolen their brain candy."

"Indeed."

Mercy shrugged. "Works for me. We can head back up the tunnel we came in when we are done here. Collapse it. Problem solved, right?"

"Indeed."

"Good thing we came down really"—I grinned at Mercy— "otherwise, we'd never have known about the big pointy bomb."

This time it was her gritting her teeth to say, "Indeed."

There were more and more svart in the streets ahead, and dozens became hundreds before long. Yet they were even more lost in their own minds than the ones that we'd already encountered. Maybe the whole moth and flame analogy wasn't too far off. Maybe being this close to the blazing light of the pyramid was melting what little intelligence they had left. Some of them seemed to be talking to one another in their croaking un-language, others were going through the motions of jobs they could never have held, and more than half were doing nothing at all, lying fetal and comatose at the sides of the street, like all the life had just been drained out of them.

After a few streets of this, we gave up all pretense of sneaking anymore. They were completely oblivious to us, so we acted like they weren't there, rerouting around the bigger heaps of them where they lay twitching and hopeless.

"Are they all going to go berserk when we turn the big lamp off?"

Mercy chuckled. "Knowing our luck."

By the time we got to the grand square where the pyramid sat, the svart were thin on the ground again. If their experience of the pyramid was anything like Asher's ecstatic excitement, it was probably for the best. He kept involuntarily reaching out towards it when he was distracted, and his eyes kept turning towards it, even when he was trying to look elsewhere. It was like some sort of religious experience for him being this close to that much magic. It was a good thing that

Mercy and I had skipped that skill-set, or we might all have been rendered completely useless in our distraction.

We strolled around the boulevard beside the pyramid, hands at the level of our eyes to keep the worst of the blinding light at bay. I wasn't expecting there to be an off switch, but there was the vague hope that Asher would snap out of it long enough to tell us what to do.

As we turned the right-angled corner, the light abruptly dimmed. This side of the pyramid was not as bright as the others. It wasn't just dim it was…infected. Within the perfect white light, a darkness lay coiled, like a plume of smoke in the pristine space within the pyramid—a darkness that trailed away all along this side until it reached the only imperfection in the whole structure. There was a chip out of the smooth crystal plane. Something solid was wedged in, corrupting the purity of the whole thing.

"Five bucks that thing is the problem."

Mercy was almost as bad as Asher. She wouldn't turn her head away either. "What?"

"The black smoke stuff." I nodded towards it. "I bet that is what is turning things bad down here, attracting the svart."

"Sure. Yeah. Maybe."

I rapped my knuckles on the side of her head. "Hey, are you still in there?"

That seemed to shake her out of it. She pushed me, but it didn't do much.

Asher's mouth was hanging open, his hands outstretched towards the pyramid's surface, and I could swear that the black fog inside was drifting closer, swirling into the shape of his shadow, reaching out towards his hands like it was some big plasma ball. I caught him by the back of his robe and tugged him away. "Hey. Something isn't right. No grabby hands."

"What?" He turned to look at me with eyes as vacant as the svart's.

"What is happening?"

The arrow hit him in the throat. As if by magic, one moment he was standing there talking, and the next there was a bright feathered fletching jutting out between the creases of his neck. He opened and closed his mouth and blood trickled out. He grabbed onto my arms, and I guided him down to the ground.

This was an easy fix, I just had to pull out the arrow and use *Restoration*. The next arrow went right through my hand as I reached for him.

[281/520 Health]

"Son of a bitch."

Mercy had her back to the pyramid now, her eyes too slow in adjusting to the dimness beyond. It was only now that I realized we were sitting ducks in front of the big light. Whoever was taking potshots at us could have been anywhere in the vaulted buildings around this square.

Mercy raised her bow at the first glimpse of movement and was rewarded with an arrow right through the haft of her own bow. The tension of the string snapped her bow as she was aiming it. She yelped. "What the hell?!"

Slipping out of my body, I squashed my sword out into as broad a shield as I could muster and crouched over Asher before the next arrow fell. "Mercy. Here!"

She dashed over, and under the haphazard cover I'd managed to make, I had time to smooth my shield out into a solid square of steel.

The next flurry of arrows was deflected with a rattle. I caught the one that was jammed through my hand with my teeth and yanked it through with a little whimper.

Mercy was tucked in tight at my side, as if she liked me or something. She snapped, "They broke my bow!"

The next flurry of arrows rattled off the shield. Rhythmic. "One thing at a time. Pass me Asher."

She finally turned to look at him, and that cursing really wasn't ladylike. "Oh, dude. It's okay. Let me just."

There was a gruesome sound of twisting sinew and wet meat from behind me. "Arrow's out."

"Pass him to me."

It hadn't even occurred to me that she wouldn't be able to move him around as easily as me, but there was nothing I could do. It wasn't like I could move with the massive bulwark strapped to my arm without putting us all at risk.

I reached out with my punctured hand, stretching back towards them as far as I could. Making the distance that poor Asher had to be dragged as short as possible.

"How is such a skinny lizard so damn heavy?!"

I hefted the shield off the ground to take a step back, and I was rewarded with an arrow immediately skittering under it. That was all the encouragement I needed to slam it back down. "Come on. Come on."

At the first touch of scales to my bloodied skin, *Restoration* sprang to life, and I used it. I turned back to glance at Asher, to make sure the wound through his neck was closing, then I let my hand drop away. "Okay, bow next."

"Here." She thrust the tangled remains of her bow out towards me. It was already inside my *Sphere of Influence*, but when I closed my eyes and stretched my will out to it, it was as unreachable as the crystal all around us. The materials were too refined for my Artifice to touch.

I took the weapon delicately from her hands, then swung it at the ground. Part snapped off, but most of it remained intact, vibrating along its length but not shattering.

"What the hell are you doing?!"

I thrust it back out towards her. "Break it. Break it down."

"How are you this dumb? I need it fixed, not more broken!"

I swung it again, and this time she leapt out to intercept the sweep of wood before it could hit the ground, reaching out past the side of the shield.

An arrow went right through her wrist and out the other side, plinking off the pyramid. She let out a scream, more rage than pain, as the bow snapped.

I took what was left of the wooden haft and rammed it into the back of my shield, closing my eyes against the shower of splinters. "You complete and utter moron. What the f—"

Slipping out of my body, time slowed. The broken remains of the bow were now little more than scrap wood. I could work with scrap wood. With one quick drag, I pulled all the parts back together into a new configuration, rough and ready but functional once more. I even used the same string that her fancy Dvergar one had been made from.

I tossed it to her as she came at me with her fists raised. On instinct she caught it. "I... You..."

"Shoot back!"

She hefted her bow, checked the tension on the string, and then leaned out to sight her shot. An arrow scratched by her shoulder and set her ducking back inside the cover of the shield. "Son of a bitch!"

She looked to me for answers. "What do we do?"

"I can walk us out if you can carry Asher."

"I can't carry Asher."

"Uh. Okay, new idea."

A big slab of metal was easy for my Artifice to produce. It was well within the bounds of the rough hewn equipment I was limited to. Punching a hole in that metal was trickier—it required more time, more concentration. With sweat beading on my forehead, I dragged the metal apart and made Mercy a peephole to shoot out through. An arrow-slit.

She crouched down to peer out, searching the buildings for our attacker.

She flinched back from the rat-a-tat of arrows on steel, then pressed her face up to the shield to look out. "Where are you?"

For the long moment between volleys, it was almost eerily silent. It felt like there should be some great humming noise behind us in the pyramid, but it stood as silent as the grave. All that I could hear was the echo of Mercy's breathing on the shield. Then, on cue. The rain of arrows.

Rat-a-tat-pop?

Mercy fell back, feathers protruding from where her eye used to be, arrow-tip sticking out from beneath the fluffy white hair around her nape.

"No. No. No. No."

She was lying right by my feet. She wasn't dead. She would have faded away if she were dead. All I had to do was reach down and touch her, and she could be healed, but that would mean letting the shield tilt. That would leave Asher, still unconscious and propped up against the side of the pyramid, exposed.

"No. No. No."

There was no way that I could choose between them. No way that I'd sacrifice one for the other. They were both my friends, and we were all getting out of this alive—even if it killed me.

One of that volley made it through the slit too, hammering through my armor, into my pec, and notching the rib beneath.

[268/520 Health]

With an awful screech, I dragged my shield closer to the pyramid,

hauling Mercy along ahead of it like a bulldozer's blade. She rolled
and tumbled beneath my feet as I moved, and all I could do was hope
that I wasn't driving the arrow in any farther.

I kept on backing up until my heel nudged Asher, and only then
did I let the shield tilt down towards us and reach for Mercy with
my other hand.

I felt hair, then skin, and then leather. I backed up and groped
around some more until I could feel the arrowhead pricking my fingers.
As carefully as I could, I took a hold of the flats of the blade and drew
it through, my fingers slipping in the wetness of Mercy's blood. Every
time that the flights caught on something inside her and I had to tug
them loose, I felt like puking. Finally, the arrow pulled free.

I only had a moment to notice that the head was as smooth and
perfect as all the carefully constructed crystal around us before I tossed
it aside. *Restoration* sprang to life the moment that I touched Mercy,
and running my fingers along the back of her neck, I could find no
sign of the hole, so I had to assume it worked.

All alone, I had to make some decisions. I couldn't just stand here
and wait for the other two to get better. I couldn't. My luck wasn't
that good. Either the sniper was going to find a new position or send
some friends down, and we'd all be sitting ducks. The only way out
was forward.

I ducked down, letting the shield topple to rest on the side of the
pyramid and protect Mercy and Asher from sight, and then I rolled out.

In an instant, the arrows were flying after me, but I did not stop
moving. I could hear them buzzing past, clipping off my armor and
my horns, but none of them stuck. I was almost as far along as the
black mark on the side of the pyramid when I saw the archer running
alongside me. Sprinting along the side of the buildings that faced out
towards us as though they were nothing, and lining up the next shot.

The creature was a svart—there was no denying it. From the big floppy ears to the elongated face, it was a svart, but something was wrong with it. Where the rest were built to scale, this one had long spindly limbs. On the flat, it would have been almost as tall as me.

I stopped dead, and the carefully aimed shot went sour, zipping by in front of my eyes. The gangly svart needed momentum to stay on the wall, but I didn't need it to stay here.

As it tried to slow and aim back for me, it lost altitude, kicking away from the wall at the last moment to flip out and land at the end of the boulevard. Ninja svart. Great. Just what I needed. I stretched out to the very limits of my *Sphere of Influence* for anything I could use and found nothing. The only way it helped was I got to watch the arrow flying at my face in slow motion.

Slamming back into my body, I launched it aside so that the arrow ripped off an ear instead of going right through my brain.

Instead of the "Ow," I tried to say, I let out a guttural roar. Tucking my head down, I charged.

The awful rhythm of the arrows on my shield came back to me. The precision and the speed. I was running down a shooting gallery, giving the svart an even bigger target with every passing moment.

The first arrow clipped off one of my horns and down into my cheek. It hurt like hell, but it wasn't enough to stop me.

When my shoulder sprouted feathers at the joint in my armor, it hurt like hell, but it wasn't enough to stop me.

The svart was just standing there with a smug little smile on its face, lining up shots like it was playing a game of pool. I was going to wipe that smile off the face of the earth when I got my hands on it.

My left knee stopped working, and I had to glance down to realize it was because there was an arrow wedged right through it.

I lumbered on, dragging the dead leg behind me until my other knee locked up in just the same way, and I fell to the ground.

The svart was so close I could hear it now. Hear the nasal, "Kek,

kek, kek," of its laughter. It was strolling towards me, lining up its kill shot. I didn't even have a weapon to fight back with. I had nothing left.

I looked up to watch my death approaching. The tatters of a black dress hung about the svart, so old and crusted with filth that it had turned solid in places. There were gems sewn into it, almost all fallen away now. More crystals. This close, the albino skin was translucent. I could see the black blood pumping through its veins and the movement of the muscles beneath her bare skin as she drew back the arrow that had my name on it.

If I was dying anyway, I was going to go out on my own terms. I reached out with Artifice and tried to grab everything. My will skittered over the worked surface of the crystal all around me. Searching for anything, anything at all that I could touch or move or work with. Anything.

Within the pyramid, I touched the shard of iron. Barely enough to make a dagger but something. I pulled with all my will, and the metal twitched. It was wedged into a hole made perfectly for it, but still, it was just metal jammed into a hole—there for the taking. I pulled, and with a soft grinding sound, it came free.

Then all hell broke loose.

CHAPTER 20

The pyramid lit up. Without that little flicker of shadow inside it, the magic seemed to hit critical mass. It shone brighter and brighter and brighter until me, the svart, the whole city vanished in the glow. It was only at the last moment before the whole world faded away that I remembered nuclear reactors have control rods jammed in them to keep the reaction inside under control. Had I just pulled the wizards and elves version out of this big nuke? The pin out of the grenade?

Falling forward, I touched the crystal beneath me, just to prove to myself it was still there, and the arrow with my name on it zipped by over my head. As fast as the light had come, now it died, not back to darkness, but to a solid impenetrable white. Not only was the pyramid perfect once more, but the whole city, one great magical circuit, was also lit up to exactly the same level, no longer pulsing or dazzling or anything else. Just solid light.

The only dark thing on the pristine white beneath me was the iron hunk I'd hauled out of the pyramid. It looked like it had a sharp tip on it. Maybe it would serve as a dagger if I didn't have the time to shape it. Gods knew, the svart was quick enough that it probably wouldn't give me a chance.

But the svart that had seemed so intent on ruining my day had stopped dead. The bow had fallen from her hands, and her arms dangled limply at her sides. Her head was thrown back like a howling wolf, and the garbled gibberish that the svart spoke transformed as I looked on in horror into a bellow of, "NO!"

It was perfectly clear and easy to understand, which was weird, but not nearly as weird as what happened next.

When her head fell forward again, those beady black eyes changed. Her whole face changed. Her body too. The long gangly limbs smoothed out into the kind of anorexic elegance that runway models back home used to pursue. The transparent, spring-roll skin which had been so twisted and sickly took on a new hue, a new vigor—it was like watching a corpse coming back to life. The flopping ears and the stretched face snapped back into their true, elegant place. The corruption that pumped through the svart's veins was being purged. The black lines of her veins faded, and a hint of pink flushed her as she fell to her knees.

I wasn't idle through all of this. Bizarre as the scene in front of me was, this was still an opportunity to get out of this alive. Fumbling around at the backs of my knees, with my ass stuck up in the air, I managed to find the arrowheads where they were jutting out. Pulling them through hurt. It was right up there with being mauled by a wolf or being bitten by a spider god, yet when I yanked them free and my blood started to flow, relief was the most powerful sensation. I used *Restoration* immediately. No point finding out if the knees would work without healing.

[292/550 Health]

So there we were. Both of us on our knees. Both of us creeping back to our former glory. She was Alvaren. There was no doubt about it now. All the ugliness of the svart had melted away to beauty. All of her twitching movements had become elegant now that the curse was broken. Her words, when they came, were smooth as water, little more than a whisper. "You fool."

The stone beneath us tremored. "Uh, you're welcome."

"I am Briar By Moonlight once more. I am myself. Why have

you done this? You imbecilic animal. Do you have any inkling of what you have done?"

Rude. "Brought you back from the svart life?"

"Put it back." She stretched out those newly elegant hands towards me. Raven black hair had sprouted from her head between words, replacing the stringy mess that had clung there before, so dark it held a shimmer of blue. "Return the shard to its rightful place within the Keystone, swiftly, while time enough remains. Before the working is undone fully."

Huh, apparently, she chose the svart life, the svart life didn't choose her.

I met her eyes for just a moment. Her face looked so young, but in those violet eyes, there was the weight of ages, all of that weight, bearing down on me. Without really thinking, I reached out to do what she asked. I always was a sucker for a pretty face.

But when my hand closed over the shard of metal, something inside my head made a little pinging noise.

Quest: Return of the Void God
Acquire Rusted Blade Shards: 1/6 Complete
400 Glory Gained

No way.

I lifted up the little blackened chunk of metal, barely the size of my palm. I could see the shape of it now—it was the snapped-off tip of a sword covered in a patina of rust so thick it might have run all the way through. Her tone changed now, wheedling instead of imperious. "Give it unto me that I might replace it. Swiftly, before the rest of them turn."

My fist closed around the shard. "Well, hold on now, I need this."

"Buffoon. You cannot even know what you hold in your clumsy

paws." She didn't trust her legs yet, that much was obvious, so this gorgeous holier-than-thou Alvaren woman had to crawl towards me. "Give it to me, and I shall furnish you with some trinket of value. Meat to eat. Another beast to rut with. What say you?"

"I say hold up just a minute." I pushed myself up off the ground, back onto my feet. The healing had taken. My knees bore the weight. "Did you just say that you turned yourself into svart?"

"It was the only way to prevent a greater evil, a decision of gravity that you cannot possibly understand. Know your place, boy. Return the shard. Now."

I held up the fist containing the shard, then raised my middle finger.

"Did you know what you were doing when you were monsters?"

She was rising now, standing with all the grace that she had lacked as a svart, pouring herself from the floor into her new position. Even in rags, she looked regal. "What relevance has that to…"

"Did you know your people were killing the Dvergar?" I tried to meet her gaze as I asked her, looking for any hint of remorse or emotion. "Torturing them for kicks?"

"What matters the life of a few Dvergar? If you only knew the—"

"We're done talking." I tucked the shard into the back of my belt.

With a soft sigh, she answered, "I can see that we are."

I started to back away towards the others. "I'm leaving."

"I can assure you, you are not."

She raised her hands towards me, and almost immediately my progress halted. There was a low thrum in the air, and as I turned my head to look around me, it was as though I was moving through molasses.

One of her open hands began to clench into a fist, and the air around me constricted. With her other hand she beckoned, and all the air in my lungs was torn up and out of me, so sudden and rough that it brought blood up with it.

There was no hint of a strain in her body, no suggestion that she was casting a spell at all, yet this was surely magic—magic beyond Asher's wildest dreams. Plugged into that big battery beside her, it was hardly surprising that it took no effort to throw me around. "Now that you can more accurately comprehend your situation, would you care to relinquish the shard?"

She allowed a trickle of air back down my throat, and I gasped it down. "Eat my big gray ass."

For a moment, the cultured perfection of her expression froze in disgust, before she snapped. "Coarse."

With a bob of her half-clenched hand, she hefted me into the air and smashed me into the ground.

"Relent, and I shall be merciful."

"My whole ass." It came out as more of a groan than defiance.

This time she was less gentle. She flung me so high into the air that I thought I was going to hit the stone ceiling above the city. It gave me a wonderful view of the place coming back to life. The solid light permeated every part of the crystal city, and the places where it had been broken were now filling themselves in again—the crystal growing over the gaps, the toppled walls righting themselves, and the svart falling to the ground and rising up as Alvaren once more.

She brought me down again hard, not beside her on the boulevard, but on the very tip of the pyramid. The big pointy rock went straight into my spine, and those strong limbs of mine went completely limp as the pain roared through me.

I lifted all too slowly off that pointed stone, floating up above the city once more, level with the spreading patterns of transparency that were opening up on the surrounding buildings so that the Alvaren within could peer out at the spectacle.

Despite all of those distractions, I looked towards Briar By Moonlight. Even through the pain of what she was doing to me, I could still see her as beautiful, wreathed as she was in a cloud of the same invisible power that let her toss me around. Her hair was floating around her face as though she were underwater. There was no mercy on that face. No pity.

An arrow flew right at her face, avoided only by a snap of her neck to one side at the final moment. Mercy was back on her feet, Asher rising behind her. They were alive. They could still make it out. The air had been driven from my body by the impact of the pyramid, but I had enough to muster a croaking scream. "Run!"

The shot to her face had been distraction enough for Briar to release me. I dropped once more, narrowly avoiding the point of the pyramid and sliding down the side, right back towards her. If I could keep her attention, the others might get away. None of the other Alvaren seemed all that hostile. Just her.

Kicking off from the pyramid before I hit the bottom, I launched myself at her. Even as dumb as everyone said I was, I wasn't expecting it to work, it only had to distract her long enough for the others to get out of range. Just as she had the arrow, she leaned out of my path with contemptuous ease. I hit the ground by her feet and was rolling back up to my feet when the sudden pressure all around me returned. Her magic, her will, forcing my face down into the ground, crushing me like a bug beneath her heel.

She reached for the shard. "I believe that belongs to me."

Mercy's arrow would have hit that extended hand if Briar hadn't jerked it away at the last moment.

The weight lifted off my back, and I was able to scramble away, not to my feet, not yet, but I was at least moving as Mercy's arrows rained down around the Alvaren.

There was an awful scraping noise from over Mercy's way, and for an awful moment, I thought that she'd been caught in some magical trap just like me, but it was Asher. He was dragging my shield along despite it being bigger than him and probably about the same weight. "Maulkin, catch!"

He could not have lifted the shield with his stick-thin arms, but that wasn't the only power he had available to him. Spinning on the spot, like a shot-putter he sent the shield skidding a few feet. That was when the gravity snare caught it, accelerating it across the ground until the shield took off. The little black hole blinked out just before the shield hit it, and that same momentum carried it in a beautiful arc right into my *Sphere of Influence*.

My shield became a sword, my sword flew into my hands, and the same momentum carried through, turning me to face her in slow motion.

She ducked under the blade without even troubling to look at me. I was beginning to feel like there was the slight—slight—possibility that I might be a little outclassed.

"Okay. Okay." The tip of the blade glanced off the floor without leaving a mark. "You win."

She raised a hand, and Mercy's arrows froze in the air. A perfectly plucked eyebrow rose. "You submit?"

"We give up!" I shouted it louder for the Eternals in the back. "We give up!"

Mercy stopped firing more arrows up into the bristling mass that hung in the air already and made a little sound of dismay.

Briar held out her hand. "Return the shard to me, and I shall grant my people their blissful ignorance."

I reached my hand behind my back, and brought a lump of dark iron back around, holding it out to her. She moved so fast, there was no way that her eyes could keep up with the reaching of her hand. She was already touching the iron hunk before she realized it was nothing more than that.

I caught her by the wrist and grinned. "I lied."

She tried to twist out of my grip, to throw herself out of reach, but she couldn't. I had her.

I hefted my sword up into the air above us one-handed and hammered it down.

She broke her own wrist twisting out of the way. I felt it strain to its limit, then crack beneath my hand. She didn't even let out a whimper.

If the sword was too slow, I had other options. She drew back her unbroken hand, power shimmering around it. No time to think. Only to act. Yanking on her arm, I hammered my head into her pretty little face.

She wasn't so pretty anymore. Bruises blossomed beneath her brows, and that aquiline nose was now crooked. She had a mustache of blue-tinted blood. Still, she didn't cry out, but her hand fell limp to her side.

Spitting blood and teeth she snarled, "You dare to lay a hand on—"

I headbutted her again.

As silently as she'd suffered every other injury, she went limp. I gave her one last shake for good measure to make sure she was out, then I dropped her.

Mercy and Asher sprinted over while I leaned on my sword, panting for breath. Mercy gave Briar a kick for good measure. "What was that all about?"

"So the missing Alvaren? They turned into svart. She turned them into svart. With this."

The fragment of the Rusted Blade really should have been more impressive. The fake hunk I'd made behind my back had looked way more dramatic.

"A turd?"

Asher's eyes narrowed to slits. "A shard of the Blade. The Prophet spoke true. Destiny led us here."

"Pretty sure the glow led us here. Or the Dvergar. Maybe even this knuckle-head." Mercy slapped me on the back. I must have looked wrecked, she really pulled the punch.

"We can worry about destiny later. We've got to get out of here. All the other svart or Alvaren or whatever will…"

A bolt of lightning hit me in the back.

[18/550 Health]

For a moment I could see my bones and taste pennies, then it passed. I was smoking all over, but at least it didn't arc out to hit the others too.

Mercy returned fire. "Too late."

Asher caught ahold of me as I fell, slamming his boney shoulder under my arm and keeping me upright. "Mercy, we must go."

I opened my mouth to say something, and a puff of steam came out. The svart were up to something. They were making the whole city spin round and round. The light in the ground. The light in the walls. They were flicking that on and off too. Mercy was under one of my arms, Asher the other. My sword was back on my back, how did it get back there?

We stumbled through a doorway sideways, and they dropped me. I landed face down, but my horns caught me before my face hit the stone. "Ow."

"He's too big to carry him." Mercy's voice. She was so sweet. I loved those guys.

Asher's hiss. He was so sweet. I loved those guys. "Do you propose that we leave him here?"

"I can walk."

They both looked at me, lying face down on the floor, and then carried on the conversation as if I wasn't there. "I'm not saying we leave him, I'm just saying that this isn't working."

"Give me a moment, I have a potential solution, but it shall be... unpleasant."

Mercy held up a hand to stop him. "For me or for him?"

"Oh"—Asher paused—"for him."

I couldn't see it, but I could hear her smiling. "Then go for it!"

Again, I said, "Ow."

Either I blacked out again, or nothing happened for a few minutes while I lay there staring at the floor, but I couldn't really say which. I became aware of things again when Mercy crouched down beside my face. "Hey, buddy, how are you doing?"

"Ow."

"Yeah... you're a real mess. Asher's going to fix you up, but he said something about searing pain, so I'm here to distract you while he..."

Flames enveloped me, every nerve ending caught fire, and my skin blackened to a crisp.

[8/550 Health]

A moment later the heat passed. I was charred but still alive. If barely.

"That hurt."

Asher's voice was little more than a whisper in the aftermath of my own screams. "Steel yourself, my friend. What comes next shall hurt even more."

"Can I vote no on..."

This time the heat was not a sudden wave, it was a single burning point of white-hot heat. Asher's claw had touched down in the hole that the pyramid had put in my back, and it felt like he was filling it up with a nice pot of freshly brewed lava.

Listen, I'm a tough guy. I think we've established that by now.

Monsters? No problem. Solar blast to the face? I don't even flinch. So when I tell you that I cried like a baby as that lava sensation burned its way out through my whole body, you'll understand just how much it hurt.

My throat was hoarse from screaming by the time that Asher was done, but there was no denying that it was effective.

[338/550 Health]

My voice wobbled when I said, "Let's never do that again."

Asher sighed. "I am truly sorry, my friend. Cauterize was the only healing spell within reach of my accumulated experience."

"Thank you. But…wow, that hurt."

Mercy kicked me in the head, but in a friendly way. "Come on, you lazy ass, let's get moving. This whole city is out to kill us, and now they're smart enough to do a good job of it."

"The returning Alvaren seem to be quite proficient in the arcane and martial arts. It would also appear that the one you rendered unconscious was their leader, so they have a minor grudge against you. It was solely Mercy's talent for subterfuge that got us to this temporary sanctuary."

Back on my feet, I retrieved my sword from where they'd dumped it and looked around. All the imperfection in the city had been burned away. The broken furniture had stitched itself back together again, and the same dull glow that made the walls opaque was barely visible within the cracks. Whatever Alvaren family lived here were gone or hadn't found their way home yet.

I rolled my shoulders, feeling the bones and muscles slide back in their proper place after days of injuries. "So the whole city is after us?"

"Uh, honestly, no." Mercy was counting her arrows—they'd been depleted pretty badly since I last looked. "They're pretty distracted with the whole 'turned into albino goblins for millennia' deal."

"That's fair." I smashed the remade table apart with the flat of my sword. "Kind of hard to get past a thousand years of goblin-hood."

With the splinters and some more iron siphoned from my sword, I refilled her quiver. As she checked them for balance, Mercy sighed. "I guess we've solved the svart problem."

"Hey, that's true! We kind of did."

Asher had no preparation of his own to do, but he watched us intently. "And the gods shall be pleased that we have returned the race of the Alvaren to the world."

"Yay. A whole city of Orphia-clones."

"To be fair to the Alvaren, I believe that your experiences with them so far may have been outliers. The others that we have encountered have been relatively neutral towards us rather than the more violent response you provoked."

I huffed. "Wait, are you saying I'm the problem?"

"A Faun Lunar Eternal does seem oppositional to many of their beliefs and philosophies."

Mercy leaned in close to me and smiled. "Plus, you're kind of a dick."

"And you're just sunshine and delight, aren't you?"

"Hey, I'm a solar eternal. Sunshine literally shines out of my—"

The ground beneath our feet trembled. Asher was crouched down with his hands spread out before I even had a chance to ask. "Magic is afoot."

Even I could have worked that one out. "What are they doing?"

He cocked his head from side to side, as though he could hear a tune that eluded the rest of us. "We are moving."

"What?"

"The city. It has risen."

Mercy and I made eye-contact across the room. "The whole place looked like it had crash-landed here."

"Or melted through the mountain."

Mercy was on her feet. "We need to get out of here."

The next rumble was enough to set the newly revitalized furniture dancing across the room. "We really need to get out of here!"

With the city rebuilt, running like hell actually wasn't all that hard. The boulevards were curved, but with no fallen buildings or broken paving cluttering them up, we were able to make good time across the city. We saw Alvaren as we ran, but they seemed to have no interest in us.

They were tall and lithe and beautiful, scantily clad in the ruined tatters of whatever the svart had clung to. They moved with a grace and purpose that made the rest of us look like stomping toddlers. There was no hint of malice in them now, just blank-eyed stares of confusion as they loped like gazelles toward the city's pyramid heart, and we barreled in the opposite direction as fast as our legs could carry us.

Once in a while, one of them would see me and slow, hands beginning to trace a spell before one of their buddies dragged them on. I guess there were more important things than nuking Faun in passing. Maybe I had just run into some of the worst examples of Alvaren so far. Maybe they were all totally reasonable people who didn't have to be convinced not to lob fireballs at me by some more pressing crisis.

The only time that I got to see the Alvaren fighting at all was when an abomination came lumbering out from one of the side-streets, lobster-claws flailing. I hefted my sword, ready to get back into the ass-kicking swing of things, but I was too slow.

Some of the Alvaren used magic, some used weapons, but all of them moved with the smooth efficiency of dancers in a waltz. They made me and the gang look like amateurs. Cut by cut, blast by blast, they took the abomination apart. At first, I was kind of jealous, then I got mad. "Kill stealers!"

Mercy caught ahold of my belt and tried to stop me from moving on them. "What?"

"They can't even get glory, and they're killing our abominations." Mercy dug in her heels, and Asher latched his arms around her middle. "This is bull."

"Dude, this is really not the time to be worrying about—"

With a grunt of effort, I dragged them both forward. "I need that glory, Mercy. I need it for things and…stuff, and they're just wasting it."

"We have more pressing concerns at this moment," Asher hissed from the back of the train. "There is a great spell-work in progress, and this entire city is its target. If we do not depart before it's completion, I cannot foresee the results that we might suffer."

The Alvaren were already slipping away without even a glance in our direction like we were so beneath them that we didn't even warrant zapping and chopping. "But…Glory!"

"Survival first." Mercy punched me in the kidneys for good measure. "Glory after."

They both had to dive back to avoid the business end of my sword as I spun it back into its fancy Dvergar baldric. "Fine! But there better be a lot of Glory after."

Now that I was feeling more like myself again, the going was a lot quicker. Mercy and Asher had to move to double-time to keep up with my long strides, and where they'd been steering clear of big crowds of newly reborn Alvaren, I was content to plow right through the middle of them since they didn't seem inclined to pick a fight about it. The other two followed in my wake, and we made good progress back to the buttress where we'd started out.

That was when we hit the roadblock. All the Alvaren that had spread out into the mines, the offshoot tunnels, the Dvergar khag, and everywhere beyond that were all hurrying home. They were elegant and graceful and all that jazz, but there were still a thousand of them trying to come down the same little stretch of crystal together. There just wasn't enough room for them all.

Some seemed to have worked out how to use their magic and were drifting like leaves on the wind to touch down in the city unharmed, but just as many were tumbling off the sides of the buttress and crunching to the floor. That wasn't going to get better. I put my head down and charged.

Some of the Alvaren saw me coming and threw themselves off to avoid the pointy end of my horns. Some didn't see me coming and got knocked off by the parting of the tides ahead of me. Either way, I only had to trample my way over maybe a dozen of the wayward Alvaren before we got to the real plug of bodies up at the cave entrance.

I couldn't even work out how many Alvaren were in the crack in the stone that we'd made our way in through—there were heads and limbs poking out of it at all angles and a constant press of bodies on the far side pulsing the screaming ones at the front through even as the jagged stone ripped at them.

Asher let out a huff of disbelief when he saw it. "How do we get through this?"

"I can cut our way through." With a heavy heart, I reached for my sword.

Mercy let out a yelp. "How about we keep mass murder as Plan B?"

"What is Plan A then?"

She pointed to the wall above the mess of bodies. "Make a door."

"That's going to take ages." I reached for my sword, getting ready to transform it. "Making a pick-axe then chopping through. I thought we were in a hurry?"

She pressed the heels of her hands into her eyes and tried not to scream. "You have divine powers. You idiot."

"Oh. Oh!" I shut my own eyes and let my *Sphere of Influence* sweep out. After so long in the crystal city, I'd almost entirely forgotten just how much I could change away from refined materials. With a rumbling giggle, I lifted up the roof of the caved-in tunnel, and the plug of tangled Alvaren popped right through. Stone flowed like water, taking the shape I willed on it, but only for as long as I concentrated on it.

The hurly-burly of Alvaren came pouring through, breaking on my empty body like the tide on a rock and slipping down into the city. It was impossible to hold the tunnel and be in my body at the same time, so I had to keep flitting back and forth between them.

"You've got. To go. Can't hold."

Asher and Mercy looked from my stuttering, hollow body to each other, then shook their heads as one. "We aren't going anywhere without you."

"It's cool…I've got…a plan."

Mercy let out a sound somewhere between a sob and a laugh. "Oh, gods."

They went for it, wading through the crowd of Alvaren, going against the flow and getting buffeted about for their trouble. It didn't matter, so long as they made it out.

The moment that they slipped out of my *Sphere of Influence*, I forced more will into the stone, and I hauled on the roof of that little tunnel, raising it as high as I could until it was taller than me, than two of me, a chasm stretching between this cave and the next, unstable and crumbling the moment my attention left it.

I slammed back into my body and ran as if the whole mountain was about to come down on me. Because it was. The solid-looking roof began crumbling the moment I let go of my grip on it, and any Alvaren that had the misfortune to get in my way got slapped aside.

I didn't have time to be nice. Rocks were falling, and I was going to die. I shouldered the ones out of my path that I could, knocked down the ones I couldn't, and ran full pelt as the falling rocks filled the air with a cloud of dust so thick I couldn't even see the other end.

I felt the tunnel collapsing behind me rather than seeing it. I heard the screams of the Alvaren being crushed as the mouth of the tunnel snapped shut. The far wall of the cave was only visible when I banged into it, and even then the air was so thick with dust that there was a bit of assuming the best going on.

Mercy called out, "Maulkin!"

I coughed back, "Don't worry, babe, I made it!"

Her laugh sounded snotty. Must have been all the dust. "Don't call me babe, you prick."

"I was talking to Asher." I moved towards the sound of her voice, feeling my way along the wall and trying to ignore the squishy Alvaren flesh underfoot.

Asher loomed out of the dust, looking up at me curiously for a moment before saying, "I am pleased that you are well."

I patted him near the base of his tail as I passed. "Thanks, babe."

Victory!
Potency increased to 43
Vitality increased to 15
Brawling: Rank 6/10
Phalanx: Rank 4/10
294 Experience Gained

Farther up the tunnel there were dozens of Alvaren still milling about, stricken now that their highway back home was closed off. "Try taking the long way around." I grinned at the closest cluster.

CHAPTER 21

Apparently, we were still beneath contempt or attention. The Alvaren continued chattering among themselves. That same language that had resurfaced ever so rarely when the svart were chanting, "Kill, kill, kill."

"No time."

"Who can touch the Keystone?"

"Returning to the sky soon."

"What do we do?"

We barreled on by them—no time to take in the chatter. The vibrations we'd felt beneath our feet back in the Alvaren city were escalating now, and the tunnels around us shook, the stone quaking as the city beneath us moved.

We made it back through the tangle of tunnels, wall-bound Dvergar, and panicking Alvaren to the main shaft and the brass rails that would lead us back to safety. The rails were humming like there was a freight train coming our way, but we ran up between them all the same. The Alvaren fading away as we got closer and closer to the khag above.

Dust rained down on us from the murder holes as we approached the mine entrance. We were so close to home I could almost taste it. Which was when everything went to hell.

The tremors from below abruptly stopped. There was dead silence for a moment, then a resounding boom sounded from down in the deep. A huge, sudden expulsion of wind swept up the tunnels behind us, throwing up massive banks of dust and buffeting us off our feet.

I scrambled back to my feet, reaching for the other two only to discover they were already up. Guess we were all getting used to getting knocked on our faces. "What the hell was—"

There was no time for an answer, nor even for the rest of the question. The mine behind us bucked like some living creature in its death throes, then it began to fall. The stone gave way behind us and began to slip down. The heart of the khag was broken. The brass rails stayed straight, but the stone beneath tipped, tearing them free.

We raced alongside them, falling to all fours when we needed to, doing anything we could to keep moving. Anything to outpace the collapse. We threw ourselves out of the mine entrance and into the long-walled avenue that I'd built, but the collapse kept on coming. It seemed like it was going to stop at the city's edge, the careful construction that had stood firm against the centuries held it back for a moment.

But did not stop it.

The stone sang above us, groaning and moaning all the way across the vaulted roof. Dust rained down. Cracks chased their way across the cavern walls, across the floor beneath our feet—even up my temporary walls, sending hunks of them flying down to pepper our path.

"The whole thing is going down." I didn't need my godly architectural skills or *Dungeoneering* to tell me that, my eyes were more than enough. The cracks were spreading faster than we could move, and the glowing crystals that had been embedded in the roof were starting to tinkle down.

"Oh gods, oh gods, all the Dvergar in the mines." Mercy was trying to run and freak out at the same time. All respect to her ability to multi-task.

"We must warn those that are still living!" Asher barked. "They must evacuate the city!"

By the time that we reached the barricade and climbed onto its ramparts, the evacuation was already well underway. The guards that had been stationed here were long gone, and any sign of habitation looked to have been stripped away too. We couldn't even see any Dvergar as we ran through the perfectly parallel streets. Here and there was the hint of them, a piece of furniture dropped and discarded, a scrap of silk, but no actual Dvergar until we rounded a corner and almost hit Gunhild's caravan broadside on. She and her men were frantically loading in supplies as fast as they could move.

When Gunhild spotted us, she very nearly stopped, but instead, she turned that attention into more furious energy for the loading. I rushed forward to try and help but all it earned me was a growl from one of the Dvergar guards. "Let us help."

"Help?!" Gunhild's thrown axe spun past my face to lodge in the wagon's side. "You did this. Never should have been trusting you."

Even Mercy seemed to think axe-throwing was too harsh a response. "Gunhild. We had no way of—"

"No way of knowing and no care neither. What matters it to you if the last standing khag be fallen? What matters it to you if the Dver die out? Not a damn!" Gunhild spat. "Not a damn!"

Asher stepped forward with his hands up in the usual placating gesture. "With respect to your suffering, there was no way that anyone could have foreseen.."

Gunhild shoved him, and my hand went for my sword without any conscious thought. "Just be closing your flapping jaws, snake. We be done with you. You're no kin of ours, so get out. Out with the lot of you."

The floor cracked beneath our feet. Cobwebbed patterns of darkness spreading beneath the dust. With another buck and rumble, the buildings by the barricade began to disappear. Slipping over some fast-approaching horizon. The pit was coming for us all.

Above us, the crystals that had lit the chamber shattered. Sparks rained down around us as the whole khag was plunged into darkness, the last glimmers of light dying.

We could see in the dark. The Dvergar could not. The floor rocked. "Go! Go!"

Fumbling in the darkness, the caravan managed to assemble around their half-loaded wagon, but blind as they were, they couldn't get it moving. "Climb on. Everyone on!"

Gunhild snarled. "I be in charge around here."

"Then act like a leader!" Mercy snapped as she shoved the Dvergar woman towards the wagon. "Get your people out of here!"

I grabbed onto the struts at the front of the armored wagon and pulled hard enough that it rolled right over the blocks that had been tucked under the wheels to keep it in place. Mercy and Asher darted around, grabbing those few Dvergar who'd wandered off and guiding them to the wagon. It was huge, fully loaded, heavy metal, and covered in Dvergar, but it was on wheels. This train was leaving the station.

We picked up speed fast, which was lucky because the collapse was right on our heels. Now that the central cluster at the middle of the cavern was gone, the whole roof seemed to lose its integrity. All of that stone, the whole mountain of weight pressing down, was finally being unleashed. You could hold off gravity for a long time if you were smart enough, but in the end, it always won.

Hunks of stone bigger than the buildings hammered down around us, and I had to swerve from one street to the next to find a clear route. Mercy rushed on ahead of me, hauling any straggling Dvergar that she could find out from their doorways and onto the wagon. There were kids. I hadn't seen any Dvergar kids throughout the whole time we were in the city, but now they were being hauled out of whatever seclusion they'd been kept in so that they might survive.

We were almost out—I could see the shining brass of the entrance reflecting my eye-light—when the whole thing came crashing down. A slab, the size of a mountain in its own right came down on top of us. I raised my hands, I surged my potency, and it didn't even slow. It was a force of nature. Something so far beyond the limits of mortal power that resisting it seemed impossible.

I slipped out of my body and threw out my will.

This was not what Artifice was for. The cracks in the pillar started blazing with stuttering light all over again as I abused it. The stone slab hung there above us, caught in one tiny spot by my *Sphere of Influence* but still bearing down on us with all its weight. On me, specifically.

Blood streamed from my eyes, my ears, my nose, and my mouth. Momentum kept the wagon rolling, and something like rigor mortis kept my hands locked to the bars even as my legs dangled like useless noodles. I could see Asher and Mercy gawking up at the stone above, hanging from the side of the wagon, their expressions filled with confusion and something else. Something I didn't recognize until I saw it on Gunhild's bared and stone-blighted face too. Awe.

The slab pivoted down to close the way out of the city behind us as my *Sphere of Influence* was pushed along, centered on my empty and halfway-to-broken body. We'd be the last ones out of Khag Mhor. The last ones to ever leave it alive.

The wagon lost its momentum about the same time that I snapped back to my body.

I couldn't see for all the blood in my eyes, and I couldn't breathe through the blood bubbling up from my throat. This wasn't my first time dying, and it wouldn't be the last, but it was the first time that it was no surprise. I knew what I was doing when I screwed around with the Pillars of Divinity. I knew that if I overreached the limits of the rules that Amaranth ran on, I would be spanked for it, but I did it anyway.

Pain didn't begin to describe what I was feeling when I saw the red-tinted light at the end of the tunnel. It was bright enough now for the Dvergar to haul me out of the way so that they could latch in. They passed me back up onto the top of the wagon and dumped me there like a deer carcass splayed on the hood of a truck. I wished I felt as good as a dead deer.

Have you ever hurt so bad that it is the only thing you can think of? Pain so insistent that it became your whole world. Where ending that pain became your only goal? I'd say it felt like I was full of molten lead, that my organs had been put through a blender, or that some tiny bastard gnome with a chainsaw was going hog-wild under my skin, but none of those things did it justice. It hurt so bad that I lost all hope of ever not hurting again. It hurt so bad that I forgot that there was any world outside of my hurt.

When I felt Asher's cool scaly palms on my skin, they brought no relief, just a new dimension to my suffering. Even when I saw flames coil up around his clawed fingers, my brain couldn't comprehend what my eyes were telling it.

He *Cauterized* me again.

I was so messed up that having every nerve ending in my body set on fire was an improvement. I might have called him some choice words in the moment, but folks have been known to curse when they are feeling extra-good just as much as extra-bad.

[331/550 Health]

I jerked upright, with only the restraining hands of Asher and Gunhild to stop me from jumping right off the wagon. I spat out a mouthful of soot-swirled blood and gasped in a breath. We were out. The sky opened up above us, wide and bright and blue. I'd almost forgotten what it looked like. I slumped back onto the wagon with a groan. "I thought we said we weren't going to do that again."

To his credit, Asher actually looked sad about it. "My apologies, it was necessary to maintain your survival."

"I'm joking. It's… Well, it isn't fine, but thanks for doing it."

"It was no trouble at all. My only wish is that there was a less painful solution to your injuries."

"You and me both."

Gunhild kicked me. Not in a playful way. In the angry way that only solid steel toe-caps can ever really convey.

"Get off my caravan." Asher had to help me up, and by up, I mean mostly sideways as he poured me off the side of the wagon to land on the road into the dead khag.

All around us, the Dvergar that had escaped lay around, stunned and sobbing. There were dozens of them, maybe hundreds. I had no way of knowing how many didn't make it out. Even when they trusted us, the Dvergar were private people, devoted to keeping out of our sight and hiding their marks of shame. This could have been the whole khag or a tenth, and I'd never know. The mountain itself seemed to shrug as the caverns within collapsed, the peak tipping to the side and one last great wave of ash and dust sweeping out the mouth of the cave to coat us all.

Back on my feet, I started to search. We found Mercy with a family of Dvergar, all huddled around a dreadfully still little bundle of silk. Everywhere I looked, the injured seemed to spring up. Gunhild was right. We did this. I did this.

I spotted a Dvergar I thought I knew, scurrying around with a water skin and bandages. Catching him by the shoulder, I spun him on the spot but he wasn't Gorm. Well, I had this guy here anyway. "Where's Gorm?"

"The elders needed seen to."

Mercy let out a little gasp. "What?"

The Dvergar shrugged my hand off his shoulder, infected with the same directionless fury that seemed to be emanating from Gunhild. "Were we to be leaving them down there to starve if they survived the collapse? To rot? To be taken by some beast of the deeps. Gorm knew his duty, and he did it."

Everyone else had tried to escape, but duty came first for Gorm. I barely knew him, but I believed it.

There was nobody left to lead the Dvergar. They looked around for their elders, for the spokesmen of the elders, for any sort of answers, and they found nothing at all. It had all been buried.

Gunhild was still standing atop her wagon, surveying it all. Counting heads and making plans. She scowled every time her gaze turned our way, but she was practical more than she was angry. She kept to her work. With nobody else to turn to, I approached the wagon. "Gunhild. You need to know what happened."

"Why don't you be going away and boiling your head?"

Mercy tried to be reasonable. "Gunhild."

"You did something down in the mines. Made the whole khag move to collapse, even though we warned you to be careful. Even though we offered you sappers and miners. You did whatever you did knowing you might bring the whole mountain down, but you didn't care because you can't be dying with us. When our lives are ruins, you can just move on along. You're Eternals, and we don't matter."

"You cannot comprehend the situation in which we found ourselves. The svart were Alvaren. Transformed by a spell," Asher tried to explain. "Their city was buried beneath your own. It was not our actions that brought on the collapse, but…"

"Always you be spinning more of your hearth stories. Alvar and legends and curses and magic. Our lives aren't fodder for your big story." She spread out her arms wide, her voice booming out over the refugees. "You see these folk? They'll all be dying out here. The khag was the last safe place for them. We've supplies enough for a few days, then the starving starts. We've weapons enough for a guard here and there, then the beasts of the wilds start chewing on the stragglers. This isn't a story, these are real people, and they'll be really dead. Thanks to you."

There would be no argument from me. I had the shard tucked into the back of my trousers still, the cool metal a comforting roughness against my skin. I could have put it back where it came from and kept everything the same, but I made the choice. I decided that I needed it more than the Alvaren, and this was the price for that.

Mercy wasn't as ready to take it lying down. "Hey. We went down there risking our lives to help you people. We weren't looking for trouble, and we weren't looking for glory. You had a problem, and we were trying to fix it."

Gunhild roared, "And what a grand job you be doing of it!"

I spoke too softly, "Mercy."

"How the hell were we meant to know that you'd built your khag on top of an ancient Alvaren city?"

Gunhild was down off the wagon now, screaming in Mercy's face, "Why did we ever trust that you buffoons might be knowing what you were doing?"

Asher caught Mercy by the shoulder. "Mercy!"

"What?!" She turned with a snarl.

The shadow of the Alvaren city swept up over her face at the same pace as realization. The great vaulted white city hung in the sky among the clouds, blocking out the sun.

"Oh no."

With an impact like a thunderclap, Briar By Moonlight's voice boomed down on us from above, "If the artifact is returned without resistance, you may all depart unharmed."

The sparse grass on the mountainside bowed to the sound of her, and the refugees of the khag fell to their knees in terror. The Alvaren were things of legend for a reason—flying cities, and magic voices shouting down from on high. No wonder the Dvergar were afraid. That wasn't cowardice, it was sanity.

I took a few steps away from Gunhild. "We've got to go."

"Aye, that be about right," she spat. "Drop us in the shaft, then run away."

I'd been letting all this slide because she was right to be mad at us, but even I had limits. "It is me that they want. It is me that they'll chase."

Gunhild let out a triumphant little laugh. "I knew it. I knew it be all your fault. You robbed their tomb, and now they're after you."

I let out a sad little huff of air, then turned to the other two. "Do you want to come with me or stay with the Dvergar?"

Asher shook his head solemnly. "Until fate parts us, we are with you, my friend."

"Thanks, babe."

Mercy burst out laughing. Not a smirk. Not a sigh. A big, ugly belly laugh. Forget the rest of the day. I was counting that as a win.

CHAPTER 22

There were no supplies to gather and no goodbyes to say. The panicked Dvergar were already on the move down the mountain road, so we struck off in the opposite direction, skidding and sliding down the scree-strewn slopes where we could and dropping right down the muddy drops when we couldn't.

I didn't look back. If the Dvergar were going to make it, they were going to make it. If we stopped and hemmed and hawed about it then the Alvaren would come down on us all.

But just because I wasn't looking over my shoulder, it didn't mean that nobody was paying attention. Mercy grunted as she leapt down off a ledge into my waiting arms. "We've got to go faster. They're coming."

I spared a glance to the sky and saw what she was talking about. The city was still hanging in the sky, but there were things streaming down from it. The svart might have had no idea what the flesh-forges did, but the Alvaren already had them back in action, pumping out some sort of winged animals to use as mounts.

The Alvaren themselves were little more than glints of metal on the back of the darting beasts in all their rainbow colors, but one thing that was easy to make out was that they were coming right for us. "Faster. Right."

Our heady pace turned to reckless. There was no more controlled drop when we hit the edge of a rock shelf. I flung myself down and caught the others as I could. Sometimes I missed, and Mercy rolled to her feet with an angry grumble. Sometimes I missed, and Asher fell flat on his face and needed to be scooped up to get him moving again. At least gravity was on our side, dragging us ever on towards the tree-line, where the bloody red forest consumed the base of the hill.

If we got to the forest before the swooping whatever-the-hells that were chasing us then we could lose them under the cover. Maybe we could even camp out there until the sun set, and we could use the cover of darkness. Gods knew I could use a rest after the day I'd had.

Of course, gravity was on their side too. The bird-cat things spread their wings wide, but their momentum still nearly carried them right into us. Gryphons. They were gryphons. That wasn't *Bestiary* filling in the blanks, it was me. Head like an eagle, body of a cat, wings up top, these were gryphons—although the fantasy art I'd seen in my old life hadn't prepared me for their fully feathered bodies to range in color from electric pink to neon blue.

The claws and the beaks though were black right to their razor edges, and they were what held onto my attention as the gryphons raked at us in passing.

We weren't going to make it to the forest. I dug in my heels and skidded on for six more feet, just avoiding the gryphon that swept through the space where I would have been if I'd kept on moving. The abrupt stop saved me in another way too.

The Alvaren who'd missed with their dive-bombs were circling overhead, and now they'd started to rain down arrows with an accuracy that would have been lethal if I hadn't stopped dead ahead of the shimmering wall of pointy arrows they were laying down. "Mercy!"

"I'm on it."

It couldn't have been easy returning fire on moving targets, but Mercy did a damn fine job. Even though she didn't seem to be hitting all that often, the shots she did manage to land were all that kept us alive. A notch knocked out of a beak turned a gryphon's head and sent it crashing into another. An arrow flying past an Alvaren's pointy ear made his next shot miss me.

She held them off for the whole moment it took us to think—the most vital moment in any fight. Asher threw back his head and belched out a voluminous gout of flame. It exploded out in a great red flash, sweeping up over every gryphon in the spiral above us and setting the tips of their feathers glowing like kindling.

Just like the static clinging to victims of his electric spells, the embers lit up the Alvaren and gryphons. But unlike the mindless svart, these enemies knew the significance of that glow. Some of them broke off, and the rest scattered into a wider whorl. They had no intention of getting caught in an area of effect spell together. Clever girls. Six of them were left.

With the extra range, Mercy found it even harder to hit them. "Will you just stay still!"

If we stayed in place, the Alvaren could take their time peppering us with arrows from a distance. If we ran, they could start swooping us again. It was win-win for them and lose-die for us.

Briar's voice echoed across the hillside from where the city still hung, still and solid in the air. "Submit and we shall be merciful."

The gryphon gyre widened out a little more as if they were giving us time to think it through. "Hey, Mercy, do you think she'll forgive me for stealing her shard and headbutting her in the face?"

Mercy snorted. "I wouldn't."

"Asher?"

"I do not trust in her words." Flames were trailing from his hands. "Her actions belie them."

"Right then." I drew my sword. "Let's kick them in the ass."

The next dive-bomber came swooping down, launching a steady staccato of arrows my way, but I had the wide flat of my sword out and ready to turn the shots away from anything vital.

As the rider yanked on the reins to turn the gryphon's nose up from the ground, I launched myself. Rough Hewn Architecture threw up a messy clay platform to give me as much height as I could get, then surged Potency let me kick off from that displaced earth like I'd just learned to fly.

Inside me, the cracks in the Pillar of Artifice blazed.

If I'd timed it right, I would have soared up, hit the Alvaren in mid-flight, valiantly wrestled control of the gryphon away from her, and soared off into the sunset to kick the asses of all the rest of them.

I didn't time it right. I jumped too soon.

I hit the gryphon in the chest with all the cannonball force of my jump.

To fly, these things had to be pretty light, which meant hollow bones, which meant I punched through its ribcage like it was a paper cup. Blood rained down on the hillside below, and the last few spasmodic twitches of the gryphon's wings kept us from plummeting the whole distance. Even so, I hit the ground hard with most of my torso still embedded inside the dead bird-cat, entrails coiling out around me.

Mercy spared a glance at me to say, "Ew," before launching her next shot.

With a heave of my shoulders, I freed myself of the dead gryphon, even if its guts still clung to me like streamers from the worst surprise party ever. The rider launched herself at me before I could even remember she was there.

Her armor flashed silver in the light—so bright it left after-images. Beneath it, she wore plain white robes. Not simple like Asher's, more like the minimalist simplicity of some elegant eveningwear. The short swords in her hands were no dimmer than the armor. They spun and darted like wheeling fireworks as she came on.

A crisscross of wounds opened up on my stomach. She was too fast to follow. Too fast to block. I'd hoped it was only Briar that could move like that. I swept my sword in a wild arc towards her, and she hopped over it as though it were a game. Maybe she had hollow bones too.

I was starting to feel seriously outclassed by these Alvaren, and that was before one of the gryphon-riders swooped down and put an arrow clean through my calf.

"Damn it."

The leg gave out, and I fell to one knee as the Alvaren on the ground came at me once more, poise and superiority written on her every feature. The flat head of my sword found the ground, and one hard push brought me back up to my unsteady feet. I wasn't dying, but even if I was, I wasn't dying on my knees.

Her head tipped back to follow my movement, but her sneer didn't move an inch. Not even when Mercy fired an arrow, and she had to cock her head aside to avoid it.

There was no way I was going to win a fair fight with the Alvaren. There was no way I could match her speed or her skill. Good thing I had no intention of having a fair fight.

Reaching out to the limits of my *Sphere of Influence* I pushed down. I couldn't do much with the topsoil, but the clay and rocks beneath us gave way readily to my will. Everything pushed down until only the soil was left with no structure beneath to hold it up.

Her next step forward, her shiny boots sank into the dirt up to the ankle. Her smirk vanished just as my grin cracked.

I launched myself at her with no care for the blades in her hands or even the sword in mine. All I needed to do was bear her down.

With a blade jammed in each shoulder, I carried her to the dirt. My blood was pouring, turning the loose soil to mud, coating her pretty white clothes and her pretty silver armor in mud, bringing her down into reality with the rest of us.

She wormed and squirmed about beneath me, but my weight was enough to keep her from escaping entirely. It took some scrabbling about, but I caught hold of her arms, pinned her legs with my knees, and paused in triumph for just long enough for one of her friends to hit me in the back with an arrow.

That little bit of pain gave me the drive I needed. I reared up and slammed my head down into the Alvaren's pretty little face.

Now the blood in the mud wasn't just mine. Her face was a mess, and my forehead was wet and tingling. I reared up again. One more thump should have been enough to knock her out. That was when the next Alvaren arrow hit me in the cheek.

My head twisted with the impact, my teeth jarred as I bit down on the metal arrowhead, and I completely forgot what I was in the middle of doing at the worst possible moment.

There was a sound like somebody stamping on a bunch of grapes as my horn dug in through her eye.

I tried to pull back immediately, but the eye socket was locked tight around the conical spread of my horn. The Alvaren who'd been so lethal and scary just a moment before was now a really ugly hat.

Mercy interrupted her barrage to call over, "Ew!"

Despite the situation, I could feel laughter bubbling up in my throat. I shook my head from side to side, making the dead Alvaren wiggle and jiggle. "It's stuck."

With that Alvaren out of the way, in every way but one, I finally had enough attention to spare for the next one swooping down. I saw the tell-tale shimmer as arrows were loosed and had at least a chance of dodging by flinging myself aside. One missed, punching down into the mud where I was wallowing without a trace. The others struck home, and I braced myself for pain that didn't come. I'd definitely felt the impact, yet they hadn't hit me. My fancy new hat looked like a pincushion.

As the gryphon pulled up from its dive, Asher's spell caught it. He was sticking with fire magic now that he'd unlocked it, and I could see why. The lightning had been impressive, but there was something primal about setting people that you didn't like on fire.

The gryphon, with its soft downy feathers, went up like it had been doused in lighter fluid. It went from the elegant curve of a well-executed swoop to wild flapping panic in an instant, then on to falling like a lump of charcoal a moment after.

The Alvaren leapt from the saddle, flames licking from his skirts. Falling through the air, he could only move in one direction. It didn't matter how fast he could twist or turn, he was coming down beside me.

My sword came up at the same time.

Two halves of the Alvaren tumbled to the ground on either side of me. "Good shooting, Asher!"

When I glanced around at him, it was pretty clear that he was only standing by force of will alone. If I'd thought my head-Alvaren looked like a pincushion, it was nothing compared to the hedgehog bristle of arrows that made up Asher's torso. I ran for him, mud sucking at my ankles, my own trap turned against me.

He took another stumbling step towards me, then fell. I had to jump to grab him before he hit the ground. *Restoration*, don't fail me now.

I poured my divine power into his swiss-cheese body, but the wounds couldn't close. The healing stalled out. Oh, this was going to suck. Grabbing them by the handful, I started to yank the clusters of arrows out of him. His cold blood sprayed all over me as I worked, but even as he gasped and shook, I could not stop. Not until enough was out that I could heal him. His desperate grasping hands caught at my wrists, trying to stop me, but there was no time to be gentle. I ripped out the last fistful and poured in my *Restoration*. He let out a little sob, but the wounds closed before his knees hit the churned mud of the battlefield.

He was going to live, so long as the Alvaren didn't replace those arrows with new ones. With a growl, I ripped the Alvaren from my horns. I was so busy having a good time that I hadn't even noticed my friend being murdered. It was enough to put anyone in a bad mood.

I called out, "Mercy. Come here!"

Artifice was still creaking and groaning each time that I used it, but it wasn't like I had any other options. My sword shifted in my grip, transforming into the big tower shield I'd used so often down in the mines. On their next pass, I heard the Alvaren arrows chittering off it.

Mercy skidded in underneath it, looked down at Asher and the ripped-up bits of Alvaren, and sighed. "Again?"

"Stay under the shield; we'll head for the trees." I hefted the shield as she got her grip under Asher's armpits. "They'll need to land if they want to chase us into the woods."

She rolled her eyes, but she stuck close as we moved. "I know how shields work, thanks."

Under my breath, I replied, "I know how your face works."

I guess the shield kinda made that reverberate back down louder than intended because she sniped back, "I know how your mother works."

My grin came unbidden. "I know how your mother's face works."

Her next reply was drowned out by another rattle of arrows.

The forest was so close I could taste the sap on the air. Just one last skid down a slope and we'd be safe. Which was when the gryphon hit me.

That wasn't completely accurate. If the gryphon had just come slamming down into the shield, I probably would have been alright. I already had an arm braced against it and…well, it was a shield—that was what they were meant for, being banged into. The real problem was that the gryphon barely bumped the shield as it swooped down and latched its claws on each corner of it, then lifted off again.

I was yanked off my feet, and the swing of my dangling legs set Mercy and Asher tumbling down the hill into the shadows of the forest. At first, it didn't look like I was going to fly thanks to weighing about as much as a small hippo, but the gryphon really had some strength in its wings. First, it had me hopping and skipping to hold onto the shield, then finally it took off just before we crashed into the trees. Or at least before *it* crashed into the trees. I got a face full of blossoms and branches.

Thankfully, it pulled up after that first sweep through the boughs, soaring up into the sky with me dangling beneath it. Higher and higher it went before looping and plunging right back down towards the forest again.

It was trying to shake me off and let the drop kill me. That's the problem with Alvaren these days, no work ethic. Don't make gravity do all the work for you, kill me yourselves.

The gryphon rider didn't risk going as low as the trees this time around, choosing instead to spiral up again when we were only halfway there, swinging me out to the side like I was in a centrifuge. Good thing I didn't get travel sick.

At the top of the spiral, it did another flip and plunge, but this time I was expecting it. As I hung for that moment, weightless in the air above my shield and the gryphon, time slowed to a crawl. My shield became my sword, slipping painlessly from the gryphon's claws as it transformed. Time snapped back into action, and suddenly, the gryphon wasn't dragging me down, I was plunging down at it with my weapon ready.

The beast itself seemed to realize that something was wrong, but the rider, on the opposite side to me, couldn't see what had happened, and she kept spurring the poor thing on in its dive.

If we'd all gone on falling forever, I guess that might have saved them, but just before we hit the red forest, she hauled up on the reins, and my sword came swinging down.

The gryphon ripped apart at the touch of steel, but the Alvaren herself seemed to be made of tougher stuff. The bone of her thigh stopped my swing dead, and she screamed, shrill as a dog-whistle, as the remains of her mount toppled apart around her in a mess of viscera and gore.

We tumbled end over end around the fulcrum of my sword, her trying to aim her bow at me, me trying to get a good kick in and separate us. I only had an instant to realize that we weren't going to fall forever and to use *Restoration* before we burst through the canopy.

Then we hit the forest floor.

I lay there groaning for a good long minute, wondering how much of the red around me came from me and how much of it was the fallen blossoms. I hoped most of it was trees, but after that fall, I could find my legs on the other side of a stream and wouldn't be too surprised. My arms seemed to start working first, so I fumbled about for my sword fruitlessly until I finally found the strength to haul myself back up to sitting.

That was a mistake. The whole forest spun around me in a wobbly orbit. I was extremely done with falling from great heights. I could go the rest of my eternal life without doing it again. It sucked. The Alvaren was lying sprawled beside my sword, blue-tinted blood still pulsing ominously from the gaping hole in her thigh.

Maybe the honorable thing to do would have been to wait for her to wake up and give her a fair fight. Maybe it would have been better to just leave her to chance. Maybe she'd bleed to death, maybe she wouldn't. In that moment, after the day that I'd had, I didn't feel like it.

The sword felt heavy as a boulder when I tried to lift it, but I had enough potency to juggle boulders by now. I raised the sword up and brought it down with the same resigned movement. Butcher and meat all over again.

Legendary Foes Defeated!
Celerity increased to 19
Vitality increased to 16

Brawling: Rank 7/10
Phalanx: Rank 5/10
Acrobatics: Rank 7/10
Airstrike: Rank 2/10
176 Experience Gained
120 Glory Gained
Tier of Glory Ascended!

Life rushed back into me as the pillars of divinity flared with light.

[192/710 Health]

Right then and there I wanted to dump my glory into Primal and go on healing myself until I had so much blood in my body I swelled up like a blueberry. But I stopped myself. I'd been pretty lucky with all my impulse decisions and drunk-buying of skills so far, but I needed to start really thinking about who I wanted to be in the future before I threw too much good glory into the same pillars over and over. I'm not saying that turning into the demi-god of buffness and giant swords wasn't appealing, but now that I'd seen Asher warp the fabric of reality a few times, it was starting to look…less than optimal.

Asher. Mercy. I needed to find them before they got too far into the forest and got lost, with no idea which way they'd come in and which way we were headed. Just like I was right now. Damn it.

"Mercy!"

The trees swallowed my shout. It was so quiet in these woods, I could almost forget everything that was happening outside of them. The foliage was thick enough that a legion of gryphons could be overhead and I'd be none the wiser.

"Mercy! Asher?"

I looked up to the sky for any hint of which way I'd come in, but the trees all looked the same. There was no convenient Maulkin-shaped hole anywhere. Cartoons lied to me. Even looking down at the bits of gryphon and Alvaren didn't help. They were scattered all over the place, parts facing every which way, blood splattered out in every direction.

"Mercy!"

Still nothing. I was going to just pick a direction and start walking. I knew that I was meant to stay still and let them come find me if I was lost, but I'd never been great at the whole staying still thing. Besides, who knew what kind of trouble those two were getting into without me. They might not even be getting into any trouble, and why would I want a boring life for my friends?

I started heading for what looked like it might be a path through the trees when I heard Briar's voice booming out of her city in the clouds, muffled at this distance but still audible, "Pursue them, my paladins. Do not give them the time to use the artifact and curse us once more!"

It was coming from directly opposite the direction I'd been headed. Whoops. I turned on my heel and then pushed through the trees, crashing through the underbrush until I found some sort of path and followed it along. I kept waiting for the little birds that kept attacking Mercy last time around to pop out and peck me, but for some reason, they left me in peace—if they were in this forest at all.

Now that I knew the vague direction I should be heading, I kept my mouth shut. If the Alvaren were down here hunting for us then they didn't need any more help than my stomping on every fallen twig was giving them. With a path weaving off through the trees that turned out to be a dry riverbed, I made good time, but even as I ran, I kept my ears perked up.

The forest seemed to grow brighter as I went, and in the distance, I could almost make out light beyond the tree-line. That was when the shouting started. To my surprise, it wasn't Mercy doing the yelling. They were off to my right, so I leapt up out of the river bed and charged on through as the low-hanging branches whipped at my horns.

The next thing I knew, the forest was on fire. It didn't catch while I was standing there, I just burst through one line of trees into the next, and they just happened to be on fire. Smoke billowed up from them and clogged up the gaps where sunlight made it through, pooling under the canopy and reducing visibility to somewhere between the tip of my sword and the end of my nose.

"Mercy!?"

A voice called out from up ahead, reedy but audible over the soft roar of flames. Asher's voice. "Maulkin?"

I charged over to him. Unsurprisingly, he was at the epicenter of all the fire. There were a few blackened things amongst the pillars of charcoal that still had droplets of liquid silver clinging to them; I assumed that they were Alvaren before they got nuked.

I never thought I'd be so happy to see a lizard. It was only when I was halfway to hugging him that I spotted the other blackened thing in his arms. Mercy was barely recognizable as human. The shape was right, but the rest was bloody and blackened, her bow snapped in two, string seared away. "I did not mean to. When I awoke, and we were surrounded, I was… You must understand I would never do anything to bring either one of you harm. Never."

Mercy's flesh was sticky to the touch, still hot from the flames that had scorched her. *Lifesense* took longer than I would have liked to burrow down into her and tell me that she was hanging onto life by a thread with only two health left. "I've hurt her so badly, and I've never hurt… I would never."

"Shh." I reached up and took a grip on the back of his neck, slowing his frantic motions. Bringing him back to the moment. "Everything's going to be alright."

A groan escaped from Mercy. Not a death rattle, but something like it. When her lips split, plasma and gobs of soot drooled out. "You're going to use *Cauterize*, and I'm going to use *Restoration* at the same time. She'll be back to normal in no time."

"I... I cannot cause her pain again. I cannot make her suffer further after I did... I never..."

"*Restoration* is going to take that pain away—she isn't going to feel it." I pressed my forehead against his, making him look up from the mess he'd made. "But we've both got to cast right now. We're losing her."

His voice was a whisper. "But she..."

"Together, Asher. Before my healing undoes your fire debuff."

I saw his lips moving as he tried to decipher my gaming terminology. Then it clicked. "Char. Yes. I... Together then. One moment."

Her health ticked down to one as he prepared his spell, and I stood ready. Either one of them would save her, and I was ready with *Restoration* in case his took too long, but together we could get her back on her feet and fighting fit.

Asher hissed, "Now."

I'd never seen *Cauterize* used from the outside before. It was bad enough living through the sensations, but now I had the accompanying visual to keep me up at night. Flames lapped over Mercy, scorching away her injuries inch by inch and leaving behind pallid scar tissue. Then the wave of fire swept back over that puffy skin, bursting it open like a chrysalis to reveal the freshly grown flesh beneath. My *Restoration*'s rapid regeneration schtick looked positively pleasant compared to the juicy mess that Asher's healing made out of people.

I had to use the back of my hand to sweep away the worst of the dislodged skin and slime so that she could gasp in a breath. It came ragged to begin with as she struggled and writhed in our grip, but finally, she fell back to the forest floor and groaned. "Ew."

I patted her on the head. "Ew, you too."

She reached out. "Asher..."

He leaned in close. "Yes, Mercy?"

"Don't ever do that again."

He looked away, as stricken as if she'd told him he wasn't the father of their weird half-lizard baby on syndicated daytime television. "Yes, Mercy."

"What a truly heartwarming scene. Truly there is not only honor among thieves but also tenderness. One might even say love—if chattel could experience aught beyond their base impulses." The Alvaren stepped out from behind the smoldering trees as one, six of them arrayed around us in a circle. Each one of them had their twin blades drawn. That was twelve pointy things. That was at least nine more pointy things than I wanted pointed at me at any given time. "Now return the artifact to us or your eventual fate shall be far more painful than anything that the wyrm-spawn can conjure."

I dropped Mercy with a growl and rose to my feet. The same smug Alvaren shook his head. "Ah, ah, ah, slowly now, ox. We would not want there to be any misunderstandings that end in the perforation of your wounded co-conspirators."

They outnumbered us pretty badly, and I'd struggled to handle one of them, even after I'd just knocked them out of the sky. It wasn't looking pretty.

"This is all just a misunderstanding."

"Of course. Of course. You misunderstood the trouble that you would be in when you attempted to rob our queen of an ancient artifact. Just as your ancestors misunderstood that when they came creeping into our city and used that same artifact to defile *our very blood* that we would seek vengeance upon not only them but every last one of their putrid line."

I raised my hands up so that the Alvaren could see that they were empty and I wasn't trying anything. "Buddy, you are way off. That is not what happened."

"Hearken, sisters. Now we move on to the baseless fabrications and contortions of the truth so common among you chattel. Spin your tale then, beast of burden. Tell us all how the things that we lived through, the degeneration and degradation that we have endured for millennia, were all just a misunderstanding. Tell us as if you were there, when your lives last no longer than a candle's wick."

"I don't know anything about what happened to you back then." Asher and Mercy were making their way to their feet, slowly and shakily at my sides. "All I know is that your queen, Briar, was really set on keeping you all as pasty goblin-monkeys."

Spittle flecked the Alvaren's mouth. "You dare to speak of our empress with such irreverence? You should put your face to the filthy earth you sprung from when you talk of her. Or better yet, do not sully her name at all with your awkward gruntings."

"I can't remember exactly what she said, but it was something like, 'Give me the artifact so I can turn them back into svarts. Snoot, snoot. Relent and I shall be merciful. Snoot, snoot. You don't know what you're messing with. Snoot, snoot, I'm better than you. Snoot, snoot.'"

Mercy let out a gasp of unintentional laughter.

The paladin raised his eyebrow, a tremor of rage constrained only by good breeding, or enough emotional constipation to make Mercy look like a gusher. "Snoot, snoot?"

"Come on, dude. You know how she is, always looking down her nose at everyone. 'I'm Queen Briarpatch, I'll magic you up and down in the air like I just don't care. Look how pretty I am. Look at my big pointy…pyramid.'"

Asher let out a nasal whine. "Are you trying to antagonize them?"

I opened and closed my mouth a couple of times before finally giving an honest answer. "Honestly, yeah. These guys are dicks."

The Alvaren charged.

CHAPTER 23

"Going up!"

There was no rich heavy clay beneath our feet, but the roots of the trees were nothing if not raw wood, and the fire hadn't touched them yet. The whole interwoven mesh of them burst up out of the ground beneath us as my Artifice worked, hauling us out of reach of the Alvaren and above the choking smoke in one great heave.

Growing Mercy a new bow out of the wood was almost an after-thought. Now, all we needed was a string and she'd be ready to rock. I slammed back into my body and all its aches with a grunt. Asher was casting already, and Mercy had caught the new bow as it dropped out of thin air and was scrambling in what was left of her belt pouches to see if she could find a string of her own. I didn't have the heart to tell her that all her arrows had been turned to ash in the charred remnants of her quiver. At least, the clothing that had burnt away left her mostly decent, except for the one butt-cheek hanging out in the breeze.

Up above the forest's roof, the scale of just how screwed we were became apparent. Above us and all around us in a massive spiral, there were dozens if not hundreds of gryphons, each with their own rider. Every individual one was enough to ruin our day. The gryphons of the paladins down on the forest floor were perched up here, and my immediate thought was "grand theft bird-cat" but they immediately reared up and started flailing their claws at us the moment we broke through the canopy. I wasn't even sure I would have been able to ride one if it liked me, let alone one that was actively trying to kill me.

Down below, we could already feel the vibrations as the Alvaren started hacking their way through my hastily sprouted supports. This little platform was going down any minute, but we had a second to think. "Anyone got a better plan than a dramatic last stand?"

Mercy paused in the midst of restringing her bow. "That's your best idea?"

"I mean…" I gestured hopelessly at the hissing gryphon squad.

Mercy pinched the bridge of her nose. "Me and Asher will hold them off while you run."

"Uh no." The platform rocked beneath our feet. "I'm not leaving you to die."

"They want the shard, and we win by making sure they don't get it." She went back to priming her bow. I made her some arrows out of habit. "Me and Ash will come back if they stab us. It isn't the end of the world. But if you die, they get what you drop."

"Yeah, but you could end up anywhere on the planet. I'd never find you again."

The whole platform began to tip. They'd hacked away enough of the roots. We were going down. "Maybe. But at least you'd have the shard."

I drew my sword. "Nope. Screw that. I'd take you two over a magic McGuffin any day."

Asher's spell seemed to be ready, judging by the plumes of smoke pouring out from between his teeth, and I wasn't giving Mercy any more time to talk herself into suicide. "Going down!"

Surprise was probably the only thing we had going for us, so instead of letting the Alvaren bring us down, I slammed us back to the earth, pushing all the wood I'd hauled up back where it came from. The impact rocked us, and the roots managed to pull a couple of the Alvaren down into the dirt with them, so I was calling it a win. Not the chatty boy though, he'd jumped back out of reach. That was fine, I wanted to smack him myself.

Asher let out the flames he'd been holding back in a great gush of orange and red, and it swept out over the already burning forest around us without much noticeable effect, but the Alvaren were all dusted with cinders, so I guess the spell worked. Looking down, I noticed I was crackling a bit too, but who cared about a little collateral damage between friends.

Chatty boy had both of his swords pointed right at me, so I went with it, closing the distance between us in two strides and then taking a swing. Just like his beloved queen, he just leaned out of the way of it, not even bothering with a proper dodge.

"Too slow by far, beast."

His returned attacks were much too quick to follow, his blades nothing but a shimmer in the flames, and the inside of my arm opened up in a rush of blood. The strength left it as severed tendons pinged.

The other blade shimmered past my face, close enough that I could feel displaced air on my eyeballs, and for a moment I thought that he'd missed. Then the tips of my horns toppled down at the periphery of my vision.

"You dick!"

The paladin spun his swords to flick off my blood. "Return what you stole, and I shall leave you with your legs to limp away, beaten and broken like the cur you are."

Mercy was shooting, but the Alvaren who couldn't duck behind trees to avoid her shots still seemed to dodge them entirely too easily. Asher was casting, but who knew how long it would take to go off. The only good news was that the Alvaren were too busy watching me get my ass kicked to do much kicking themselves.

As if that wasn't bad enough, some of the dark birds that we saw in the last blood forest had decided to join the party, flitting out beneath the branches to dive-bomb at Mercy's head and foul her aim even more. The whole world was out to screw us, I swear.

With my right arm dead and dangling, I shifted my sword to the other and gave it a few practice swings since the paladin was in no rush. "Drop your blade, beast, and I shall show mercy."

"Or you could"—I leapt forward, sweeping the sword up at his face—"eat it!"

He tilted his head aside with a smirk, and my wild swing missed.

I swear I didn't even see him move against the backdrop of swarming silver-birds, but my arm came back bloodied and useless.

My sword toppled to the ground as my fingers lost the strength to hold it up. It lay there, vibrating on the turned soil, the stampede setting the whole forest shaking.

The paladin snarled, that handsome face twisting to ugly. "What is it that you do not understand, oversized cretin. You are not my match. You shall never be my match. Before you rutting beasts crawled from out the filth, we ruled this world, and now that we are returned, so too shall order be restored. The time of the savage is done. Submit."

"You know what, you're right. You used to run this place, but you've been gone thousands of years. That is plenty of time for things to change."

"It is a testament to the briefness of your lives that you think so." He rolled his eyes. "Nothing ever truly changes."

I grinned. "Tell that to them."

The giant mushroom stampede burst through into our charred little clearing. I didn't know if all the noise had attracted them, or maybe it was the heat—it didn't much matter. They came on blind and wild and crushed every Alvaren they encountered underfoot without even noticing.

Chatty spun on his heel to face this new enemy and got in a few good cuts. The kind that would have killed me, any of the monsters we'd crossed paths with, or anybody else. However, they did nothing but release spores from the spongy white flesh of the big chunky fungus.

He was bowled over by one of the trunk-legs before I had to bail on the fight and head for safety, so I was calling it a win for team me, even if I didn't get to stamp on him myself.

I was roaring with laughter despite all the bleeding. "The chungus are among us!"

Mercy rolled her eyes, but she had the right idea, and she caught Asher by a sleeve and dragged him off. I abandoned my sword and ran after them. There was no way we could stay ahead of the big mushroom guys forever, but the odds were in our favor. They'd run off in a random direction every time that they banged into a tree. All we needed was a little bit of luck and we wouldn't get trampled. We were due a bit of good luck by now. We must have burnt through all the bad stuff.

When the big mushroom guys hit the fire, it licked up their flesh with just a little bit of browning, but where the rot leaked out of them, they caught like they'd been doused in oil.

The forest was ablaze behind us, and every tree that the mushrooms battered into caught alight as their fluids splattered out onto them. All we had to do was keep the heat to our backs and the dark in front of us, and we could be sure we were going the right way.

I caught glimpses of the other two through the trees as we ran, but there was no sign of the Alvaren who hunted us. The chaos of the great mushroom fire seemed to be doing the trick. The only thing chasing after us was one persistent silver-bird that wanted a piece of Mercy and the spreading miasma of smoke and spores.

Asher was casting as we ran, flames trailing out behind his hands like the tail of a comet. I would have complained about it attracting attention or mushrooms, but we seemed to be completely alone and ignored. As we burst through the next clearing, he darted over to run beside me, tripped over a rock, and flung himself into my waiting, useless arms.

Trying to catch him with them was a lot like flopping a pair of overcooked noodles in his general direction, but he caught onto them himself, and the flames from his hands spread out across me. Cauterize. Again.

Knowing what to expect actually made the pain worse somehow, like I was tensing for it or something. Or maybe it just hurt worse every time he used it. You would have thought I'd get used to it eventually, but no. Fire still burned when it got shoved into your open wounds. Who would have thought?

I almost threw him off as new strength born of agony swept through me, but I managed to resist the urge, holding him out at arm's length instead. "I thought we weren't doing that anymore!"

At least he had the decency to look sheepish about it. "Needs must, my friend. You are of no use in battle without your strength of arms."

With shaking hands, still slick with my own sticky plasma, I felt the tips of my horns. They were back and as pointy as ever. That was a relief.

"I'm not racist, but I'm starting to think that I really don't like Alvaren."

He let out a little snort as we parted. "It would seem that the feeling is mutual."

Mercy was waiting for us impatiently at the edge of the clearing, but her scowl soon faded once we were back to running again. The forest changed around us as the sickly white spackle of fungal polyps on the wood vanished, the clouds of spores and smoke faded into our past, and the full vibrancy of the bloody red blossoms came back with a vengeance.

Asher nearly tripped over Mercy when she abruptly stopped, and I had to fling myself to the side to avoid crushing the pair of them, crashing into a tree and loosing a cloud of silver-birds to pester Mercy all over again before they finally worked out her hair wasn't delicious.

With the last of them slapped away, she let out a sigh and flung herself down to the ground. After only a moment's hesitation, Asher crossed his legs and joined her. I just let myself slide down the side of the tree. "Let's never run anywhere ever again."

Asher's head dipped down. "Agreed."

Mercy flung herself back to stretch out across the fallen blossoms. "Running is bad."

Companionable silence stretched out for a long moment, then Mercy finally asked the question we'd all been avoiding until now. "Now what?"

Asher's head snapped up. "It was as the prophet foretold. Fate led us to the shard beneath the earth. The quest that has been bestowed upon us is truly our purpose in Amaranth."

Mercy made a little hissing noise at that line of thought, but I shrugged my shoulders. "There are too many coincidences for it to all be coincidences. He wanted us to get that shard, and we did—without even knowing that we were doing it."

"Oh, come on. Fate didn't take us down into that mine. Maulkin did. He wanted to help the Dvergar—not that they appreciated it all that much."

Asher cocked his head to one side. "And in so doing he inadvertently restored the lost Alvaren race to their true form and recovered their fragment of the Rusted Blade. Who can say what planted the seed of the idea within Maulkin's mind to begin with?"

"Oh, that was video games. For sure. You meet somebody, and they give you a quest. That's how these games work."

Mercy pointed and laughed, which was a bit rude. "See, he is just an idiot."

"A savant perhaps." Asher was in my corner, but I wasn't sure I liked where this was going. "Guiding us precisely where we needed to go to achieve our ultimate goals."

I mumbled. "Uh…"

Mercy sprung to her feet. "This guy thinks that this is a fricking video game, and you think he's the chosen one?"

"The beauty of a belief in fate is that everyone has a part to play in its grand tapestry."

"I still don't buy it." She was pacing. "The white prophet had to know about the shard under Khag Mhor. That must be why he built his little study out here."

"There was no mention of it in any of the scrolls or books that he left behind."

She stopped pacing for a moment. "Key words there are 'left behind'. He knew we were going to dig through that stuff, so he took all the good shit away."

Tempers seemed to be flaring a little. Asher looked as chill as always, but I'd seen him with that same expression on his face while we were in the process of being slaughtered. I piped up again. "Guys…"

They both ignored me. "The Prophet could not have known that we would encounter the Dvergar caravan as it was under attack, nor that we would even head in the direction of the Dvergar city."

"Of course he could have!" Oh good, Mercy was yelling now. "It doesn't take a rocket scientist like Maulkin to go up the nearest hill when you're lost."

That one stung a bit. So I put in my own little jab before I remembered I wanted everyone to calm down. "You didn't think of it."

"I was a bit pre-occupied with the whole reincarnation and giant monsters thing at the time. It kind of destroyed my whole understanding of reality." Mercy snarled at me. "Excuse me if I didn't jump right in with genius suggestions like 'let's climb a hill.'"

Asher caught her attention again, and I didn't envy him. "You believe that our actions were entirely predictable? Even if it was somehow inevitable that we would come across the hidden Dvergar city beneath the surface of the earth, what were the odds that we would offer them our services? What were the odds that we would assist them instead of pursuing our own agendas?"

"Oh, come on. Anyone with a heart would have looked at those sad-sack Dvergar on their last legs and volunteered to help."

"I would not have." Asher was still sitting, but he was stock still. "Were it not for Maulkin's intervention. I was of the opinion that it was a distraction from our greater cause of seeking the shards."

There was no way this was going to end well. "Guys, stop."

"So you're heartless. Big surprise."

"I simply believe that saving the entire world is of more importance than assisting every traveling merchant that we encounter. I do not believe this statement to be immoral." Asher's tail was twitching behind him. This was the most annoyed he'd ever looked. "If Amaranth is lost, then so too are the lives of all who dwell upon it."

"You're telling me you could have looked those Dvergar in the eyes and said no?"

"I would not have put myself in the position of looking them in the eyes, so to speak. I would not have intervened to begin with. I would have allowed the svart and Dvergar to clash, then cleared up any survivors when the svart were victorious."

Mercy spat on the ground. "Gods, you really are cold-blooded."

Asher rose to his feet. "I am not certain, but I believe that was another racial slur."

"Guys, stop!" I didn't mean to yell. Honestly, I didn't. But apparently, a roaring faun was enough to grab everyone's attention. "It doesn't matter if it is fate or luck or anything else. We've got the shard, and that means that the whole world is going to be gunning for us. We need to work out what we are going to do next."

That gave them enough food for thought that they actually stopped shouting at each other. Mercy slumped back down to the ground, and I relaxed a fraction, leaning back on my tree.

Asher spoke softly. I got the impression that he wasn't very proud of himself for losing his temper. "The next step in our journey is obvious. We must pursue the remaining shards with all haste."

"Funny"—Mercy snorted—"I was going to say we should toss it in the sea and hope that everyone forgets we exist."

Asher cocked his head at her. Quizzical. "Now who is seeking to pursue the immoral path?"

"Look, I don't know if you've noticed, but just one of those Alvaren foot-soldiers can bat us around like a cat with a mouse. We are seriously out of our depth here." Mercy leaned back until she was lying on the bed of blossoms again, trying to calm herself down. "All that is going to happen is somebody bigger and tougher than us is going to come along, stomp us, and take the shard to do... whatever the hell they want with it. Maybe if we lose it for a few years while we do other stuff and build up our strength then we might have a chance at holding onto it."

There was some good logic to what she was saying, but also, screw that. "So you want to quit now that we're winning?"

She looked almost sad when she turned to face me. "In what world are we winning?"

"We've got a shard, and we made it out without dying. Sure we didn't kick every ass on our way out the door, but we still made it. This is a win."

Her jaw made a little clicking noise. That wasn't good. She was obviously trying to hold it back, but it still came out a shout, "I nearly died!"

"Nearly doesn't count." I shrugged. "I've died for real. Twice already! Who gives a damn. We got the shard."

If she kept rolling her eyes like that, eventually they were going to fall right out of her head. "Yeah, for ten minutes until you die again."

I grunted. "Hey!"

Asher intervened once more. "Perhaps not."

"Oh yeah, maybe Mister Fight Everything That Moves isn't going to end up running into something tougher than his thick head."

He bowed his head to her. "Apologies, I have not made myself clear. There can be no question that Maulkin will almost inevitably lead to his own death through mismatched combat..."

Ouch. "Hey!"

"... but while the two of you have been learning more about the world around us, I have turned my attention inwards towards the Pillars of Divinity and the powers that they can provide us. Within the domain of Aether, there is an ability that allows us to bind a physical object to our spirit. A soul bond, so that when our physical forms are destroyed and fade from this world, a single object in our possession remains in our possession, to travel through the realm of the dead and be reborn along with us."

My mouth was hanging open, so I closed it carefully before asking, "For real?"

"I would suggest that the next time one of us has accumulated enough glory to..."

"I've got it!"

A quick glance told me I had eight hundred and fifty-five experience to spend. We'd been in such a rush that I'd never even had a chance to look at them. I hadn't checked my character sheet either. I had 43 Potency now. That was awesome.

Turning my attention towards the Pillars of Divinity, I immediately dumped all my accumulated glory into the Pillar of Aether. It lit up just like the others had in the big circle in the darkness— although on the opposite side to all of my more physical focused abilities so far.

Once it had crystallized, I hopped right over to skills and narrowed my search down to the divine ones that my new pillar offered me.

Aether Tier 1: Abjure Spirit
  Forces an unanchored spirit to depart from an area.
Aether Tier 1: Astral Projection
  Slips your spirit loose of the physical form to travel over great distances and observe.
Aether Tier 1: Soul Bond
  Forms a permanent bond with a physical object, so that even in death you cannot be parted.
Aether Tier 1: Soul Stone
  Binds an unanchored spirit within a physical object.
Aether Passive: Psychometry

I was only meant to be picking up Soul Bond, but I had to admit that the rest of them sounded kind of awesome too. If I was meant to be a part of Chernghast's little death cult thing, all this spooky scary skeleton stuff seemed like it would be a good fit.

At first, I nearly selected Soul Stone because I'm such a genius that if two separate things have the word soul in them, I mix them up. Soul Stone did look pretty cool. It let me put a disembodied spirit into a physical object to stop it from wandering off, but that didn't really help me with my current situation.

Soul Bond came first, so I didn't get any more wires crossed later. I felt the weird tickle of experience draining and knowledge bubbling into my brain. At a glance, it seemed to do exactly what Asher had said, so that was all good.

Psychometry sounded like a prog-rock band to me, so I had to look into it to discover that it was some sort of touch-based psychic magic thingy, where any spirits with an attachment to an object I was touching could talk to me. Great. Ghosts. Just what I needed.

I dallied for a minute on the list, considering hopping over to Ascension and grabbing another one of those tasty, tasty Surge powers, but then I felt a firm slap around my head and snapped back to reality.

Mercy was yelling at me. "…many times do I have to tell you to stop doing that in the middle of a conversation!"

"Sorry!"

Asher was standing over me too, looking concerned. "I must admit that it is rather rude to abandon your body in the middle of a—"

I hopped up and pulled out the shard. "I said I was sorry! But look, I got Soul Bond!"

Mercy's frown deepened. "How did you Tier Up before the rest of us?"

I grinned down at her. "Maximum effort."

"This world does seem to reward direct conflict more than strategic approaches." Asher sighed.

"Look that doesn't matter right now, what matters is…"

I focused on the shard in my hand and concentrated on *Soul Bond*. Immediately, the whole world darkened and slowed around me like it did when I was using *Artifice*.

Chernghast's awful nails-on-a-chalkboard voice scraped along the inside of my skull. *"This is a permanent decision, with irreversible consequences. Are you certain you wish to do this?"*

Guess that made sense, if you only got to bond one item per Tier of *Aether*. "Yes."

The bond formed like a trap snapping shut. Suddenly, I could feel the shard in my hand, not as an object I was touching, but as a part of my body. As a part of myself. I was this rusty lump of metal, and it was me.

In itself, that would have been a weird and unpleasant experience, but what came next blew it out of the water. Every one of my Pillars of Divinity cracked.

It wasn't as dramatic as when I'd pushed *Artifice* too far, but something had definitely gone wrong. When I turned my attention inwards,

I could see the moonlight was dimmed within them, tainted with tiny fracture lines of pure darkness. "Oh, what the hell?"

When I snapped back to reality, I could still see them like I'd been staring at the sun, shadows dancing from the center of my vision to the periphery. I could feel the darkness too, like a chill inside me that no amount of heat could ever clear.

Mercy jumped back from me. "Oh, what the hell!?"

"What?"

Asher took a step back from me too. "My friend, your appearance just changed."

I grumbled. "Well, I haven't exactly got a mirror. You want to be a bit more specific?"

They crept a little closer. "I can kind of see your veins. But they look sort of, black?"

Looking down at my arms and particularly my wrists, I could see what she meant. Beneath the dull grey of my skin, all of the visible veins that my pumped-up muscles had given me definitely looked darker now. "Okay...that is weird."

Asher was all up in my face. "The color of your eyes has also changed. They are no longer shining so brightly."

"Yeah, my pillars got a bit dimmer too. Maybe that is just a soul bond thing?"

"Perhaps it is a weakening of the soul as it is spread thinner." Asher was peering and prodding at me like I was his science project and I'd just gone bloop. "We have no means to test this hypothesis."

I gently pushed the pair of them away. "Anyway, the shard isn't going anywhere, so what is step two of the plan?"

Mercy didn't even seem to realize that she'd lost the argument until she opened and shut her mouth a few times. Eventually, she grumbled out, "I still say we head for the coast."

"You really want to see me in a bikini that bad?"

She ignored me. Wisely. "From what the Dvergar were saying, inland there is nothing but warlords and monsters for miles and miles in every direction."

Asher acquiesced all too easily. "It would be tactically advantageous to have at least one direction we cannot be attacked from."

"Oh, come on." I grinned. "This place has got to have sea monsters."

Mercy shrugged. "I'll take sea monsters over Alvaren any day."

"So there is nothing but crap inland. What's at the beach?"

"The Dvergar were kind of cagey about that. From what I could piece together, I think they used to trade with ships somewhere along the coast, or there was a settlement somewhere. Maybe a fishing village? I don't know. The khag hadn't run anything out that way in a while, but that might have just been because the mine dried up and they had nothing to sell."

I clambered to my feet and stretched. Funny how sitting still for a few minutes let all your aches and pains catch up to you like you'd been outrunning them. "Alright. Beach episode. Let's do it."

Mercy knew which way to go. I had no idea how she knew which way to go, but she did. In all the fighting and running and giant mushroom attacks, I had completely lost track of where we were in the forest, yet somehow she had the map fixed right in her head. Either that or she was leading us all in circles, and we were too dumb to know the difference.

In the quiet of the forest, we sometimes heard the rapid beating of great wings overhead. Travel had become gentler without Alvaren attacks, sprinting for our lives, or giant mushroom monsters—which *Bestiary* now informed me were called Myconormorians. That was a mouthful. I was going to go ahead and keep calling them giant mushroom dudes.

Where I felt the tickling presence of the mushroom's spores trying to take root, I batted them off, but, for the most part, the spores seemed to have been burned away or sweated off during our great escape. In a few places on my armor, I could see little mushrooms starting to spring up, but at this point, I figured I'd just let them. They saved us from the Alvaren, I was happy to give them a free ride.

As the day rolled on, the red glow of the trees above us began to dim as the sun headed down. As well as keeping our ears open for any sign of the Alvaren or the chungus fungus, we'd been listening for any more bellowed orders from Queen Briar, but it seemed like she'd finally switched her magic megaphone to airplane mode.

We didn't rest often, but we didn't need to. Stamina did not seem to be an issue for Eternals. I guess that was a side effect of the whole immortality thing. It also explained where all the other Eternals had gone—giant millennia-long orgy in a cave. Or at least that was what I was betting on. Most of the time we stopped so that Mercy could get her bearings or because we'd heard a lot of gryphon activity overhead. Long silent pauses with nothing to do but think.

During one of the pauses without the threat of bloody death descending on us from above, I hauled a big slab of stone up out of a dried-out riverbed and cobbled together a new sword with Artifice. The going was definitely tougher. Stuff that had felt intuitive before, I now had to really think about. Maybe it was the crappy materials, but it felt a lot more like it had more to do with whatever had gone wrong with my pillars interfering in the smooth flow of work. The end result may not have been as sharp as the metal sword I had to abandon, but anything that survived being whacked with a big slab of rock probably deserved the chance to take a swing at me.

Of course, most of the traipsing through the woods was long periods of quiet with nothing to do but think too. I kept on going around in circles about what to do with the five hundred and fifty-five experience that I had leftover.

Celerity boost still wasn't going to put me on the same level as the

Alvaren, and since we were hauling ass away from the Alvaren at the moment, I didn't even know if it was worth planning around fighting them again any time soon.

There were swathes of regular skills that it would probably be a good idea to invest in, but all the shiny new divine ones kept on calling to me. What kind of demigod did I want to be? A meathead who smacks things with a sword really good? A blacksmith for all my buddies? A spooky spirit wrangler? There were so many options, and the decisions I made would be with me for all of eternity.

In the end, I decided not to make a decision. I had no intention of dying any time soon, so that meant that the float of experience could just come along with me until we ran into some problem that needed solving, and I needed a new skill for it. Problem solved by ignoring it.

CHAPTER 24

We broke out from under the trees long after darkness had fallen, and we kept our heads down. The stars hung bright in the sky above us, but my patron moon was nowhere to be seen—which was probably good news since it meant spotting us sprinting across the grasslands was probably harder for all the Alvaren in the big floating, glowing city that still hung in the air over the collapsed mountain.

After the stroll through the forest, it almost felt good to run again now that we were out in the open. Though we kept glancing at the sky, even if there were any gryphons overhead we wouldn't be able to spot them. At best we might see the stars blink out for a moment before catching a face full of bird-cat. If they were still circling up there we couldn't see them or hear them, so the best we could do was ostrich our way along, pretending that they weren't there. If they were. Which they might have been. Or not. We didn't know. It was pretty stressful.

So we ran through the night, crossing more of the sparse grassland that seemed to be all this bit of Amaranth had to offer—more sparse grassland than I would have wanted to see in my lifetime. Sometimes there was a rock. Sometimes there was a rock that looked a bit like it might have been a building once, but then it turned out to just be another rock. It was boring. Not everything is giant monsters and bitching underground cities. Sometimes maps have empty patches, and we were crossing one.

The light of the Alvaren castle in the sky faded as we went until finally, it dipped under the horizon, and I started to feel vaguely safe again. Maybe safe was too strong a word. I didn't feel like I had a whole city of deranged, murderous prehistoric murder ninja-wizards staring directly at the back of my head anymore. That was it. That was the feeling.

By the time that the sun rose ahead of us, we could smell salt on the air, and the smooth, rolling dales we were used to had gotten lumpy. The hills as we came towards the coast weren't as big as the minor mountain that the Dvergar had been living under, but they were big enough that we couldn't see as far as the horizon anymore. I kind of missed it.

When I crested the next hill, Mercy and Asher were just standing there staring. It didn't take a genius to work out why. The ocean spread out before us, glowing golden in the rising sun. "Oh pretty."

We all just stood there for a while, watching the sunrise. It probably wasn't the first time that nothing was actively trying to murder us since we first arrived on Amaranth, but it certainly felt that way.

I put an arm around Mercy and Asher's shoulders and gave them a squeeze. "This is the life."

Mercy sighed, "Shut up," but she leaned against me all the same.

As the sun broke free of the horizon and blue began to fill in where the light had been, things became a lot more visible. Asher pointed and said, "What is that?"

There was some sort of structure out in the sea. It was visible from where we stood but right on the edge of the horizon. A great sun-bleached white pillar platform covered up to its rims on all sides with a patina of seaweed, and above the stone, a ring. It looked like gold in the morning light, but it could have been made just as easily from silver or anything else that was super shiny.

Mercy nodded. "Big floating ring."

"Yup." I nodded too. "Big floating ring."

Asher let out a huff. "It is emanating a low level of magical energy. Inert but still present."

"The big floating ring is magic?"

"No. Really?" Mercy added, completely deadpan.

"While your droll commentary remains as hilarious as always, this…ring could provide us with the guidance that we require. We have not encountered any mindless creatures capable of magic as of yet, so the presence of such a thing would seem to indicate civilization of some sort."

Mercy shrugged. "Or it has been sitting there for thousands of years doing nothing but float."

"Even if that were so, these constructions must have borne the test of time unflinching. It seems likely to me that anything constructed by the same hand would still stand and that such a place would soon become inhabited once more."

You had to give that to him. "It is free real estate."

Mercy groaned as I set off down the other side of the hill. "So which way, left or right?"

Asher held up his clawed hands and fell silent. His fingers twitched, as if he was plucking unseen strings or wiggling them to look like he was doing magic. "I believe, left. The flow of magic through the ring extends in both directions, but I believe that to our right, it flows farther from the coast towards parts unknown."

"Left," Mercy grumbled all the way down the hill. "All you had to say was left."

"And all that you had to do was attune yourself to the fundamental powers of creation rather than become marginally competent at shooting pointy sticks at things, yet here we both are."

The shade may have been cast her way, but even Mercy laughed at that one.

Scabby grass gave way to sand, and soon the hills became dunes as we cut to the left while following along the curve of the coast. Eventually, we slid down to the beach—where nobody appreciated my awesome joke about crabs keeping their money in sandbanks—and kept plodding on.

There was no sign of another giant floating ring anywhere, and I was starting to get a bit dubious about the whole mystical energies thing that Asher kept feeding us until we rounded a dune and saw the first sign of human civilization since we landed on the planet.

Picture the oldest, most pimped out gothic church you have ever seen, with nine million gargoyles and big pointy roofs and bell towers and all that jazz. Then imagine it was made out of white stone and covered in more ivy than you could shake a big hedge-trimmer at and that instead of building straight up, it had sprawled out into a courtyard and a few outbuildings and…okay, so not so much like a church except for all the gargoyles and roofs, but still, very cool-looking.

What it was missing was any giant floating rings. "Uh, are we sure this is the right place?"

"It is brimming with arcane energy, and it appears to have been constructed from the same material as the pillar in the sea."

"Yeah, but"—I pointed—"no ring."

"We do not know the purpose of the ring, as of yet. Nor of this building. There are a multitude of reasons why this place may not require one."

"Or it fell in the sea," Mercy quipped.

There was an old trail leading up from the beach onto more of that scrubby grassland that we knew and loved so well. We followed its meandering path around the dunes and up to the outer walls of the mystery buildings. The smooth stone of the wall had been overrun with creepers, but the opening where the gate used to hang was still clear enough for us to move inside—which we almost did before I spotted the flooring situation in the courtyard. "Hold up."

Mercy snapped around, bow at the ready. "What?"

"Look!"

They looked, and they saw what I was worried about. Underneath the scattered leaves and the accumulated sand that had blown up and in, there was no denying that there was a mosaic on that floor, and if there was one thing we knew about mosaics in Amaranth, it was that they were all traps.

With all the accumulated crap of the years, we couldn't make out what the design on the thing was, though it looked very big and dramatic—mostly monochrome to go with the white walls, but with the odd silvery tile here and there that shone in the sunlight. There were a couple of outbuildings that were now open to the elements after their doors had rotted away, and from our viewpoint on the periphery, it looked like all the accumulated crap in the plaza was just a prelude to the giant mounds of sand and rot inside those buildings.

At least the other side of the courtyard looked a bit more promising. From the bigger, fancier main building, somebody had extended out the roof to make a little porch, protecting it from the worst of the elements, and some of the stained-glass windows over there were still in one piece, even if they did look a lot thicker at the bottom than at the top.

"I'm just going to go for it, guys. There is no other way in. I'm just going to do it."

Mercy grabbed at my arm. "You can't, it's suicide."

"Maybe it is the first ever un-trapped mosaic. Maybe I'll get lucky. If not. Don't worry. I will find you both again, no matter how long it takes."

I took the leap of faith and stepped out onto the plaza. The other two flinched back, just waiting for me to explode into ludicrous gibs of bloody meat, but it didn't happen. I took another step, then another. I strode out onto the mosaic, a belly laugh rumbling up out of me. "The trap must have broken down from being here too long!"

The silvered tiles leapt up into the air. "Oh crap!"

With a buzz like a swarm of bees they flew at me, and even moving as fast as I could, there was no way I could draw my sword and swing it around to block them before they hit. I was doomed. Closing my eyes, I braced myself to be minced.

I stood like that for a long moment, waiting for the pain to come, but it didn't. I opened my eyes.

Standing before me, there was a man made of mirror. When he moved, the gaps between the shards of silver showed, but the rest of the time, he was a perfect representation of a robed human being with long flowing hair and a little goatee beard. "I bid you welcome, my dear students of the arts arcane, to Witchglass Overlook, the premier school of magic in all of Amaranth."

Mercy and Asher crept closer. The mirror-man was still standing there, perfectly still, like he had stalled out. I reached out and gave him a prod, setting the tiny plates that made up his torso rippling. "Uh, guys. I think we got the answering machine."

Asher was beyond enthused, of course, not that you could really tell from his tone. He was practically dancing around the thing, with his hands up to feel the magic vibes or whatever. "Fascinating. Truly fascinating."

That would keep him happy for the foreseeable future, so I turned my attention to Mercy. "Okay, so we are in. It is wizard school. You know what that means?"

"We have to put on a hat that assigns us to a gang based on random personality traits?" She smirked.

"It means books!"

"You…don't really strike me as a book person."

I clasped a hand to my chest, wounded. "Okay, first off. Rude. Second, the books are going to tell us where to find the other fragments of the Rusted Blade. Wizards always know everything about everything. There is no way that they didn't write down where the most important magic items on the planet are."

Her mouth was hanging open a bit. "That might actually work."

"Why are you always surprised when I have good ideas?" I crossed my arms over my chest.

"Really? You really want me to answer that? Again? Really?"

I sighed. "Okay, so where is the library?"

We all jumped when the mirror-man started talking again. "The Library of Witchglass Overlook is located beneath your very feet. Seek it out, searchers for wisdom, by navigating the grand hall and then down through the spiral staircase to the rooms of trials."

Asher clasped his little hands together in excitement. "My goodness, what a fantastic magical construct, capable of responding to verbal commands long after its caster was—"

"It's a robo-tour-guide." Mercy poked it in the goatee, setting the face rippling all over again. "We get it."

Asher's mouth snapped shut, and if looks could kill, there would be bits of Mercy scattered from here to Khag Mhor. Got to love a tetchy lizard man.

With no time to lose, and another argument to avoid, I headed off for the main doors of the main building, which honestly, probably should have been my first port of call anyway. The wood of the doors had all rotted away, but the filigree was still standing there, like the outline of the ghost of the door, all the silver gone green in the sea air. Beyond it, there was only darkness.

I drew my stone sword and gave it an experimental swing, knocking what was left of the silver away in a sparkly cloud of crumbling dust. Guess they didn't bother to magic the doors. That boded well for my chances of getting through the rest of them.

I stepped through into the grand hall, then stopped and went back outside, nearly crashing into Mercy and Asher as they continued their bitching and moaning at each other. I took a long hard look at the outside of the building, then looked in through the door again. Out then in. Out then in. Mercy caught me on my third pass. "What is it?"

"This is bull."

They stepped into the hall with me this time and gawked as it opened out before them. It was three times the size of the building outside, with vaulted ceilings to match the sort-of-gothic architecture and stained-glass windows depicting some guy with a goatee doing all sorts of magical shenanigans. Apparently, goatee guy thought a lot of himself. We couldn't even see all the way to the far side of the hall, and by my calculations, it should have been off over the edge of the damn cliff that this place was standing on.

Down on top of the plain flagstones that were blessedly not a mosaic, there were tables lit up with candelabras and still glistening with food. Delicious-looking food. My mouth started to water as the smell of it hit me. I hadn't eaten properly since we arrived, and while it didn't seem like I needed to, the urge was still there.

There was a whole roast chicken sitting on the closest table with my name on it. The skin looked so crispy I could already feel it crunching between my teeth. "Oooh. Come to daddy."

Mercy snorted. "Should we leave you two alone?"

"You really should." I hefted the whole chicken by its leg and grinned. "This is going to get weird. I'm going to make it weird."

I could feel the steam rising from the skin of the chicken on my lips before it was unjustly yanked away from me. Asher had slapped it out of my hand. "Rude."

Grabbing a ham-hock, I went hog-wild on that instead. Or at least I would have if Asher hadn't slapped that away too. "Dude!"

There was a big rack of ribs on the next table across, so I made a dive for it face first, sending the silverware and side dishes flying. My teeth were just about to close on it when Asher's voice finally cut through the meat-madness. "Wait!"

I stopped, my teeth an inch away from the succulent surface of the beef. Maybe I shouldn't have eaten that one, what with my horns and whatnot. Maybe it was my cousin or something. At this point, I was too hungry to care. "Maulkin, I beg you, use your mind before your actions lead you to folly. How could food have persisted here all of this time? Why have none of the local predators picked this feast clean? There is something wrong here, my friend. Something terribly wrong."

"But...beef."

"Hold on now," Mercy said. "He might be on to something here."

I was practically begging now. "But beef!"

Asher crept forward and edged the plate away from me as I whimpered. "I promise you, my friend, at the next viable opportunity, I shall furnish you with a meal that is neither an illusion nor a curse."

My head fell forward onto the table, horns digging into the lacquered wood. "Ugh."

"Come on, beefy"—Mercy gave me a prod as she passed—"we've got a wizard school to explore."

"Will there be snacks?"

"Knowing our luck, there will be traps and monsters."

That perked me up. I put the palms of my hands down on the table to push myself up to standing, and abruptly, the hall filled with ghosts.

A glimpse of a forest. Tools. Carvings. Hundreds upon hundreds of robed figures flitting through, too fast for me to see any features. Chatter in a dozen different languages, too fleeting to follow a word. Flashes of light. Spells being cast. Colors all dampened to milky white whisps. The man with the goatee, eyes glowing, standing in the empty hall, casting one last spell. Deathly silence. Flitting shadows that might have been birds. A monster, like some great crocodile on two legs striding in. It took a bite out of the food, and its face melted off in a shower of meaty gobs. Dvergar came and met the same fate. A whole posse of human settlers taking shelter from a storm, the first humans I'd seen on Amaranth, melted away to nothing when they decided to trust in the bounty. More Dvergar. More silence. More memories all piled up. The long empty stretch of eternity.

I jerked my hands off the surface of the table with a gasp. *Psychometry*. I'd forgotten all about it. It was a fair guess that I'd been making some weird noises from the way that the other two were staring at me. "So…I got a new ability—a freebie with Soul Bond. A history-sensing kind of thing. Anyway, you were totally right. Nasty curse on all the food. Acid trap stuff. Thanks for slapping my lunch."

Asher seemed pleased that my very brief irritation with him had passed. Maybe he was a bit sensitive with Mercy ragging on him all the time. "You would have done the same for me, were I caught out in such a manner."

"You know what, you're right." I grinned down at him. "I would have. I would have slapped the crap out of your snacks."

Psychometry felt like it was going to be a problem. I couldn't touch anything without seeing its history? That was going to screw me up real bad if it did ever get to be snack time again. Eating pork, fine by me. Eating an adorable little piglet looking up at me with puppy-dog eyes? Piggy-dog eyes? Anyway, I needed gloves—preferably gloves that weren't made out of either puppies, piggies, or eyes.

We made our way across the great hall, and the distant shimmer of sunlight coming in through the doorway faded away until only candlelight and the glow of our eyes was left to guide us. Despite mine being markedly dimmer, I didn't seem to be having any problems seeing just as well as the other two. Maybe their eyesight just wasn't as good as a Faun's? It took us considerably longer than it should have to hike to the far end of the room, and everywhere that I looked, delectable dishes designed to delight were there, tempting me. When we passed the dessert buffet, I nearly broke down and wept until I remembered the dissolving gator dude.

The back wall of the grand hall was in sight now, but even as we kept trudging on, it felt like it kept on moving farther away like it was a bad dream or somebody was screwing with the focus on the camera in a Hitchcock kind of way. "Okay, so this is some more wizard stuff, right?"

Asher cocked his head to the side. "The ambient magic of this place has left me tragically bereft of any more specific sensory information, but I believe it is fair to say so."

Mercy fired off an arrow at the rear wall, and we stood there and watched as it flew and flew and flew without ever reaching anything. "Huh."

When we traipsed a little farther, it was there, hanging in the air above us, but the far wall was no closer. Again, Mercy said, "Huh."

I clapped Asher on the shoulders. "Okay, buddy, this is all you. You are the magic wiz in this team. You are the one who can zap stuff. You are the brains of the outfit. You can solve it."

Asher looked genuinely uncomfortable. "The brains would probably be yourself, as a matter of fact. Your plans are the ones that we most often actively pursue."

"Oh gods, he is the brains? I thought I was the brains."

"Guys, guys. We're all the brains. Or maybe none of us. We're all good at our own things. I'm good at swording. Mercy is good at bows. And, Asher, you're good at magic. So since this is magic..."

He sighed. "I shall make an attempt."

Mercy and I shuffled back a bit as he began casting a spell, coils of crackling electricity gathering all around him, twisting and reshaping according to his will. It was pretty impressive-looking.

"Bet it doesn't work."

I glanced down at Mercy where she was leaning on the side of my arm like I was a wall, picking her nails with an arrowhead. "I'm not going to bet against my own team."

"I'm just saying, this doesn't feel like the kind of problem you can solve by throwing a fireball at it, and that is the only magic your boy there seems to do."

"He does lightning. And healing. And he breathes fire now. Plus the gravity stuff from being an Eternal."

She flicked a little mushroom sprout out from under her nail. "Uh-huh. It still isn't going to work."

Asher unleashed the lightning at the back wall, and while it traveled just like Mercy's arrow for far longer than it should have, eventually it did seem to make contact with something solid. There was a sound like a giant bubble popping, and abruptly we were nose to nose with the sooty little mark he'd left on the rear wall.

"It would appear that the addition of my spell destabilized the workings of the spatial folding."

I pretended that a word of that made sense. "Cool. Cool. So is it going to stay popped or?"

"It seems unlikely that it would have stood the test of time if a little alien magical energy could permanently disable it."

The air around us rippled and popped. Like there were bubbles rising to the surface from somewhere. Mercy's head looked like it was swollen to twice its usual size when she looked back at us through one of the bubbles. "So...run?"

"Indeed."

We took off for the spiral staircase that we'd been promised, and we weren't let down. It wasn't as oversized as the hall had been, but it was still wide enough for the three of us to run down it side by side, feet skidding over the smooth white stone and hands scrabbling at what was left of the silverwork banisters for balance, even though they had a nasty tendency to crumble and twist beneath your fingers.

Halfway down the stairs, we realized that Mercy's head was back to its usual size, and the bubbling of the air had stopped, so we all skidded to a more reasonable pace for the rest of the turn. Down at the bottom, we were confronted with pitch black beyond the open doorway to the next floor.

Once again, it fell to me to do the stupid and/or brave thing and go wandering through. At once, the room began to light up. Huge braziers that must have been sitting empty since the place was abandoned suddenly sprang to life. Green-blue flames flared up out of them, bathing the whole place in their eerie glow. This room was nowhere near to being the size of the hall above us, but it was still pretty substantial.

Along one wall there was a row of dummies carved from the same pale stone as the rest of the building, the rotten tatters of clothes and armor long fallen away from them, but the sooty marks where they'd been spell-struck were still abundantly obvious to even my untrained eye.

Along another wall the sagging remains of a great storage cabinet ran the length of the wall, rotten wood held together by filigree, and the glass panels sloughed down into lumps along the countertop. Whatever had been inside before the place was abandoned had long since degraded or dissolved, but here and there was a hint at the weird and wonderful stock it once held. In one corner, dazzling clusters of crystal were growing up the side of the cabinet and beyond to crawl along the wall, all set shimmering in rainbow colors by the brazier light. On another shelf, a solid cylinder of something too coated in dust to discern still stood at a jaunty angle as the shelf below it had tilted to one side.

I drew my sword and crept into the room. At the far wall, there were a half dozen doors, leading who knew where. In the floor, the flagstones gave way in places to holes that might have been fire-pits but were now filled with nothing but rust and dust. There were other channels carved into the floor, crisscrossed with more of the surviving filigree, deep enough to cause a problem if you weren't paying attention and stepped right into one. Which, of course, I immediately did with a hideous creak of metal. Asher jumped on the spot, but Mercy was too busy digging into the potential bounty of the cabinet to bother.

She'd dislodged the filigree and was now tossing aside filthy scraps of rotten cloth and leather along with the odd marble or glass instrument. The marbles bounced across the floor to fall into one of the other channels, and the glass merely shattered. At last, she came to the dusty cylinder and gave it a wipe with her sleeve, revealing the glass beneath and the brain within. "Ew."

"Wizards, man." Laughter rumbled up from my belly. "They keep the weirdest stuff."

Which was about when the critter in the pit reared up and took a bite out of me.

CHAPTER 25

"Ow!"

It took me a while to work out what I was even looking at, but by the time that I did, *Bestiary* was already feeding me more details in that same dry academic drone it always gave me.

Akin to the ashen-waste dwelling dholes, the more aggressive Khorkhoi were ambush predators that relied on their ability to conceal themselves among silty substances to gain the element of surprise when first encountering prey. Their worm-like bodies typically take on the color of whatever materials they are using for concealment, but after a period of gorging when prey becomes available, and the subsequent swelling, the khorkhoi's natural blood-red coloration became more apparent.

None of which helped me with the four pincer-like hooks arrayed around the thing's mouth, or the fact that it was currently latched onto my thigh. "Argh! Kill it!"

Asher rolled his eyes. "Certainly, allow me a moment to simply incinerate it with one of my many terribly precise spells."

"Now hold on, Asher, don't you waste your energy. Let me shoot it with my janky broken bow and arrows. I'm sure I won't miss it many, many times and leave Maulkin full of holes."

The pincers gnashed at my thigh as I grabbed it by the tail and tried to haul it off. The skin beneath the ash was slimy and slick, and my hands slipped right off it. "Guys, it is eating me!"

Mercy sighed. "Maulkin, it is a bug. Just pull it off and stomp it."

"I'm..." I growled to a halt. "Fine!"

Snatching the sword from my back, I swung it with all the force

I could muster at this awkward angle into the khorkhoi on my leg.

The tail fell off, and the jaws that had only been clamping in place now went into chompy overdrive.

[414/710 Health]

"Ow."

[411/710 Health]

"Ow."

[409/710 Health]

"Ow!"

This time I didn't play it safe. I swung right for the bug-eyed head of the khorkhoi as hard as I could. Which was, of course, when it decided to let go.

"Oh, come on!"

The severed parts of the chompy little monster wriggled around on the flagstones for a bit, then stopped moving. I gave it a stomp for good measure—with the leg that didn't have a big bloody sword hole in it.

"Did you just hit yourself?"

I grumbled. "Would you rather I hit you?"

"Try it, beef boy."

I did not try it, despite my flaring temper. If there were any more worm-friends waiting in the ash pits, my prodding around with the tip of my sword did nothing to dislodge them. What I did find down among the ash was a whole load of rusted-out hunks of metal that probably started out life as cauldrons or something. I hauled them out with Artifice and remade my big rock sword as a big iron sword and dumped the hunk of stone on top of the khorkhoi's remains for good measure. That helped my mood immensely.

With nothing else to do, I wandered over to the doors and was about to haul one open when Asher let out a little yelp. "Wait."

I waited while he did his little wavy hand thing, feeling out the magic in the room. "I believe that this is another trap, curse, or illusion. Only one of these doors will take us onward, while the others may do us harm."

"So we've got a one in six chance of getting the library?"

"Three in six if we all try a different one." Mercy abandoned her search through the ruined cabinets. "That is fifty-fifty odds."

"It is my expert opinion that triggering multiple traps simultaneously may not be in our best interests." Asher's sarcasm was so dry you could have used it as kindling.

"Alright then, expert opinion, which door is the right one?"

He did more feeling around while Mercy mouthed, "Jazz hands," behind his back, and I tried not to laugh.

"I cannot say with any certainty which of these doors is correct. I assume that this was some sort of test for the students of the arcane, or perhaps a security measure to prevent anyone unfamiliar with the library from gaining access to the trove of knowledge that was secured here."

Great. More wizard nonsense. "Want me to go back up and ask the campus tour guide?"

"I cannot believe that the automated respondent would give away the secrets of the place so readily, and you would most likely be snared by the trap in the room above."

I groaned my frustration to the heavens and sat down heavily on the floor. "I'm no good at puzzles."

Mercy opened her mouth to make a crack about how dumb I was, then sat down and shut up. Guess she wasn't any good at puzzles either.

Asher continued pacing back and forth along the rear wall, examining each of the identical-looking doors in turn. Back and forth. Back and forth.

"Can't we just zap this one with lightning too?"

"It is my belief that direct interference with the doors will likely result in the triggering of whatever magic hangs ready here."

I groaned some more. I couldn't believe that my grand plan to find out where the hell we were meant to be going to find the shards could be derailed by some ancient book-burglar alarm. The same irritation that had been building up since I got chewed on by the khorkhoi boiled over, and I slammed my fist into the flagstones.

The room filled with ghosts. I was so startled that I snatched my hand back, and they all vanished again. More carefully this time, I laid my hand down on the flagstones. The ghosts of students past swarmed all around me, and the air filled up with the wispy ghosts of spells cast long ago and the chatter of excitable voices. It was too much. Too many people. Too much noise. All buzzing at once. Maybe *Psychometry* would be useful out in the wild places of the world, but where so many people had lived all it did was give me a headache as all the information tried to cram its way in at once. Individual ghosts were like blurs in the midst of all the others, impossible to discern. All I could really make out was the flow of them. Like a big abstract shape made out of all the people who'd been here before.

I blinked a couple of times trying to make sense of it all, then I saw what I was looking for. Over to the rear wall, the tides of ghosts that had been flowing everywhere narrowed down to a single channel. All heading into the second door from the left.

Pushing myself up off the floor, I headed for it. The ghosts of the once-bustling place vanished as I lost contact with the ground, but it wasn't like I could forget where I was headed. I crossed the room in a few strides and both Mercy and Asher had only just started screaming,

"Wait! Stop!" and all their other usual negative stuff when I reached for the door handle and swung it open.

The screaming cut off abruptly. "How did you…"

"You could have…"

"Of all the stupid things that you've done since we got here…."

I had no time to listen to the haters, so I stepped through into the library. The first place in all of Amaranth that didn't look like it had been set on fire or trampled over by giant monsters. Civilization.

There were lamps hanging from the ceiling giving out a lovely blue-green glow, and fur rugs, comfy chairs, and shelves as far as the eyes could see. Hundreds upon hundreds of shelves all stuffed to bursting with books. Asher literally gasped when he saw them all. He was going to be in little nerdy heaven. Even Mercy looked suitably impressed by it all.

I sank down onto one of the longer chairs and it groaned alarmingly, but by being ever so careful as I shuffled around and lay down, I managed to not collapse it. In prime napping position, I finally let myself relax and close my eyes. Mission accomplished.

Mercy kicked me. "How the hell did you do that?"

"Lucky guess?"

"Don't lie to me, beefy." She jabbed me with an arrow. "Don't ever lie to me."

"Oh, for the gods' sake. I used my new spirit touch thing to see which door people used to use. It isn't rocket science."

The latest prod was even more brutal than the last. "Why are you acting like this isn't a big deal? You can see the past!"

Begrudgingly, I opened my eyes. "And Asher can fart out black holes. We've got god powers now. Did you think they were all going to be small-fry stuff like making you new arrows out of thin air?"

That seemed to leave her speechless, but Asher was kind enough to let out a squeal of delight from the far side of the room that gave her an excuse to run off without admitting I was right. After that, I've got to admit things got a little bit hazy for a while. I was warm and comfortable. That old book smell was wafting through the place, we were making progress towards the next shard, and nobody was actively trying to kill me. I fell asleep with a big smile plastered on my face.

If I dreamed, I couldn't remember, but I was still pretty warm and content when I opened my eyes and saw a manic-looking Asher hanging over me with what I assume was a grin on his face. "We have learned so much, friend Maulkin. So very much."

Mercy was draped upside down on one of the smaller chairs, feet in the air and a book covering her face. Her snoring sounded kind of like a buzz-saw. It was kind of amazing that I'd slept through it for so long.

"Asher, did you sleep?"

"What need have we Eternals for sleep? And who among us could sleep in the face of such a cornucopia of wonders. Look here, a book on the sentient species of Amaranth. And here, a treatise on the workings of magic. I could spend the rest of my eternity here learning and not consider a moment of it wasted."

"Shame we've actually got to use that information to do things really."

"Ah yes, indeed. Quite a pitiable plight. Regardless, there is so much that I have learned, even though I have tried to restrict myself to pursuing information pertinent to our quest. I believe that I have tracked the provenance of several of them through historical accountings of the Revelation of Araphel."

"Awesome. What have you got?"

"The shard bequeathed to the wyrms is likely still in the possession of the Great Black Wyrm Tsangaanax, known also as the Twilight Betrayer and the Alvarsbane. While a great number of the wyrms allied themselves with Araphel during the revelation, mostly in opposition to their ancestral enemies, the Alvaren, Tsangaanax turned against him in the latter years of the war, providing vital intelligence to the mortal races before finally joining in the final decisive battles to drive the Voidgod's armies back."

From beneath her book, Mercy groaned, "Did we not already know this?"

"Ah, we knew the shard was passed to a wyrm, but now we have his name, and supplemental reading has confirmed to me that the lifespan of wyrms is such that the very same wyrm is still liable to hold it."

I sighed. "Okay, so we know the wyrm has one in his wyrm hole, wherever that is. We have the Alvaren one. The human one is at the Shattered Bastion, wherever that is. What about the rest?"

"The Dvergar shard appears to have passed into the hands of a smith-king by the name of Vidar Forgeborn who set off to found a kingdom somewhere in the frozen north beyond the ash wastes. Its guardianship seems to have been passed down his bloodline, though little information seems to have come south about it."

Mercy moaned, "Super helpful."

"The Faun shard was passed into the hands of an individual known as the… Well, I believe that the word translates into War Chief or Hunt Leader? It does not seem that Faun typically share their given names with outsiders, or rather, not a given name but an earned name—one bestowed upon them for some great feat of martial or hunting prowess. As a matter of fact, it is interesting that—"

I didn't slap him despite all of my instincts screaming at me to do so. "The shard! Asher."

"Ah yes. The chieftess did not feel that any of her replacements were suitable bearers for the shard, so it seems that she, uh, died with it. Carried it with her into the realm of the dead? There seems to be a translation issue. I imagine, and intently hope, that it simply means that there is a Faun burial mound somewhere where the shard has been entombed."

"Super specific." Mercy let the book fall off her face to land with a splat. "Good job. So helpful."

Asher let out a little huff of irritation. "The study of shard-lore appears to be a fringe interest in this world at best, more mythology than anything of substance. There seem to have been true believers circulating the stories that they had available but little in the way of active research or archiving. It was pure luck that we seem to have stumbled upon the trove of someone with such an active interest."

She tried to scoff and choked on her own spittle because she was upside down. "So even the dorks of fantasy land thought that this guy was a dork?"

"I believe that they considered him to be a scholar of great esteem, and a master of the arcane arts of such power and renown that when the time came to found a school for magic, it was to him that they turned." He pointed to the weathered oil painting upon the wall of the same long-haired and bearded man as in the auto-greeter. "The Archmage Talon."

He said it with so much of a dramatic pause that even Mercy had to respect it. She sat there in awed silence for a whole second before blurting, "Who?"

Maybe I laughed just a little bit, but I didn't mean to. Doesn't that count for something? Asher looked at me with betrayal in his eyes. "If you had been pursuing the actual research that was required of us, as I so desperately pleaded with you to do, then you would already be aware that the Archmage Talon was an Eternal. One who waged war upon Araphel and claimed the Eternal's shard in recompense for his efforts."

That was enough to finally get my attention. "Wait. So that shard was here too? Talon was here?"

"Indeed. Not only was he here, but it seems that he remained here for centuries after the downfall of Araphel. Here he gathered all knowledge of magic in the wake of the unanticipated annihilation of the Alvaren to preserve it against the passage of time and to ensure that it was available to all who sought it out. Dvergar, humans, and even Inyoka were welcomed here to study."

I found my voice dropping low. "Not faun though."

Asher looked uncomfortable for only a moment before saying, "I could not find any record of Faun that applied to attend."

"Bet nobody was too upset about it," I grumbled to myself.

Mercy rubbed her temples. "Guys, nobody cares about faun school attendance right now. The immortal wizard with the shard. Where is he?"

"Given that this was our most promising lead, this was where I directed most of my attention during my research. It is my belief that as the student population declined, our man Talon began to devote himself more and more to research before finally withdrawing entirely from public life to give his passions full focus."

Mercy was practically vibrating with irritation. "Yeah, but where?" I was starting to wonder if Asher was taking his time with every answer out of pure spite. If he was, it was pretty funny.

"Well, my friends, that is where things began to become more interesting from the standpoint of a researcher. Talon withdrew from public life with the intention of being left in peace, so most references to his private estate have been deliberately left out of the records here. However, I have found students' notes that refer to him traveling from his estate to lecture and then returning to his estate on the very same day."

"So it is somewhere nearby?" Mercy cocked an eyebrow. "That seems…weirdly convenient. This guy is some kind of expert on the shards, and he doesn't know anything about one on his own doorstep this whole time? They could be anywhere in the world, but they just so happen to be right here?"

"Perhaps we could account for it with the inevitability of our fated arrival at a later date, but alas no, I do not believe that the mage's keep is anywhere close to us." Asher sighed. "The same student accounts mention him bringing tropical fruits and exotic birds with him to their classes, sometimes for study but primarily to amuse. Rather than dwelling nearby, I believe that he had a means of traveling great distances swiftly through magic."

"Which leaves us with the entire world to search." Mercy flopped limp again. "Oh no, only the warm parts. Great."

Asher clapped his hands in delight. "Yes, of course, let us wander aimlessly because there could not have been any information on this frankly miraculous piece of arcana being performed for the first time in history in the library of a school of magic."

Mercy rotated herself until she was sitting upright and opened her mouth to snarl a reply. Then she closed it again. Then finally when it seemed she might actually burst, she mumbled, "You can be a real smug dick, you know that."

"With insights like that, I am amazed that you were not the one to find the extensive documentation on the Waystone Project."

Before the bickering could start again, I jumped in, "The big floaty ring thing?"

Asher's attention snapped back to me. He seemed to come alive when he was lecturing, like the cold fish of our little gang just needed a bit of reading time to get warmed up. "Indeed. A series of them were constructed with the intent of providing safe passage between the remaining bastions of civilization, while thwarting the movement of the monstrous species that overrun the world yet seem for the most part incapable of magic."

I grinned, rising up from my seat. Finally, some good news! "Wait, so we can just go through the magic rings and go anywhere?"

"Unfortunately, no." I sank back into my seat with a groan as Asher rambled on. "It seems that construction of additional pylons in the network was reliant upon agreements of co-operation between the various kingdoms that had sprung up in the aftermath of the Revelation and—"

"People acted like people and screwed it all up." I pouted. "Figures."

"There was no small number constructed, even if the more extensive network was not completed, and if we were to follow them along, it is likely we would encounter other bastions of civilization from the years following the Revelation. However, it does appear that by the end, the only one using the Waystones was our reclusive friend, Talon. The spell required to activate the Waystones seems to have been scrubbed from the records here quite thoroughly. It seems that Talon did not wish to face the possibility of visitation through magical means when he retired to solitude."

Mercy's scowl had not diminished in the time since I'd last looked her way. She'd be so much prettier if she'd just smiled. And I'd be full of so many arrows if I suggested it. "So all of this helps us how?"

"Quite simple, dear Mercy. All that is required of us is to follow the Waystones along their course, and we shall find our way to the reclusive Talon and the shard that he retains in his possession. An ally and the vital object that we require."

Mercy let out an exasperated grunt. "I don't know if you've noticed, but we can't fly. How are we meant to follow those floaty rings out to sea?"

"Well, I did wonder if perhaps Maulkin might provide us with that solution." He couldn't smile without lips, but he made an attempt. "Do you have any experience points left with which to purchase the Sailing skill?"

I grinned. "You know what? I just might."

For all that we had worried, Witchglass Overlook really wasn't all that imposing on the way out. The biggest challenge was convincing Asher to part with some of the books that he wanted to borrow so that whatever boat I built didn't immediately sink to the bottom of the ocean under the sheer weight of paper. As it was, he had me carrying so many of the damned things that even my Potency was strained to its limits.

We traipsed up the stairs, and I was fully expecting to have to make some mad dash across the ever-extending hall again, but as it turned out, the Overlook wanted us out again as quickly as possible. The distance between the front and back of the room felt like a few strides, even though a backward glance still showed it sticking out way over where the land should have stopped. I took back what I said about magic before, being able to shoot lightning out of my elbow wasn't worth all the weirdness it entailed.

The upper levels of the building, the halls of residence, and the classrooms remained unexplored. If it got to the end of the day without our boat being finished then maybe we'd go looking for beds, but right now, aside from the mountain of reading material I was laden with, I was feeling more energized than I had been since we landed on this rock.

We left Asher in the sunshine, curled up with what I have to assume was a good book from the fact he didn't even look up from it when we left, and headed down to the beach to see if there was enough driftwood to work with or if I'd need to go looking for a copse of trees to make into planks.

Down the rabbit trail we wandered, sun glinting off the big floaty ring and the shimmering sea. There was a little breeze in the air, like early autumn back home. I didn't want to jinx anything by saying I was content, but it was nice.

"I don't think you're stupid, you know."

I stopped in my tracks. "Huh?"

Mercy wasn't looking at me. She was very deliberately looking at the sand, hunting around for wood to build our boat. She was technically meant to be along to watch my back while I did Artifice stuff, but I appreciated the help. "You keep getting annoyed when I say you're dumb. You aren't dumb. You're sort of smart. Kind of."

"Thanks. You're not a bitch." I grinned at her when her head snapped around. "You're sort of nice. Kind of."

Her exasperated sigh was so familiar at this point that I could probably recognize it anywhere. Descending from a hiss to a huff. "I'm trying to apologize here."

"You think that is an apology? And you call me dumb?"

"You...f... Okay. Okay." Her knuckles were white on the handle of her bow, and I couldn't see the other side, but I'd bet good money it was a fist too. "I deserve most of that."

"Okay." I got back to work, slipping in and out of my body, and sending pulses of my will out through the sand to search for anything useful in my *Sphere of Influence*. There were a few hunks of wood down beneath the surface, some shells, and things too, rocks here and there, but nothing substantial enough to make it worth the effort of hauling up to the surface. Not yet anyway.

Mercy scuffed her heel in the sand. "So are we cool, or?"

For the god's sake. "We were cool until you kept making things weird and awkward."

"Okay. Uh cool."

I loomed over her and practically growled. "Cool."

Along we went with me pulsing all the way, my body going limp and vacant as I jumped out of it then hopped back in again before it took the next step and stumbled. My face was slack and empty when I was out of my body, looking like the face I'd see when my computer back home powered down and I was left staring into my own reflection on black. "I am pretty stupid."

She almost stumbled. "Hey, what? Is this because I said... No, you're not. You're not stupid."

"No, I really am. It is okay. It's better. I'm good with being stupid. Stupid is fun. Smart people are miserable. Just look at Asher. So smart he killed himself."

"So smart I'm going to kill him too," she muttered under her breath. "But even if you aren't, uh, traditionally smart, I shouldn't be ragging on you for it."

"Hey, it isn't your fault. What other bad things could you say about me? Nothing." I grinned. "I'm a half-ton of sex on legs."

She broke down laughing. Real laughter for the first time in days. It was like music to my ears. Really wheezy music. Bagpipes?

After that we settled back into companionable silence, for the most part, finally giving up on driftwood and heading back over the dunes to scout out some promising trees. I didn't really fancy bringing down any of the red-blossom trees—I had a nasty suspicion that they were going to start bleeding or screaming if I cut into them, and I just didn't have the bandwidth for that today. Screaming shrubberies would have to keep until tomorrow.

There was a bristle of dead trees out among the dead grass on the far side of the Overlook, dried out and salt-crusted from their time by the seaside. I didn't even have to chop them down really, just pull on them and they'd pop right out of the ground.

With my new sailing skill, the shapes of ships were floating around in the soup of my brain now, and with the careful application of Rough Hewn Architecture, I was fairly sure I could get us something rustic-looking but waterproof to work with.

Getting the wood down to the beach was a little bit trickier but not much. Using the dead grass and Artifice, I was able to spin out some ropes, which I figured would come in handy later in the boat building anyway, and Mercy spent a good half an hour giggling while she tied the various logs onto me like I was a dog on a leash.

It took some straining and puffing to get all the wood moving, but once it was going, there was no stopping me. I took the dunes at a run, feet skidding beneath me even as every single log tried to dig into the sand and anchor me in place. Mercy's cackling followed me everywhere that I went, an endless litany of snorts and wheezes all the way up each slope and all the way down again. I would have complained that she wasn't doing anything to help, but honestly, there wasn't much that she could do. This was a job for a beast of burden, and I was our best available version of that.

With all the wood down, I set to work. This wasn't as simple as banging together the bits of a sword. I had to go slow and steady, assembling parts of the boat rather than the whole thing. Every time I tried to make something too complex, the blackened and cracked pillar of Artifice began to tremor, and since I really didn't fancy bleeding out through every orifice in my body again, I opted to take my time. It wasn't like we were in a rush anyway. The other benefit of a day with nothing frantic happening was that I actually got the chance to fully heal up, using *Restoration* every time it flickered back to life. By midday, I was back to my full load of hit points. I felt great.

The only downside of slow and steady was that Mercy got bored fast. "Careful that rope doesn't loop around your neck and hang you."

I pointed behind her without looking up. "Careful you don't sink into that quicksand."

"Careful you don't fall over and impale yourself on your own horns."

"Careful you don't fall over and suffocate on your own giant ass."

She paused for a second. "How would that even work?"

"On normal people, it wouldn't. With your giant ass, anything is possible."

She stood up and twisted around to get a look at herself, finally noticing that one cheek was dangling out and sandy. She slapped the sand off. "My ass is perfect."

"Are you kidding, that thing? Have you seen the buns they gave me?" I got up onto my knees and bent over the length of prow I was working on curving, giving her a full-on view of my rear. "You could crack an egg on this thing!"

She sank back into her seat. "Careful you don't fall and sit on any eggs."

"Have you really got nothing better to do?"

She grinned. "Nope."

As the sun started slipping back down behind the cliffs, Mercy and I headed up to see how much of his stack Asher had managed to read through. We made it as far as the gates of the Overlook before the back of my neck started to prickle. "Uh."

Mercy slowed to look at me, and then stopped dead. "What?"

I closed my eyes and let my senses swoop out into my *Sphere of Influence*. Something wasn't right, but I didn't know what. My senses just couldn't reach far enough. Regretting everything, I dropped down to one knee and placed the palm of my hand on the dirt of the path.

Swarms of ghosts rushed through me. This was the only entrance to the courtyard from the outside, so everyone who'd ever come in had walked right by here. The choke point of the library was nothing compared to this. Thousands upon thousands of people through the centuries all passing right through me, making me shudder at their touch, making me hear snippets of their memories. Tiny fragments that meant nothing. Then abruptly the flow slowed to a trickle. Then to droplets, a Dvergar. The croc monster. Some humans. I rode it out. A long silence. Then I saw us come strolling through. Then the Alvaren. "Oh shit."

Mercy looked from me to the open gateway. "Trouble?"

"Always."

From inside, a lilting voice called out, "It would appear that the two of you have finally become aware of our presence, but I would remind you that we still have your pet snake hostage. Come on in slowly, and do not even consider reaching for your weapons if you wish for it to remain on this side of the veil of death."

I wondered if there were some special elocution lessons that they sent little baby Alvaren off to so that they could learn how to talk to people like they were dirt. Mercy met my eyes. "What do we do?"

"Stay behind me."

Before she had the chance to argue, I walked in.

There were a pair of Alvaren paladins with their blades drawn on either side of the gate, lounging there like unruly teens. The other Alvaren were slipping out from their hiding places now that their cover was blown, and a pair of them dragged an unconscious Asher out from behind his stack of books by the tail. A few more with bows sidled out of the out-buildings, and a couple more of them dropped down from where they'd been hiding on top of the tiled porch area in sniper positions. If any of them had decided to hide in the main building then the various traps and curses must have still been holding onto them. I gave Mercy a quick glance and a meaningful nod towards that door. If she could get in there and run, they'd all be stuck in an endless loop, and she could take her time shooting them. That was Plan B.

Another Alvaren unfolded herself from behind the book stack and sauntered out. Her swords were still at her hips, her smug expression impenetrable. "There is a good boy. Who's a good boy? Come on over here now, boy. Come on over and nobody has to cut into your friend."

Step by begrudging step, I moved into the courtyard. Mercy turned so her back was to me, keeping an eye on the duo by the gate who'd sidled over to block our escape. Grabbing Asher and smashing out through them was Plan A. I didn't like our odds against all the archers, but if I kept my body between Mercy and them, we had a chance of making it out. Or she did at least. If I made sure that my pin-cushion body dropped in the doorway, it was liable to give her some good running time, and it looked like they'd sent away their gryphons—if they'd even ridden them here to start with.

"Such a good boy." She turned to the other Alvaren, her golden hair flowing and shimmering in the sunset. "You see, it is just as I always told you. The lesser species can be trained so easily with a little praise and the promise of kindness."

I snorted in disbelief. "Kindness?"

"Is it not kindness that stays my hand and leaves your wyrm-spawn breathing?"

Mercy deadpanned, "I'm going to go with no?"

I held up my hands to show that they were empty. "Listen, why don't you let them go. I'm the one that you want. I'm the one with the shard."

Mercy kicked me in the back of the leg. "Don't tell them that!"

"Shard?"

"The thing you are here for. The shard. The shard of the Rusted Blade? The one your queenie wants to jam back in your big glowing pyramid to turn you all back into svart?"

There was no sign of confusion among the Alvaren, their carefully schooled facial expressions did not change, but there was a sudden stillness that gave away just how desperately they were trying not to show anything.

Blondie appeared entirely unfazed. "You believe that you can sow dissent among us? You think that you could make us turn against our empress with such blatant deception. I must inform you that it will not work."

"Honey, I've got nothing to gain here. You got the drop on us. You've won. We've lost. You're going to kill me and take the shard anyway. I don't care about that. I just want you to let my friends go."

She scoffed as she strolled over to meet me halfway. "What possible purpose would it serve for the illustrious Briar By Moonlight to corrupt the consummation of our magical power and render her willing servants into those degenerate beasts?"

"The hell would I know? Why don't you ask her?" I shrugged. "Maybe before you hand her the shard."

This close I could really see how pretty this Alvaren was. I mean, they were all pretty, but I've always been a sucker for blondes, and this one even had little freckles across the bridge of her nose. I didn't think I'd seen a single hint of a blemish on any of the other ones. Though the prettiness was kind of spoiled by her expression of utter contempt. "You were the ones who corrupted us. You were the ones who used that stolen artifact to transform us into mindless rutting animals."

"Honey, I haven't even been here a week. You've been svart for thousands of years. That doesn't add up."

"Your kin, your ancestors. The slave-beasts and wyrm-servants, risen up to drag their betters down into the filth alongside them." She even smelled nice. How do you spend millennia as a goblin and come out smelling like flowers? That didn't even make sense.

"Then why does Briar want the shard back so bad? Wouldn't she want it as far away from your floaty castle as possible if jamming it in the pyramid makes you all monsters?"

She clearly didn't have an answer for that, so she went with the default. "It is not our place to question her judgment."

"Well, whoever's place it is better do it quick." I paused and thought about it for a second. "Actually no. I've changed my mind; just give her the shard without asking any questions. Svart were way easier to deal with than you assholes."

"You impudent filth." Her open palm clattered across my jaw.

[708/710 Health]

I gave her a bloody grin. "That's it, baby, talk dirty to me."

She stepped back with disgust breaking through her neutral mask, and I called after her, "Wait, come back. I'm not done yet. Hit me harder."

She went for her sword, and everything was about to get really messy when Mercy's laughter swept over us. She was laughing so hard she ended up breathless and doubled over on herself. "You just can't help yourself can you?"

"Hey, if I've got to die, at least I can have fun doing it."

"Rest assured, scum, your death is now a necessity for my continued wellbeing. Yet first I shall complete the quest that has been granted to me by the most gracious Briar By Moonlight. Return the artifact to me, and I shall ensure that your suffering is minimal."

"Ooh, swing and a miss. Counter-offer. Why don't you get down on your dainty little Alvaren knees and suck my—"

Her blades were drawn faster than I could see them moving, one spinning towards my throat and the other darting out, point first, aimed at the region of my anatomy that I had been pointing to just a moment before.

I tried to jump back, but Mercy was there, and I ended up bowling her over as I fell in a heap. "Oh my gods, your giant ass."

Blondie didn't come after me, she hadn't even moved from the spot, but her sneer said more than words ever could. That same playground bully smirk. Why are you hitting yourself? Why did you flinch? That was when it finally clicked in my head, they weren't monsters anymore, they were something worse.

Mercy wriggled out from underneath me, and I clambered back to my feet, every one of the Alvaren arrayed around us had that same expression of amused contempt. Screw that.

I reached up and drew my sword. "Meet you in the library."

She glanced from me to the Alvaren all around. None of them had reached for weapons. None of them thought that we were any sort of threat anymore. Good. Let them underestimate us. "Asher?"

He was still lying immobile and bloodied up by the pile of books he'd been so happy with just a few hours ago. "I'll do what I can."

"You want a fight, do you?" I spun my sword overhand. Still, the archers didn't even twitch. They thought I was a joke. They thought their little leader was going to knock me about. Good. "Come on then, blondie. You and me. Let's dance."

"Please do not embarrass yourself further. You are…livestock." She looked me up and down without any change to that sneer. More posturing. "It is obvious that I am far beyond your capabilities."

"Oh yeah?" I bellowed. "Which way to the lecture halls?"

She raised a perfectly planed eyebrow. "What?"

The silver tiles exploded up out of the ground and came zipping over towards us. Blondie was fast, way too fast for me, but even she couldn't outpace a hundred mirrored fragments flying straight at her. She parried them away in a blur of blades, knocking them aside only for them to come buzzing back in a moment later. There were a hundred of them or more, all in orbit, all trying to form a helpful tour-guide and being interrupted by some unknown obstacle.

I couldn't have asked for a better distraction. My sword glinted in the dying light as I held it aloft, then made a beautiful hiss as it descended. In the midst of the intricate dance of parries, the blonde Alvaren caught a glimpse of me, and her sword came up to meet mine. It made no difference. She might have been skilled and fast and beautiful, but none of that did jack when you had a massive slab of metal coming down on you.

She managed to turn my blade enough that it didn't hit her straight in the face, but there was no stopping that kind of momentum. The short sword in her hand pinged out of her grip and skidded across the plaza, the flat of my sword hammered into the top of her head, and she went down in a delicate heap.

Mercy was off and running. The girl knew how to work a distraction. The Alvaren meanwhile seemed to be paralyzed with surprise. Perfect.

I charged at the two guarding Asher. They stood their ground, but they made no move to kill their hostage. I was going to call that a win too. I came at them with my blade whipping around in a horizontal arc, just above the level of my waist and just about the level of their face.

They probably would have dodged it quite readily if it weren't for my dear friend Talon. The mirrored form of him finally assembled behind the Alvaren and loudly declared, "The lecture halls are located on the eastern end of the second story in the main building, please take care to access only the halls to which you have been assigned as preventative wards are in place outside certain lectures to prevent the unwarranted spread of certain techniques without the proper training."

Both Alvaren spun on the spot to face this new threat, and my sword carved clean through their beautiful flowing locks and their elegant necks.

Blood sprayed over Talon's mirrored face, but the automaton didn't flinch. That was more good news. I really didn't fancy dealing with psycho magic robot security systems as well as all these Alvaren.

Enough time had passed for their faculties to come back online, and the remaining Alvaren all had arrows trained on me now, except the two who'd been blocking the gate who were sprinting over at full pelt. Both of them ran at exactly the same speed, with the same motions. They were like synchronized swimmers, except fully armed, armored, and set on causing my painful death. So only a bit like synchronized swimmers.

Lucky for me I didn't have to fight them. I grabbed Asher by the back of his bloody robes, put my head down, and ran.

Maybe I could have dodged the arrows if I'd been thinking straight, but in that moment, all that I wanted was to get Asher out of their reach before they could kill him. *Restoration* pulsed through my hand

and into him as we moved, but he was in no fit state to run for himself yet, and I wasn't convinced I could have put him down if I wanted to.

We passed between the two archers by the great hall entrance while they were lining up their next shots, and we made it over the threshold before the next pair of arrows hit me in the pits of my knees.

With one last grunt of effort, I managed to fling Asher into the room so I wouldn't land on him as I came down like a fallen oak, but I doubted he'd be thanking me for it after he bounced off that table leg.

It hurt like hell when I snapped the arrows off in my legs, but I didn't have any other options if I wanted to move, and I really needed to move.

"We should look upon this thing with pity. It is a beast not even fit to be served on these tables. It is cast aside like an offcut." The archers had moved in. Great.

"Pity was what Serendipitous Winds showed to him, and you saw how her kindness was repaid. I say we put the creature out of its misery and be done with it." I wasn't sure if they thought that I couldn't speak Alvaren or if they just didn't think I could understand speech, but either way, I was getting sick of them speaking over me.

With a roar of effort, I flung myself forward. Their bowstrings sang behind me, and I waited for the pain, but it didn't come. The hall had stretched out deeper when I moved into it, and now their arrows were stuck in that same infinite loop as me, never making it any farther forward. All of us were trapped in the distortion.

Every time I slapped my hand on the ground to drag myself forward, a cloud of ghosts rushed in around me. I could barely see in front of my own face. Reminder to self. Gloves. The chatter of the long-dead deafened me. Their feet flowing by my face left me blind to the death creeping up behind me. My hand squelched into the dropped chicken before I saw it. I didn't even know the Alvaren had caught up to me until I felt one grinding a boot-heel into the bloody back of my knee.

"A clever trick for an oaf, but the magics of your betters shall not avail you." The bows had been stowed and daggers drawn. I rolled onto my back like an animal submitting, tummy in the air. Just like they thought I would. What else would a wounded animal do? They stepped away from me smirking, and I pulsed *Restoration* and closed the holes in my legs.

[710/710 Health]

The chicken was still in my hand, so I held it up. "One last meal?"

"You expect us to stand by and watch you eat? You must jest."

"Not a last meal for me. For you." I lunged up and smacked him in the face with the chicken.

I had the element of surprise on my side—partly because they had no way of knowing I'd healed enough to jump up like that, but mostly because nobody ever expects to be smacked in the face with a chicken.

He reared back from me, spitting as he went, but it was too late. The curse took hold. One minute he was snarling at me, pretty as a picture, and the next his whole face turned into a bubbling mess of meat and gore.

He wasn't even dead yet, he was still screaming as his throat bubbled away to nothing, but I guess that he was dead enough for Amaranth to count it. Either that or the gods had just decided to grant me glory for killing a man with a chicken.

I spun to look for the other Alvaren, but she'd already crossed the distance to Asher and had her dagger to his throat. "Not another step, trickster."

My sword was still lying on the ground useless, so I held up my empty hands to show I was harmless, manfully resisting the urge to lick my fingers clean of chicken grease. "Let's just be cool here. Okay."

"What matters the temperature? Your pet dies if you take another step. Mark my words."

"I'm marking them! I'm marking them."

That was when Asher's eyes snapped open, revealing his two sets of eyelids to me once again and sending an unsettling shiver down my spine. His voice came out croaky, "Maulkin?"

The Alvaren pressed her dagger in tighter against his throat. "Not another sound from you wyrm-spawn or I'll slit you down to your gizzard and call it a good day's work."

"Let's just be calm here." I was using that special voice I saved for small children and dangerous animals. "Talk things through rationally."

Her eyes bulged in her head. Turns out the minute they lost their cool, all the elegance of the Alvaren was overtaken by their weirdness. "There is nothing to be spoken of. You will not move or I shall slay him."

I was very careful not to move. "Okay. Then what?"

She snarled, her perfect white teeth shimmering in the dull glow of my eyes. "Then he shall be deceased. He shall be no more."

"And then I'll shred you."

All the color drained from her face. "You dare to threaten me as I hold a blade to your..."

Maybe I could have phrased that better. "No you don't get it. If you kill him, I'll kill you. We both lose." I held my hands up a little higher. "So let's talk about how we can both win. Yeah?"

Her eyes darted from me to the glow of the door to the outside world. I pretended that all her buddies weren't out there planning their next move. "There is naught that you have to offer and no promise you could make that I would trust. In this, we are at an impasse."

"If we swap places real slow, you can walk away." I sidled a step to the right, and she tensed up. "I won't come after you. I won't try to hurt you. Even if I wanted to, you could outrun me, yeah?"

"You think that you can outwit me, you idiot-ape?" She dragged

Asher tight against her chest. "I will slit his throat and then yours just as readily. Neither of you is a match for me. While you were but babes in the cradle, I had already mastered the blade and bow twelve hundred times over. You think that you know strength? You are nothing to me. I shall return to my queen with your head as a prize."

I took another step, and blood trickled from Asher's throat. "I mean, maybe? But hadn't all your other dudes mastered the bow and sword and stuff too? I made chunks out of them."

"Trickery. They were bested through trickery. Not by your skill or your strength of arms."

It is hard to shrug with your hands up. Feels a bit like a one-man Mexican wave. "A win is a win, right?"

"Of course, lowborn scum like you would think it so. Honor has passed your people by since they first crawled from the mud." She wasn't loosening her grip on Asher, and I didn't like the look of helplessness in his eyes. I'd felt like that enough in one lifetime to know just how much it sucked.

"Kind of missing the point here. If you kill him, me and my bag of dishonorable tricks are coming for you."

A dismayed shout echoed out from behind us, then the thrum of bowstrings. I was out of time to do this without bloodshed. The rest of the Alvaren were piling in through the door, rattling off a volley at my back that was never going to make it. The paladins from the gates would be crossing the stretched distance towards us even now.

The Alvaren in front of me was watching them closing in on us with a grin. "It seems that your well of tricks has run dry."

It didn't have to end this way. I sighed. "Asher. Light my candle."

It only took him the length of a blink to realize what I was saying. He had been right when he mentioned that cantrip before, it was instantaneous. He just made a little flick with his clawed fingers, and one of the candelabras I'd knocked over throughout the day suddenly flickered back to life.

The spell on the hall reverberated and died once more, and it snapped back to its usual length an instant after the candles were lit. The arrows that this Alvaren and her dead buddy had fired at me earlier hammered into the flagstones a few feet back, and the arrows that her friends had fired at me from the doorway continued on their smooth arch through the air and right into her.

Never let it be said that I can't do math. Adding and subtracting, maybe I'll struggle a bit. Multiplication and division, yeah okay that is hard. Algebra? I don't know her. But angles? I've got that on lock. Maybe it was the kind of math you learned playing pool rather than the kind you learned in a classroom, but you had to admit it was effective.

One arrow took her high in the chest, one flitted past her ear, another went clean through her cheek, and the last one slammed home with a juicy pop, right into her eye.

She toppled over backward, and Asher shrugged her limp arms off his shoulders. "We must flee. They are coming in great numbers."

He mostly said that to my fleeing back as I pounded across the room, pausing only long enough to scoop up my sword and glance back. As it turned out, the reason they'd been waiting outside was for reinforcements. Either there had been one hell of a lot more Alvaren still hiding out there that I'd missed, or more had shown up. Neither option made me happy.

"Run faster!" Mercy bellowed from the stairwell as she launched arrow after arrow over our heads and managed to hit absolutely nothing. The Alvaren were too smart and too fast. They used cover when they could, and dodged easily around the shots that couldn't be avoided entirely. I never knew that I could miss the svart so much. Maybe giving them back the shard wasn't such a bad idea if it meant they all turned back into tiny goblin morons and left us alone.

I caught Mercy around the thighs as we passed through the door, and she went right on firing up at the Alvaren on our heels over my shoulder as we darted down the stairs. "We need them distracted before we hit the library."

Asher started mumbling a spell as he stumbled breathlessly down the stairs, but Mercy interrupted him. "I got it."

He cocked his head. "You do?"

"I do." Slinging her bow behind her back, Mercy closed her eyes for just a moment before spreading out her arms.

Like a miracle, a wall of fire leapt up behind us, blazing blue-hot but just transparent enough for me to see the vapid looks on the Alvaren's faces when they nearly plowed into it. If any of them had eyebrows left, I'd be extremely surprised. "Nice."

All of this time, I'd been using Artifice and all the rest without thinking how it must have looked to the people around us. Even here in this world of magic and monsters, it was something spectacular. Something awesome—in the original meaning of the word. It filled anyone that looked at it with awe.

Mercy jostled herself into a more comfortable perch, grabbing onto my horns like they were handlebars. "I had to start using some god powers eventually. Now seemed like a good time to show off."

Asher wheezed with what might have been laughter. "A most impressive display of Creation. Bravo."

At a full sprint, we crossed the testing rooms and into the library, slamming the door shut behind us. Asher doubled over, trying to catch his breath. I tossed Mercy onto a sofa, but she bounced off and onto her feet. "How long will your fire last?"

She looked sheepish. "Without wood? A few seconds maybe? I don't know. It's my first time."

I clasped my hand to my chest. "Aww, you gave up your fire virginity for us."

"Thanks for making it weird."

"Any time."

Asher had his hands up and his eyes closed, his other senses doing their thing. "The way is shut, the illusions and traps have been restored to their rightful place, and the Alvaren will struggle to find us here if we simply remain quiet."

"Then what?" Mercy came around and gave my shin a gentle kick for throwing her. "Just hope they get bored and wander off?"

"Quite the contrary, my dear Mercy. My hope is that they immediately begin opening doors in the hopes of finding us, triggering whatever lethal surprises the Archmage Talon left in place to defend his library.

Judging from the sudden sonic boom from the other side of the door and Asher's lipless smile, it seemed likely that was exactly what had happened. There was some screaming and thumping too, though the thick walls and door of the library worked wonders to keep the volume low.

Only a moment later there was a roar and squelching noise loud enough to make it through once more. Door number two.

"How many do you think are left?"

Asher shook his head. "Too many."

I joined him by the door, ostensibly to brace it with my shoulder but also to stretch out my *Lifesense* to its limits and see what there was to see. There were a dozen Alvaren in reach of my *Sphere of Influence* and twice as many dead. A dhole lay in finely chopped pieces on the floor—the super-size-meal death worm had the dying flickers of a good few Alvaren inside it, so at least it died doing what it loved. Eating people. The added bonus of that big dumb worm was that most of its corpse was heaped up against our door, making it more likely the Alvaren were going to be dumb enough to open one of the others.

Sadly, they weren't quite that stupid. They retreated out of my *Sphere of Influence* into the stairwell to regroup. "Okay, there's still at least twelve of them out there."

Mercy rolled her shoulders and plucked her bow off her back. "Four each? I like those odds."

"I do not care for them, personally," Asher whispered back, speaking so comically quiet that he was obviously trying to make a point about how loud we were being. "Even a single paladin has proven the match of any one of us."

I shrugged. "Speak for yourself. I've been kicking their asses up and down the road all day."

"We lack the numbers required to brute-force our way through this situation. A more finessed plan will be necessary."

I turned to face him with a grin. "Alright. Hit me with it."

"I beg your pardon?"

"Your plan," Mercy groaned. "What is your plan?"

"I have no plan. I was merely observing the necessity of developing one while we have a moment's reprieve."

Mercy pinched the bridge of her nose. "You are the most useless—"

I cut off her rant before it could get any steam. "She was really worried about you when they had you prisoner you know."

"I... My thanks to you both for the swift rescue. I was taken quite unawares."

I chuckled. "We figured from the fact that you hadn't burned the whole place down that they got the drop on you."

Something tickled across the top of my head, and I reached up to brush away the imaginary spider before I realized that it wasn't my physical body but my *Sphere of Influence* that was being touched. I closed my eyes and let my life-sense stretch out.

The Alvaren had returned to the grand hall at a sprint, and though I couldn't hear their voices, I could feel the vibrations of their panic. Some of them I had felt before, and others were passing through my *Sphere of Influence* for the very first time. There were more than twelve left. My count was way off. There had to be twenty or more. But despite their weight of numbers, they had broken and run. "They're running for it."

Mercy's head jerked up. "They're what?"

I yanked the door to the library open. "They're running away!"

Asher called after me as I clambered over the dhole corpse, "Let them!"

"Are you kidding me?" I called back over my shoulder as I ran. "This is our chance."

I was too far away to hear Asher and Mercy groaning and moaning about it, but not too far to hear them cursing as they clambered over the reeking dhole chops.

Up the stairs I ran and out through the hall too as it contracted to reject me. I skidded to a halt by the door instead of charging right out, and that was when the sound of battle swept over me. The Alvaren hadn't been running from us. They'd been running towards this.

Blood filled the cracks between the tiles in the courtyard. Shimmering by torchlight. Red blood. Not blue. Red. I charged right out into the melee.

Dvergar in their full metal plate armor were a sight to see, like walking tanks wading through. The Alvaren were faster, of course, able to dodge away from every swing of the Dvergar axes, but nothing they did to the Dvergar made a dent. Their arrows ricocheted away, and their blades did nothing but scrape paint from the metal. The only dead Dvergar were the ones who'd come without armor. The common folk of Khag Mhor, with their silks shredded and their rocky skin exposed in death.

Until now I had seen fighting in Amaranth. This was the first time that I had seen war. The Dvergar had come back for us. They were here, dying...for us. The same rage I'd felt in my gut when I saw the Dvergar who'd been tortured by svart was back. A cold dead weight inside me. I didn't even notice my body moving until it did.

My sword was straight out to my side, and I couldn't remember swinging it. One of the dodging Alvaren had leapt right into its arc as the one I'd been aiming at dodged away. It didn't matter if they were faster than me in the press of battle. It didn't matter if they were better. They'd all die just the same.

There was so much death all around me. Life sense might have felt like a tickle over my senses, but death embraced me like a long-lost lover. I was soaked in it. The world around me seemed to slow to a crawl like it did when I was using my divine powers.

I stepped between the smooth blur of an Alvaren sword and a silk-shrouded Dvergar woman using a frying pan as a shield gladly and felt the pain of it like it was from a great distance away.

The blade bit through my armor and lodged against my ribs, but I didn't give a damn. All I cared about was the paladin failing to jerk it back out in time to stop my fingers locking around his wrist.

Just like his queen before him, he dodged out of the path of my sword with a twist, but at the cost of breaking his own arm. The treacle slow swing of my sword was only ever a distraction. I had another weapon now. With a grunt of effort, I lifted him off his feet and swung.

The archer caught her companion across the back, and they both went down in a heap.

I lifted him up and hammered him back down again for good measure.

The broken corpse collided with another of the dervish Alvaren as I tossed it aside, knocking her down for the Dvergar to hack her to pieces. There were glimpses of the Dvergar's faces in the twilight and torchlight, their expressions fixed, their actions methodical. The same precision they used in everything they did traveled through into the swing of each hammer and axe.

Crossbow strings thrummed, and the Alvaren had to fling themselves down to avoid the line of death stretched across the courtyard, passing harmlessly over the heads of the Dvergar but right at chest height for their foes. It only took a glance to confirm my suspicions. There was Gunhild on the top of her grand wagon with a cadre of crossbowmen already reloading for the next volley.

In normal circumstances, the Alvaren could run rings around us, so we had to ensure that they never got any normal circumstances to work with. Flames roared across the courtyard from the entrance to the great hall, sweeping over us all harmlessly but dressing us in embers so that even in the dim light, every target was perfectly outlined.

Knowledgeable in the ways of magic in the way that Dvergar born in this century could never be, the Alvaren began to panic. A whistle came up from amongst them, a lilting wavering sound. They were calling down their gryphons to make their escape. To hell with that.

I roared, even as I charged for the biggest cluster of Alvaren where they were trying to regroup. "Gunhild, look up!"

Mercy already had arrows flying up into the shadowed sky above us, and where they made contact, blood and feathers rained down on us all. I had no time to spare a glance to that battle when the one all around me was still raging. The armored Dvergar were forming a battle line on their side of the courtyard, the stragglers of their more haphazardly-equipped kin scrambling to get behind them.

I was on the wrong side of that line, as were Asher and Mercy if you wanted to get technical, but it didn't much matter. Apart from their archers, the Alvaren seemed to have given up on attacking altogether, pulling back into a cluster near Asher's trampled heap of books. He wasn't going to be happy about that.

In a straight fight, regrouping like that was smart, but it didn't account for magic. When Asher unleashed a great blazing sphere of fire into the mass of Alvaren, it avoided all of the rest of us thanks to their retreat.

Those books were not making it out alive.

Even the braced Dvergar rocked back from the explosion of the fireball, and I was kicked clean off my feet. It was probably for the best. If I'd kept up my charge, I would have ended up full of more shiny swords like the one that was still jutting out my side, and I might have lost my eyebrows too.

As it was, the Alvaren's attempt at careful formations came to an abrupt and fiery end, and the survivors, of which there was a surprisingly large number, made the latest in a long line of stupid decisions.

They didn't get back on their feet faster than me.

I was up and scrambling into a run before they'd even finished shaking the concussion from their ears, and I was in mid-air before they made it up onto bended knees. Nobody was fast when they were lying down.

The first of the Alvaren archers split cleanly in two beneath my blade. Blue blood spritzed me, soothing and cool.

Next up was a paladin, half her face crisping away and tears flowing down what was left. That one almost felt like a mercy.

[63 Damage]

Her head hit the next one.

[61 Damage]

Then his head hit the next.

[64 Damage]

I could have gone on like that all day, but the last of the Alvaren were up and running by now, choosing the uncertain death of the

Dvergar line over bloody dismemberment at my hands. Almost a good idea. Almost. I cut one of the stragglers down as they passed.

This wasn't a battle anymore, it was a slaughter. The Alvaren were beaten, but there was no question of letting them go free. If they got away, they'd bring back their whole city, their queen, and all their spell-casters. Even one of them could overwhelm us, and we'd seen thousands upon thousands of svart. If all of them were Alvaren now, we would be too hopelessly outnumbered to stand a chance. Briar could probably take on the whole lot of us by herself if she deigned to get her hands dirty.

The gryphons above had scattered, so Mercy's arrows were raining down on the fleeing Alvaren too, most missing, but enough making contact. There were barely a dozen Alvaren by the time they hit the Dvergar line. Maybe hit was the wrong word. At the last moment, every one of them launched themselves into the air.

It was more of the same Alvaren crap, beautiful and elegant to behold, the prancing arc of a gazelle over a mountain stream. Crossbow bolts punched them out of the air.

The bodies hit the ground, and the Dvergar set in on them. This was not elegant or beautiful. It wasn't even the carefully ordered movements of the Dvergar in battle. It was pure barroom fighting. Hit the guy on the floor with whatever was in your hands. Thousands of years of training meant nothing in the face of that wild hate.

In a blink, the Battle of Witchglass Overlook was over, and the Alvaren who'd ruled the world a thousand years back learned a whole new lesson.

Legendary Foes Defeated!
Potency increased to 44
Brawling: Rank 8/10
120 Experience Gained
380 Glory Gained

"Can't be leaving you alone for a minute, can I?" The battle-line parted, and Gunhild came strolling out, the crossbow still balanced on her shoulder.

I grinned down at her. "I could have taken them."

She laughed, and the rest of the Dvergar took it up. The only one still scowling was Mercy when she pulled up alongside me. "Oh what? We're all friends again now?"

"I mean, they did just save us from the Alvaren."

Asher joined her on my other side. "For which we are, of course, grateful, but you must admit that we parted on less than pleasant terms."

"Aye well. We did some thinking on that after you be tearing off with all the knife-ears chasing you. We...That is to say...I be..."

"People died." I sank down to my haunches so that I was level with Gunhild. "I can't think of a better reason to get upset."

"Aye. The grief had us." She came over and wrapped her arms around me, the studs and spikes on her armor digging into my back. It wasn't easy to apologize at the best of times, and she was trying to do it in front of a whole caravan of refugees who were looking to her to lead. Her next words came low as a whisper. "We know you did right by us, best you could."

Mercy still looked skeptical, but at least she wasn't openly hostile anymore. "And that's why you came chasing over here to save us?"

"Well..." Gunhild had the good grace to look sheepish. "We were hoping you might be saving us."

Asher let out a snort of laughter but got himself under control fast.

Still too late to stop Gunhild leaping back and snarling up at him though. "You thinking it be funny, wyrm-flakes? Without walls to keep them, what hope have these folk of surviving? They don't be fighters. They be needing somewhere to keep them safe and folk to keep them safe until they get there."

Mercy was still smiling, but there was no cruelty to it. "So you want us to babysit."

"Not forever!" Gunhild snapped. "Just…until they be settled."

Asher pressed the heels of his hands to his eyes. "This is so clearly a bad idea."

I grinned. "How do you all feel about boats?"

CHAPTER 26

Serendipitous Winds woke up to the feeling of her namesake brushing the hair away from her pretty little face. The gentle rocking of our ship at sea had been swaying her like a cradle so far, but as we moved out from the shore into deeper, choppier waters, that gentle rocking was starting to stutter as we cut across grand waves. I'm assuming she had one hell of a headache from the whimpering little groans that she made, but for all I knew, Alvaren thrived off headwounds.

Now that she was stirring, I felt less guilty about poking her with the end of my sword. She let out a little grumble. I crouched down over her, drew in a nice big breath, and then shouted, "Good morning!"

Her eyes snapped open, but otherwise, she was perfectly still. Now some of that was probably because we had her trussed up in chains, but I got the impression that this was more of that weird grace or discipline or whatever that the Alvaren liked to show off all the time. She spoke softly and calmly. "Release me."

Asher glanced over from his book. "Absolutely not."

"It is a great crime to bind an Alvaren. A deadly sin. You cannot know the punishments that shall be rained down upon you." She struggled now, trying to turn and take in the sights and sounds around her.

Mercy passed us by with a train of her Dvergar friends in tow. She called back over her shoulder. "Unless it is worse than what you guys already had planned for us, I'm not exactly worried."

Serendipitous Winds' eyes turned back to me. Gods help her if I was the sane person she had to appeal to. The voice of reason? Me? "Torment. Tortures of the like that mere mortals could not even comprehend."

I settled down beside her in the belly of the boat with a grunt. "You keep using that word. I don't think it means what you think it means."

Her eyebrows jumped up. "My grasp of this language…"

I carefully placed my hand over her mouth. If she tried the old licking trick, I couldn't feel it through the new gloves I'd made myself. "You are mortal. You get that, right? You might not get old, but I've seen your lot die. A lot of you. Eternals on the other hand, we're here forever."

She glared at me until I lifted my hand away from her face again. "Eternals? You claim the title of the…"

Glove. Meet mouth. Again. "We don't claim a damn thing. Use your eyes and your brain instead of your mouth for a minute."

This time when I lifted my hand away, she was already snarling. "You dare to—"

"They dare, we have established that they dare." Asher was almost shouting. "Daring is well within the wheelhouse of their behavior. Kindly work from the assumption that they dare and move on so that we might move the conversation forward." I hadn't even needed to cover her mouth to cut her off that time. Asher's vitriol had stopped her dead.

Mercy crowed from up in the rigging. "Damn, Asher. Go off."

Asher settled himself back down with his book and tried to pretend he hadn't just lost his temper. "The pomposity of these Alvaren begins to grate."

"So let's take it from the top." I smiled down at blondie. "Hi. I'm Maulkin. I'm an Eternal. This is Asher and Mercy. Also Eternals. We're here to put the Rusted Blade back together so that we can kill the Voidgod."

"Hah!" she snapped. "Your lies will not avail you. The Voidgod died before the tragedy that befell my kind at the hands of your ancestors. You cannot deceive one who lived through those dark days."

"He's coming back. Or, at least that is what the prophecies say." I paused to consider it for a moment. "Or…that is what they told us the prophecies say."

"Then you have been deceived also." She slipped on her most ingratiating smile. "You have been led into conflict with the most glorious Briar by Moonlight through no fault of your own. Return the artifact to her, and I am certain that an accord can be reached."

Asher glanced up from his book again. "It is my belief that the White Prophet was correct in his assertions. Everything that we have experienced since our rebirth in Amaranth tells us that the prophecy was true."

Mercy swung by on a rope, presumably doing something useful about the boat and not just having a fun time. Without me. "Still not a hundred percent on that, personally."

When it seemed like glove was no longer going to need to make the acquaintance of face again, I settled myself with my back on the curvature of the wood. "Either way, I don't trust Briar. She's shifty."

"Did you truly just say that the Empress of the Alvaren is…shifty?" For one glorious moment, blondie had been stunned into silence, but now she was spitting mad all over again.

"Yup."

"She who led the allied armies of the free people to defeat the dark one? She who has reigned throughout millennia beyond reckoning? She who slew the wyrms of dread and despair before the sun or moon first rose? She who…"

"Don't know. Don't care. Don't trust her." Serendipitous Winds gaped at me, but I pressed on. "She lied to all of you. She was using the shard to make you into svart. Something is seriously not right there, and there is no way I'm handing myself or the shard over until I know for sure what she is going to do with it."

Apparently, this was basically sacrilegious for Alvaren. Serendipitous Winds spoke as soft as a sigh. "You should trust in her wisdom."

"She should give me a reason to trust her."

Asher intervened before blondie could lose her temper all over again. "It appears to me that there was some dark power within the shard. Some remnant of the Voidgod that the weapon slew. Perhaps it was this corrupting influence that led to her current course?"

"Briar by Moonlight is incorruptible." Blondie sniffed.

"Oof." I lay back with a groan. "That is like saying a boat is unsinkable."

Asher groaned. "Perhaps you could refrain from jokes about famous shipwrecks while we are traveling in a shoddily constructed ship that lets in water."

I opened up one eye to stare at him. "You want to build the boat next time?"

He turned back to his book with a sigh.

"Yeah, that's what I thought."

I wasn't going to pretend that this was the prettiest ship on the seas, or that some of the boards I'd used in the construction didn't occasionally let a tiny bit of water through their gaps even though we'd slathered it with all the tar Gunhild had managed to salvage from her wagon, but it sailed, and with all the Dvergar on board taking turns at the oars, we could even keep going when the wind wasn't doing us any favors.

The boat had been considerably more work than I'd bargained for. The Dvergar had been a great help in hauling wood and offering up their meager supplies for the other fixtures, but they also had opinions. So many opinions. None of them had ever sailed before. None of them had ever even seen the sea except for Gunhild and her lot, yet somehow everyone knew exactly what every length of wood should look like, and how I was doing it all wrong. To start with I thought it was just more of the usual abrasive Dvergar personality that we all know and love so much, but no, they actually all thought that they knew better than me. The annoying thing was, of course, that they were right. I might have been able to slap things together, and I could sail a ship just fine after dumping a few skill points into Sailing, but when it came to the complicated math parts of engineering, I was mostly sticking my head in the sand and pretending they didn't matter.

It took me almost a full day to construct my boat, then another day to reconstruct it so that it would actually sail, carefully guided by a nursing mother Dvergar who had once led an expedition through some sort of underground lake, making her their resident expert. Even her baby gave me contemptuous looks. Damn judgmental baby.

I shook the thought of his beady little eyes away. "Anyway. Serendipi…Windy…Seren. Here's the deal. We found you in a pile of corpses, nursed you back to health, and brought you along with us because I think we could help each other."

She turned her head away. "I shall offer no succor to the enemies of my queen."

"Well, you just said yourself that we probably weren't actually enemies." I gave her another prod with the end of my sword, making her snap back around.

"I beg your pardon?"

"You said we were being misled, this is all a big misunderstanding, all that jazz." She blinked when I mentioned jazz but paid it no mind. Maybe they had jazz here? "Told us to trust in Briar, right?"

The ingratiating smile was back. "Yes, I am glad that you see reason."

"Well, a good way to earn some trust would be to help us out a little." I smiled back at her, making it look as real as I could while desperately wanting to stick a bag over her head so I didn't have to deal with the condescension any more. "You want us on Team Briar, you need to help us."

"What could you possibly believe that I could provide to you?"

Asher glanced up again. This was his plan, after all. "Information."

"I shall not betray my queen's trust in any way, wyrm-spawn. I shall not share her secrets or those of my people. I would rather be cast into the sea still bound in chains than speak a word that might be used against her."

I shrugged. "That's fine, we didn't want the codes to the nukes or anything. We just wanted to talk to you about history."

She ignored anything that she didn't understand and zeroed in on the stuff that she did. That must have been handy. Of course, if I did it then I'd never interact with anything. She pursed her lips. "History?"

"Yeah, seems like you lived through some history that is pretty relevant to everything that is going on now. You're a firsthand witness to all the Revelations and Voidgod stuff. I don't know if anyone has explained to you how long you were svarted…"

The false good humor had begun to fade again. "We were informed in no great detail of the millennia that your kind stole from us."

"Anyway, there isn't a whole lot of reliable information from back then to work with. If you could give us the short version, it would be much appreciated." I settled back. That was my pitch made.

Asher and Mercy had argued back and forth over keeping this Alvaren alive as our prisoner, sniping at each other throughout the whole of the construction process and keeping their distance from one another now that we were on the boat to keep tempers from flaring. Mercy thought that we were being too generous, that Seren was going to stab us in the back at the earliest opportunity. Asher thought that the risk was worth the reward. I just didn't feel comfortable murdering someone in her sleep.

After weighing it for a moment, Seren asked, "And, in return, what would you grant me?"

Mercy dropped down beside us, ready to join in the conversation at last. "You want to make a deal now?"

Still, Seren only had eyes for me. "You make demands but offer nothing in return, how like a savage."

I tried for the same vacant smile I'd been bandying about all day, but at this point, my temper was starting to fray. "Hey now, no need for name-calling. We're all friends here."

"You are not my friend, beast. You are not my equal or my ally." Her face narrowed as she let her mask of civility slip until all the sharp edges seemed to jut out. "You could never claim my friendship, nor cultivate any bond with me that goes beyond master and hound."

"Alright. That's how you want it. Bark for me, bitch." I rose to my feet in one movement. Sword clattering to the deck.

Asher startled. "What?"

I took hold of Seren's chains and hefted her up. She weighed less than the metal she was wrapped in, and that weighed less than nothing to me. I roared in her face, "Bark for me!"

Her eyes were wild in the mask of civility, darting from side to side. "What are you doing?"

I took a step to the edge of the boat, put my foot up on the rails, and dunked her into the waves below.

Asher was scrambling to his feet, calling out. "Stop!"

I yanked Seren's head back out of the water. All that beautiful hair was in her face now tangled and sodden. I snarled, "Bark for me!"

Mercy rushed in to stop me, but she was too slow. I already had Seren back in the sea before she could grab onto me, and then anything that she did might have cost me my grip and the Alvaren her life. "Maulkin, what the hell!"

The rage had come on so suddenly I didn't have a chance to catch myself before I moved. Bypassing the rational part of my brain and seizing control. I'd never been so angry in all my life. Not either one of them.

Seren was every sneering bully to ever look down their nose at me. She was everything wrong with the world. "If this is what she wants, this is what she gets."

I hauled the Alvaren back up out of the water, and she came up barking. Pitiful little yelps, like a child's impression of a dog. A child that had only ever read about them. I threw her down onto the deck. "Happy now. One of us is master. One of us is dog. Just like you wanted."

She managed to roll herself over and was wriggling like a worm towards Asher where he stood like she was going to hide under his skirts. "You wanted a deal? Here is the deal. You tell us what we want to know, and you go on breathing. How is that for a deal?"

Asher held up his hands as if he were going to do something. No idea what he thought he was going to do since throwing a punch was just going to end in him hurting a hand, and casting a spell was going to end in him going for a swim. "Maulkin, this was not what we discussed."

I spat on the deck. "You can't reason with them. You can't treat them like they are real people and expect them to listen to sense. This is all that they understand. Violence. Threats. Fear. They're no better now than when they were svart. They're just taller."

He crouched down now over Seren straining to lift her back up against the side of the boat by his book-stack. "We shall discuss this later."

The rage washed away with the next spritz of seawater on my face. Gone as fast as it had come. I clamped my mouth shut before I could say anything else stupid and stormed off to the back end of the boat to give myself a time-out.

After a few minutes, Gunhild of all people came along to join me. "You be right enough about them Alvaren."

I still didn't trust myself to speak, so I gave the shortest answer I could. "I lost my temper."

"Well, you'd be doing well to keep losing it. Auld knife-ears is flapping her mouth like nobody's business. Whatever you wanted to know, she'll be spilling it all now, just to keep the big bad chagnar away."

My face fell into my hands. "Great. Great! I just love it when people are scared of me."

"Well, you'll be glad to know a fair few of my crew be too afraid to come anywhere near you now too, in case you decide to go dunking them. I actually be proving how hard I am right now, sitting my arse on these splinters you call a boat beside you."

It was meant to be a joke, but I couldn't muster up more than a snort.

She put her arm around my back. "Listen good, you big lump. You might live forever, but it seems to me I've been around longer than you already, so hear my words, and you keep them close. You might be wanting to go through a life full of hugs and flowers, but that don't be the world we've got. This is a hard world, full of bad folk who'll take one look at kindness and call it weakness. You can't be a friend to a monster, even if it be a monster with a pretty face. Best thing you can do is show it you're too strong to be prey."

I unclenched enough to put my arm around her too. "Thank you, wise old woman."

She elbowed me in the ribs. "You're not too big to be going over my knee."

"Don't threaten me with a good time."

She cackled as she pushed herself up off me, then sauntered off to boss around some more of her Dvergar. I don't think there was actually much of anything to do, but she was keeping them busy. Keeping their mind off things. No point in looking back at what they'd lost or out at the drowning deeps of the sea when there were barrels to move or crates to stack.

I should have been doing the same, taking over the rudder or heading to the prow to see if I couldn't spot the next Waystone on the horizon to keep us on course. I was just about to get up and get to it when Mercy booted me in the back.

"What the hell was that?"

I rocked with the kick but didn't turn around. "You know, if I ever feel you hitting me..."

"No. No jokes. What the hell was that? You were waterboarding her for talking back to you?"

"You've never heard of good cop, bad cop?"

"One: they aren't meant to be the same person!" She punctuated it with a kick. "Two: you are meant to tell the people on your side that you're doing it before you start doing it." Another kick, even more half-hearted than the last. "And three: it is good cop, bad cop, not good cop, CIA torture technician."

"It worked, didn't it. She's over there spilling her guts to Asher right now."

"Yeah, it worked. She's scared of you now." Her voice dropped to a whisper. "But so am I."

That was enough to make me turn around when all the booting didn't. "Oh, come on. Just because I lost my temper a little bit..."

"You would have killed her. Even with me and Asher together, we had no way of stopping you. I don't even know if Asher would have tried. If she hadn't...degraded herself like that. You would have killed her. Just like that."

"I wouldn't have." Denial is a versatile tool to help you get through the day.

"You would." She sank down beside me but still held her distance. All that companionable shoulder-bumping thrown overboard. "I saw your face, you were so... It wasn't even like you were angry. It was like there was nobody in there. Like Maulkin had checked out, and your body was on autopilot."

I put my elbows on my knees and my horns in my hands. I didn't want to look at her right now. I didn't want her to see me. Denial could only stretch so far. "I was still here. I was just... I just got angry."

"Angry is swearing when you stub your toe. Angry is yelling at me when I call you a dumbass. I know angry. This wasn't angry."

"Seren. All of them." A growl crept into my voice that I didn't want to be there. "They think they're so much better than everyone else in the world. They think they own it, that we should all be groveling for whatever place in it that they want to give us. That doesn't make you angry?"

"Yeah, they're rude, but that doesn't make me want to drown a chained-up girl. That's some serial killer shit."

I let that sit for a minute. The sound of the sea lapping against the boat and the distant calls of the Dvergar to each other the only sound. It was a good thing that it was so quiet, or she might not have heard me when I rumbled, "You're right."

"Usually am."

"That... That wasn't me. I'm not like that." I pulled on my horns like you'd drag your fingers through your hair, and it felt so natural that I didn't even remember I hadn't even had horns a week earlier. "I mean, you know me."

"I've known you like a week, dude," Mercy said, cold as her namesake. "Luckily, you are as deep as a puddle and as open as a book, so a week is plenty of time to get to know everything about you. I know you aren't... I know you aren't like that. That's why I tried to stop you."

Now that I was talking about it, it felt like the floodgates had opened. I couldn't string my thoughts together. "I don't know what that was. I don't know if that was this new body or something the gods put in me or... I don't know."

Mercy leaned in to nudge me with her shoulder. It was literally the nicest thing anyone had ever done for me, and that was kind of sad too when I thought about it. "Well, next time I see it, I'm putting an arrow between your eyes, just to be safe."

I let go of my horns to nod. "Probably smart."

The waves crashed, the Dvergar shouted, and the wind dragged us ever on. Silence again, but the tension was gone. A death threat probably shouldn't have made me feel better, but honestly, the idea that there would be somebody to stop me if I went off the deep end was kind of nice. At least I wouldn't hurt anybody else. I did a double-take when Mercy started talking again. "You know what your problem is, right?"

"My sassy sidekick?"

"Hah. Okay, you need to think that one through because you are definitely the sidekick around here." She gestured up and down me. "Look at you. Nobody is rooting for the big cow-man."

I shook my head in mock sorrow. "So sassy."

She gave me a punch in the shoulder, but she was smiling again. Not her big genuine smile that you had to work for, but the little smirk that meant she didn't want you to know she was smiling at all. "Nah, your problem is that for the first time since we got here, there is nothing for you to fight. It has been a whole day since some giant monster tried to kill us. You're wound up! You're itching for a fight! You're—"

The ship lifted clean out of the water as the serpent hit us from below. One minute we were sailing straight without a care in the world, and the next we were catching air and the ship was lilting over to one side before it hit the water again.

I grabbed an arm full of barrels, surging my Potency to take the strain, and sprinted over to the starboard side. That is the right side, for those of you without skill points in Sailing. The combined weight of me and the barrels was enough to right the ship before anyone got thrown overboard, but whatever had hit us was still down there.

Mercy caught up to me, laughing. "You're the luckiest son of a bitch alive."

The rest of the boat did not seem so amused. The Dvergar were mostly screaming except for the few under Gunhild's direct command who were trying to batten down everything they could. Asher was clinging to the central mast with both arms and a look of alarm on his face that was honestly kind of adorable. Like a gecko.

I launched myself right past him onto the mast and started climbing. It swayed the whole ship violently as I went, but it was still better than the rocking that whatever had hit us was doling out. As long as I ignored the creaking and cracking noises that the mast was making, that justification seemed enough.

From my awkward vantage point, I could see the shadow beneath the waves. Some huge eel-shaped thing, coming around for another run at us. Like I was going to give it another chance. "Asher! My sword!"

He realized what I was doing before I kicked off from the mast to leap out into the sea, with just enough time to press-gang a bunch of the burliest Dvergar in reach into throwing the thing. They could throw it about as far as I trusted Seren.

The black hole opened up ahead of me, and once more the whole ship rocked as some new force was exerted against it. Water leapt up all around the boat to reach for the dark singularity in the sky, but so did my hastily flung weapon.

Between the gravity snare and my own Artifice, the sword made its way into my hands before I reached the water, and I brought it down hard and double-handed on the shadow below.

I had just enough time to roar, "Nice!" before I was pulled under the water. Enough time to wonder if I still knew how to swim, too. Guess I was about to find out.

Beneath the surface, there was a torrent of bubbles blinding me to nearly everything going on. I got my feet set on the slippery, shimmering, scaled surface of the serpent to either side of where my sword was wedged, but that was as far as my progress went. There was a vague impression of frilled fins at either side but no certainty. Then we dove down into the crushing depths.

It seemed to be bucking and twisting in the water—it certainly felt like I was being flung around—but my potency was always going to be too much for simple turbulence to dislodge me. I bent down and took a hold on the edge of the wound in its back, cutting down my profile and the drag of the water. There was blood pouring out of the serpent in a great tail behind us. I wished that I'd remembered to wear my shark cage today.

With a solid grip on the rough edge of the scales, I started to work my sword loose. Back and forth. More and more blood bubbled up around me until I couldn't see a damn thing through the red cloud. I probably wouldn't have seen much anyway, between the sudden drop in light as we went deeper and the bubbles.

With one mighty tug, I finally got my sword free, just in time for the serpent to reverse direction. It shot straight up into the air like a bottle rocket, and I lost my footing, clinging to the rubbery tissue inside its wound with one hand and hoping like hell it didn't shake me off. My ears popped, then a moment later there was light enough to see what was ahead. Beyond the great pointed wedge face of the serpent, I could see a shadow on the surface. The ship—as big as the serpent itself. The only solid object for fathoms around. That is miles for those of you that don't have points in sailing skill. Maybe. I only had one rank in sailing.

It planned to bop me off its back, and I was here for that plan. Riding the back of a sea serpent might sound awesome, but my lungs were burning. I really should not have wasted all that breath saying, "Nice."

I leapt free at the last moment, but I still got carried along in the column of displaced water, dragged up to splat against the side of the boat at about the same time the serpent scraped across it, sending the whole thing swinging violently to the side.

The water dragged me on, bouncing me along the bottom of the ship in the wake of the serpent.

Maybe I didn't have enough ranks in sailing to be sure, but I was fairly confident that I had just keelhauled myself. Still, I was free. I broke the surface and gulped in air greedily. There wasn't much in the way of handholds on my crappy little boat, but with Artifice it didn't take long to yank a few boards around and clamber back on deck.

My head had barely come up over the edge before I had to duck back down again. A bolt of lightning cracked over my head and then dispersed harmlessly over the surface of the water. It made a pretty light show, and it might have shocked a few fish dumb enough to be anywhere near this mess, but the serpent had dived back down out of reach.

"Maulkin!" Asher cried out in dismay when he realized that he'd nearly crispy fried me. That was nice. It was good to know it hadn't been deliberate.

Dvergar swarmed forward to help haul me up onto the deck, but I shrugged them off fast. "Crossbows! Cannons! Have we got cannons?"

Gunhild was among the crowd. "What be a cannon?"

Asher shook his head at me as I staggered to my feet. "Right. Sorry. Yeah. Uh…"

The latest hit had knocked some of the rigging loose. I only had wood to work with, so it was hope as much as anything else holding most of the ship together. "Crossbows…"

I closed my eyes and slipped free of my soggy mortal shell. I'd made almost everything on the ship with Artifice, so I could remake it just as easily. The careful work of assembling the mast was undone in a moment, with the Dvergar up in the rigging leaping to safety on the deck as I reshaped it nice and slow. It wasn't much of a job for my Artifice, even weakened as it had been by my soulbonding.

One big cross of wood with ropes strung across it was remade into another one of the same but with a whole new purpose. I caught ahold of the ropes as they dropped in a great stretched tangle, and then I started to pull. My sword was the biggest hunk of metal that I had lying around, so it had become the tip of the giant crossbow bolt. My armor became the fixtures holding this string in place. Yes, I was naked again. No, nobody cared about it when they were being attacked by a giant eel. I made a mental note to make a joke about two giant eels attacking later.

Grunting, I made my way across the deck, every muscle in my body working to draw this string tight enough to spring back. The Dvergar worked out what was happening faster than Mercy and Asher, but it didn't take long for both of them to spring into action either. Mercy grabbed hold of the rudder, lining up our shot, and Asher started casting his electric spells on the metal head of the bolt so that when it struck home, it was really going to do some damage. I could distantly hear Mercy and her Dvergar ninja buddies up on the railings shouting back and forth to each other, but the meaning escaped me. All I knew in that moment was the rush of blood in my ears, the creaking of my shoulders, and the inexorable passage of the boards beneath me.

I hit the far rail of the ship and tucked my chin over it as if the forces involved weren't going to rip my head clean off if I stopped pulling. Behind me, I could hear the bolt being rolled into place, too big to be lifted by anyone but me.

The ship bucked as the eel passed under us again, and it took all my concentration to hold on. There was a thump you could feel across the whole ship as the bolt was knocked out of place. Screams and calls for help followed as Dvergar were flung from their positions, creating splashes when a few unfortunates hit the sea. Beneath the water, the keening cackling call of the eel echoed out. I wished that I could see, but I was also grateful I couldn't. There was no way that the serpent wasn't coming back to eat our lost crew, and if Mercy hadn't have taken her shot before then, then I didn't know what I would have done.

Saltwater had splashed up onto the deck, and my feet were slipping out beneath me. If I lost my grip now, not only would it all have been for nothing, but all the Dvergar frantically trying to roll the bolt back in place would have lost their heads in the bargain.

The chittering came closer, and the waves rolling off the back of the eel set the ship rocking once more. I felt the bolt bump into place rather than saw it or heard the Dvergar bellowing. Now all that was left was the sweet release, when my suffering at least might end. My arms, each thicker around than my whole body had been as a human, were shaking.

Mercy screamed. "Now!"

In the moment of truth, my janky crossbow fired just fine. It wasn't pretty, but it worked. The bolt launched, and it wobbled through the air towards the peaked wave of the rushing serpent. It hit with a sound like a thundercrack.

[314 Damage]

The surface of the water flared white as the spells Asher had heaped into it detonated.

Legendary Foe Defeated!
Celerity increased to 20
Airstrike: Rank 3/10
63 Experience Gained
200 Glory Gained

The chittering sound of the eel's charge stopped abruptly.

The charge did not.

Even though it was dead in the water, the eel was still coming at us fast. Momentum carried the dead and mindless doom-noodle through the water, right at our ship. With the only brains the thing had leaking out into the water behind it, there would be nothing to make it turn away instead of plowing right into us.

"Oh, crap."

"Brace for impact!" Gunhild roared. "Brace!"

This time when the eel hit, it wasn't a little love tap, intended to toss some tasty treats overboard. It's punctured skull hit the side of the ship like a battering ram, busting clean through my shoddy work and bringing the sea in with it.

As the first wave of it washed up my legs I slammed my eyes shut and abandoned my body. All around me, I saw the people I'd brought along on this fool's errand preparing themselves to die. Asher had bowed his head. Mercy was screaming, trying to haul the Dvergar away from the water as it rushed in. Gunhild had her arms wrapped around one of the Dvergar that had no business being anywhere but safe at home. The sea was going to swallow us all.

CHAPTER 27

Now that it was dead, the eel was just a heap of materials, no different than wood, stone, or the rest. I couldn't rework it the same way, but I could use it. Where the wooden slats were too broken to be repaired, bone ribs plucked out of the eel slid into place. Where the water was leaking in through little cracks between the boards, the whole thing was sealed with a coating of the serpent's waterproof hide. Even the wood and metal of the bolt still lodged in the skull could be used again.

The careful painstaking work of days—building and rebuilding—had embedded the knowledge of every part of this ship firmly in my brain. Now all I had to do was follow the instructions I already had. The ship was still sinking, water lapping up around my body's knees, but by the time that the skull of the eel floated free of our side, it was whole again—and probably better made than before. I slipped back into my body, grabbed a bucket, and started bailing out. This could still work. We could still survive this.

That was about the moment that Mercy set everything on fire.

Firewalls worked fine in the open air, but under the water, they flashed into being then faded just a moment later in a mass of bubbles. If that had been the extent of it, then we probably would have been fine, but Asher saw what she was doing and joined in. "What the hell!?"

The water started to boil around my shins from Mercy's flash-fires but at least they were mercifully brief. When Asher's flames leapt out from his mouth, they were anything but. A torrent of flames poured down into the water, throwing up a massive cloud of steam that obscured everything. It was like we were in the middle of a fog bank in an instant, and the only thing we could see was the distant glow of the sun above and the blazing flames pouring forth from Asher's face.

Their plan was working even if the Dvergar were terrified. The huge plumes of steam hid it from view, but the water in the bottom of the ship was definitely going down. Lumbering over to the side I caught sight of the Dvergar scattered around us in the water, clinging to bits of the ship, bits of eel. A few of them that were feeling brave were paddling around, helping their friends. It couldn't have been easy to stay afloat when you were part-rock, so all due respect to those guys. The steam was floating up, so it was easy enough to see that they were all doing alright. As long as they could tread water for a few minutes while we got ship-shape again, we'd have no trouble picking them up.

Which was about the moment that I remembered Seren, bundled in chains.

Pushing through the fleeing Dvergar and the mildly scalding water, I ran to where I remembered her lying against the side of the boat and found nothing. "Seren!?"

I splashed around through the water, hands seeking her beneath the surface and finding nothing. I caught a Dvergar as she passed. "The Alvaren?"

She shrugged and scampered out of sight. Someone must have seen something. I roared, "Where is my Alvaren?!"

There were murmurs of confusion from the Dvergar. Chatter amongst themselves. Finally, one of the braver children called out from his father's arms, "It went over!"

That was exactly what I didn't want to hear. I took off running, and while I'd like to say I did a graceful swan dive into the water, it was one hundred percent a belly flop.

Gasping in some air, I went under.

Without all the chaos of the eel in motion, the water was relatively clear. There was a kelp forest down beneath us, so deep that my ears popped just looking at it, but there was no sign of Seren. I let my *Lifesense* stretch out in every direction, and I was inundated with the Dvergar, the fish, the kelp, and even the plankton and tiny shrimp too tiny to make out. Everything was alive in the ocean; everything was static to my senses. Swimming down deeper and deeper, I pressed my eyes shut and listened to my *Lifesense* exclusively. She had to be down here. She had to be alive.

At the edge of my senses, I felt the familiar prickling of an Alvaren. She was still alive, if only barely. Either that or there was another Alvaren down here, and I really didn't have the mental bandwidth for that right now.

Down into the forest of kelp I headed, pushing the tendrils aside as they did their damnedest to tangle around me. Was there sentient, murderous kelp here? Was it just regular kelp? Was this even kelp? I didn't spend a lot of time underwater back on earth. I assumed it was kelp.

The shimmer of metal caught my eye, and I plunged on. She was still alive, and she was glowering up at me with pure unadulterated hatred in her eyes. The more things changed, the more they stayed the same.

I reached out with my Artifice and broke her chains. In an instant, she shot up out of the kelp like a champagne cork, zooming right past me without a second glance. The need for air outweighed the need for vengeance. I was feeling much the same. My lungs were burning as I floundered about and then started swimming back up towards the ship.

Either sharks or the native equivalent was going to be showing up any minute now, so I put on another turn of speed, burning my Potency Surge to get the hell out of the water just a moment after Seren was hauled up onto the deck by the waiting Dvergar. If they tried to help me up like that, they were going to end up in the sea. I launched myself up like a performing seal and caught onto the edge of the boat myself, rocking the whole thing with my bulk.

On the deck, I rolled onto my back to catch my breath. That was not fun. I did not like the sea. The sea was not my friend. There was some shouting from among the Dvergar and Mercy at the sight of the unbound Alvaren amongst us, but I pushed myself up and groaned, "Give it a rest."

Gunhild scrambled for her crossbow. "You be setting her free?"

"Where is she going to go?" I hooked some seaweed off my horns and threw it overboard. "We're in the middle of the ocean."

Mercy already had an arrow drawn. "She's going to murder us in our sleep!"

Seren looked like a drowned rat. All of the glitz and glamour of the Alvaren had been washed away by a good dunk in the sea. Her hair hung lank about her face, and bereft of her armor, the elegant black cloth she wore beneath looked about as imposing as a wet potato sack. I looked back to Mercy. "No, she isn't."

Seren and Mercy both snapped around to demand the same thing, "What?"

I lay back on the deck and waited for the sun to dry me off. "She isn't going to kill us. I just saved her life."

Out of sight, I heard a scuffle, then my eyes bulged open as Seren landed hard on top of me. She had a knife in her hand, snatched from one of the Dvergar. "You attempted to drown me yourself but a moment ago. Give me one good reason that I should not end you here and now."

She had landed on my stomach, so it took me a moment to catch my breath and answer, "Because you're smart enough to know that there is more going on here than your boss told you. Because I risked my life to rescue you for no good reason except I wanted to. Because you've got some sense of honor going on, even if it is all messed up. And if all of that wasn't enough…because I'm sexy as hell?"

She pressed the point of the dagger into the hollow of my throat. Prickly and tickly. "What does your carnal appeal matter to the debate?"

I waggled my eyebrows as Mercy groaned. "So you do think I'm sexy?"

To my delight and surprise, a tiny blue tint crept over Seren's nose and cheeks, beneath the freckles. She was blushing. And she was mad about it. Her eyes blazed with fury. "You are a beast. Beneath my notice."

"I'm beneath you alright." I rolled my hips, and she shot off me like she'd been burned. The knife was dropped on the deck, and she was cowering behind Asher. "Right, glad that is settled."

Mercy pointed her arrow at me now. "I swear to the gods, if you don't put some pants on right now I'm going to shoot another wiggly serpent in the head today."

"Pants are at the top of my to-do list," I grumbled and rose to my feet. The poor Dvergar were right at head-height for the danger zone. "If everyone stopped threatening to murder me, I'd get to them a lot quicker."

There wasn't much in the way of spare metal or leather about the boat, even if I had reclaimed the bolthead to remake my sword, but at the edge of my *Sphere of Influence,* more material than I could ever use was still drifting just beneath the surface of the water.

The Dvergar ducked as fragments of scale and bone came fluttering up out of the sea to encase me. Sinews coiled through the torn skin to latch it into place, bone fragments chattering as they pulled together into a brand-new suit of armor that somehow managed to look even jankier than the old one that had been made out of kitchenware.

An armor rating of 55 wasn't bad, and it definitely felt a lot lighter than the last set—also marginally less likely to drag me down to the bottom of the ocean if a certain Alvaren decided to roll me overboard while I was napping. Not that she would. I was totally confident about that. So confident that I was going to do all of my sleeping hugging the mast.

With clothes on my body and the ship back in ship-shape, it didn't take long before we were underway again. Progress seemed slower now, but it might have been because I was paying so much more attention, waiting for a knife between the ribs that never quite seemed to come. I mostly kept to the back of the boat, steadying the rudder and adjusting as Mercy and her spotters silently directed. The fact that nobody could sneak up behind me there was a total coincidence.

I could see the whole ship from where I was. I could see the Dvergar swerving to keep out of Seren's way as she paced. Now that she was free from her chains, she seemed less inclined to help Asher out with his research, but hopefully, this was a step in the right direction. It was hard to make people trust you when you had them chained up, and in the end, we needed her to trust us if we were going to learn anything useful about the War, Araphel, and the shards.

The hours rolled on, with the waves rhythmically thumping and the Waystones passing by on the horizon, guiding us farther and farther out to sea. The air was thick, and clouds that had started out as delicate little puffs in the big blue sky were now grey slabs blotting out the sun and the blue alike. The wind whipped up, and while I appreciated the turn of speed, I didn't like the slight tingling sensation that I was getting on the back of my neck, like Asher was preparing one of his lightning bolts somewhere nearby. Despite all of that, I was fairly sure that it was actually getting warmer.

Just when I thought I might have to slough off my lovely new eel-skin suit to cool down, the rain came down. Just a gentle spritz rather than the downpour I'd been expecting. Refreshing rather than a danger to the safety of the ship. The only downside was that it cut visibility down to the point that we had to drop anchor in sight of the next Waystone and work out our next move.

Mercy and Asher came to me already arguing, her voice getting louder and louder with every step.

"…blow us all up in the bargain!"

I blinked. "Who is blowing us up?"

Asher stepped in front of her. "There shall be no explosions, not any need for hysterics. I have simply devised a plan that will allow us to continue through the foul weather."

Mercy's head popped over his shoulder. "Or blow us up."

I held up my hands. "One at a time. Asher, what is your idea?"

"The Waystones are designed as a conduit, to conduct magic between them. Were I to cast a spell into the ring, I believe that we could follow the course that it traced out to the next site without the need of constant visual confirmation."

That made sense. I nodded. "Okay. Mercy?"

"That is totally going to blow us up. It is like throwing plutonium in a coal stove, or coal in a nuclear… It is like mixing two things that are totally different, and there is no way of knowing what will happen. The stones are only meant for transportation, if he shoots lightning up the hole he might wreck them all or explode us."

That also made sense. I nodded. "Okay."

Mercy looked to Asher, then back to me with annoyance. "So what should we do?"

"Nap."

Asher cocked his head to one side. "Nap?"

The Dvergar took up the call along the length of the ship, "Shift is up!" Groans of relief rippled along them.

My presence was going to be required to pull down the sails and convert them into a tent to cover the ship's deck and provide us with some shelter through the night. "The crew needs to rest. It is getting dark. The rain might pass in the morning, and if it doesn't, then we can think about the zap-a-ring plan."

Mercy stepped in my path, and I nearly tripped over her. "And what happens when another giant eel shows up and takes a bite out of us sitting here like a...duck."

I smirked. "We're wearing the skin of the last sea serpent to try it. I figure we don't look too appetizing about now."

Asher cocked his head the other way. "A fair point. Very well, let us take some rest."

Mercy was less impressed. "Come on, you lazy ass, you slept all the way through all the research back at Witchglass Overlook, you can't be tired again."

"I wasn't tired then either, I just didn't want to do my homework."

She held up a vibrating finger towards me, staring wide-eyed at Asher, and he gave a little nod of concession. She told him so. "Then what the hell?"

"You, me, and Asher can go forever. Everyone else can't. Cut them some slack."

Mercy grumbled away. Asher gave me a polite nod and went back to his books. It took me only a couple of minutes to clear the rigging and rebuild the ship into a floating tent.

The rain drummed on the canvas above us gently, as if the sway of the ship wasn't going to be enough to bob us off to sleep. Dinner was sparse for the Dvergar and even more sparse for us. I didn't want to tap into their very limited supplies of food when I didn't even technically need to eat. The fact that most of it looked to be dried mushrooms really helped seal the deal. Mercy's fire was used sparingly to heat up some soupy-stew, and I made a mental note to put together some fishing nets come morning. Maybe we should have held onto some of the eel chunks.

The chatter was subdued. Nobody was feeling the party spirit after seeing their whole civilization fall into a hole a few days ago. Funny that. Even the lucky few who'd fallen in the sea and been retrieved without any harm whatsoever weren't sharing their stories. A whole boat full of sad sacks.

There was no clear sign of when to go to bed, but at some point, they all went their separate ways. Some of Gunhild's boys positioned themselves outside the tent to keep watch, the rest trying to make up beds out of whatever soft material they could find. I was made of tougher stuff. I'd been a boy-scout for almost three whole weeks in my last life. I could sleep on a heap of rusty screwdrivers and like it—and that was before I grew skin thick enough to make an elephant think that some exfoliation might be required. Asher had retreated to his nest of books, and Mercy was off with her ninja Dvergar buddies, messing around with the spare rigging trying to make hammocks. I plopped myself down at the back end of the tent-boat in case I needed to jump up and get us going fast for any totally non-eel-related reason through the night.

The crew didn't need my night-light eyeballs waking them up if I stirred, so I put my back to them all and settled down, nothing in front of me but canvas and the sound of the sea lapping away. With nothing left to do in the day, I closed my eyes; trusting in my other senses to warn me of danger if it came along.

I got about a minute of darkness before all my senses started screaming, "Danger! Danger!"

I didn't jump up, but I did open my eyes rather abruptly. Seren jerked back, that same blue tint coming to her cheeks. She said nothing, but after an ambivalent moment, she dropped to the deck and turned her back to me. She curled up a little, but from the rigidity of her back, it was pretty obvious she wasn't going to sleep. "Uh…"

"I am attempting to rest, do not disturb me."

That had me opening and shutting my mouth a good few times before I decided I had to ask, "You know you could sleep anywhere you wanted on the boat?"

"This is the position that I have chosen. Be silent." She shuffled a little closer to me as another breeze swept under the canvas. What the hell?

I wet my lips. Apparently, I was already dreaming, so I might as well go with it. "Lady, if you are trying to get some of that sweet faun loving, you are going to have to be a lot more obvious about it."

The look on her face when she turned around was pure disdain. If they ever did a photo-book of facial expressions, that would be the one they pick for the disdain page. Ultimate disdain. "If you were capable of thinking beyond thy animal impulses to rut for just a moment, you might understand that I am surrounded by enemies here upon this ship. Most would be delighted to slit me from throat to gizzard were they given the opportune moment. Of all these enemies, only one has proven with action that they intend to preserve my life. The only one willing to stand as my advocate and protect my freedom."

I smiled at her. "Does that mean you forgive me for the uh... dunking in the sea thing, from earlier?"

"I believe that you too are possessed of some stunted sense of honor." The blush had returned in full force. Not the anger I'd been expecting. "And in debasing me so, you claimed a degree of ownership over me. Just as I had you with my jibes. It has reinforced to me that you are... Let us just say for now that you are the one who holds my chains. The one that will keep and protect me from harm until I am returned to my queen."

Sometimes I swear that my brain and my mouth have no connection. "Is this a kinky thing or a feudal thing?"

She looked puzzled at both terms—thank the gods—and after a moment's pause, she said, "It is an act of trust."

Feeling like even more of a heel than usual, I gave her an awkward little sideways bow-nod thing, but she had already rolled back over to go to sleep after her dramatic pronouncement, all the tension that had been thrumming through her since we first crossed paths gone in an instant. Great. Glad she was feeling better.

Meanwhile, I could already feel my shoulders tightening up every time anyone so much as stirred behind me. Seren was right. Any one of the Dvergar would happily see her dead, and they'd said as much while she was still passed out and the debate about what to do with her had raged on. The ones that didn't want to decapitate her in her sleep wanted to throw her in the sea. The Dvergar were not big on forgiveness as a general rule, and their approach to prisoners of war was entirely rooted in the practicality of their living situations. The Dvergar had never lived without some degree of rationing in their underground home, or while traveling between khags, and that meant that every time they choose to put food in an enemy's belly they were taking it out of their own, weakening their own defenses to keep somebody alive that wanted them dead. It was a pretty simple calculation for people living perpetually on the knife-edge of extinction.

Maybe I wouldn't be sleeping after all.

CHAPTER 28

B y the time that dawn rolled around, I was good and grumpy. I'd been lying there, not quite sleeping, for a solid seven hours. Solid as in, solid wooden planks digging into my side, my horns bumping on the wood every time that the ship rode over a wave, and my eyes snapping open every time a pair of Dvergar stirred to swap out for those on watch or to go to the toilet over the side. I was starting to suspect that it was some kind of practical joke. Surely, they couldn't all need to pee.

At the first glimmer of sunlight on the horizon, I was up and tearing the ship apart, slamming the mast back up, slitting tents into sails, and restitching it all with a flex of will. There were eel-skin patches on the wax-cloth that I didn't even remember making, but given how much of the ship was coated in the stuff at this point, it was hardly surprising.

Seren was up and at my side by the time that I had finished the re-assembly. Gawking. "What kind of magic is this? Even my queen could not..."

I cut her off with a laugh. "I already told you we're Eternals. This is what we can do. Well, part of it."

She was looking at me coyly. Not angry the way that she had been before but still dubious. "There is no need for deception. It is no surprise to me that progress has marched on since our time ruling this world. Thousands of years have passed–of course, magic has been improved upon."

This was going to be awkward. How do you tell somebody that their utopia turned into a post-apocalyptic wasteland while they were having a nap? "Uh, you might want to talk to Asher about that, he's our magic expert, but from what I hear, you guys are still top dog when it comes to spells and wands."

She flinched at the word "dogs" and I immediately regretted the turn of phrase, but by then Mercy was bounding over. "Aw, did you two make up?"

I gave Seren a sideways glance. "Well, I think we've agreed not to kill each other."

She gave Mercy a curt nod. "This is so."

That was enough Alvaren weirdness for one morning. I clapped my hands together. "So how is it looking?"

"Still drizzling."

"Ah, drizzle." I turned my face up to the grey sky. "The most fun of all weathers."

She was not getting distracted. "Are you going to let Asher blow us up?"

"Yeah, probably." I shrugged. "He seems to know what he's doing."

She fell into step beside me as I strolled along the ship, checking that my repairs were sticking. "What he's doing is blowing us up."

I stopped in my tracks. "Hey now, he is probably only going to blow up the Waystones. And we can always follow the trail of wreckage."

She prodded me in the side and abruptly, Seren was there, glowering at her. Mercy gave me a confused look and stepped away. "When we all die, I'm going to say I told you so. A lot."

"I wouldn't expect anything less."

Asher hadn't moved from his book heap since we got on the boat, and he didn't show any signs of moving now. He didn't even look up as we approached. "Are you aware that you can unlock new skills from reading?"

"Yeah, I think I got some ancient history back when we were digging through the prophet's papers."

"It would have been helpful to know that in advance. I would have made a broader selection from the Witchglass Library instead of focusing upon my areas of interest, we might have all improved ourselves."

"Yeah, but if we'd brought all the books you wanted to bring the boat would have sunk, so…"

"You wish for me to cast the spell now?"

"Please."

The clouds above us roared and rumbled as Asher gathered lightning between his clawed hands, and I started to wonder if calling up lightning in the middle of bad weather was maybe a bad idea. Just as I was about to say so, he snapped his arms apart.

He hit the bullseye on the first shot the lightning bolt jumping straight through the center of the great floating ring of metal before abruptly looping back on itself and coiling around the metal. Round and round and round it went until the whole ring was crackling with electricity that seemed to have nowhere to go.

Dvergar were already frantically hauling up the anchor. Gunhild called over, "Do we be needing to run?"

Mercy said, "Uh…"

I said, "Um…"

Asher shook his head. "This is as it should be."

Strangely his confidence didn't do much to calm everybody down. Nor did the increasingly high-pitched whining coming from the ring or the fact that every metal object on the deck now seemed to be slowly sliding over towards that starboard side.

Seren stepped behind me, and I only had half a moment to consider I was about to get a knife in the kidneys before I realized that she was only using me as cover in case of explosions. Mercy was doing the same on my other side. Real classy, ladies.

Just when I thought I was going to have to cover my ears, something gave. The coiled lightning leapt off in a great crackling white-blue line over the horizon. "That's where we're headed, folks! Let's get those oars moving and the sails trimmed!"

I wasn't completely sure that any of the boat terminology I was using was right, but none of the Dvergar knew better, so I got away with it. They sprang into action. Even the ones that had still been lying on the deck blinking at the dawn light were up and moving by the time that I made it to the rudder.

"Follow that lightning bolt!"

And so our day went. Sailing in the light of Asher's lightning to each new Waystone, then pausing there for the last leg of our journey to go dark and the lightning to leap on. The rain came down heavier and heavier the farther we went, but it was not the chilling rain that I'd come to expect. The water falling from the sky was warm like we were all getting a comfortable shower, not the kind that was meant to make bad and naughty thoughts go away.

Seren spent her day chatting intermittently with Asher in his book nest, supplying answers to questions I probably wouldn't have even thought to ask, and slowly but surely relaxing. Every time she got an answer back from him, I could see the same little line appearing between her brows. That same expression of doubt that she treated every statement we made with, but at least she wasn't screaming that we were all lying liars who lie anymore. She might not believe everything she was hearing, but at least she seemed to be hearing it now.

More often than not, when I glanced over at her, she was looking right back at me. After looking away awkwardly the first few times, I spent a solid minute or two locked in a staring contest with her. Asher didn't look up from his books often enough to notice, but Mercy definitely did.

While she was doing the rounds, handing out some of our sparse rations at what was probably lunchtime, she stopped to lean against me and singsonged, "Someone's got a crush."

I scoffed. "Are you kidding me? That psycho was trying to stab me a few hours ago."

"Yeah, but you're both freaks." She jostled my arm, and I had to reset our course again. "A little bit of attempted murder is like foreplay for you. It is like pulling a girl's hair on the playground. You smack her with a sword. She stabs you in the side. You both snark at each other for hours…"

I grinned down at her. "By that logic, you'd have killed me from sexual exhaustion by now."

"Ew."

I gave her a little shove. "Why don't you go worry about your own love life. How many of the seven…Dvergar have proposed to you so far, snow white?"

"And again I say, ew." She glanced up at the rigging to make sure none of her little ninja buddies were around. "Those guys are like… work friends."

It was my turn to look dubious. "Uh-huh?"

"I… You… Shut up." She went back to her rounds, and I let out a little sigh of relief. Sneaking around, trying to make people talk about their feelings. What was she thinking?

Asher had the right idea. He was keeping his head down, his eyes on the prize—assuming the prize was a big old pile of books. In Asher's world, it probably was. I certainly hadn't ever seen him happier than he was right there on the deck of the ship, researching to his heart's content.

Seren was staring at me again, but this time I chose to ignore it. Wouldn't want to give Mercy the wrong idea about things.

It was almost nightfall when the call came down from on top of the mast that they had spotted land. I still couldn't see it, but I knew it had to be coming up soon. The lightning had dispersed in a great pulse across the darkening sky when it reached the final waystone, so there was no question that the chain had been broken, one way or the other.

Duties were abandoned as the Dvergar and Mercy scrambled forward to get their first glimpse of our destination. Even Asher rose stiffly from his place on the deck to take it in. At the back end of the ship, steering, I was probably the last person to get a glimpse of the jungle rising up on the horizon.

The island wasn't huge, maybe a few miles across. It was small enough that from our approach we could see it from end to end. Jungle from beach to beach, like a castaway's dream. Rich and lush and green—the way that nothing back on the mainland had been. If you aren't clear on the difference between a forest and a jungle, it is pretty straightforward. You just take the green and crank it up to eleven. Everywhere that something living could go, something living does grow. Like somebody took the magic plant potion that everywhere else gets a little sprinkle of and dumped a whole vat of it out.

"It would be unwise to make landfall before the coming dawn." Two bells. I needed one for around Asher's neck and one for around Seren's. It could be like a team uniform. I'd wear one too, I was cool with it. You can never have too much cowbell.

I was too startled to come up with a comeback. "Yeah?"

"It would place you at a great disadvantage to enter such terrain by night." She leaned back against the railing, staring off towards the distant shore, backlit by the setting sun. Did she deliberately pose at every opportunity or was that just how Alvaren stood?

I pointed to my glowing eyes. "We can see in the dark."

"You can see as well as by daylight?" She rolled her eyes. "When all the night predators are astir? When you cannot call upon aid from thy runtling chattel?"

It took me a second to catch that last bit. "Runt... Hey! Don't call the Dvergar names."

She scowled across the ship. "They deserve worse than rude words for their sins."

I waved a hand in front of her face, bringing the glower back to me, where it belonged. "No. They don't. These Dvergar aren't the ones you knew. These are just people. And it isn't like they haven't paid enough for the bad decisions their ancestors made."

"The curse of theirs? Your wyrm-spawn spoke of it in passing. Though anyone with eyes could see it. Let us just say that the Dvergar in my time were less modest in their dress. Still, the curse is but a small recompense for the evil they have unleashed upon this world."

I needed to nip that in the bud. "It wasn't them."

"Who then if not the Dvergar greedily delving?" She waved a contemptuous hand out at my crew, and a few of them seemed to notice that she was speaking about them. This was not going to end well for anyone. "Who if not for these runtling curs could have unleashed—"

"It wasn't these Dvergar." I cut her off dead, my voice more of a growl than I'd intended. I tried to ease off, keep the conversation light and breezy. If this turned into a screaming argument there was no way the Dvergar weren't going to overhear and throw her overboard, no matter what I said. "You aren't every single Alvaren. I'm not every single eternal. We are all just people, and you need to stop blaming these people for things that they had no control over. This whole world needs to move on."

Her voice had dropped deep in fury. "Easily you speak for someone that never suffered the depredations of the Voidgod's Revelation."

"They've done their time."

"Amaranth is in ruins by their hand, and you expect that I will grant forgiveness to the ones who unleashed that ruin?" Now it was more of a hiss. That pretty face was thinning down again, her pupils shrinking to pinpricks. Time for the truth bomb.

"Amaranth is a battlefield. A game for the gods. A wargame where they work out their differences. There was never any chance that this place wouldn't end up trashed. What I don't understand is how you geniuses never worked out that the only way you'll survive it is by working together."

She crossed her arms with an air of finality. "When the Alvaren empire ruled the skies and our vassals ruled the land, we had the unity you speak of. Perfect order across the lands. A shining empire that would have lasted out eternity. Your Dvergar ruined that."

There really wasn't a nice way to say this. "You understand that people can work together without most of those people being slaves, right?"

"Once more your wisdom is that of a back-birthed child. For there to be order, there must be leadership. For there to be leadership, there must be hierarchy and obedience."

The boat went into a swerve when I let go of the rudder, but I didn't care. I slammed my arms down on either side of Seren. Face to face with her. The cold anger wasn't back, thank the gods, but I was still prickling with rage. "You can lead people without owning them."

She didn't even flinch. If anything she seemed more comfortable nose to nose with me than she'd been all day, and that old infuriating sneer was back on her face. "The limits of thy experience are cleanly marked. Given enough time, you will come to understand things the way that we elder races do. All leaders make slaves of their followers. It is the true nature of things. There is a beauty in purity. In honesty. We Alvaren have abandoned the pretense. If we must subjugate a people so that order can be created, then we make no false promises. They obey us because we are the powerful and the perfect. We command them because they are the lesser."

I don't know when it happened, but the next thing that I knew I had leaned in so close that I could see my breath displacing her hair where it hung around her face. "You think I'm less than you?"

"Not you." Those tiny black pinpricks in her eyes blossomed out until they were taking up my whole field of vision. She turned her head away, a blue tint playing over her cheeks. "If you are Eternals, as you claim, then you are my equal. We would have a place for you in the new world that we must make, by our side."

Mercy coughed so aggressively I'm surprised she didn't dislodge a tooth. "Am I interrupting something?"

My train of thought derailed, and all that prickling anger washed away in a wave of embarrassment. I turned around so fast Seren had to duck under my horns. "We're mooring off the coast until morning."

Mercy looked back and forth between me and Seren. "Uh-huh."

"Don't uh-huh me, Snow White."

Her eyes narrowed. "I will shoot you right in the eel."

"And I shall disembowel you before the arrow is drawn."

We both turned to look at Seren with dismay, and she flushed again. "Is this not the manner in which you speak amongst yourselves?"

Mercy didn't laugh, but it was a near thing. "Tone was a little off, sweetheart."

I pushed away from the two of them, bellowing to the Dvergar, "Drop anchor and get dinner started!"

There was another round of relieved sighs. They didn't want to be on the boat, and they'd been pretty clear about that from the get-go, but the Dvergar seemed even less enthusiastic about heading into a jungle at night. Seren had a point. I was willing to admit she had one good point. Only the one.

After our little flare-up, Seren and I had kept our distance throughout dinner, made a lot easier by the fact that she ate and I didn't, but when it was all over and I'd settled myself down at the edge of the tent, she came and curled up beside me again. "You know you'd be just as safe sleeping with Asher or Mercy, right?"

She shuffled back towards me a little. "I disagree with thy assessment. Your bulk makes you a far better shield."

"Are you trying to make a joke again?"

She stopped shuffling. "Perhaps."

"Good night, Seren."

"And unto you."

By dawn, she'd made her way close enough that I could smell her hair. Honey and lavender. She'd been chasing us for days, been dunked in the ocean, and somehow, she still smelled like honey and lavender. I'd managed to sleep through the night this time around, only stirring once when a Dvergar made the mistake of stepping too close to me, so the presence of a warm body in arm's reach came as something of a shock.

I was on my feet with my hands up before I even knew I was awake. "No touching!"

The Dvergar around about me startled from their sleep, then rolled over when they realized it was just more Eternal nonsense. Seren glanced back at me but said nothing. Desperate for a distraction, I started breaking down the tent and remaking the ship before anyone could say anything about anything.

With the sun up, the rain cleared to another gentle and sporadic patter, and the cloth of our makeshift tent moved aside, I felt like I was getting my first good look at the island. Off amongst the trees, the sun glinted off something white. The same shimmering stone that the pillars of the Waystones had been carved from—and Witchglass Overlook too. A tower of it, so tall that it rose above the canopy of the jungle and beyond, reaching up like a grasping hand with three jutting fingers trying to snatch the sun from the sky. Asher joined me at the prow. "Talon's Keep."

I spread my arms wide. King-of-the-worlding. "That's her."

He looked at me sideways but kept his peace. "Do you mean to bring the Dvergar into the forest with us?"

"Do you want to leave them on the boat to be eaten by sea-serpents? At least if they're with us, somebody will try to protect them."

"Do you be thinking we've no say in this, boys?" Gunhild elbowed her way between us, pointing a brass telescope off towards the tower. "We'll be marching right along with you. Outpost like this would be needing a lot of infrastructure. Farms and the like. Might be there's someplace to restock our supplies. Maybe even a dry patch to lay our heads."

I put a finger over the end of her telescope, and she grinned as she yanked it away from her eye. "You don't like sleeping on a boat?"

"The rock, solid beneath me. That is what I be liking." She spat over the side. "The sea can away and drown itself."

"Not sure if that would work, but I get what you mean."

With a full complement of Dvergar on the oars, we moved in towards the shore, the gentle ebb and flow of the waves bouncing us as we went. Despite my eel-skin repairs, the ship still looked ragtag at best and decaying at worst. We were lucky it had served us this far. I really needed to upgrade my Artifice so I could start making better boats. And weapons. And armor.

We started bumping over rocks before we even got close to the white sands of safety, with only the toughness of the eel-hide I'd coated the ship with stopping us from springing a half-dozen leaks. Even with it, a few of the Dvergar were scampering around, stomping boards back into their rightful places and pouring out our last precious supplies of tar. I wasn't even sure it was worth it. Sure, we were going to need a ship to get off this little slice of heaven when we were done, but there was a whole island's worth of fresh trees they could use to make one. There didn't seem to be much point in hanging onto this one for anything except materials.

For all their protestations of hating this ship, the Dvergar sure did want to keep it in one piece.

It wasn't an ego thing when I insisted that I was the first off the boat, it was practicality. Whatever this new island had in terms of hideous monsters, I was the one most likely to survive being smacked in the face with them.

Okay, maybe it was a little bit of an ego thing. I felt a weird impulse to stick a flag in the ground, even though I knew there had already been people living here. A lot of world history suddenly made a lot more sense.

Asher, Mercy, Gunhild, and Seren came on down next. All the best fighters we had on offer, just in case the jungle was as full of dinosaurs as it looked like. I crept up the beach towards the trees' edge, then realized how stupid I was being. The whole point of me going first was to draw the attention of anything nasty that might snack on the Dvergar later. I whistled, long and shrill.

Whether it made it any farther than the edge of the jungle I couldn't say. We could certainly hear bird calls coming from inside, a cacophony of them, but if anybody heard me, there was no sign. I turned back to the rest of them and shrugged. "All clear?"

Mercy shouted over from beside the boat. "You are so bad at this."

"Oh, like you know any better."

Even unarmed, Seren moved like she was ready for a fight, slinking up behind my position on the beach. "The decision was tactically sound."

"Get a room!"

Seren raised an eyebrow, but when I didn't even attempt to explain what that colorful little turn of phrase meant, she seemed to discard it. I drew my sword and marched on into the forest. Gunhild called after me, "And where do you think you be going?"

"We're headed to the tower, yeah?" I shrank my sword down until it was more like a meat cleaver again, a machete to hack my way through the dense vines. "No point hanging around."

With the excess metal, I made a second chopper and passed it back to Seren. Distantly, I could still hear Gunhild back on the sand. The jungle muffled sound amazingly. "And what about our supplies?"

"Leave them on the boat?" I bellowed back over my shoulder. "It isn't like there's anyone about to steal them!"

That was when I noticed Seren looking from me to the blade in her hands and back again. Ah yeah, I forgot she wanted to kill me. Slight error in judgment there. "You cannot mean for me to have this weapon. Forged of your own blade, no less. Thy are testing me."

Progress was slow through the jungle. A few faltering attempts at using *Artifice* to do some serious deforestation had ended up with me face down and my Divine Pillars aching. There was too much alive in the forest for me to work it. Chopped down, I could probably use these trees for whatever I pleased, but not as long as they were alive, enmeshed in the rest of the tangled web of roots, parasites and symbiotes. Not to mention being filled with critters all happily living out their fuzzy little lives. So we chopped.

It probably would have been a lot quicker if somebody was using their cleaver-machete instead of talking about it, but she was clearly having a moment here. "I'm not testing you, I'm trusting you. Let's see how it works out."

If she found any happiness or pleasure in me trusting her, it didn't show on that carefully schooled face of hers. If anything she looked annoyed with me as she stepped up by my shoulder and began slicing away. "Your kinfolk shall not approve of this, you must know that. Even the wyrmling is cautious of me."

"Well, you did beat him unconscious and tie him up that one time."

Her blade seemed to dance as we moved in deeper. Her cuts weren't as powerful as mine, but up against an enemy as tough and fearsome as some vines they didn't really need to be. "The favor was returned, post-haste."

"What's a little beating and bondage between friends, eh?" I grinned, but she wasn't looking.

"We are not friends, Eternal. I am your hostage. It is merely advantageous for me to assist you as it grants me freedoms that I would not have expected to enjoy." She reached over where I was cutting, deftly severing a knotted vine that was supporting the one I was trying to hack down, arms and blade weaving through mine like it was a dance.

"So you're finally admitting I'm an Eternal?"

She paused, glancing at me. "I am willing to entertain the possibility that every word you speak is not a twisted lie."

With a snort, I pushed on. "Thanks."

Mercy had the good grace to make some noise as she ran through the jungle. No cowbell for her. "Hey, Maulkin, tag out. They need you to help haul supplies."

I groaned. "I told them to leave them on the ship."

"Yeah, well in a shocking twist nobody gives a damn what your opinion is. Go carry heavy things."

"Ugh. Fine! Try not to chop your own leg off." I tossed her the cleaver as I passed.

She stopped dead when she saw Seren at work. "Uh…"

"Got to go carry heavy things. Have fun. Bye!" I power walked away from that conversation before it could even start.

In my absence, the lovely Dvergar had lashed all the supplies that they could manage onto a big sled and made a nice big loop of rope to tie around me. I was literally being used as a beast of burden now. Great.

Gunhild sat on top of the stack of barrels and crates as we wobbled up the beach and into the trees. "Don't you be whining now, big lad. You might be the best fighter we've got, but you're not worth the dozen men it would take to haul this without you."

"Next time I get reincarnated in a new world, I'm coming back as something small and feeble, so nobody makes me do things."

"Aye, that be working out well for your boy Asher." That prick had the Dvergar carrying his books for him, a stack of them balanced in each set of arms he could find. Apparently, he was concerned about water damage. I had no idea how we were going to get him to go on adventures again now that he'd found his one true love.

With a heave and a growl, I got the sled over a buried root. "I swear, I'm going to burn those books while he's sleeping."

"Don't you be daft now," Gunhild said, letting her silence linger for a long moment before adding, "They'd make fine kindling. Burning them up for no good reason be wasteful."

I was still laughing when the attack came.

CHAPTER 29

I didn't even have a chance to see what was coming at us before it burst out of the woods and bore me to the ground in a tangle of ropes.

There were teeth locked in my arm—a bite that had been meant for my neck. Whether it was pure luck or instinct that got my arm up before the beast hit, I couldn't say. All I could say was that it hurt like hell. Even nose to nose with the creature, I couldn't get a good look at it. There was a vague sense of crocodile about the snout, but the eyes behind it looked more like the bulbous cones of a chameleon. One looked on me, the other turned back to stare at Gunhild where she fumbled her crossbow.

Chameleon. That was why I still couldn't make out more than the outline of the thing. It was shifting colors to blend in with the jungle. Stupid monster-mash lizard. I hammered a fist into its face.

[21 Damage]

"Let."

[19 Damage]

"Me."

[20 Damage]

"Go!"

[18 Damage]

With every bop on the nose, I could see the eyes swivel around and the colors ripple out from the point of impact. Still, the damned thing wouldn't let go.

There was a thumping, pulsing sensation in my arm where it had bitten, which I'd first taken for the thumping of my own heart, but now that it was slowing, I realized that it was venom pumping out from the hollow needle teeth that were locked in my flesh.

Numbness spread out from the bite, not cold, just…nothing. Death crept out, leaving that whole side of my body feeling bloodless. Good thing my other side was still working.

Instead of another wild swing, the next time that I twisted my body around, I stretched out past the snout and grabbed hold of the eye-cone.

That got its attention. The grip on my arm loosened, but not as much as it loosened when I squeezed and twisted.

An awful noise vibrated out around my dead arm. A trilling wail somewhere between nails on a chalkboard and a spider set on fire. The eye turned to mush in my hand, and I flung it away.

Uncoupled from my arm, the lizard leapt back out of reach just in time for Gunhild's shot to go wide.

The numbness was spreading across my chest from the shoulder, and the grey of my skin turned pallid and lifeless, the black veins beneath growing ever starker. When it passed over the midpoint, my upper-body went full ragdoll, the dead muscles no longer holding up my weight. I managed to stagger around for a moment before the weight of my own bulk pulled me down.

My face hit the mulch. Gunhild was scrambling to reload as the lizard waddled back in. Could a partially invisible lizard look smug? It looked smug.

I was going to die. Worse than that, I was going to die to some big reptile in some jungle in the middle of nowhere. Death by beast, the gods had called it. It seemed cruel for it to happen to me three times in a row.

Closing my eyes, I was surrounded with everything I could possibly need to make a weapon—metal ore in the crates, wood all around me, even rope to tie things together—yet none of it mattered because my body would not move. My unbitten arm still had some life in it, but even my head was lolling uselessly to the side.

When I opened my eyes again, I wished that I hadn't. The jaws of the lizard were opening, and then the jaw dislocated with a pop as it spread wider and wider. It was going to swallow me. Just what I needed. Slow and painful death being digested alive. Even better than just dying.

Poison Resistance: Rank 10/10

The trait shone with moonlight as it was written permanently into my being, and the number faded away.

Suddenly the numbness felt a lot less numb, allowing me to clench a fist.

The lizard lunged for me at the same moment I flung myself up. The jaws tried to snap shut on me, but they were spread too wide, and the stretched-out muscles were too slow to clench tight again. With one hand on each of its jaws, I pulled them even wider apart.

That same screeching keening noise came out of the crocodile face, but I had no time for mercy. This thing would have made me its lunch if I'd let it. With a flex of my shoulders and a boost of Potency, I ripped the jaws apart.

Now it was the gator's turn to feel its parts fall useless. It tried to scramble backward still wailing, but I was having none of it. A stick leapt into my hand, sharpening itself into a spear point as I thrust it between the dangling jaw and the fixed row of venom-dripping fangs.

The tip burst out through the back of the lizard's head, and the whole thing collapsed to the ground in a heap.

Victory!
Potency increased to 45
Celerity increased to 21
Brawling: Rank 9/10
Polearm: Rank 1/10
70 Experience Gained

Dead, I could see what had been hidden by its color shifting before. The whole thing was massive and over-muscled beneath the scaly skin, and the jaws and head, in particular, seemed to be grossly overdeveloped, but even so, the monster was obviously from the same family tree as Asher. Gunhild let out a hiss. "Wyrm-spawn."

"Feral Inyoka."

Up ahead, I heard another reptilian screech, and without even thinking, I launched myself into a full-on charge. Mercy and Seren were in the jungle up ahead. All alone against the…

I slowed to a jog when I caught sight of the girls ahead of me. Mercy was drenched in blood and still furiously hacking away at the remains of the Inyoka on the ground, even though it was clearly dead. Seren, meanwhile, was moving through a series of elegant moves with her cleaver, as though it was some delicate fencer's tool instead of the big metal hunk I'd handed her. Every time it overbalanced her, that little furrow appeared between her eyebrows. I was breathless. "You're alright? Of course, you're alright."

Mercy left my cleaver buried in the back of the Inyoka's skull. "I have had enough! I'm done. Everywhere we go, something is trying to kill us!"

Seren launched herself at me with a snarl. I wish I could say I wasn't expecting it, but she'd spent the whole time that she had a blade in her hand casting me sideways glances like she was just waiting for her opportunity. Weird that she'd pick now, with Mercy standing witness, to kill me.

One foot kicked off my knee, the next off my shoulder as she launched herself up for a killing blow. I managed to get a hand up as if that would stop the cleaver coming down, but she just used that as another foothold to gain more height, impossibly fast.

She soared past me to collide with Asher as he emerged from the bush, hammering him to the ground. "Wyrmspawn!"

Everyone was shouting all at once, but I won out in volume, if not the contents of my bellow. "Stop! That's our one!"

The blade was already coming down on Asher, but with a deft twist of her arm, Seren managed to embed it in a tree root beside his face instead of the face itself. Alvaren and Inyoka stared at each other for a long moment, then she gracefully dismounted him, and he gasped for air. "My thanks."

I plucked the chopper out of Seren's unresisting hands. "How about we don't murder all the people on our side?"

Her empty hands flexed at her sides. "Your side, not mine."

"Just don't stab Asher, yeah?"

"As is thy wish," she said with a sneer. One step forward, two steps back.

You could have cut the tension with a knife. Luckily, we had an even blunter object available, Mercy. "So what? Talon keeps pets?"

Asher and I both shrugged, but Seren was quick to reply. "These wretches are wyrm-born and make no mistake. Inyoka bred for war rather than"—she cast a glance at Asher—"domestic duties."

I swear, I tried not to picture Asher in a French Maid outfit, but it was like my brain was set on betraying me. The sniggering started, and it just wouldn't stop. Mercy rolled her eyes. "But what does that mean? There's a dragon here?"

"Mayhaps. More likely one passed through in the past, leaving its cast-offs in its wake. Even at the height of our war with the wyrms, their spawn was more capable…feral you named them, and feral I'd mark them."

"Wait, how did you hear me calling them…"

She tapped her long, pointed ears. Apparently, they weren't just for show. I froze for a second, trying to mentally backtrack through every conversation that I'd had with Mercy and Asher back on the ship, searching for anything embarrassing or incriminating, and oh gods, Mercy had to go and blurt out all that stuff about me having a crush on Seren.

Turns out Faun can't blush. Which was a relief, but I still turned on my heel and ran back along the path we'd been cutting. Mercy called, "Hey!" after me.

"Checking on the Dvergar!"

As it turned out, the Dvergar did not need checking on. Gunhild was fine, and her boys had formed a solid defensive line down on the beach to protect the civilians when they heard the sounds of fighting. When the time came to move them through the jungle, we'd all go together, but from how few of the ferals had shown up for their big ambush, I had a suspicion that we weren't going to have too much trouble. With surprise on their side, camouflage and venom probably would have let them whittle us down, but they'd lost that now. Everyone was on high alert. Yet again I had to admit Seren was right, these things were not very smart.

Before the hour was out, I was trussed to the wagon again, and we were underway, close enough behind Mercy and Seren that I could see the vast difference in their skill with the blade. Handing the chopper back to Seren, consciously aware of what I was doing this time around was a different experience, but I figured that if I didn't make a fuss then she wouldn't either. She took the tool without comment and set to work.

Inch by inch, we cut our way into the jungle, pressing on over the freshwater streams with only a little more humping and bumping around than before. Asher was perched up on the back of the wagon alongside Gunhild by now, ready with his spells in case of any more nasty surprises. If he was missing his books, he didn't complain out loud.

It was hot, humid, and tense—and not in a fun way. Every time a bird took flight or twig snapped off in the jungle I froze, just waiting for another lizard to cannon into me. Every time a cut vine dangled down to whack me in the horns, I fumbled at the ropes around my middle. It was barely past midday when we broke through into the clearing surrounding the tower, but I was so done with being a pack-horse.

From this close, at this angle, I couldn't even see the top of the tower, it just seemed to go on and on forever, fading into the clouds above. Uncoupled from the wagon, we began a tentative exploration of the area. The tower itself dominated one side of the clearing. I wasn't even sure if clearing was the right word; this place had been very deliberately purged of all plant life. I wasn't sure if Talon had salted the earth, and I didn't fancy taste testing it to be sure.

At the other side of the big bare circle from the tower, there were outbuildings that looked practically identical to the ones back in Witchglass Overlook. The same hand had crafted both of these places, without a doubt. The big difference here was that the jungle had provided some sort of shelter from the elements. The wooden doors had rotted away, but there was no pile-up of filth inside. Sticking my head in through one of the doorways, I could see rusted metal rings stacked up in neat rows; they must have been barrels, once upon a time. In the next, there were hunks of wood that were unmistakably furniture. Rows of beds. Talon had hosted students here. More of the same exciting nothing could be found in every building, with the exception of one round-shaped one that had a firepit sunk down into the middle of it, which was inexplicably intact, and even more inexplicably still burning with the same blue-green flames we'd seen in the Overlook.

Seren pushed past me without a glance, in sharp contrast to the constant stares she'd been giving me until now. "Ignem Aeternum was once a common sight, but from thy face, I can see it is a shock to you. If so small a thing is startling, I begin to believe your wyrm-spawn's tales of the decline of magic."

Beyond that, there was a well set off towards the jungle's edge and very little else. The Dvergar would have a roof over their heads tonight, a fire to warm themselves around, and clean water to drink. It was hardly paradise, but it would keep them alive.

Once Asher had gone around doing his jazz-hands thing, confirming that there were no hidden traps, curses, or monsters, we all went back to herd the Dvergar through. I'd reclaimed the metal of my sword and recombined it, but before we headed out, I went for a rummage in the back of the wagon until I uncovered Seren's gear. Her bow had been broken somewhere along the line, but her two swords were intact and too finely worked for me to have used them for scrap even if I'd wanted to.

Presenting them to her felt like it should have been even more of an event than giving her the cleaver. Asher, Mercy, and Gunhild were all making meaningful eye contact with each other when I passed the blades over, but Seren was careful to let nothing show on her face. She strapped into her greaves and breastplate without assistance. Some enchantment must have been helping, because speaking as somebody who has contended with the evil alien intelligence of a bra clasp before, there was no way that you could do up all of the fastenings around the sides and back without assistance.

If I had to pick a word to describe the rest of the day, it would be uneventful. No. If Asher had to pick a word, he would have chosen uneventful, I would have chosen boring. It was boring. We went back and forth, escorting groups of Dvergar through the big scary jungle. I probably wouldn't have minded if there had been a single lizard attack, but nothing. Not a damn thing. Not even an oversized gecko.

It was late afternoon by the time the Dvergar were settled into their new accommodations. They'd put me to work ripping up trees and building a barricade fence around the outside of the clearing once it became clear that we weren't going to get lizards to the face every time we went outside. I didn't really know if the fence was necessary. Even the birds seemed to steer clear of the air above Talon's circle of dirt.

Regardless, I did my time and raised the walls, and the Dvergar nodded approvingly instead of providing me with helpful advice. Maybe they knew I was itching to hit somebody. Yet when all that was done, the gates—that I'd just made—were slammed shut, and I was ready to get going, everyone seemed oddly reluctant.

I clapped my hands together. "Come on, guys. This is it. This is what we've been waiting for. A proper dungeon. Crazy wizard tower full of traps and monsters and…this is going to be awesome!"

Asher didn't look up from his book. "I do not believe you are using that word correctly, nor assessing the dangers in such a place with any rationality."

"Oh, come on. This is going to be so much fun!"

Mercy rolled her eyes. "You're an idiot."

Gunhild was nodding right along with her. "Aye, you be a fool and a half, true enough. If you be seeking excitement, there are ways to find it without putting your boot in the Chelic polyp."

Bestiary helpfully explained that she was talking about a species of cave-dwelling scorpion-spider things. The polyps were their nests. Like a wasps' nest but lethal.

Asher hadn't even taken his eyes off the tower since we arrived. I could already tell that he was obsessed. He wanted to jazz-hands it so bad. Yet even he betrayed me in my hour of need. "The ladies are correct. Our best course of action would be to begin our exploration once the new day has begun."

"Oh, come on!" I looked around desperately for any help. "Seren! Seren thinks we should go in now, right, Seren?"

"There seems little reason to delay the inevitable." She looked up at the tower, pupils blossoming huge and dark in the day's dimming light. "This fortification must be taken, and thee must take it. Cover of darkness can only aid in your egress."

Mercy raised an eyebrow. "Does she get a vote?"

"If the trees were voting his way, I suspect that Maulkin would be marching for arboreal suffrage." Asher didn't smirk—he didn't have the equipment for smirking—but he radiated a smug aura.

I groaned all the way to sitting on the floor. "Why do you all want to be boring and have a nap?"

Gunhild coughed. "Because I be asking them to. There be no way of knowing what be out in those trees. I'd sleep easier knowing you folks would be here. At least for one night until we be seeing what comes a-crawling out."

This time my groan carried me the rest of the way down until I was completely horizontal in the dirt. "Ugh. Why didn't somebody tell me that instead of letting me argue with you all and look like an asshole?"

Mercy stepped on my chest on her way to help the Dvergar settle into the bunkhouse. "No force on Amaranth can stop you looking like an asshole."

As she passed over, I used Artifice to patch up the hole in her trousers. She let out a little yelp as the leather tightened back around her ass, then glowered back at me.

"You're welcome!"

And then after I went out of my way to do her that favor, she flipped me off. What a class act.

That night, as all the Dvergar lay asleep in their beds, I got to stand watch. It was my own fault really. I shouldn't have made such a fuss about not being tired earlier in the day when I was pushing to get on with the actual adventure parts of our adventure.

Seren stood sentinel silently behind me, her armor and weapons shining in the moonlight. Part of the reason I'd sort of volunteered to stand watch all night was to get away from her, but she went ahead and actually volunteered anyway. Mercy kept wiggling her eyebrows at me behind Seren's back. Ugh.

After about half an hour I was bored. Don't get me wrong, it was pretty and there were a lot of interesting new noises to be heard out in the jungle, but none of the wildlife had any interest in coming into the circle of dirt that Talon had left behind. Asher had confirmed my suspicions that there was some sort of magic at work, but he had been vague about the details. Something about it being unusually subtle. Given that every spell he could cast ended in an explosion, I suppose anything would feel subtle after that.

My attention drifted around to the tower itself. There was no way that a wizard didn't have some monsters inside as a security system. That was what wizards did, right? That was their whole schtick. Anyway, that was the justification that I needed to keep my eyes locked on the doors of the tower instead of the tree-line—anything might come wandering out.

I literally jumped when Seren spoke. "Your companions do not accept me as you do."

"I think they're waiting for you to switch back to being a psycho killer." There wasn't really a tactful way to say that.

"That is not my nature, though I'll warrant they have good reason to fear so." She let out a sigh, then leaned back against me. "Will they accept my presence in your party come the dawn?"

Her armor was too smooth to dig in, and it was retaining the heat from the air so that it felt almost as warm as the body it encased against my skin. I had to remind myself we were in the middle of a conversation. "Yeah. Maybe. Probably."

"I would not trust in the hospitality of thy runt"—she switched seamlessly—"the Dvergar, were it not for your presence."

I shrugged, and I could feel it shifting her too. "Well, they've got a good reason to be mad at you. You destroyed their home."

She pushed away from me with a snarl. "You counsel me to forgive and forget the sins of their ancestors, yet you expect me to shoulder the blame for—"

I held up a hand to cut her off. "When your city teleported back into the sky, it collapsed the mountain that their city was built in."

She wet her lips. A brief flicker of the tip of her tongue. "This escaped my attention."

"Yeah, turns out they built Khag Mhor right on top of where your sky castle crash-landed. Or maybe you teleported under them later?" I shrugged. "Either way, you moved, the cave collapsed, their friends and family died, and they lost everything. Then afterward, you kind of waged war on them for a bit there. Are you surprised that they don't love you?"

"Yet…you do." She quickly corrected herself. "You have a care for me though my people wrought the same ruin upon thee."

I pretended not to hear that first bit. "Hey, I did plenty of ruining right back. Besides, you didn't know any better. You thought we were bad guys."

"I have not abdicated myself entirely from that belief. Your acts of kindness matter to a prisoner, but should I win my freedom, then we shall be foes once more. My resolve does not so easily weaken."

I rolled my shoulders and drew my sword. "Come at me then."

"I beg your pardon?"

"You're free. You already gave Asher the history lesson he wanted. You've got all your gear back. I'm not keeping you here. If you want to go then go. If you want to take another swing at me, I'd be happy to kick your ass all over the island."

"I am your prisoner. You bested me… Bound me…"

"You're free to go. I've got no use for prisoners, and I figure that even if you do haul ass back to Queen Psycho, we'll be long gone before she catches up to us here."

"Speak no ill of Briar By Moonlight."

"Yeah, gods forbid I mention that she turned you all into drooling apes."

Her swords were in her hands without me even seeing her move. Maybe I had not thought this plan all the way through. "I told thee, speak of her no ill!"

"Yelling doesn't make the truth go away. Pretending doesn't make it go away. The truth doesn't change just because we don't like it." Seren lunged for me, blades crossing at my neck as I barked out, "She did it."

I could feel the razor edge of her swords on either side of my neck, stilled in their path by Seren's will alone. "Why?"

"Ask her." Even speaking was enough movement to cause a trickle of blood to seep out on either side of my neck.

"Not her!" Seren spat. "You! Why are you doing this? Why are you saying these things when you know I must reply with my blades. How is your cause helped to have me at thy throat?"

"Maybe I think you deserve better than being made to kill for a lie."

Her hands shook as she stood there, paralyzed by indecision. No, not indecision. Ambivalence. She knew I was telling her the truth. She knew it because I had no reason to lie to her. But on the other side of the scales was her whole lifetime, devoted to the service of the mad queen who'd put us both in this situation. Not just one lifetime either. Who knew how many hundreds of years Seren had seen before losing herself to the svart? Every moment of it had been devoted to believing every word that Briar by Moonlight spoke as if it was natural law.

It was genuinely amazing that I still had a head.

Agonizingly slowly, the swords moved away from my neck, then in a flash, they were sheathed again as if nothing had happened. My new bloody neckbeard was the only evidence that anything had happened at all. Seren's face was the locked down mask of no emotion that she seemed to save for when something was really bothering her.

She swiveled on her heel to stare back out into the jungle, as though guard duty actually mattered, and she'd been unforgivably distracted. The same tension that had stripped her face of all emotion was still there, obvious in her forced stillness. Great. More weirdness. Just what I'd hoped for.

"The Dvergar. They could find the permanence that they seek here." I jumped. Again. I swear this one woman had me twitchier than a whole mine full of svart had.

I cleared my throat to make sure the little yelp-scream I'd caught there didn't come out. "Same thought crossed my mind."

She pressed on. "There is an abundance of fodder in the jungle, this earth could be cultivated, and the water flows pure and clean. All that they need to survive is here."

I was nodding along, even though she couldn't see me with our backs turned to each other. "Everything but a mine."

She scoffed. "What need have they for stone and metal in such a place?"

"They're Dvergar, it is like…their religion or something."

I could almost hear all of the less than polite things that she wanted to say about Dvergar religion running through her head. Wah, wah, they killed the world looking for a god underground and now you want to give them a new hole to go digging in. Yes. Yes, I do want to give them a new hole. Shut up. See, two of us can play at this internal conversation game. "Should fertile soil be turned aside, there shall be stone, no doubt. Given time, they could make of this place what they wished."

I nodded to the tower. For my own benefit, presumably. "You think Talon would be cool with new neighbors?"

She glanced back over her shoulder; some measure of composure must have been back. The mask wasn't slipping exactly, but her face didn't look like it had been carved out of marble anymore. Marble with freckles. "I do not believe that the master of the house is at home, lest we would have been bid to depart as soon as we arrived."

"Only one way to find out."

"Let us be courteous guests and make our presence known to our host—if he is present."

I sighed. "As soon as the rest of them wake."

CHAPTER 30

Was I a little bit excited to go and explore a wizard's tower? Yes. Yes, I was.

Did that justify running into the bunkhouse at dawn, picking up Mercy and Asher around the waist, and carrying them off to the doors of that tower? Maybe not.

While Asher tolerated being manhandled with all the good grace that I was accustomed to, Mercy was not, by her nature, an early riser. She was, an early kicker, an early groaner, and an early tantrum thrower.

I had to drop her halfway across the dirt circle before she did Asher an injury. Suddenly, all the sleepiness seemed to leave her as she sprinted back towards the bunkhouse. "Oh, come on!"

"Nope. Still sleep time. Go away."

I called after her, "You're already up!"

"Not for long!"

I put Asher down without incident at least. "Might I return to the bunkhouse and retrieve my supplies, or do you mean to have me enter with nothing but myself."

Oops. "Oh yeah, you normally have robes or something."

"Indeed. I shall see if the judicious application of one end of a stick to our indolent companion might not part her from her bedroll."

"Thanks."

After several long hours of doing nothing, Seren and I had taken shifts napping under the starry sky, if only to avoid the awkward silence that was still hanging over us. I didn't want to say anything that might set off her murderous rage again, and she seemed reluctant to delve into any conversation deeper than commenting on the various birdcalls that she heard and speculating as to what bird that we had observed through the day they might have been coming from. I had not been paying all that much attention to the birds, so I found myself with little to contribute.

If there were any murderous beasties hiding out in the jungle, waiting to pounce on all the innocent sleeping Dvergar, they never made an appearance or even a noise. I was betting that the chameleon-crocodile things we'd run into yesterday were pretty sneaky, but Seren's big pointy ears could pick out every single sound in the woods. She even made me go patrol around the outside of the fence once or twice when she heard a twig snap too close by.

Well, she didn't make me. I just wasn't willing to let her go wandering off into the jungle at night to get chewed up by whatever Jurassic Park reject we encountered next.

A judicious application of some *Restoration* and well-water had dealt with the blood on my neck, and Seren very deliberately avoided looking at me while I cleaned up. I wondered if she was embarrassed about her decapitation-threatening outburst or more ashamed of herself that she hadn't gone through with it. I'd hoped last night might have cleared the air between us, but it just seemed to have made her even more introverted and tense.

Mercy emerged from the outbuildings with a scowl that would have killed a lesser man and paused only briefly in checking over her gear to give me a kick in the shins. Luckily, the long and pointless night, along with the rusty fixings of some of the old doors that had rotted away, had given me the time to make some new arrows for her—a gift that seemed to ease her grumpiness a little bit. "Gunhild is staying with the rest of the Dvergar. She wants to get them settled in, start building…something or other."

"She wasn't invited anyway."

Mercy's glare was now directed at Seren, who was checking the doors of the tower over for any obvious traps. "But she is?"

"Well, yeah."

"There is little point in having an expert on ancient history along if you do not have her accompany you into the ancient ruins that you are exploring," Asher piped up, now fully dressed in his Dvergar-made robes. Mercy hadn't snapped him into lizard-chunks in her rage. That was nice.

Mercy had no response to that but a growl. She closed the distance with Seren in a few strides. "Alright, little miss, let's get a few things straight. The second that I see you so much as point one of those pig stickers in the direction of one of us, I'm shooting you full of arrows, then setting you on fire. Are we clear?"

Seren looked askance to me, and I shrugged. "I consent to your latest barrage of demands. In return, I seek the concession that you heed my words within Talon's demesne. Where the expertise that your wyrm-spawn prizes shall be at its most valuable."

Mercy loomed over her. "You think you can tell us what to—"

I cut her off before this got too stupid. "Yeah, that's fine, Seren."

That earned me a curt nod from Seren and a betrayed look from Mercy. "Then heed me now. I can find no mechanical traps upon this door, but if there is some arcane ward, thy wyrmspawn shall have to seek it."

Asher was radiating smugness again. "Before your inspection today, I took the liberty of ensuring that there was no protective spell upon the door, beyond that necessary to preserve it against the passage of time. No harm shall befall us."

I stepped up and pushed the big doors open. They were taller than me, so they were massive to the rest of them, carved from some rich dark wood, and worked with the same silver fixtures we'd seen all over this place and the Overlook.

Light flooded into a place that hadn't seen it in so long, even the rat skeletons on the floor must have had long-beards. A moment after the door opened, torches around the walls blazed to life, tinting everything green. A great spiral staircase started at the far side of this round chamber, but you could hardly see it past the statue dominating the room. Talon himself, yet again, but this time it was carved to be twice the size of me. I'm not saying that he was compensating for something, but if he turned out to be over six foot, I would use Artifice to make a hat...and then eat it.

Asher let out a hushed whisper. "Astounding."

"It is a big rock."

"The craftsmanship, the artistry, it looks almost alive." Maybe he should have just married it.

I sauntered closer and gave the statue a solid prod in the crotch region of the robes. "Nope. It's dead."

Mercy and Seren managed to get out a garbled call of warning before the statue slapped me.

Have you ever run into a solid stone wall? It felt a lot like that. Or maybe more like getting hit in the side of the head by a truck going full speed. Either way, one second I was standing there thinking up clever jokes about being rock hard, and the next I was in motion, soaring through the air to smash into yet another stone wall.

For a second there I was pretty sure I was dead. The flash of light that rang through my head like a thunderbolt was all too familiar to somebody who'd died a few times. Yet I could still feel things, and the encroaching darkness retreated as I fumbled my way to my feet and blinked the whirling room back onto an even keel. Good thing I still had my sea legs.

I managed to stagger a few steps into the room before the thing wobbling at the periphery of my vision caught my attention, and I reached up to brush it aside. Ow. Again. Ow. I fumbled at it for a second, not understanding what it was until I dragged the tip of it in front of my face again. My horn. "He broke my horn!"

"Nobody cares!" Mercy snarked as she took a dive under the living statue's sweeping arms. A few of her arrows lay broken and useless on the floor. Asher had retreated out of the room, and only Seren was actually attacking the thing, her arms and blades a blur of motion, a green-silver shimmer, chipping away uselessly at the robed legs of the thing, filling the air with stone-dust.

If it were me, I'd be dead. Sadly, this thing was made of tougher stuff. I drew my sword and charged in with a roar, surging my Potency as I went. The statue saw me coming, and it brought its arms back around, swinging for me, meeting my attack head-on.

Both arms shattered below the elbow and spun off into the room from the force of that collision. The statue's arms, not mine, although it kind of felt like mine might too. My trusty sword was still vibrating from the impact, and that same tremor was spreading through me, carrying aches along with it.

The statue reared up, lifting the stumps of its arms up until they were level with Talon's stupid smug beard. Maybe it was a wizard thing. You spent too many skill points on spells, and suddenly, you couldn't stop smirking at everyone like you knew something they didn't. Something other than a load of spells, I mean.

Seren didn't waste a moment, sprinting across to me, running up the flat of my blade, and then kicking off from my shoulder to fling herself at the statue's face. Both of her silvered blades slammed against the stone chest of the statue but found no crack or purchase. She fell just as quickly as she'd launched herself, and I had to throw myself forward, abandoning my sword with a clatter to stop her hitting the ground.

The shock of bodily dismemberment had passed, and the guardian statue, the golem—my *Bestiary* helpfully mentioned—moved back onto the offensive. The arms may have ended at the elbow now, but my strike had turned each of those elbows into a lethal jagged mass of mineral spikes.

Spikes it was now raising up to bring down on me.

With no better plan, I threw Seren at it, hoping she might score a better hit in passage, but her blades skittered across the golem's stony robes, leaving a trail behind her but no marked effect.

Mercy had started up the stairs in search of a better vantage point, but now she had frozen in place with an arrow pulled back, taking careful aim, as if the whole target wasn't made out of impenetrable stone.

Asher's spell was unleashed through the doorway—a bolt of lightning that struck the statue square in the gut and did absolutely nothing. Even the static charge that usually clung to enemies that he'd hit dissipated down the length of the statue and spread harmlessly across the flagstones. Magic wasn't getting us out of this one, apparently.

Through all of this, the arms were coming down, and I had no hope of getting out of their way in time. That didn't mean I was defenseless though. Artifice swept out through the room, filling my awareness. The worked stone and the careful craftsmanship of the golem put them all well beyond my reach, but my sword was still as rustic as ever.

I slapped together a shield as thick as I could muster above my head and just barely caught hold of it before the crushing blow of the golem came down.

My potency surge had abandoned me, and all I had was the raw strength of my body against the crushing blow of this stony giant. It wasn't enough. The hit knocked me to my knees and slammed the shield down into the top of my head and shoulders.

The snapped horn fell by my feet, whatever few strings of material had been holding it gone. The ache that had reverberated up my arms spread out all through me now as my shield rang like a bell. I could only see the golem's feet from this vantage point, and standing up seemed like it was a virtual guarantee of falling over in my dizzy state. All I could really do was tilt up the edge of the shield to see when the next hit would come down.

It never did.

Mercy unleashed the arrow that she had been holding back, but it was more than just a stick with a metal point this time. It was the eye of the storm. Every one of the torches in the room flared as the air was sucked away from them, and every speck of stone that Seren had chipped away took flight. Imbued with the power of the wind, Mercy's spiraling arrow hit the golem with the power of a hurricane.

Legendary Foe Defeated!
Vitality increased to 17
Phalanx: Rank 6/10
44 Experience Gained
300 Glory Gained

Hunks of stone the size of my fist tumbled out of the golem as it died, clattering and battering off my shield. Seren slipped under the rim and set her shoulders against the curve of metal above her. That blue flush was back in her cheeks, and she seemed to be breathing again for the first time since I'd knocked her out. Life was back in her now that the fighting had started. She wasn't uncouth enough to be smiling, but she didn't seem to be actively fighting a frown anymore either. That was the Seren version of a frigging parade.

I'd make a comment about her being bloodthirsty, but honestly, who was I to talk. Fighting was my favorite thing to do too.

My shield became my sword, and I put it away before I accidentally hit somebody with it that I didn't mean to. Mercy for instance. She was just stepping off the stairs when I caught her and hoisted her into the air. "That was awesome!"

"I know, right!" She squealed. I might have been squeezing her too tight. Very carefully, I put her down again, but that did nothing to curb the squealing. "Every fight until now we ran into something too big and tough for my arrows to breakthrough, but I still love my bow, so I had a look at the divine skills and found..."

She rambled on and on in her excitement, bouncing up and down with every word and, gods damn it, that enthusiasm was infectious. I found myself bobbing along too.

"...and I could have tried imbuing the shot with fire, but then I thought no, because rock doesn't burn, but a strong enough wind can knock almost anything down."

I started clapping. I really didn't mean to. "Can you do other flavors or just wind?"

"Just wind for now, but I can unlock the other elements with more experience."

"Oh, we've got to try mixing this up with some of Asher's magic. Or I could make like... shrapnel!"

"When the two of you are quite finished." Asher sighed. "I do believe that I preferred when they were fighting all the time."

Seren cocked her head to one side. "This is not fighting? Then why do they shout so?"

Another lipless smirk. "I believe they attempt to make up for in volume what their conversations lack in substance."

"Rude!" Mercy snapped, all the joy draining out of her in an instant. Why couldn't people just let each other be happy?

I guess that was it for the ground floor, and there didn't seem to be any basement on this place—or at least not one that my eyes, Seren's probing fingers, or Asher's magic wiggling could discover. That left the stairs heading up, which Mercy had kindly, accidentally, searched for traps while she was lining up her shot on the golem. We set off up the spiral staircase.

"Hell of an ego on this Talon guy, right?"

Mercy might have been back in her shell, but that had never stopped her snarking before. "The giant statue of himself is a bit of a giveaway."

Seren piped up, "The guardian golem could have been given any form. Perhaps he had it graven in his likeness to allay suspicions about its true purpose."

"So what, it used to be normal to have giant statues of yourself standing around?"

"I cannot speak to the norms of thy kind, only my own." Her eyes flicked back to the rubble. "We would find a display like this to be… lacking in taste."

Asher let out a little chuckle.

There was no chance that we were going to get lucky enough for this spiral staircase to take us all the way to the top of the tower, but I had hoped that we'd make it farther than the first floor before we came to a solid wall. "Oh, come on."

"You are the one who wished to move at a crawl through a dungeon."

"Dungeon crawl, Asher. I was excited to go on a dungeon crawl."

Seren was very deliberately not smiling again. "Has that excitement abated?"

"Uh no. This is going to be amazing."

The door to the next floor was made of the same wood and silver as the ones I'd swung open earlier, and I was already reaching for it when Asher let out a little yelp of warning. "Trap?"

"I cannot say for certain. Magic lingers about this door, but…it lingers all throughout this tower. The ambient charge makes it impossible to identify any specific…"

I pushed the door open. Nothing happened.

Asher yelled, Mercy hit me, and only Seren stood back with a fixed expression on her face that might have meant anything. Maybe she thought it was funny, or maybe she had been hoping I'd be filled with exploding centipedes. Who knew? Not me. Probably not even her.

Inside the next room, things started to look a lot more like what you'd expect from a wizard's tower. Beyond the yellowed wallpaper and hardwood floor, there were great brass apparatus in motion and orbs of gemstones embedded in some pieces and floating around in a fixed position next to others. Every so often a beam of light would shoot from one gem to another, timed to some imperceptible rhythm to ensure that they never struck any of the moving parts.

I winked at Seren. "Still think this place is abandoned?"

She blinked back at me, frowned, blinked again, then moved into the room to give it a more thorough examination.

Whatever rhythm the gyroscope rings and gemstones were moving to escaped me, but she seemed to get it, ducking and leaning as she moved along to avoid contact. It wasn't like the spinning things were taking up the whole room or anything. We could have strolled right by them to the door at the far side, but no, Seren wanted a good close look. Asher was as much of a dumbass, he just didn't have the timing down, so he had to approach in an awkward crouching crabwalk, following along after Seren like a really messed up pet dog.

I met Mercy's eye. She was vibrating with contained laughter. "What? You don't want to go sniff around too?"

"I've seen enough wiz-biz for one lifetime, thanks."

A light darted from one side of the room to the other, passing through the space where my damn horn was meant to be. "Oh right."

I used *Restoration* as I ambled on, feeling around the horn so I could enjoy the weird experience of feeling it grow back.

[710/710 Health]

"That's still weird to watch." Mercy looked a little green around the gills.

"If you ever want to touch instead of watch"—I winked at her—"just say the word."

"Ew."

Across the room, I saw Seren blinking again, the same little frown line appearing between her eyebrows. She put a finger upon one eyelid, then blinked again, holding one eye open. She was trying to wink. That was adorable. If I ever told her it was adorable she'd disembowel me, but that didn't make it any less adorable. Like cats, except even more murderous, somehow.

She jerked her head around, and I looked away as quick as possible. I was definitely going to be winking at her more. "We can move on."

Asher nodded his agreement. "These devices are for the measurement of the flows of magic, not anything that may impede our movement."

"Magic detectors." Mercy sighed. "Great."

She had almost strolled all the way across to the door at the far end when one of the darting beams of light hit her in the shoulder. Abruptly, every part of the machinery stopped dead. I threw up my hands. "Not my fault this time!"

We all waited for the other shoe to drop, but the moment stretched on and on. Asher's hands raised up too, feeling for the magic death that was almost certainly going to be coming raining down on us any second.

Nothing.

We didn't relax yet, but Mercy moved again, going for the door even quicker than before. The other two broke into a run as well. Everyone was so convinced that something awful was going to happen now that Mercy had set off the magic tripwire laser thing, that nobody was thinking about what that awful thing was going to be.

It was the door, as it turned out. When Mercy grabbed onto the handle, it melted like pudding in her hand. "No, no, no."

The silver slithered up her hand and then on to a brave new world beneath her sleeve. The wooden boards of the door burst apart too, each one moving independently, lashing out towards the other two as they got too close.

My shoulder hit her in the mid-section, knocking all the air out of her even as I knocked her out of the silver tentacle's reach—or so I'd hoped. The metal followed along with her, still clinging to the tips of her fingers and beginning to spread again the moment she stopped moving away.

Hauling myself to my feet, I stumbled to a starting position and on towards the other end of the room. The silver stretched and stretched until it was as thin as a thread of spider-silk. Yet even at that limit, it would not let her go. All of my pushing and pushing, and all that I managed to do was make Mercy scream out in pain. Judging from the little popping noises, I'd dislocated our archer's fingers. Oops.

I drew my sword, still bracing her at the limits of the silver's reach. Predictably, she started yelling. "Oh, hell no!"

The moment I stopped pulling, the metal began creeping back up her fingers. "You'd rather it smothers you?"

"Asher!" she yelped. "Asher! Have a better idea!"

Ducking under the stretched silver, he closed the distance fast, eyeing along every inch of it as he went. "I believe that if I apply suf-ficient heat to the—"

Mercy cut him off. "Okay, cut it off."

I hefted my sword and rolled my shoulders.

"Alright, don't move. On three. 1, 2…"

I hit on two before she could tense up or jerk back.

Mercy bowled over, the abrupt impact on the metal holding onto her hand so tightly yanking her off her feet. Her face hit the stream of metal, and it swallowed her. Her whole head vanished into silver in an instant. Seren and Asher both leapt in, trying to haul her out, but it was too late. Her whole arm, her whole head, both were enveloped as she was dragged across the room.

Who could have guessed that after all my antics and accidents, Mercy was going to be the first one to die?

CHAPTER 31

She was still struggling, flailing around frantically as the tiny little doorknob pulled her in. She slapped Asher across the face in her panic, and Seren bobbed back out of reach before she could suffer the same fate. "I must attempt a fire spell."

I caught hold of his hands before they could start the casting motions. Every time I had to be the voice of reason, something felt fundamentally wrong with the universe. "Metal conducts heat. You'd melt her face off before you made a dent in it."

"What other choice is available to us?" He yanked his hands out of mine. "If she is burned then so be it. I shall cauterize her wounds when it is over and done."

As he set off after Mercy again, and I caught him by the tail. "You'll kill her long before you melt it off!"

"Damn your hypotheticals." Panic was written all over his face. "She is dying now!"

Crossing the room in three strides, I jammed both my hands into the silver pooling over Mercy's head. At once it leapt up me like quicksilver to a magnet. It fled from Mercy's face and up across my arms, up onto my chest. The silver that had covered Mercy from her waist to the top of her head barely stretched up over my massive pecs. Where it had slipped under her armor and coated her skin, it could find no entry to mine. Gloves to the rescue again.

Mercy gasped for air, then realized that we were now attached to each other and groaned. "Oh, man. Attached to you? Why couldn't you just let me die?"

"Stick with me, kid. We'll get you out of this."

Mercy wailed, "Oh gods no, not the puns."

I grinned, even as the deathly cold of the metal crept higher and higher, seeping through my armor. "Seems like you got yourself in a sticky situation here."

She tried to pull away, but the metal dragged her in closer to me. "Bring back the smothering. It would be kinder than this."

"No need to get choked up about it."

"Oh come on! That one barely even worked."

Seren's elegant fingers interlocked beneath my chin, and she hauled back with all her strength. Asher was there at our side in an instant, embers already dancing from his fingertips.

"I already told you that isn't going to work!"

Seren was the one to answer me, grunting in my ear. Asher was too lost in his spell. "If thy can be divided, he might strike with flame at the sorcerous bond between."

I had heard worse plans. "Fine! Asher, if you melt my arms off, I am going to be pissed."

"Fear not." Seren grunted in my ear as she pulled for all that she was worth. "You shall be avenged if you fall to his foolishness."

"Uh... hold off on the vengeance part. I mean he isn't deliberately going to—"

Asher's spell fired off into the broad stretch of metal reaching between me and Mercy. The flames shimmered over the quicksilver's surface and then were swallowed down into it an instant later. "Huh."

For a moment, it seemed like nothing was going to happen at all, then the surface of the metal began bubbling. Maybe it was actually going to work. Maybe it was going to melt away the...

More liquid metal came pouring up out from among the bubbles— as much as had managed to spread from the doorknob and more. It rushed out in a wave, completely encasing Mercy in an instant. I only had the time to gasp in one last breath of air before Seren jerked her hands away, and it rolled up over me too.

The suffocation would have been, well not fine, but manageable? As would the deathly chill that swept over me everywhere that the liquid metal touched. I still would have been able to function and think with the trap doing its best to crush the life out of me. What I couldn't cope with was my own *Psychometry*.

The history of this metal washed over me, into me. Everything it had been before. Everyone that had touched it and succumbed to the same slow choking death it was trying to inflict on me. The centuries bombarded me, bearing me down to the ground under their crushing weight, and through it all that voice? Talon.

The same words repeated again and again through the years, centuries apart but still echoing the last recitation. A lecture. Practiced and spoken in this room, in the Overlook. Murmured to himself as he sat by his desk, working the raw liquid metal between his fingers. The glow of magic cutting through the shadows of intervening decades. "To defeat a mage, we must defeat his casting."

The metal creeping up over the hands of some lost and weary traveler. A human, or something like it. Surrounded by the silver. Consumed by it. Not even his corpse escaping as it was crushed down smaller and smaller by the metal.

"To defeat a mage's casting, we must take two things from him. His hands and his voice."

I had only a moment back in my own body as I felt the metal pushing its way up into my nose, into my ears, pressing against my lips. Trying to get inside me.

"With this simple trap, any who would seek entry to my tower are stripped of both. So when I tell you that I do not accept visitors, do not think that I am merely a recluse." Pause for laughs. The doorknob set down.

He was handling it freely. It was keyed to him somehow. He had some way of making this spell stop. I bucked and struggled within the metal. I tried to scream, but that just gave the cold steel darkness all around me ingress, and it rushed down my throat, squeezing the little air I had left out of me.

Words still echoed. Words spoken hundreds of years ago. Months or years apart. Words I couldn't understand. Eternals could speak and understand every language on Amaranth. Even the svart's degenerate screeching could be translated by our God-given powers. How could there be words I didn't understand?

Over and over, he whispered them to himself. What the hell were you saying, Talon? Were they just noises he was making? Some language he was coming up with himself?

The metal ripped back up my throat, out of my nose and ears and mouth, and away from my face entirely. Feeling swept back in everywhere it had been. My lungs, my throat, everything burned. Light flooded in as the metal parted. I was lying on top of Mercy, both of us encased. Asher was frantically trying to cast something else.

It was Seren who'd saved me. She stood encased in the same metal that coated me and Mercy, her foot placed strategically on my collarbone, to tease the metal up and away from my face. Even running up the full distance of her body, the metal that had been required to encompass mine had no difficulty swallowing her whole. I caught only a glimpse of her expressionless face before the metal rolled up over it.

Gasping and desperate, already feeling the metal coming rushing in, I yelled out the words as best I could remember them. "Ah peero la me-ah bocca!"

The metal slowed to a crawl as I scrambled to remember the rest of the nonsense the old wizard had been spouting. "Con oona parabola?"

Now that I needed it, the trap was no longer touching me. Any second now it was going to realize I was just spitting out noises. I strained against the straitjacket of metal until I was able to brush one cheek against it again. I recited the rest of the little phrase in time with Talon. "Diro cose nascoste, cose del passato."

The metal became inert, splashing to the floor, and soaking down between the floorboards. I flopped back on the ground and enjoyed the feeling of air on my skin and in my lungs. Mercy was beneath my legs, dry-heaving and gasping. Seren collapsed on top of me, too. Asher stalked over to look down at the heap of us, shaking his head. "What was that all about?"

"French? Maybe. Italian?" I lifted my legs to let Mercy crawl out with some measure of dignity. "Something euro-trashy anyway. I guess our boy Talon came from Earth, same as us."

Seren did not seem to be so quick to escape from the dubious comfort of lounging on me. She lay there, still as a wolf waiting for a deer to pad out into a clearing as she listened to our conversation without saying a word. She was really good at not saying anything and not showing any emotion. It was like having dinner with my dad. Asher crouched down beside me. "And you knew the exact phrase to speak?"

"Oh, uh history sense or whatever. *Psychometry.*"

"It would seem to me that we grossly underestimated the power of many divine skills."

Wrapping both arms around Seren to stop her from being flung across the room, I sat up. She looked from my arms around her to my face with the beginnings of a scowl. "What is this?"

"This is a hug. We use them to say things like 'thanks for saving my life back there.'"

She didn't wriggle around. She was so still she might have been dead. "Release me at once."

I spread my arms as wide as I could, and she leapt up like she'd been burned. "Alrighty then."

Mercy had finally stopped retching long enough to get a word in. "That. Was. Dumb."

"It was certainly not your finest moment," Asher snarked.

She started up another coughing fit. "Eat. Me. Asher."

With that trap out of the way, I pulled the door to the next stairwell open. All of the bare floors and sparse walls were done with now that we were out of the public parts of the tower. This was pure opulence. There was thick plush purple carpet running all the way up the spiral of stairs around the outer wall, and candles replaced the torches of the lower floors. There was even a little railing to hold onto as you climbed, although I was reluctant to touch anything at this point in case it tried to eat me.

Once again, we only made it one floor before hitting another dead end and door. "There has got to be a quicker way up this tower."

Seren scoffed. "Had I my mount, we could have flown at once to the top."

"If you had your mount, you'd be halfway across the ocean screaming for reinforcements by now." As it turned out, being asphyxiated and probed by an angry metal puddle had not improved Mercy's mood.

"Hey now. She saved our asses back there."

"I am a paladin myself, I need no gallant to charge to my rescue." Seren sniffed. "Thy companion has made it clear she has no care for me, and who among us could lay the blame for that at her feet when I set myself as your enemy from the off. Yet this I say unto you, Mercy, the ill-named, had I the desire to depart, then many opportunities have already presented themselves—opportunities that offered up the chance to see you all deceased in the bargain, if I had so wished. So understand me now. Your leader has declared me free, against all wisdom, and it is only by my volition alone that I remain in your company."

Suddenly, everybody had something to say. Asher politely inquired, "Maulkin has freed you?"

Mercy bellowed, "Leader?!"

I pushed the next door open before the argument could start, betting that a smart-ass like Talon wouldn't put the same trap in twice. I was right, for the first time in living memory.

The next room looked like something out of a fairy-tale. I didn't even know the words to describe it until *Dungeoneering* helpfully supplied "Solarium." So it was a solarium. Apparently. Floor to ceiling windows surrounded us on the east and west curves of the wall, there was an honest-to-the-gods fountain in the middle of the room, as tall as me and tinkling out sparkling water that shimmered in the sunlight, and everywhere else that I looked, there were flowers.

Underneath those flowers were plants and fancy carved marble planters and all the rest, but after a week in Amaranth, I think that room of flowers was the most color I'd seen. I was drunk on it. Forgetting all about the arguments and the dangers, I stepped out into the room and drew in a deep breath. Beautiful.

I didn't even hear what Asher and Mercy were yelling when they came through the door after me, just the sudden intake of breath. Seren was not stunned into silence. "What could be the purpose of all this?"

"It's pretty." I had moved farther into the room without even realizing it, drifting closer to the abundance of life and color that I thought we'd left behind. Talon had left that world behind too, I suppose. Maybe that was why he'd tried to remake a little slice of home here.

"Beauty without purpose?" She scoffed. "I do not believe thy predecessor would think thus."

Mercy dragged her gaze away from something like a lily of the valley. Yeah, that's right, I knew some plants. I wasn't a complete couch potato. I mean sure I knew them from video games, but I still knew them. "So what, you think the flowers are going to eat us?"

Asher shook his head. "They bear no hint of magic within them beyond that which has sustained them through the ages. I cannot even say that is a spell. It feels as though the pillar of Cosmos and magic have been intertwined somehow. It is no wonder that Talon was hailed as an Archmage if he could blend his gods-given gifts with the principles of magic."

A butterfly flitted out from between the flowers I was sniffing, its wings silvery even in the golden sunlight that was streaming in. Leaning back I could see there were dozens of them dancing around the room. Those reflective wings picking up the colors of whatever flowers were around them. If I was about to be murdered by ninja-star butterflies, I was going to die mad about it.

But strangely enough, for Amaranth, they didn't seem to be all that interested in brutalizing us. Instead, they just fluttered around. Mercy slapped a hand over her mouth when she started to make an "ooh" sound, but it was enough to set me off laughing. That got me a solid kick in the ass.

"I don't know, Seren, I think this might just have been someplace for him to relax, I mean… look at it."

Her eyes were darting around frantically, staring suspiciously at the butterflies as they fluttered by, and avoiding getting too close to any of the flowers. I suppose if you grew up in a world that was out to kill you, you'd be a bit suspicious too. "Were it for his relaxation, it would be closer to his chambers. Given thy assumption that those chambers lie within the uppermost portions of this fortification… I am dubious."

That was a valid point. Why would he build it down here? I squeezed between some ferns to look out the windows. We were just up above the tree-line, and I could see out over the forest as far as the sea. Maybe there would have been a better view higher up, but I doubted it. A butterfly flitted by me, startling me out of my thoughts, but not before I saw the tops of the trees rustling in some unseen breeze. More than a breeze. It was as if a gale-force wind just whipped over the top of the forest in a line. A line stretching out from where I was standing. Or right beside me at least.

"Oh my gods, they're hurricane butterflies."

"What?" I dragged Asher over to look. He jumped when he saw what I had seen.

After a moment of contemplation, he let out a little huff of surprise. "It would seem that your Alvaren friend's suggestion of flying around the defenses of the tower has already been considered."

My mouth fell open when I understood what he was saying. "Oh, no way. That is so cool. And also so weird. Who thinks of butterflies when they're playing tower defense?"

"It would appear that the Archmage is a man who can think… laterally." His robes whipped around him as a butterfly passed us by. He met my gaze with trepidation.

"Alright. Everybody out before we get tornadoed by the bugs!"

Seren was already at the door on the other side of the chamber, examining it without touching anything. Asher darted over to begin his own probing. Mercy was not moving. She was still standing there by the fountain, perfectly still. "Mercy, come on."

She still didn't move. It was only when I closed the distance with her that I understood why. One of the silvery butterflies was on her nose.

"You are having the best luck today."

She tried to answer without moving her face. It was kind of hilarious. "What do I do?"

"Blow on it?"

A bead of sweat ran down her face. "If I make it angry, will it blow my head off?"

"Uh… maybe?" When I turned to quietly call for Asher, I nearly bumped into Seren, two bells around her neck. Two.

Her eyes were locked on the butterfly, practically shimmering with her excitement. "I am most certain that I can kill it before it moves."

That seemed like a bad idea. And I knew bad ideas. "Or we can just wait for it to fly away on its own?"

Seren's little frown returned. "You value the life of this insect over that of your companion?"

"I'd rather not have a sword near my face," Mercy mumbled through lips she was scared to part.

The butterfly's wings twitched, blowing Mercy's bangs back and spritzing the beaded sweat off her face. I moved in a little closer, raising my hands.

"Don't."

I moved my hands a little closer, coming in from the sides of Mercy's face.

"Don't!"

Ever so slowly, I cupped them around the butterfly. My knuckles grazing over Mercy's cheekbones.

"Do not do what you are doing!"

I pulled my hands towards me ever so slowly, just barely brushing the edge of the butterfly's wings. It stepped off Mercy's nose and onto my fingers, and she let out a sigh of relief. A sigh of relief that tickled across the backs of my hands, through the gap between them, and startled the butterfly.

It took flight, and so did I.

Blasted backward, I shattered the fountain. Ow. Fragments of it were flung across the room. Hitting flowers, cracking the windows, and most importantly of all, pissing off the other butterflies. Oh no. "Go! Go! Go!"

Mercy and Seren were already running, and the same blast that had knocked me on my ass had launched them across the room to bowl into Asher. The three of them were scrambling over each other and wrestling the door open when the tempest kicked up.

Me against a room full of butterflies? I'd normally put the money on me, but with all the fragments of pots and fountain scattered around, the odds were a little bit skewed in their favor. Back on my feet, rainbows swirled around me as the water from the broken fountain picked up. Rainbows with sharp teeth.

[685/710 Health]

The first shard of stone glanced off my cheek, leaving a stinging mark.

[684/710 Health]

Then came the next.

[683/710 Health]

And the next.

[682/710 Health]

Every step I took I was buffeted by the winds, scratched and pounded from every direction.

It was death by a thousand tiny cuts, and to make matters worse, I couldn't see or hear anything beyond the swirling rainbow. The wind wailed, and the grit and dirt got in my eyes even when it wasn't trying to slash them out of my face.

Staggering forward another step, my knee hit the broken edge of the fountain. I'd gone in a full circle.

"That is enough!"

I threw out my arms and my will. Every fragment of stone, grit, and dirt in my *Sphere of Influence* froze, and I hammered them down into the ground. There was nothing I could do about the wind or the water, but I could see clearly enough now to run at the open door where the others were waiting

The wind slapped me off course, and I bumped into a couple of butterflies that were more than happy to launch their own violent gusts in my direction, skidding me about the room like I was stuck in a pinball machine, but I made it through the door and slammed it shut behind me.

I slumped down to sit with my back to the door. "That…was not fun."

Mercy nudged Seren. "Wow, that is like…the most negative thing he's ever said about anything."

"I've said worse about you." I managed a grin.

She stamped on my shin. "I've said worse about your face."

I hoisted myself back to my feet with her outstretched hand, almost toppling her over in the process.

"I've said worse about your mother."

Asher turned around and walked away from us. More purple carpet, more stairs. Another disappointment just around the corner. "Any magic?"

Asher held up his hands and then cocked his head to the side. "None."

"Well, alright then." I pushed the door open to see another identical door. Seriously. I pushed on the one. It was locked. "Great."

Rolling my shoulders, I got ready to barge it down when Seren stepped up beside me and said, "Wait." I followed her pointed finger up to the mechanical apparatus attached to both doors. Interlocking cogs covered the roof of this little antechamber. It took me longer than it should have to work it out. "Oh!"

Asher was poking his head through the door, still puzzled. "Oh?"

"It is a one or the other kind of deal." I snapped my fingers. "Like an airlock. Everyone squeeze in."

Seren was already so far up in my personal space that it was sheer skill on her part that we weren't touching, the other two managed to make it in without too much complaint. Although Mercy did say, "Why does a tower need an airlock?"

"I cannot believe that these doors are airtight regardless." Asher shrugged. I reached over to slam the door shut behind us. The one ahead sprang open at the same time.

Asher dropped like a sack of spanners, all awkward angles and flopping. It was mostly luck that let me catch the scruff of his robes before he hit the floor or Mercy. At least the floor would only have hit him back once. "What the hell?"

Mercy got an arm around him too, and all together, we carried our napping companion into the next room. The décor was…different in here, less sumptuous summer getaway and more 'rusty dungeon'. Mercy covered it pretty well with, "Ew."

There were no windows here, no pretty flowers, just metal plates riveted into the walls, bones scattered around the outside—I kept an eye on them in case this turned into a living skeleton kind of situation—and a podium in the middle of the room with a big ingot of some dark metal sitting on top. Or at least I assumed it was. I couldn't actually see whatever was sitting on top of the podium, it was too dark for that. Not the room, the ingot. So dark it swallowed up all the light that touched it. So dark it kind of hurt my eyes to look at it for too long.

Seren had stepped gracefully clear of the toppling Asher and now darted forward. "I have heard tell of this. It was a legend even in my time. A theoretical puzzle for the magisters. Inimicus. The un-magic."

Mercy rolled her eyes. "Why would a wizard have the opposite of magic in his house?"

"Why would a noble wear blades at their hips as they walk their own streets?" Seren snapped back.

"Downstairs, the uh doorknob thing. Talon was setting things up to protect himself from other magic users. That trap was meant to stop them casting, it used the magic we threw at it to become more powerful. I guess this is just the natural escalation of that."

"As fascinating as these insights into the mind of the mad mage are, what are thy intentions for departing from this place?"

The door behind us had swung shut as we focused more on Asher's fainting spell than our surroundings, and the door at the opposite side of the room was equally devoid of doorknobs, handles, or any other way of opening it. Another glance around reminded me of the bones on the ground. All the people who'd made it this far then starved to death, trapped in this room. Great.

Asher began to stir on the floor, groaning and grumbling all the way.

"Okay, so there is no magic in this room. But our guy, Talon, he'd still need a way to get through it, right?"

Mercy and Seren had split up, each one trying to pry open a door on either side of the room. What had been wood on the outside was plated with iron here, rusty sheets of it that neither woman's fingers could hope to part. They couldn't even force their fingers between them. Seren drew her sword to make an attempt at using it as a prybar.

Something was wrong with the blade. The same rust that covered the walls seemed to have worked its way inside them, blossoming out across the smooth silvered surface like oil over water. Seren held it up to eye-level and glowered as the artistry that had forged her weapons crumbled away to nothing. Without a sound, she reached for her other sword. The hilt snapped off in her hand, then even that crumbled away into chunks.

My sword. I grabbed for it and hauled it out of the Dvergar-made baldric which had somehow survived all this way. It was fine. No rust. It was a little blunted and scratched from walloping a big stone boy downstairs, but otherwise, it was perfect. Seren's eyes darted back and forth from her crumbling rust to my pristine great-sword and scowled. "The Inimicus. My blades were spell-wrought by the high magister himself."

"Well, if it is any consolation, trying to use them like a crowbar was probably going to wreck them anyway." Awkward, who me?

"It is of no consolation. They were a symbol of my service, and now, so like that service, they are sundered."

Asher gasped awake on the floor. "What? What is happening? Where am I?"

"Anti-magic room, buddy. Knocked you right out."

He scrabbled up the podium to his feet, leaping back from the black lump like it was covered in electrified hornets. "How can this be?"

"Ask your man Talon. Even Seren's people didn't have this stuff lying around." Mercy sauntered back over with a smirk. "My gods, for the first time since we got here, we can't just say 'magic' as an explanation of everything."

I offered Asher a hand up, but he refused it, staying right where he was, head weaving from side to side as he tried to keep us all in focus. "Even if such a thing could somehow be made, why would any mage consent to having it anywhere near them?"

"Talon kind of seems like a paranoid wreck. Maybe that's why."

"Paranoid he may have been, but a fool he most certainly was not." Asher tried to look at the tiny black obelisk, but it seemed to be hurting his eyes. He flinched away. "I cannot believe that he would place something so detrimental to his own position and power within his home."

Seren nodded her agreement. "A man would not drink poison in the hope of his enemy supping from the same cup."

Mercy didn't like to be left out. "So he'd lose his magic powers if he was in this room. So what?"

Both Asher and Seren looked horrified. "To sever a mage from their magic is a barbarous act. It should come as no surprise that thy condone it."

"I'm not condoning a damn thing, I'm just saying it wouldn't matter to Talon if he lost his magic for a while. He wasn't just some mage, was he? He was one of us."

I snapped my fingers. "He could get through this because he was an eternal! He had his divine powers, even when his magic was offline."

They all turned to look at me. "What?"

Mercy started tapping her toe, Asher covered his eyes with a hand, and Seren looked embarrassed on my behalf. "What?!"

The penny dropped.

"Oh!" I slapped myself in the head. "I'm an Eternal. I have Eternal powers. I could do my Artifice thing. Right. Sorry. Yeah."

My *Sphere of Influence* encompassed almost the whole room, but I figured we were going forward not back, so I hopped back in my body and strolled it over to the door on what I guess was the south side. I'm not great with directions.

Stretching out my will, I got ready to dramatically pull the door off its hinges when I abruptly stopped. I couldn't touch the door. I couldn't touch anything in the room. All of it was carefully worked metal, some sort of alloy that looked like iron, rusted like iron, but was out of reach of my basic bitch Artifice. I went behind that to the doors and the walls themselves, figuring I could just pull things apart brick by brick, but they were too complex for me too. There was something like clockwork running through the whole room—complex machinery locking the doors in place, running beneath the floor and through the roof like a great technological cage containing my abilities. "So uh, Artifice isn't going to cut it. There's some sort of mechanical stuff inside the walls."

Seren looked me up and down. "Can you not simply break down the door?"

"I mean, maybe?" I rubbed the back of my neck, inadvertently flexing arms that were as big as Seren's waist. "It is a metal door covered in metal plates."

Asher piped up, "And if there is a mechanism that would allow for our release, bending the door out of shape would inevitably prevent us from using it."

They were all still looking at me. Damn it. "Anybody else have any bright ideas?"

"Perhaps it would behoove us to consider which of the Pillars of Divinity it is likely that our friend Talon would have pursued."

"I haven't seen anything elemental, so probably not Creation." Mercy scowled. "Omnis for sure."

"Oh yeah, he seems like an Omnis kind of dude for sure."

"Do we believe that the power of Primal would have been required for the creation of his guardian golem?" Asher was literally stroking his chin. Unbelievable.

"My people crafted golems during the Voidgod's reign of terror," Seren interjected. "It is an act of craft and magic, not divinity."

"He might have needed it to make the butterflies though."

"Thy course is true. Those were not natural beings." She turned that little frown of hers on me. Always suspicious. How was that not exhausting? "How did you know of them? What did you call them? Butter flies?"

"We had butterflies back on our world. They didn't make storms though." I paused for a moment. "Well… I mean some philosopher chaos theory kind of people said they did, but it was a metaphor or something. Probably."

Mercy was smirking. "Stop confusing the poor Alvaren. Ascension is a maybe." She counted them off on her fingers. "Artifice is probably a no?"

I shrugged. "If I was building someplace for myself, I wouldn't make it too complicated to artifice."

"He might have been artifice-ing a lot longer than you, though. Maybe he is actually good at it."

"Bite me."

Seren chirped, "Refrain from biting him."

"Why does everything have to be so difficult." I groaned. "Cosmos and Omnis. Maybe Ascension, maybe Aether."

I snapped my fingers. "Aether!"

Fumbling with my gloves took longer than it should have. I still wasn't used to wearing them, and they made dexterous movements trickier. Seren and Mercy eventually sighed and pulled one off each in opposite directions. I wiggled my fingers at them. "Who wants to see what my magic hands can do!"

Predictably, Mercy said, "Ew," but Seren was nodding with an almost childlike excitement until Mercy leaned over and whispered in her ear. The first hint of a smile that had been playing about her lips instantly vanished.

"Grotesque."

Oof. I didn't know how much more damage this old ego of mine could take. One more hit like that and it might need to be moved out of the matchbox I'd been keeping it in throughout all my dating years and transfer it to something smaller.

I slapped my palm down on the rusty dusty floor and immediately regretted it. There was a lot of death here. Long, *long* bouts of silence, then the sobbing. The slow and agonizing decline as bodies ate away at themselves. Cannibal in their desperation. Panicked and screaming. Then silence again, heavier than before. Still, I plunged back and back through time until the dead were all gone and there was only the most distant sense that anyone was passing through the room at all.

Nothing useful. Well, it was just some random patch of floor, what had I been expecting? Sauntering over to the exit, I gave the girls a big grin before slapping my hand to the metal.

Movement behind the sheets. The rumble of mechanisms. Grinding open, grinding closed. The door in motion. Swinging along its axis. Fingers brushing over it. Hands that were wracked with tremors. Talon's hands. The same, blue-gemmed ring I'd seen him wearing in my last vision. Then gone again. Gone without a clue how the door was opened, except that it gave Talon the shakes.

I yanked my hand back in frustration. Had he done this deliberately somehow? Using his Eternal powers to block my view of how he escaped? Was I getting as paranoid and weird as him? Had I started out as paranoid and weird as him? I was talking to myself. That probably wasn't a good sign.

The rest of the gang was all staring at me like I had descended from on high to bring them the answers to all of their woes and worries. On the one hand, I liked the vote of confidence, on the other, I really didn't appreciate the pressure that I was being put under to perform. "I swear I can open this door, just…just give me a minute. This has never happened to me before."

There was only one thing left in the room that I could touch, and even though I was about as magical as a brick, there was something unsettling about the Inimicus. Maybe it was the way it swallowed all light, making it look like there was a hole in reality. Maybe it was the way it made Asher pass out just from being near it. Who could say for sure? The main thing was I really didn't want to touch the little cuboid of black-hole. I really didn't. Yet still, I forced my hand out, just waiting for the sting of it disintegrating me or sucking me into hell or whatever it was going to do.

It was cold, but not the death-chill of the void between the stars, just regular metal left at room temperature cold. I let out a little sigh of relief before *Psychometry* kicked in, and I was hauled into the swirl of ghosts. There were so few of them throughout all the ages that this tower had stood. So few who'd made it this far. The history of the Inimicus felt as devoid of life as the metal itself. I plunged even further back, back to the moment that it was forged. "And so you see, magic, like lightning and the pull of the earth beneath us, is just another force for Cosmos to master. All things have their antithesis, and I have made…"

A sudden lurch forward and there Talon was again, hand hovering perilously close to the top of the Inimicus, unwilling to touch it but pushing it down into the podium with something like Asher's gravity snare. The block sliding down into the podium, the cogs within turning. I yanked my hand off. "This is it. This is how you open the door."

Asher cocked his head to one side. "I do not understand."

Curling my fingers into a fist, I punched the block down into the machinery. It groaned and creaked, rust dislodged, and the door at the far end of the room swung open. Mercy grinned. "Talon wasn't scared of monkeys like us, he was scared of other wizards."

Seren finished the thought. "Those that would not dare to lay a hand on the Inimicus."

When the block was level with the top of the podium, it stopped moving with a click. I held out my hands, and after two attempts at trying to hand my glove back to me, Mercy grumbled through putting it back on my hand like Seren had. "Thank you, Seren. Thank you, Mercy."

Seren gave a slight bow while Mercy sing-songed, "Oh thank you so much for touching things with your big sausage fingers, Maulkin, you've saved the day again. Let me repay you by dressing you and telling you what a big strong man you are."

"I know it's sarcasm, but I honestly think I like Mercy better this way."

She kicked me in the shins, and Asher jerked his head around so that his own laugh couldn't incriminate him. Seren watched all of this unfolding with the same expressionless mask as always, but I could tell that she was filing it away for later. This older-than-human-civilization dog was still learning new tricks. Absorbing the way that we spoke, the way that we interacted, everything. I didn't know if it was because she was planning our deaths or because she was trying to fit in, and honestly, I wasn't sure if I'd ever know at this rate.

CHAPTER 32

The next set of stairs coiled up around the outer curve of the tower the same as all the rest. The same plush carpets were there, the same candelabras, and the same fancy silver-filigreed handrails. You had to respect the interior designer's consistency if nothing else. I took hold of the handrail and hauled on it. It was pretty well embedded in the stone. I couldn't make it budge until I surged my Potency. Even then it came away screeching and bending in my grip instead of popping out clean. That was some solid construction work. Mercy came running back down the stairs. "What the hell are you doing?!"

"Stuff."

"Could you focus for five frigging minutes, please?" She rolled her eyes and walked away, calling up to Asher, "It is alright, he's just screwing around. Again."

Beneath the shiny exterior, the metal was just iron. Nothing clever or fancy or hard to come by. With a few good twists, I could get at that iron, and with a few seconds of work in the slowed-down space of Artifice, I was able to cobble together a pair of swords.

Seren took them from me cautiously. "These blades are forged by thy own power?"

"Yup, sorry they aren't as fancy and shiny as the old ones, but they should still work alright. Maybe not as sharp or as…"

She sheathed them in one smooth movement and dropped to one knee on the stairs.

I was one hundred percent not ready for marriage. "Uh what are you—"

"I pledge myself to thee, Maulkin. As I did my empress before thee."

Flustered, I stepped down to grab her shoulders and haul her up. "Hey, no. No uh... no need for any of that."

Mercy stuck her head around the curve of the stairwell, and I leapt back from Seren guiltily. That sing-song voice was back again. "What are you guys up to down there?"

I tried to shout, "Nothing," but Seren barreled on.

"I am pledging myself freely to your kinsman, to serve him in all ways until such time as I am returned to my people."

"Awww." Mercy's voice grated over my nerves. "Asher, come quick, they're getting engaged!"

Once more I tried to cut off the conversation and failed miserably. "I will kill you."

"The pledge to one's lord is a more serious matter than mere promises to wed. I swear on these blades that I shall give my mind, body, and life as Maulkin commands me. Whatever use he should have for me..."

Mercy's eyebrows started waggling so wildly I was concerned that they were about to take off. "Oh, I know exactly what use he's going to have for you."

I'd had enough. "Everyone shut up now!" I shoved my way past Mercy and ran up the stairs only to bump into Asher, who cocked his head to one side.

"Is the honeymoon at an end?"

I was going to kill them both. It didn't matter if they wouldn't stay dead. I was going to chop them up. If the next door was trapped, I was going to die. My boot met the middle of the door, and it burst open.

There was something to fight inside. Thank the gods. These golems weren't giants like the one in the entry hall, each one about human size, give or take, but each of them was unique in a way I wouldn't have expected automatons to be. The first one to come charging at me had its marbled shape carved into a suit of armor, but it wasn't all stone. There was a solid-looking maul in its hands, made from some brassy metal I didn't recognize. It was swinging for me before I even had my own sword out.

[651/710 Health]

Bang, right in the middle of my chest, setting me sliding and stumbling back out into the hall. My eel-scale armor held up well against it, with all the scales snapping together solidly against the impact, but it didn't seem to do much to actually temper the blow. The wind was knocked out of me. If Asher or Mercy had been the one to catch that swing, they'd have been on the floor.

I wheezed, "Let's go!"

With my own sword drawn, I charged back in, ducking under a flitting arrow that embedded itself in the door. I only had eyes for the big guy with the maul, but there were many other golems on the move. The archer was Dvergar-sized, but the armor it was carved into looked distinctly different from what we'd seen the current generation wearing. Theirs were all blocky brutalist efficiency. This thing was a work of art, rune-marked all around the borders of the armor plates.

There were a pair of porcelain-looking Alvaren with the same twin-swords that Seren and her paladins had used, and they looked exactly the same. Some things never go out of fashion, apparently. Farther back, guarding the archer, was another human in a different style of armor, something closer to my own piecemeal. That one had a solid-looking shield and a short sword held ready, but it looked like it had no intention of moving from the spot, so I ignored it.

After the relative silence of the rest of the tower, the sound of metal meeting metal was almost deafening. My wild swing arrested hammer golem's precise chop at my mid-section with a shower of sparks.

"Fight!" I hefted the mass of my sword back and swung overhead. "We've got a fight! Finally!"

The strike could have halved any normal fighter, but this one caught it on the haft of its hammer and turned it aside all too easily. Bringing the head around at my head, I had to jump back or risk losing my jaw.

Damn. This golem actually knew how to fight. It knew how to fight better than me! Which admittedly wasn't hard since most of my skillful swordplay came down to whacking stuff as hard as possible, but even so.

The next arrow went through the gap between the hammer golem's legs, right into my foot. Pinning me in place. *Ow.*

They were a lot more competent than I'd expected mindless automatons to be. I went into this expecting more of the slow-zombie stuff from downstairs, and instead, I was getting knocked around by a team of professionals. It was like fighting the damned Alvaren all over again.

Fire swept through the room in a wave, washing harmlessly over the golems but covering me in flickering embers. Asher's contribution. Great. Hot on his heels, Mercy and Seren came storming into the room with their weapons drawn, yelling out whatever battle-cries they still had breath for after running up the stairs.

When I glanced back, the hammer-golem was up in my grill—as the kids say. I saw my own double-handed overhead strike being returned to me with interest, and this time, I had no hope of dodging out of the way.

In my panic, I reached for Artifice. My sword became fluid for an instant, then solidified into a solid boxy shield above my head.

It worked, technically, but the shield buckled under the weight of the hit, folding around it like it was made of corrugated cardboard instead of metal.

I barely even had time to grunt my dismay before I caught a glimpse of shimmering metal under the rim of the twisted metal umbrella. The upward swing of the golem's hammer lifted the whole thing out of my hands and launched it into the air.

"Hey! That's mine!"

Mercy's Tempest Arrow hit the golem square in the chest, right where it had bonked me, and the concussion as it went off knocked everything sideways.

The golem slid back across the flagstones with a screech, and I flopped right over onto my back and landed with a crunch, still pinned by that one arrow through my foot. An arrow that had been in flight was knocked straight up into the roof and tumbled down to land beside me. My trashed shield clattered down beside me a moment later.

That wind arrow thing was cool as hell, but it really wasn't a lot of fun being this close to it when it went boom.

Inevitably, hammer golem was quicker to recover than me, and he came charging back with his hammer upraised, ready to turn me into pulverized Maulkin jelly.

I started to babble the words that had disarmed the last trap frantically, memory failing me. "Ah peeing lame bocky con oona parabola dire nose no cost, cozy del pasta!"

Somehow, that didn't work. The hammer was coming down.

Seren hit it head-on. Not with the clumsy tackle I would have used, but in a blur of blades and motion. Competent as the golem was, he couldn't match her speed. Skill didn't matter when a blade had already struck home twice before you saw the enemy moving. I'd never seen her going all out before. Not really.

No hit that she landed was enough to actually break through the golem's armor, but there were so many of them coming from every direction that it didn't have a chance to react before something new was happening around its other side.

She was buying time, but any second now, she was going to be buying it with blood. The Alvaren-looking golem were moving up on her, their own blades spinning in their hands like they were food processors gone wild.

This was going to suck. I took a hold of the arrow, and after two tugs failed to pull it out, I snapped it off in my foot.

[605/710 Health]

I was right. That did suck. But even as I bled and groaned, I was able to haul my foot free. Artifice remade my sword for me as I rose, and I set the flat end of it to the stone and pushed myself back up onto my sore feet with a grimace.

Asher's next spell rolled through the room, a great blast of flame that narrowly missed me and Seren but washed right over the Alvaren, archer, and shield-guy golems. When it cleared, they didn't even have a sooty mark on them, and I was genuinely starting to wonder what Asher was playing at before I heard the frankly hilarious twang of the golem's bow-string snapping. The bow, the shield, they were all on fire, even if the golems themselves were fine.

Through it all hammer-golem was still chasing after Seren, every swing a little too late, every step dogged by the beautiful Alvaren's deadly swordplay. In desperation, it swung its maul around at waist height in a great circle, hoping to buy itself some space, but Seren leapt neatly over the hammerhead as it came her way, turning a little sideways somersault in the air.

I was staring again. Whoops.

While the golem had his back to me, still chasing Seren, I rushed him with the same clumsy, crazy swing I always used, and this time it connected.

The statue crumbled around the site of the hit, and my sword punched right through it. No wonder they were so fast compared to the big ego trip downstairs, they were hollow, like plaster casts of golems instead of the rock-solid one we'd faced before.

"They're soft. You get through the shell and there's nothing inside!"

I was corrected a moment later when a huge plume of dust burst up out of the broken golem. A column of particulates blasting up into the air, spreading itself out across the beams of the ceiling and then vanishing just as quickly.

They might have been soft, but their weapons certainly weren't. The Alvaren golems moved like Seren, fast and smooth like dancers running through a well-practiced routine. They were closing on her as she let a hint of a smile play over her lips.

I kicked the dead golem at the one on Seren's left, and it had to leap aside or be crushed. The armor plates all fell apart now that there was no force animating them, but it didn't matter. It was a distraction while I rushed to Seren's side. As the golem continued their slow stalk towards us, we ended up back-to-back pacing around in circles to keep them in sight. "I did not speak in jest when I swore myself to your service." Her golem darted in, and she matched every blinding thrust of its silvery swords with a parry. "You have been gracious to me beyond my deserving, and though I mean to return to my queen, there is no reason that for now I cannot take comfort in your leadership."

My own Alvaren golem was less willing to test at my defenses. It came on hard and heavy, and only the bulk of my sword serving as a bulwark managed to hold it off.

Mercy's arrows flew true through the dust and the spinning blades, never quite punching a hole through the plates of stone that comprised the golems but knocking them constantly off balance. It was as much as we could have asked of her while she waited for her epic explosion arrow thing to charge up again.

With the bow-wielder rendered useless, the shield boy was shuffling forward to have his try at us too, but Asher was having none of that. With fire proving useless, he unleashed one of his classic lightning bolts at the shield-golem.

That shield did not hold up well against the fury of an Asher scorned, and fragments of it flew across the room. Even though the golem itself was yet again untouched, there was something really satisfying about seeing their weapons being slapped out of their hands.

The next time my Alvaren darted in, I yelled, "Swap!"

Seren hit my back in a roll, flipping up and over me as I stepped in, dragging my blade-tip in a shrieking arc along the flagstones to come up right into the Alvaren statue Seren had just dived away from.

The delicate, intricate dance that it had been conducting was shattered, its cunning parries slapped aside by the one sweep of my blade. It even tried to fling itself back, but it was too late.

The tip of my sword caught it under the chin and lifted the whole head up off its shoulders in two halves. "Hah!"

Meanwhile, the one that had expected an immobile object to hack at got the deadly dance of Seren. It's initial slower, more powerful swings were like a joke to her. She darted in past them, slapped at the insides of its wrists with the flats of her blades, and then thrust both swords into the weak point where neck met armor on the torso, twisting the swords as she withdrew to pry the seam apart.

It was enough. The same rush of dust escaped her golem as had burst out of mine. Only the archer and the artist-formerly-known-as-shield-golem were still standing. Seren and I met each other's eyes, and that almost smile was there again. I was grinning like an idiot, personally.

Asher had simply retreated out of the room when it became apparent that his magic couldn't help us anymore, keeping himself safe in case he had to give one of us a handy cauterize. I really, *really* hoped that he wouldn't cauterize me again. I know, I was being a wimp, but I just really didn't like feeling all my organs set on fire.

The remaining golems lacked the power or speed of the others. They had the competence down, but Seren had that in spades, and I made up for what I lacked with enthusiasm and size. The newly dubbed short sword golem ducked under my initial swing, not even realizing that there was an Alvaren hiding in the shadow of my blade, just waiting for it. She shot out between his splayed legs with her swords up. Scoring a long line across the joint of its legs. Good thing it wasn't a boy golem, or it would have just lost its stones.

I reversed my grip and brought my sword back around along the same arc. It would have missed entirely if Seren hadn't chosen that moment to stamp down into the back of the golem's knees. We were like a well-oiled machine out here on the dancefloor. Her all graceful, and me all choppy.

Sword met stone face.

Another impressive pillar of dust blasted up at the roof, but Seren and I were already in motion towards the last of the golems. It had no weapons, no armor, and thanks to the curse of stone, it really didn't look all that different from all of the other lost little Dvergar we'd left outside. The only difference was that this one had an out.

As Seren closed on it, it slammed both hands into its chest and pulled the breastplate in half. The torrent of dust was unleashed without us having to land a single blow, pattering off the ceiling and joining the cloud of impending coughs that was lingering up there among the rafters.

Legendary Foes Defeated!
Vitality increased to 18
Phalanx: Rank 7/10
165 Experience Gained
120 Glory Gained

"That was surprisingly painless." Asher wandered in, his eyes upturned towards the cloud.

"Easy for you to say," I grumbled without much malice. "Nobody hammered and shot you."

Mercy grinned. "I can still shoot him if you want."

Seren gave the suicidal golem's shell a kick, and it toppled into pieces. "Disappointing. For a moment, it seemed that we might face a challenge."

"Once again, shot and hammered."

"Oh stop whining." Mercy smirked. "You're hardly even bleeding."

They were right, of course. My ever-expanding health pool had rendered even these horrific wounds fairly mundane, but that didn't mean I had to like it. *Restoration* spread out along my skin, closing me back up, filling my health up to its maximum once more. I checked over the other three, but there didn't seem to be any damage despite the golem's best efforts. Despite being toe-to-toe with the golems the same as me, the worst that could be said about Seren was that she'd broken a sweat.

Now that the golems were out of the picture, we had a proper look around the room, but it was as devoid of interest as it had initially looked. There was dust, broken bits of golem, stone slab floor, and stone block wall. I suppose that if the intention were to use this as a killing ground then adding in fancy décor was probably a bit counter-productive, but damn it all, if I was going to get murdered by animated pottery then I wanted to die in style.

I dug around in the remains of the golems for the silvery swords of the Alvaren-looking ones, and I offered them to Seren, but she pushed them away with a shake of the head. "I would not shame myself by wielding a blade that I did not earn."

"They're better than the ones I made you. This isn't like a test or something, they're just better. Go on take them. I'm not going to be offended."

"Your concern is noted."

Either she was really bad at taking orders, or I was really bad at giving them. Probably both. She'd wandered off before I could get it together enough to demand she take the damn things.

The gang had this down to an art by now, Seren checking things over while Asher waggled his hands about. Personally, I was convinced that we weren't going to run into any trapped doors. Talon was too impressed with himself for that. Every floor would be something new and different. Not necessarily anything pretty or even interesting—this was the guy that had the biggest most boring library in the whole world—but something at least.

My hunch proved correct yet again and then we were onto a much dustier version of the same spiral of purple carpet that had joined up every floor. "Hello, purple carpet, my old friend, my old nemesis."

Mercy called from behind me, putting on a butchered accent, "Want that I should toast him, boss?"

"Nah, he's suffering enough. Just let him get walked all over for the rest of his life."

Seren looked askance to Asher, who just threw his hands up in the air. "Your guess is as good as mine."

The next door was different from the ones before, finally. The wood was pale, the silver so covered in the patina of years that it was almost milky. I was almost touching it before the chill took me by surprise. The door was the same as every other, the silver-workings too. The only difference was that this door boasted a thick layer of frost.

I snatched my hand back. If it was cold enough to feel through my gloves, I didn't feel like touching it. I mean, there was a temptation to lick it, obviously, but I didn't want to touch it other than that. "Ooh, are we doing the classic elemental dungeon thing? Ice floor. Fire floor. Earth floor. Water floor. Air floor. Lightning floor…"

Asher was beside me examining the frost. Cowbells. So many

cowbells. "I do not believe the tower to be that tall, my friend."

"Maybe just the classics then? Earth, wind, and fire?" I started and abruptly stopped doing an awkward little boogie when I realized I was doing it. "And water."

Mercy helpfully pointed out the blindingly obvious. "That's ice."

"Could you count that as the water one?"

Seren looked on bewildered, as though we were speaking a foreign language. Well, as bewildered as she got anyway, which was mostly expressionless with a hint of a raised eyebrow.

Asher interrupted before I could lay down some elemental evil knowledge on these fools. "I do not believe that this ice is magical in origin."

"Pretty sure it isn't natural." Mercy rolled her eyes. "I'm not seeing a lot of glaciers around here."

This was getting us nowhere, so I kicked the door open. Or at least I tried to. What I actually did was shatter the whole thing into clunky frozen fragments that scattered into the room, tangling up in the drapes, hauling some of them down off the ceiling, and just generally making as much noise and mess as you could possibly imagine. Oops.

"At the very least, we know of one element that we shall not be encountering on this floor." Seren brushed past me. "The element of surprise."

"Maybe this is the fire floor"—Mercy smirked as she went by—"because you just got burned."

It wasn't any kind of elemental dungeon floor as it turned out. All the plush pomp of the stairwells had spread out across this room. There were the purple drapes breaking up the space, interspersed with honest-to-the-gods lace curtains dividing up the room even more, all of them fluttering in the breeze as we stepped into the room despite being weighed down with a fine rime of frost. It was only after we were all in that I realized there was no breeze. The air in here was still.

Which to me, meant… "Invisible monsters, guys. They've got invisible monsters in here."

Seren and I drew our swords, and the other two drew back behind us. Yet the invisible monsters did not immediately and conveniently leap out at us. The rippling of the drapes slowed and stopped as we did. Rude.

"Monsters… Come out and play!"

Still nothing.

I stormed forward into the room while Seren hung back to protect the others, swiping my sword through the first set of drapes. It wasn't sharp enough to cut them cleanly, but it was heavy enough to rip them, get tangled up, and haul the whole thing down off the ceiling with a clatter.

Still nothing.

I reached out with my *Lifesense*, stretching it to the very limits of my *Sphere of Influence*, straining for any hint of a living creature in the room. If there were golems, that would be useless, but on the off chance that Talon had magicked up some ghouls and goblins for us, I wanted to be ready. Still, there was no hint of anything alive in the room.

There was a door at the far end, and we were obviously meant to go wandering back and forth through this maze of curtains, getting more confused and stressed with every step, waiting for the ambush to pop. I wasn't falling for it. The door was in a straight line, so I was going in a straight line. With a bit of tugging, I managed to haul my sword free of the velvet and step up to the next one. I was cutting us through.

I took my next swipe and hit solid metal behind the cloth. My arms jarred, and I had all of a half a moment to wonder if I'd hit some sort of supporting column before it twisted, turning my blade aside and sending me stumbling off balance.

The Alvaren leapt out at me from behind the lace to my left the moment I was compromised. She slammed both blades into me and bore me to the ground.

[616/710 Health]

The noise that came out of me when I hit the ground was barely human. There was a sword in my lung and a roar trying to fight its way up out of me regardless. It came out gritty and burbling. I tried to grab for the Alvaren, but my hands passed through the empty air above me.

I must have blacked out for a second. I grabbed for my own weapon and was halfway to upright when the knight with the maul stepped through the curtain I'd been trying to slash and slammed it down into me. I barely even had time to flinch before all the air was literally hammered out of me.

My ribs bowed inwards and snapped, and blood sprayed out of the hole in my side like I was a punctured water balloon being stomped flat.

Mercy's arrows flew, passing right through the white knight to tangle up in the curtain behind him. It was like he wasn't even there. The frost that coated his armor gave him shape, and that had been punched away in a shimmer, but the pale glowing light inside of that crust was still there.

I did my best to shout, "Ghosts!" but mostly what came out of my mouth was a whole load of blood. I mean, a lot of blood. I didn't even know I had that much blood in me. Uh-oh. I reached inside myself for *Restoration*, but it was still out of commission. I'd squandered it on the whole "shot and hammered" thing on the previous floor.

The ghost knight lifted his maul high in the air, and I could already tell that this swing was coming for my face. What would life be like as a pancake?

Nobody was coming to save me. I rolled out as the hammer fell. Broken ribs tinkling against my organs like a xylophone of pain. Everything hurt, everything was terrible, I was going to chop this ghost right in the crotch.

The usual energy wasn't there, but I made it to my feet and managed to pick up my sword along the way too. With his attempts at an easy slaughter thwarted, the ghost knight struck a defensive pose and waited for me to come at him. It wasn't much, but that little pose did serve to remind me that this guy had actually trained all his life with the weapon he was waving around while I was just some guy who hadn't existed until last week. What the hell was I doing going toe to toe with these people? Ex-people. Whatever.

I charged in with another gurgle. Sweeping my sword down at him with all my strength and embedding it in the flagstones beneath his feet. It had passed through him without leaving a mark. Oh yeah. Ghost.

I couldn't tell if he was grinning inside that helmet, but I had to assume that he was. He jabbed forward with the head of his maul, catching me in the chin and bowling me over backward again.

As I fell, I saw how the others were faring behind me. It wasn't good. The two Alvaren were running rings around Seren, dipping in and out, slashing her, then leaping out of reach before she could return their strikes, even though they could have just stood there and chopped her to pieces. Old habits die hard, I guess.

Asher was down with a peppering of blood staining his robes in different places. Presumably, the ghost version of the Dvergar archer at work. Mercy seemed to have realized that her arrows weren't doing a damn thing, but that didn't mean she was out of the fight. With a clap of her hands, she threw up a wall of fire between them and me, blinding the archer to their targets if nothing else.

I rolled over and started back to my feet again when I heard, rather than saw, the hammer coming down again. A whistle of displaced air. Ending right in the middle of my back.

[362/710 Health]

There was a crack, and I tasted salt. My legs went cold as ice. I could feel them, but I couldn't move them. I couldn't use them. I got my arms under me and started dragging myself forwards.

The whistling again. Then another crack.

[299/710 Health]

If only he'd hit me in the back a little bit harder and properly broken it all the way through, I might not have felt every bone in my ankle shattering. It didn't seem fair that it still hurt.

Even my scream of pain was all messed up. I spat up more and more blood, leaving a trail of it like a snail as I tried to crawl away from the ghost knight. I didn't dare to look back. I didn't dare to do anything but haul myself forwards with all of my strength, surging my potency to balance out the hopelessness that seemed to be seeping out of my wounds and turning all my efforts to nothing.

It was enough. Each drag of my arms flung me a foot forward now as I breaststroked across the scraping, ragged flagstones. I couldn't hear the ghost's footsteps behind me, only the soft roar of the wall of flame.

There was no other way. I threw myself through it.

I barely had time to blink before Seren and Mercy threw Asher right on top of me. At least he was intact enough to scream about it. If you've never heard a lizard-man's scream you are really missing out, Inyoka have got some range. He could have fallen back on a career in opera.

He landed on me heavily, knocking what was left of my breath away. The embers still clinging to me from the wall of flame were briefly dampened, taking that stinging away, but he was grinding all of my broken bones together inside me.

Spluttering blood in complaint, I looked back to see the women darting towards the door as the Alvaren ghost twins pursued them. They were leaving us here to die. Lovely.

Throughout all of this, I'd been desperately reaching for *Restoration*, and now, finally, I realized it was alight again, not for me but for Asher. I pulsed my divine power into him, closing up the holes that the arrows had made.

With a gasp, he rolled off me but not to his feet. Throughout all of the aerial antics and his healing, I realized that he had been speaking softly with what little air he was able to draw, words of power, words of magic. Familiar ones. Oh no.

He lowered his hands to me and cast Cauterize.

[607/710 Health]

Every bone snapped into place amidst the licks of flames, seared into the right position. My lungs burned shut where they'd been opened, and even the masses of bruises that the mauling had left behind wisped away as red steaming vapors into the air.

Life flooded back through me, and I moved, scooping up Asher and tossing him through the door where Seren managed to catch him without bowling over. I tore off my gloves as I charged the Alvaren specters, and at the call of my much healthier-sounding roar, they turned to face me with their blades at the ready.

My own sword was somewhere back there beyond the wall of fire and the burning drapes, but it wasn't what I needed right now anyway. I was all that I needed. The power was in me. The most annoying passive divine power I'd picked up throughout my whole time on Amaranth. *Psychometry*. Also known as Spirit Touch.

I drove right between the Alvaren's darting feints without flinching and grabbed them by their heads. More specifically their faces.

A gentle kiss placed on each of Talon's whiskery cheeks. Standing together in a trench as in the distance a wyrm roars. A squeeze of each other's hands a cold comfort before launching into battle with the Voidgod's spawn. Chittering beasts. Burning eyes. Not sunlight. Not moonlight. Burning darkness. Metal and scale and death made flesh. Screaming. Blood. Pain. Talon's sanctuary. Wounds that will not heal. Scars. The shard. The shard must be protected. Evil seeks it even now. We can still serve. "Even if your bodies are broken, there is a way that the five of you can still help me to protect it from those who would use it for evil." Talon's voice. Ascent. Then the light. So bright. The tearing.

I flung the two of them back into the room. Into the wall of flame where the frost vanished in a puff and beyond, severing my connection to their histories, their sob stories. I didn't need to know what their deaths felt like. I'd died enough on my own without needing anyone else's misery in my head.

Staggering backward, I called out over my shoulder to the others. "Anyone got a plan better than me punching dead people to death?"

Mercy called back. "Working on it!"

The knight with the hammer strolled around the wall of flames, which I was sad to note was already dying down, even if some of the lace nearby had caught alight.

I shouted back. "Work on it faster!"

Without the bulk of the sword to slow me down, this was more of an even match. He swung for me with his ghost-hammer, and I was able to lean back out of reach. He whipped it back around again to continue the same lethal arc, and I managed to step inside his sweeping arms and catch hold of it by the shaft.

Once again, I wished that his visor wasn't down. The look on the dead man's face when I caught his ghost hammer would have been amazing. My own grin, streaked with blood, must have been something to behold too because he tried to jerk back out of reach.

The ghost of the hammer wasn't like the ghost of a person. There was no torrent of memories pouring out of it. No life in it, expired or not. To my *Psychometry*, it felt almost like a radio tuned to static. Dead air.

Silently, the knight twisted at his maul as he pulled away, trying to wrest it out of my grasp. But as big and tough as he was when there was nobody around who could hit him back, there was a frantic energy to his motions now.

He was only a dead human underneath that armor, but I was so much more. Even as he hauled on the hammer with all his might, I took control, sweeping the tail end up into his crotch, just like I'd promised myself I would.

Losing his grip and grabbing at himself, he staggered back. I hefted the spectral hammer, ready to repay him all the kindness that he'd shown me when I was bleeding out on the floor, but it faded away in my hands. Wrestling match then? That could still be fun.

Rushing under his half-hearted round-house punch, I caught the little ghost knight around the chest with both arms and promptly passed right through him and out the other side. Ghost touch hands. Right.

Now that he knew the name of the game, ghost knight didn't hesitate. He came at me hard with another wild swing I had no hope of avoiding while I was still trying to catch my balance.

[588/710 Health]

It staggered me, but it wasn't enough to put me down. I came back in with a swing of my own. He ducked it and caught me under the chin with an uppercut so fast I didn't even see it coming.

[579/710 Health]

My mouth filled up with blood after those hits, and it was just starting to trickle out from between my lips when the ghost hefted both his hands over his head and brought them down together at me again.

I spat the blood in his face. There was nothing for it to hold onto, so it spritzed right through, but for that one vital fraction of a second, as it was passing through the air, he couldn't see me.

Fist, meet gut.

I had that momentary flair of satisfaction as Brawling hit ten and lit up inside me, searing into my soul as a permanent addition to the beautiful tapestry that was Maulkin.

[577/710 Health]

Ah yeah, armor. Punching metal hurt. Even ghost metal. Apparently.

Too late now, he'd folded around that first punch, so I brought my other fist around into his face, knocking that stupid helmet sideways

He staggered, and I took the opportunity to switch sides, ducking right through his ghostly body and out the other side so that my back was to the door, and one angle of approach was protected by what was left of the wall of fire.

The ghost knight advanced on me again, finding his courage and pressing his fist into his palm in the universally accepted sign language for, "I'm going to hit you."

Sadly, he didn't get the chance. Mercy bellowed from behind me, "Get down!"

Never one to let a lady down, I threw myself face-first onto the floor for what felt like the hundredth time that day. The ghost knight stood over me, puzzled for only a moment before hell came rushing through.

Asher's fireball spell and Mercy's tempest arrow launched into the room together. For just a moment, I saw the two of them separately, then their paths crossed, and they became a firestorm. It was like every firework display I had ever seen in my life all rolled up into one, blazing so bright and hot that I was pretty sure I'd lost my eyebrows just glancing in its direction. The roar of fire was deafening. An explosion playing out in slow motion. Colors danced through it, every shade of fire chasing after every other one in an ever-expanding rolling burst of light that seemed to never end. When it passed, the drapes were gone, the lace was ash, and even the flagstones bubbled and buckled under the heat of those flames. It washed out through the room, stretching out from above me to encompass everything in sight before breaking like a wave on the rear wall, washing up and over the roof to chase back over to me again, lighting up the absolute devastation that it had left in its wake.

My lungs had been healed by Asher's magic, but yet again I found that I couldn't catch a breath. All the air in the room had been swallowed up to fuel the firestorm. Gasping did nothing to help. There was just nothing there for me to breathe in. I scrambled back to my feet and ran for the door, but I didn't get far.

The knight caught me by a horn and yanked me back, and breathless and confused as I was, I just went with it. Thumping to the ground on my hands and knees before him.

All the ice had been melted away, taking the crisp edges of his glowing form away, but to make up for it, the light inside him was blazing brighter than ever before. It was like he'd taken all the heat of the fire and used it to stoke himself up. Looking at him left afterimages burned into my retina. I had to jerk my head away or go blind.

All around the room the ghosts shone so bright they were like stars dragged down to earth, overwhelming in how solid they looked. They looked more real than us now.

The knight lifted a boot up to stamp on my head, and, of course, I had to look. Nobody wants a surprise head stomp. The outline of his blazing form was wavering. The solid edges of it leaping and vibrating around, like he was losing cohesion.

He seemed to feel it too, and he paused with his foot raised up, ready to kick me, and that moment was all I needed. He might have had all the training in the world at being a knight, but I'd been living in this particular slice of weirdness all week. I rose up, caught his leg on my shoulder, and bowled him over as I sprang to my feet.

That was unexpected. I had fully planned on passing right through him, but his newfound solidity seemed to be out of his control. He'd swallowed up too much heat and power to fade away.

For a moment I was all tangled up with his leg, then I was free of it, off and running out into the scorched and ruined room. Everything that wasn't glowing was covered in soot, but I didn't need eyes to tell me where the half-melted remains of my sword lay.

Artifice brought it back to me, and Artifice reshaped it into the big cleaver that I knew and loved. Even if the leather wrappings had all burned away and the hilt was scorching my palms, I was armed, and I had an enemy that I could actually hit. It was over for these bitches.

The juddering torch-Alvaren came at me in a rush now that their wits had returned to them, and I cleaved clean through them both with a single swing that they didn't bother to dodge since they were expecting to be incorporeal.

As they died again, all the energy that had been harnessed inside them exploded right out of their wounds and washed over me. It didn't hurt exactly, but it did send me sliding across the floor, stumbling over heaped embers and ash-banks.

The archer launched a shot at me, but it missed, waggling and wobbling through the air to embed in the stone by my feet. Turning on my heel, I ran right back towards the door and the blissfully cool air that was rushing in and throwing up clouds of ash as I went.

The knight loomed out at me, still unarmed, still unused to having a body again. I relieved him of the burden with a chop.

He exploded too, but I just couldn't bring myself to give a damn when there was all of that sweet, sweet oxygen just waiting for me by the door. I gulped it in greedily as the others came barreling through. Mercy and Seren caught me under the arms as my momentum and the last gasp I'd managed before the explosion ran out.

"Oh crap," Mercy groaned. "We made them stronger."

I gasped out. "Nah. You made them. More. Explodey."

Seren started to pull away, reaching for her blades with the deadly glint in her eye, but I held onto her. "Wait."

Restoration flowed through my bare hands and across both of the ladies in my life. The tiny cuts that the Alvaren spooks had been bleeding them out through sealed up. A blue flush of vigor leapt up Seren's face, all the way to her hairline.

At the farthest end of the burnt-out room, the last two ghosts stood guard by the door, the Dvergar archer lining up her shot on me, and the shield-bearer kneeling to give her the most cover without costing her the angle of attack. I grinned. "Together."

My sword became a shield as we charged, and the archer's shot plinked off it harmlessly now that the arrow was solid.

They managed two more shots as we crossed the room, but they may as well have not bothered. Asher and the girls had fallen in behind me, so close that the archer had no clear shot at them. Each arrow grazed uselessly around my shield, and even the shot at our feet was haphazard. All the precision was gone now that the archer had mass bearing down on them.

I hit the shield-boy head-on with all the momentum I'd built up. Shield to shield, I pushed him back step by step. He flailed at me with his little arming sword, but it couldn't reach around the breadth of my shield, and he was rewarded for his efforts by Seren hacking at his arm each time.

Asher had lightning crackling between his hands, ready to unleash, and Mercy darted back and forth, firing arrows at the Dvergar ghost, who I assume was doing the same little dance. My arms were straining to hold back the shield-spook, but I was far from the limits of my potency. After so much time fighting giant monsters, some guy with a sword and shield just wasn't all that impressive, even if he did glow in the dark.

Seren moved out to the side, circling around the clash of shields, looking for her opening, but for all that the ghost wasn't my match in strength, it still had skills. He started turning even as she did, sliding my shield around and exposing my side to his archer. I really still had a lot to learn about all this.

But then again, he had a lot to learn about fighting an eternal. I kicked the bottom of my shield, surging my potency and smacking his shield into his legs and flipping him forward into Seren's waiting blades. They scissored under that helmet of his, clean cuts that should have had his head exploding off his body but... nothing happened.

Seren was frozen with confusion for a moment. Only managing to whisper, "No," before the arming sword was thrust right through her guts.

CHAPTER 33

I echoed her words in a roar. "No!"

With a blink of time, my shield became a sword again and I hammered it down into the shield of my enemy. My potency was still surging. It cleft it in two, and the arm behind it too.

The explosion knocked all of us away, but before I'd even stopped skidding, I was running back to Seren—a mad dash that was halted by an arrow to the face.

[536/710 Health]

Thank the gods for my thick skull. The arrow was still sticking out of the side of my head, right under my horn, but it hadn't broken through to my brain. I could only imagine the brain damage jokes I'd have to endure from Mercy if it had.

I got my sword up ahead of the next arrow.

"Asher, heal Seren! Mercy, are you doing anything!?"

Mercy was incandescent with rage.

"She!"

She loosed an arrow.

"Just!"

And another.

"Won't!"

That one definitely hit.

"Die!"

That one passed right through the ghost and out the other side. The blinding glow clinging to it for a moment before fading away.

What was happening? If you wanted something done right, you had to do it yourself, apparently. I charged the archer, turning one more arrow aside before there was no more time for them to aim.

When it was clear that there was nowhere to run and that there was no way to avoid it, the Dvergar ghost didn't even try to fight back. She spread her arms and...

The final spectral explosion lashed out through the room, wiping away any evidence that the ghosts had ever been there at all. I was knocked on my ass, and Asher would have been too if he weren't already down on one knee, huddled over Seren.

Legendary Foes Defeated!
Potency increased to 46
Brawling: Rank 10/10
188 Experience Gained
650 Glory Gained

Seren.

I dashed across and skidded to a halt by her side. The stomach wound was brutal. Blue-tinged blood was pumping out in a wave with every slowing beat of her heart. I put my hand over it and pressed down because I vaguely remembered something about putting pressure on wounds, but I had no idea what I was doing. *Restoration* was still dormant and useless. "Asher, come on."

He was mumbling through his spells, waving his hands around as the fire gathered there, but it was all taking too long. *Lifesense* was an amazing tool for spotting when there were enemies around, but in moments like this, when I could literally feel the life draining out of someone, it was a nightmare.

The first spell cast, tiny glowing embers were coating Seren from head to toe, like she was dressed up in Christmas lights. He moved right into the next spell, but I had no clue whether it was going to be done in time. Her health was dwindling down to single digits. "Seren, you swore you'd obey me. You swore. So I'm giving you an order now. Don't die. Do not die, Seren. Don't do it."

I reached for *Restoration* again, but it was still dull and lifeless within me. I tried anyway. Maybe my Primal Pillar would shatter like Artifice had, maybe it wouldn't. I didn't care. She was not dying while I had a way to save her. No way. Not on my watch.

All the life and divine power that I had inside me, I pushed out into her. I strained, and I willed it, and it was all useless. Nothing moved. *Restoration* was just…dead. I would have died to heal her, without any question, but the universe wouldn't let me.

Of course, I would have died for her, I could come back from death. She wouldn't. Her health ticked down to just a single point, my aware-ness of the life inside her dimming until there was barely a spark left.

"Asher, now. You need to do it now."

His spell wasn't ready. I knew it wasn't from the look on his face. All that he could do was go through the motions. Say the words. Shape the fire. He couldn't change anything. He couldn't make it go faster.

I pressed my eyes closed and dug through the lists of divine pow-ers, desperately hunting for anything—anything that might stop the inevitable from coming to pass. Soul Stone was the only thing that I could see. Trapping her soul in a gemstone didn't sound like some-thing she'd want. Just the idea of imprisonment seemed to have made her physically sick, I wasn't going to throw her in a shiny rock for all eternity. I cursed myself. Maybe if I hadn't been such a flaky, excitable, jack-of-all-trades asshole I could have powered up a pillar enough that I might actually be useful. This was my reward for being me.

My head felt too heavy. Grief overpowered my strength. It fell forwards until my face was an inch from Seren's, and I whispered so that only she could hear, "Stay with me."

The final point of health did not disappear. She lingered there, right on the edge of death, the moments stretching out. Every breath I took seeming like an eternity. My hands shook where I held them over the hole through her gut. There was no blood pulsing now. No movement at all. She was as still as death, but down there, deep inside her, that final point of health was still there. She was still holding on.

Asher's spell burst out over her, and I snatched my hands back before they could be scorched. The flames rolled out over her, passing harmlessly over her pristine skin and armor until they found the hole in her stomach. They drained down into the hole in a swirl, and Seren began to jerk and jump. I pressed down on her to stop her from doing any more damage to herself, but I needn't have bothered. She was so weak with blood loss that she barely managed a few wiggles beneath my hands. When the last of the fire had faded away inside her, there was nothing left but an ugly twist of scar tissue on her bared midriff.

She huffed out a great plume of blue-tinted smoke and then panted for air. Her eyes opened. She was alive. Somehow, she was alive. I let out an unexpected little bleat of delight, then scooped her up in a hug. "Oh thank the gods."

"Unhand me." She wriggled free of my grasp as life returned to her body in stages. She flexed her hands, then pushed off me to stand.

"What just occurred?"

"You got stabbed, then Asher healed you."

"I do not speak of the obvious. I speak of your voice in the darkness. Hands of shade and moonlight. Your hands. Holding me in place. Bringing me back from the darkness. Tell me truly, what occurred?"

Asher frowned. "Maulkin did nothing. He tried to heal you, but his restorative powers are limited in their use by time."

"I saw your face. I heard your words." She scrambled away from me. "Do not attempt to deceive me. Do not treat me with such cruelty in a time such as this."

Even I was as confused by everything she was saying as she was. "I mean, I was speaking, I was holding you, but that was it."

"You commanded her not to depart," Asher piped up, helpful as always.

Her eyes widened. "I was dead. I felt the life rhythm beneath my breast shudder to a halt. Yet I live. I could not be extinguished. I could not pass on to the next life. You...you did this to me."

"Come on, guys, it isn't like I've got power over life and death."

Mercy sidled over to Seren's side. "Hey uh, not trying to cause trouble or anything, but did anyone else notice he was the only one who could kill the ghosts?"

I knew the answer to this one. "That was just because I've got the Aether Pillar and the *Psychometry* skill. That's why I could hit them."

"Even when they were corporeal, Mercy's arrows and Seren's blades could not pierce them, yet your own blunt instrument served you well."

Damn it, Asher, whose side are you on?

Mercy snapped her fingers. "You chose Chernghast."

Seren's head snapped around at the wolf god's name. "What?"

"When we had to pick a patron to make us Eternals, you picked the death god, didn't you?"

Where was she going with this? "I mean, yeah, but that doesn't..."

"That explains it! You've got some death powers! Check out your character sheet."

Asher tipped his head to one side. "Character sheet?"

I rolled my eyes. "You've never played a video game before, we get it."

My character sheet revealed nothing new. It was unchanged, bar a couple of extra codified skills and the gradual creep of my stats. Nothing that would explain my sudden ability to kill ghosts. I took a long hard look at my divine skills to see if there was anything that could explain it, but they were just the same as always.

My own voice echoed in out of the darkness. "You have become so steeped in destruction, that you now extend your reach beyond the veil. All fall before you. All turn to rot and ruin at your touch. The severed souls of your victims are now yours to command. The Psychopomp is a conveyor of souls, a guide or guardian akin to the reaper, who may push their incorporeal victims beyond the limits of the world and on into the next. If you so choose, you may guide those who have been slaughtered to the afterlife of your choosing, sundering whatever connections they have to their mortal shell."

Psychopomp.

"I'm a Psychopomp, apparently. I didn't really get all of the…uh… details when I got the upgrade last time I tiered up. There was a lot of other stuff going on at the time."

"Always said you were a psycho."

Mercy smirked, while at the same time Asher was saying, "Your pomposity has hardly been noteworthy."

I rolled my eyes at the two of them. Seren did not look amused. "A psychopomp, is he? A reaper of souls? The Voidgod was one such as thee. A slayer of mortal and immortal alike. Is that the path that thou are walking, Maulkin? Do you mean to burn all the world down for your Lunar masters?"

"Whoa." Mercy held up her hands. "Hey now, chill out. Don't go psycho on us too. You sound like Orphia."

"More Eternal secrets and more Eternal lies. Deeper and deeper into the well we must plunge. Who is this Orphia? What is the meaning of all this?" She was fumbling at her sides for the swords that were lying by my feet. Instinct was a hell of a drug.

I held up my hands. "Alright. Okay. Let's all just calm down."

I'd never seen her so incensed. Her face had narrowed until every feature seemed jagged. "You denied me a warrior's death and the eternal bliss of the Elysian. What part of that makes it seem that all is right in your eyes?"

My voice came out in a rumble when it came. "You wanted to die?"

"Of course, I did not seek death, I am no coward. Nor do I wish to be denied the afterlife that I have earned through centuries of service on the whims of one such as you."

Mercy took a little step away from her then. Supportive only went so far, apparently. "You'd be dead if these two hadn't saved you, how about a little gratitude?"

Seren scoffed, then dropped into a perfect curtsey, arms extended out in exaggerated swoops. "My thanks to thee, oh gracious saviors. How might I ever repay you for the supreme kindness that you have granted me in stripping me of my rightful rewards and dooming me to an eternity in the dark of the void?"

Mercy rolled her eyes. "It isn't like they're going to retract your invitation."

"What know you?" Seren spun on her, empty hands up as if she were ready to swing at her. "What do any one of you know of the rules that govern the lives of Amaranth. You are strangers. Fools. Charlatans. You pretend at divinity but know not the first thing of our ways or our faith. Hemeraphel is a loving mother, but only to those that obey her strictures. What happens when she judges me defiant because I denied her plans for me and returned to life? What will become of me when this flesh fades? All that I am shall be fodder for the void if not for the kindness of the gods. And you have spat in their eye."

"I'd cut their eyes out if I could."

That voice barely even sounded like me, but it had come out of my mouth. I'd never heard myself so twisted up with rage that I sounded like that. I could feel the chill of it inside me, like drowning Seren, like slicing up Alvaren. Anger without start or end.

All three of them turned to look at me. Seren's mask of calm shattered into horror at my blasphemy, and Mercy and Asher were startled by my vitriol. "They've made this whole world as a playground, filled it up with real people like Seren, and told them that if they break any of the rules that the gods just made up, then they were going to end up in the void? Sounds to me like the gods are assholes."

Even Mercy looked shocked at that. Seren's mouth flapped open and shut. "You cannot say such things!"

"Why? Is it against the rules?" I had no idea why I was this angry, but now that I'd started talking, I didn't know how to stop. "What are they going to do about it. They can't directly affect anything on Amaranth, that is their rule. They're all about rules, right? And I'm Eternal. They can't hold the promise of some fancy afterlife over my head for my whole life either. I've got tenure! I'm here forever, no matter how obnoxious I am."

Seren was yelling. Great. "I should slay you where you stand for speaking such blasphemy."

"Seriously, dude, chill out." Mercy shifted uncomfortably. "The gods have been pretty good to us. No need to piss them off."

"Oh yeah, they're real saints sending us off to fight their wars for them while they sit back and chill." I pointed right at Mercy. "If you were following all the damned rules, you'd have tried to kill me back when we first landed on this rock. You didn't. You knew that what I was saying made sense and Orphia's race war bullshit didn't."

Seren paced towards me with the other two on her heels in case this turned violent. "Who is this Orphia of whom you speak with such disregard?"

"An Eternal. A solar Eternal who thought her whole purpose in this world was to kill lunar Eternals."

"The two pantheons are at war, this is known. It is a grievous sin to aid a servant of the lunar gods."

"Then you're a sinner, baby. I'm a lunar Eternal."

"You cannot be. Such creatures, they're naught but ravening beasts.

Even in the War of the Voidgod, they were deployed not as troops but weapons, with handlers ready to put them down, should their natural treachery overcome them."

"Oh, I'm getting really tired of that crap. You've spent days with me. You know I'm not 'a ravening beast full of natural treachery.' I'm me. You know me. What difference does it make which gods picked me?"

"It matters because your true nature is opposed to order and law. You are a beast of chaos. A sower of discord. A breaker of harmonies."

"And so what?" I roared in her face. Furious enough that Seren actually backed up a step. "Some things need breaking."

You'd think I just said I wanted to bang her mother from the way that Seren was looking at me. Mercy and Asher met each other's eyes across the room and then glanced away quickly. As usual, Mercy was the one to get up the courage to speak first.

"If it weren't for Maulkin, you'd still be a svart." Seren's mouth fell open, but Mercy pushed on before she could start screaming. "I mean if it weren't for him then nobody would have gone down into your city. Nobody would have found the shard. Nobody would have changed you back. Asher, if it weren't for Maulkin, you'd still be hiding out in the wilderness, avoiding everyone on Amaranth because they might interfere in your grand purpose. If it wasn't for Maulkin…I'd have nobody to dunk on all day."

"Love you too, babe." I blew her a kiss.

"Seren is correct. It does matter that Maulkin is a Lunar Eternal. It is the purpose of such creatures to spread disorder wherever they travel. To disrupt the order as they find it. The Lunar Eternals are meant to cause trouble." It looked like it pained him to say it, but he raised up a finger and pointed right at me. "He is causing good trouble. There are structures that must be demolished before they can be rebuilt. Strictures that must be overturned. He is a Lunar Eternal, and he is making this world better."

I mimed wiping away a tear, but honestly, this was all getting me right in the heart. Whatever anger had been carrying me on throughout all this arguing died on the spot.

"Seren. If you feel like I've lied to you or I'm not worthy of trusting anymore, you're free to go. There's the door. I'll do my best to get you back to your queen as soon as I'm done in here."

"There...there is no law among my people regarding Eternals of the lunar court. There is no precedent that I must follow. I gave my oath to you, and my word is not so easily broken. To my eyes you are the same man that you were when I was on my knees before you, accepting your weapons and dedicating myself to your cause."

Mercy turned bright red the moment Seren said "on my knees before you," and the rest of the Alvaren's little speech was to the accompaniment of her uproarious laughter. Great.

"Can we just get on with the dungeon crawl please?"

"Indeed, by my calculations there cannot be much further to explore. The ah...fingers of the claw structure should begin to branch out from the floor above us. Our journey may be nearing its end."

The same spiral staircase awaited us as on every other floor, but instead of a dead-end, it opened out into a hallway with four doors branching off. "Is this going to be like the exploding crap back at the school?"

Asher scurried forward. "Allow me a moment to examine them."

Seren stood considerably farther back from the doors than the rest of us. "I recall the doors in question. Many of my paladins were slain by their curses and traps."

"It feels weird to say sorry for that since you were trying to kill us at the time?" I rubbed the back of my neck to avoid looking at her.

"Thy fought and bested a superior enemy by making use of the advantage that familiar territory granted you. There is no shame in that."

"Maulkin, might you grant me the benefit of your experience for a moment?"

I joined Asher in the middle of the room where he was stroking his chin and pondering things. "Four doors, yet only three towers." He pointed to the one on the right of the stairs we came up. "From the emanations that I can sense, I would judge that to be the library and the next to be our destination. The epicenter of magic within this grand steeple. Yet two more doors remain. What purpose might they serve."

I grinned and pointed in order. Opposite the stairs. "Bed." Overhanging the stairwell. "Bath." Then I waved my hand grandiosely to the other doors with a grin. "And beyond!"

He looked at his feet. "Of course. Even Eternals have some worldly needs."

"Are you saying I need a shower?"

"You were cast into the ocean but a day back. No." He leaned in closer to stage whisper, "It is Mercy who is particularly ripe at this juncture."

"I can hear you."

"I am aware of that, but there was no polite way to directly address your aroma, and I had hoped that overhearing this conversation might spare us a little awkwardness."

"Nope. I'm making it awkward." She strutted over and gave him a shove. "You think I smell bad? Ever been in a hot room with an old pair of gator-skin boots?"

I put a hand on each of their shoulders. "Guys, guys. You all smell terrible. Can we get going?"

Seren made a little sniffing noise. Oh for the love of... "Except Seren who smells delicious. Seriously, people, can we please go fight some monsters before I start screaming?"

The two of them fell into a glowering silence for a moment while Seren looked away, and I pretended she wasn't blushing. Finally, Asher broke the silence.

He pointed with one claw. "The most potent magical emanations are…"

I was off before he could even finish that sentence. "Let's go!"

He snatched after me with all the dexterity of a pair of oven glove-wearing noodles, but when he cried, "Wait!" I did.

"What? You don't want to see what Talon left here? The shard might still be up there! Come on. This is it. The next big step in the quest."

He hissed. "We must prepare ourselves."

That wasn't a bad point actually. After all the chaos of the rooms below, I was still all hyped up, but this definitely felt like that room right before you went in to face the boss in a video game. Shame there was no save point. Or heaps of items. Or anything helpful whatsoever.

I moved around the room, laying hands on each of them in turn and letting *Restoration* bring them back up to full health, before finally turning the Primal power back on myself and closing up all the various scrapes that I'd earned fighting ghosts. I had a more than decent stockpile of experience at this point – one thousand and sixty-six of them to be exact – and if I died to some wacky experiment gone wrong in the wizard's lab I'd be mad to lose it, but I was also in spitting distance of my next Tier Up and all the new divine powers that I might unlock there. 1750 out of 2100 Glory. That was just one abomination's worth of glory. Surely, we were going to get that soon.

Still, if I was heading into a fight, it made sense to buy up some new skills to help me. I could afford to splash out a little and still be able to afford a couple of new divine powers. I went straight into Ascension this time, ignored all the big, exciting powers, and narrowed in on the one I'd unlocked through my own efforts. Ascendant Brutality. I seemed to have maxed out the regular version of that skill tree, but I had no intention of changing how I fought any time soon, and I wanted to go on improving my damage, so I guess this was it. It flared with moonlight as it burned into my soul, a little dimmer than the ones before, but still, definitely that pale blue-tinted light.

Seven hundred and sixty-six experience in the bank for Tiering up, and new strength flooding through my muscles. Perfect. I clapped my hands together. "Alright. Who's ready for some wizard bullshit!"

CHAPTER 34

The lab at the top of the silver spiral staircase was considerably bigger than every other room in the tower despite the fact that it should have been less than one-third of the size. When I say wizard bullshit, this is exactly what I'm talking about, even though I'm sure that Asher would be quick to inform me that the effect was achieved through the Cosmos power rather than magic. It is all the same to me. Wizard bullshit.

While the rest of the tower had been pleasantly warm, just like the jungle outside, the lab was chilly. This might have had something to do with the fact that all the stained-glass windows arrayed around it were in pieces all over the rug, and we were high enough up in the air to catch a breeze, but given that it was a wizard tower, I'd have accepted the idea of magical air conditioning on the wrong setting just as readily.

Talon had made this space his own. There were bookcases covering every inch of wall that wasn't broken window. The desk I'd seen him sitting at making the doorknob trap was over to one side, stacked up with various strange ores that magical energy crackled between in multicolored sparks. The floor had the same flagstones as everywhere else, but there were rugs tossed all over the place, haphazardly. Like he didn't really give a damn about them, he just knew he needed rugs.

There was a little bit of the silvery apparatus that we'd seen downstairs, although none of it was in motion at this point. Most of it wasn't even in one piece. There were bones in amongst it, in the places where it had been melted and battered. Stains too. That grime and bones decorative flair showed up all around the room—heaps of bones by every wall and window. Scorch marks on some, and others reduced to powder.

Skulls were few and far between, but the ones that I could make out were distinctly inhuman. Elongated and serpentine. Inyoka. A lot of dead Inyoka—somewhere between the Asher we all knew and loved and the wild things out in the jungle. I spotted elongated claws on the top of one heap.

Talon was dead in the center of the room.

He wasn't standing freely. In fact, there were twisted lengths of ragged metal that passed right through his body to pin him in place—a tangle of hand-twisted barbed wire made from the silvery remains of his ruined lab that someone had fed through his flesh. A structure of wood, broken off from tables and desks, had been hammered together to support these new additions, bent around the solid backing of the structure that had already been there. The shantytown gallows held him strung up against a great stone slab that glowed from every inscription with dim sunlight.

New Divinity Unlocked! [Rough Hewn Shrine Construction]

Shrines. The gods mentioned them back when we were on speaking terms. They took away the randomization when we died. I guess that when Talon died, this was where he came back. Yet there he was now. Maybe there was some rule about dying too close to your shrine? Maybe…Talon's head jerked up. He wasn't dead.

He strained against the wire where it wound through his eyes—in one and out the other. He was blind and trapped, but he could still croak out, "Non ti dico niente."

Mercy rushed over to try and pull him free, tossing her bow aside as she reached for him. I wasn't so hasty. He was naked up there on the rack where he'd been hung, beard and hair grown down long and matted enough to cover his dignity, and the filth of ages had accumulated on his skin. His own blood had turned rusty and black where the metal dug into him, and only the outer reaches where it met his crusty skin showed any hint of red. Talon sobbed, "Non toccarmi!"

Mercy was almost to him when the stubble bristled up on the back of my neck.

The exact moment when we all lifted off the floor was different. I guess that because I was heavier it took me a little longer. That was why the rest of them let out cries of dismay before I'd even noticed my feet losing contact. I wish that I'd been completely surprised because then I wouldn't have had time to flail around and accidentally kick-off, sending me flipping end over end up into the air as gravity cut out. "What did I say about wizard bullshit?!"

Now that he'd found his voice, Talon's screech was deafeningly loud. "Get away from me, wyrm-spawn! Away! Away!"

"We aren't Inyoka!" I found myself bellowing back as I flipped up towards the speckled pattern of tiny black holes he'd opened up on the ceiling. "We're Eternals, just like you!"

He wailed, "È mio!" and the sob seemed to reverberate out through the air, and the room stretched and rippled around him. The curses back in Witchglass Overlook were like child's play compared to the raw cosmic power that this guy was throwing around in his tantrum. As I drifted from one bubble of reality to the next, my fingers, elbow, and shoulder dislocated with a rattle of popping sounds and pain. A lot of pain.

[673/710 Health]

Asher was dangling upside down, his skirts up over his face as he fumbled with them trying to see. Seren was still more or less the right way up but paralyzed in indecision, half crouched in mid-air, and tensed up with nothing to kick-off. Furniture took off too, not just drifting up into the air but being buffeted around as Talon's magic or Cosmos or whatever wizard bullshit it was came lashing out of him in every direction.

"You shall never take it from me. Kill me. It is me. We are one. Kill me! It is mine!" Bloody froth started to drip down from Talon's cracked lips. "Search all you like. Tear down my tower. Slaughter my students. Kill and kill and kill and kill and kill me again. You shall not have it, Tsangaanax! It is mine!"

Mercy had been the closest to him, and momentum had carried her forward even once she lost contact with the floor. She'd drifted too high to reach him, but the structure that held Talon pinioned in place was close enough for her to make a grab.

Her fingers brushed over it uselessly, finding no purchase but setting the whole thing shaking as she was dragged away by the currents throwing around the air. That vibration carried down through the wires, and Talon screamed in agony as fresh blood began to flow.

Blood gushed down from his punctured eyes as he jerked his head around, and the wire tore at him. It bubbled on his lips as he ranted, "No more! I beg you. No more! I cannot give it to you, Tsangaanax. I cannot, even if I wanted to."

Another roiling wave of power flooded out of him, throwing everything in the air into orbits around everything else. Asher and the archmage's desk pirouetted around one another, Seren and a heap of bones found themselves looping in intricate designs to maintain their distance, and Mercy and I spun together at opposite sides of the room, slowly swapping positions as I twisted and contorted myself, trying to stay out of the patches that looked wrong on the basis that I liked all my limbs attached, and my right arm was currently dangling uselessly like something hanging out the side of a shark's mouth.

Since I was apparently completely useless at this moment, I called out, "Talon! We're here to set you free! Not to hurt you! We're on your side."

I didn't know if he was too nuts after all these years of torture to care, whether he had been deafened as part of his torments, or whether he was just ignoring me, but I was pretty sure that when he screamed, "Non puoi prendere ciò che è dentro di me!" it wasn't related to what I was telling him.

I bumped into Mercy's bow as I drifted about and caught ahold of it more by luck than anything else. If I'd had two arms working, I might have taken a pot-shot at Talon, but my right still felt like a wet noodle and the left was none too stable.

"Mercy! Catch!"

Putting all my strength into it, I launched her bow across the room. As an equal and opposite reaction, I got launched the other direction.

If there had been a wall behind me, I would have been ecstatic about it. But instead, there was a big wide shattered window and the blue tropical sky. I was definitely going to die if I fell out of this tower. I started to frantically paddle through the air, but there was just no traction. I was going out. There was no question about it.

Across the room, Mercy caught the bow. I really didn't see that coming either. She drew one of her drifting arrows and sighted on Talon then paused. Wavering.

I stretched for the top of the window frame, the tips of my boots scraping over it hopelessly as I flipped. "Mercy, take the shot!"

She did. The arrow flew true from her bow, launching her up towards the gravity snares on the roof, and momentum seemed to carry it through. It passed through one bubble of cosmic nonsense after another, changing color, changing shape, flying backward, but when it came out the other side it was still on target. It hit Talon in the throat, and all of the chaos abruptly stopped.

Gravity snapped back on.

I fell.

Twisting in the air, less like an agile cat and more like a fish out of water, I reached for the window's rim as I plummeted. I twisted around, grabbed for the edge, and then discovered to my horror that I wasn't the first one to come by that way. Thick grooves had been cut into the solid stone where the Inyoka's claws had bitten into it. Thick grooves that time and the weather had now smoothed out into delicate little inclines that my fingers could find no purchase in. "Oh no."

I barely made it an inch down the side of the claw scarred wall before I was caught. Another tiny black hole had opened up above me. Asher's gravity trap was the only thing keeping me alive, but even it wasn't strong enough to stop my descent entirely. The farther I fell, the weaker its hold on me grew. I reached for the wall, scrabbling at it, but there was nothing for me to catch hold of. Artifice. I reached for it and found the walls with the careful carving and hidden mechanisms completely beyond my abilities, but my sword wasn't.

Claws had worked before, and they'd work again. I forged them for myself, dangling out there in the sky, and then surged my potency so that when I punched them into the stone, they stuck.

It actually worked. Between the claws and the reduced weight that the gravity trap gave me, I could climb. Oh, gods, it hurt. Every joint in my right arm felt like it was on fire. Every part of it felt like it might give out each time that I put weight on it. My whole body shook with the effort, even with my potency doubled.

Following in the Inyoka's tracks, I climbed back up the outside of the tower, avoiding all Talon's defenses against flyers and the ones he'd piled up inside. He'd been so obsessed with stopping other wizards that lizards hadn't even crossed his mind.

The pain went from awful to unbearable as my potency surge wore out. The wind tore at me, and I was left dangling there as I waited for Asher's trap to blink out and gravity to have her wicked way with me. I'd come so far to make it here. Fought through so much. All for it to end like this. Killed by the ground. It was pathetic. Laughable. I wasn't doing it.

Dragging the claw back out of the stone without surged potency sent jarring vibrations all the way up to my shoulder, and my muscles screamed. My joints felt like they were on fire. I was not having a good time, but it got easier. Every time I brought a claw up and hammered it into the wall, I got farther from Amaranth and closer to Asher's trap. I got lighter. Even as exhaustion crept into me, it was balanced by that lightened load. Inch by agonizing inch, I crawled back up the side of the tower until I was back to the shattered window.

Up over the window's rim, and I probably would have kissed the scabby carpet if everyone hadn't come running over to haul me back inside and to my feet. Seren was actually smiling, which was even more of a surprise than gravity abruptly stopping a minute ago. It was a blink and you'd miss it opportunity. Her usual expressionless mask was back a moment later as Mercy punched me in the shoulder. "Dumbass."

"Hey, it worked."

I swept Asher up in a quick hug, then deposited him carefully on the floor when he froze up.

Which was about the moment that Talon appeared back in the same spot.

Even as he blinked back into reality, he seemed to be twisting, trying to avoid his fate, but it did no good. His eyes blazed with sunlight for only a moment before they burst and went streaming down his cheeks. His arms, his legs, all of them were caught, penetrated through and through by the wires. He fell limp with metal cutting into him, and the blood began to flow anew. Starting a fresh patina.

A long and drawn-out wail of anguish filled the room, only to abruptly cut off in a gurgle. Seren crossed the room at a sprint, blades crisscrossing and sweeping apart, and his head hit the floor. His body vanished in a blaze of golden sunlight.

"We have only a moment, what are thy intentions?"

"We need to talk to him. To find out what happened to his shard." I wet my lips as I picked across the trash-strewn room to the torture shrine. "But also to not die."

Another flash of light brought Talon back to life, and without looking away from me, Seren's hand lashed out once more, and she was spritzed with arterial blood. Another flash.

"I shall stand ready. Should he make another attempt at us, he will be ended." She glanced at the empty space. "Albeit temporarily."

Mercy and Asher joined us, both shaking their heads but offering no better suggestions. Asher looked like he wanted to cry, even if his new body didn't have the necessary equipment for it. "He must surely have lost his sanity by now. Enduring who knows how many centuries of this torment."

"I don't know." Mercy's brows furrowed. "He seemed to be together enough to tell Sang Axe to shove it."

Talon appeared again, only to be stabbed through the neck before any of us could say a word. Seren flushed blue. "My apologies, it has become habitual."

Rolling his eyes, Asher recited by rote. "Tsangaanax. Alvarsbane. The Twilight Betrayer. Bearer of the Wyrm's shard."

"The Black One." Seren's eyes narrowed. "The wyrm without honor."

Hmm. "So the wyrm with eighty names was trying to gather the shards himself?"

"So it seems," Asher allowed.

Talon blazed back to life, and I caught Seren's wrist before she could complete the stabbing she was already trying for.

I caught Talon by the chin before he could flop forward, flooding *Restoration* through his body, and closing up the wounds around the wires before the bleeding could begin. "Stop screaming, stop throwing yourself around, and listen to me."

His eyes were still intact. Pierced by the wire, but not burst. Glowing golden. "Servants of the wyrm, I shall not swallow your lies so readily."

"We are Eternals. Just like you." Carefully, I tilted his head around until he could see my face. See my eyes. Glowing just like his. "I'm Maulkin. We're here to help."

"Help?" he whimpered. Golden tears flowing freely. "I am beyond all help. This is perdition. I am in hell. I should not have been deceived by false gods. I should not have obeyed them or taken their succor. When I died, I should have gone to heaven, not here. I was a godly man. A righteous man. What did I do to deserve this?"

I swallowed down my blasphemies and spoke to him with that voice you save for scary crazy people and children, who are—let's be honest—just tiny scary crazy people. "What can we do to get you out of this?"

"I do not seek escape. I am...ruined. All I want is for this to end. Please, Lord, I have done my penance, let it end."

Mercy stepped up close to him. "We can make the pain stop. If we break your shrine, you'll come back somewhere else, right?"

"It cannot be done."

"I'm pretty sure one solid whack would do it."

"Do you think I have not tried? Do you think that I have not torn this contraption apart with my power a dozen times over?" His voice broke, and Seren stepped a little closer, blades ready. "An Eternal and their shrine are bound. So long as one exists, so too does the other.

When he tried to blink, the wire cut into his eyelids and set blood running down his cheeks. He began to shake, and Seren was already in motion before we realized that he was laughing. "There can be no escape, but in my torment, I have found victory. The great adversary, the black wyrm, he cannot have that which I possess for as long as I live. And I live and live again. Flesh and blood and bone. This is the meaning of eternity, young ones. Suffering. Our suffering is without end. No matter how I try, I cannot die. No matter how I rend my flesh. All of this power, all of this mastery, it is for nothing. And so forevermore shall the shard rest within me, bound to my soul."

He soul-bound it, the same as I had mine. If someone took it away from him, all he had to do was die to get it back. Great minds think alike. But that didn't explain where the damn thing actually was. "Where is the shard? Where did you hide it?"

His laughter had turned to bitter little giggles now. "I sought to draw power from it once, as Tsangaanax does now. To draw on the power bound within this relic and to become as the gods themselves with the echoes of the Voidgod slain. It was hubris. There is only death and destruction left to us. It cannot create—just as Araphel could not—and so that which lingers cannot be used to fuel any Eternal or mage."

Mercy leaned in closer. "Where is it?"

"I knew that he would come for me. Before Vidar's body was cold in the ground, I could feel the wyrm-spawn magi prying at my defenses. I should have known then that he would not stop at two. That his hunger for power knew no end. I should have known that he would seek out all six." I tried to interrupt, but the ranting would not slow. After being alone for so long, it was like he was trying to catch up on all the lost opportunities to ramble and lecture. "It is the nature of the wyrm to hoard. It is the nature of Tsangaanax to betray those he called allies. I called him friend once. Rode upon his back into battle against the void. Now look at the bounty that his friendship has bestowed upon me."

Asher hissed. "Where is the shard, Talon?"

He cackled. "It is of great amusement to me. It had been so long since I last ate that I could not even remember how to swallow. So long since I truly lived, beyond this charnel house hell, that I had to push the piece down with my fingers, rub it down my throat like I was nursing a baby bird. Even now I can feel it inside me, cold in my stomach as the flames of torment and perdition lap all around me."

Mercy's mouth fell open. "You ate it?"

"Ate it? I swallowed it whole, young one. And trouble yourself not to let that alvar bitch dig through my innards. I'd die long before she found it, then where would we be. Back here once more."

My grip on his chin tightened. Anger prickled inside me when he spoke about Seren that way, but I quashed it soon enough. He was half-mad with pain and half-mad with being alone in his tower like this through all the years. That was two halves. Getting angry at him for lashing out was like getting angry at a fish for swimming.

Enough screwing around. Best case scenario, if we managed to free Talon, was that there would be an insane immortal Archmage running around trashing the place. It would get us no closer to having his shard or any of the others. "If I kill you, can I have it?"

"You ask for my permission? If you could kill me then I would say that you could have anything you wanted in this world, for you'd have a power above the Solar and Lunar courts themselves. Deus vult. You are young yet, so perhaps you have not learned. We cannot die. No matter how much you desire it or detest it, you must live now for all of time. Never shall I know salvation. La pace è per sempre al di là della mia portata."

I shrugged. "I mean, you probably thought that the ghosts downstairs couldn't die either."

"Banishment through the divine aether is not death, you sniveling buffoon. They shall return to guard this place again soon enough, guarding it long after you are gone and only I remain. I remember when I was like you, so sure of my power in the face of all arrayed against me. L'orgoglio viene prima della caduta. Such pride I once had." He jerked his head from my grasp in his raving, and without that support, the wire coiled behind the bridge of his nose tore his eyes apart. They streamed down onto my hand, the light within them dying. Still, he raved on. "Now I do penance for that sin. For believing I could not be touched, could not be taken. Could not be broken. Sono rotto."

I had to shout so that he could hear me over his own rambling and the pitched battle that he seemed to be doing with his own breathing. "I didn't use rebuke. They weren't banished. I hit them with my sword, and they died."

He shook his head, wire sloshing through the remnants of his eyes, cutting into his temples. "Speak not this nonsense. Such a thing cannot be."

"But it is." Mercy frowned. "He did it."

For the longest moment, Talon was blissfully silent, the cogs inside the rusted machine of what had once been a great mind turning. He added together one and one and came up with eleven. "I see your game now, Tsangaanax. Illusions and tricks will not avail you. You seek to give me false hope once more. Enchant these beasts of yours to look as Eternals. Have them treat with me under the guise of kindness. It shall not work. I shall not succumb. It matters nothing, even if I did, for I cannot give you what you seek. It is bound to me."

I groaned. We were back to square one again.

Talon bellowed, "Il Signore è il mio pastore. Non mi mancherà. Mi fa sdraiare in verdi pascoli. Mi conduce lungo le acque calme."

Seren slit his throat again, and we didn't even complain. Asher sighed. "It would seem that he is beyond persuasion."

Seren and Mercy weren't even looking as Talon's body vanished once more. They were looking at me. Mercy was the one who had the guts to actually ask me, "Can you do it? Can you kill an eternal?"

I threw up my hands. "Maybe? I've never tried. I figure that worse comes to worst, he comes back again and nothing changes."

Seren's eyes bore into me. "Yet if you succeed, then everything changes. The fundamental laws of the world are overturned."

I shifted my claws back into a sword. "Well, I am all about breaking rules."

Talon reappeared in a flare of sunlight, and before his eyes were lost, he saw me there with my sword ready. "Do it, you coward. Signore sto arrivando!"

There was no grace to my strike. It was not a kindness like Seren's quick slices. Even if I knew how to do something like that, I'd probably screw it up now that it was important. I just did the same thing that I had always done, hefting my sword and bringing it down hard on Talon with all my strength.

Blunt as it was, it cut through the naked man like butter. The wires that had been woven through his flesh plinked apart and whipped out at us now that their tension was broken. There had been hooks and barbs hidden away inside him—torments that nobody could have seen so long as he lived. The tip of my sword gouged through the golden lettering on the stone behind him, breaking cleanly through whatever had been written there, and the light in the stone went out.

Talon's body tumbled from its place to fall in two halves at my feet. There was no fanfare. No blaze of light. Just silence and stillness.

New Skill Discovered! [Climbing]
Legendary Foe Defeated!
Potency increased to 47
Climbing: Rank 1/10
12 Experience Gained
4000 Glory Gained
Tier of Glory Ascended!
Tier of Glory Ascended!

And that. Talon had been a legend in his time, immortal and powerful, and I'd just killed him, with a little assist from centuries of wyrm torture. Holy crap. I did it.

"I did it. It worked!" I dropped my sword. All the exhaustion and injuries of the day finally catching up to me. "It actually worked."

CHAPTER 35

I flopped down onto my knees, then remembered what we were here for. I crawled over to the dead naked man and started desecrating his corpse a little more. I didn't know enough about anatomy to know where his stomach was, but I did know what metal felt like, so I smooshed my way through all the soft stuff until I found something solid, then I hauled it out.

Mercy looked green, and Asher was looking away entirely. Only Seren was still watching me with the same dispassionate mask that she always wore. Observing.

With my bare hands, I tore apart the fleshy sac that contained the shard. It was bigger than I'd been expecting—almost as large as the one I already had. Well done to Talon for managing to get it down.

Quest: Return of the Voidgod
Acquire Rusted Blade Shards: 2/6 Complete
400 Glory gained

I was still kneeling there in the entrails just staring at it when Mercy said. "We should get out of here."

There was no small effort involved in pulling my eyes away from the shard to meet her concerned expression. "Huh?"

Asher was shaking his head. "There is much here that will require research and study. The Archmage's notes in this very room alone will contain a wealth of information. There is no doubt that he would have held close any information regarding the location of the remaining shards. We might—"

Mercy cut him off. "There is plenty of time for all that. This place... This is ours now. The Dvergar are settling the island, but the tower is all us."

"The shrine. We can... I can build them now."

"We can make this home." Mercy grinned. "We can stop running."

Seren shook her head. "Your quest does not end here."

"No." I shook my head. "No, it doesn't."

Asher was brimming over with excitement, tail lashing. Probably because he was allowed to hang out here and read to his heart's content. "Only the fear of separation is at an end. Should we die, then we would be returned here to the seat of our power. We need not fear scattering to the winds. This changes everything for us."

Backtracking through the tower made me realize just how big it was and how much ground we had covered in a single day. In the empty ghost room, I put an arm around Seren's shoulders, and this time she did not object. Asher snuck up on the other side of me and looked expectant until he got the same treatment. Only Mercy didn't want in on the group hug. She walked along behind us as we trailed through the broken fragments of golems on the next floor, sniggering away to herself.

I glanced back over my shoulder. "You got something to say?"

"Weirdest harem ever."

I kicked a bit of golem at her.

The Inimicus was still down inside the shielded podium, though the clockwork seemed to be working overtime to shove it back up again. I tucked an arm under Asher's armpit to give him a little extra support, just in case.

From there it was all smooth sailing until we reached the bottom of the tower and the ruined statue of Talon.

The rest of us were headed for the door, but Mercy stopped in front of the golem's surprisingly intact head. "So are we just going to pretend that we didn't straight-up murder some old Italian guy?"

"My concern is less for that which has passed and more for that which is to come. This 'old Italian guy' was one of the most powerful of our kind. He waged war upon the void god himself." Asher drew away from me to look down into the face of the man I just killed. "Yet the ruthless foe that we now set ourselves against was able to bring him so low that death was a sweet release. What hope have we against such an enemy?"

"We'll kick Tsangaanax's scaly ass." I grinned. "Same as we kicked everyone else's."

Seren pushed herself out from under my arm with disdain. "Such needless bravado."

"Oh, I'm not saying it will be easy. I'm just saying that we are going to do it."

Seren's eyes narrowed. "What could fill you with such assurance?"

I counted them off on my fingers. "Abominations?"

Mercy piped up. "Kicked their ass."

"Svart?"

"Kicked their posteriors," Asher conceded.

"A whole Alvaren city? No offense, Seren."

Mercy was getting into it now. Smirking over at the Alvaren as she said, "Oh yeah, we kicked their ass."

"Giant mushrooms, magic schools, giant eels, jungle lizards, wizard's tower, golems, ghosts. I'm all out of fingers."

Mercy clapped her hands. "Every ass has been kicked."

"So no. It isn't boasting. It is practice." I tipped an imaginary hat to the head of Talon, then turned to the door. "We are good at kicking ass, and every ass that we kick makes us better at it."

Stepping back outside into the jungle afternoon was like walking into a wall of humidity. Between the sunlight and the heat, I had to blink a few times to really understand what was happening. Trees had been felled, and there was construction work already underway inside the big barren clearing. My haphazard barricades were being replaced with solid, well-built structures, and the topsoil was being cleared away by rows of diligent Dvergar, searching for stone to work.

Gunhild was in the middle of it all, of course, perched up on top of the glorified dormitory where they'd spent the night. When she saw us, she yelled so loud that the whole place came to a halt. "They be alive!"

A cheer picked up immediately, and the Dvergar all came barreling over to us, the bravest wrapping their arms around us, and the rest applauding. Even Seren got a hug, although she looked extremely dubious about it. Gunhild scrambled down a ladder I was pretty sure hadn't existed this morning to join in the festivities. "You bested the tower then?"

"Was there ever any doubt?"

"Aye, there be quite a lot of doubt." She waded through the crowd, snatching bags that were held out to her as she passed. "And a fair few bets made too. You be making me a wealthy woman this morning!"

"Aww, you bet your money on us." Mercy was too swept up in the excitement to be too annoyed. "How sweet."

"Did you find what you be looking for?"

Asher was bopping his head along to the music that had just started up. Say what you want about the Dvergar, but they know how to get a party started. "That we did, my friend! Moreover, with the tower emptied of any potential aggressors, we name Talon's Keep our new home, and you fine people as under our aegis."

Gunhild cocked her head to me then called out, "We're staying."

A cheer went up even louder than the one heard when they realized we were alive. Ouch. Fair enough, but still, ouch.

It seemed that in fleeing from their ancestral home and across the lands and seas, some of the Dvergar had still remembered what was most important in life; there were three kegs of that mossy mushroom liquor that I'd nearly poisoned myself with back in Khag Mhor cracked open by the time that we made it over to the bonfire where one of the giant feral Inyoka from the day before was spit roasting. Asher pretended not to notice.

All of them pretended not to notice when my attention wasn't fully on the party too. Seren couldn't be convinced to share stories, but Asher and Mercy soon filled in the Dvergar on everything that had happened since we stepped inside Talon's Keep. Asher's stories were a little dry, and Mercy's were a little too focused on how funny our failures had been, but between the two of them, they covered everything.

Seren watched me, though she pretended not to. I had to admit that the whole Psychopomp thing had come as a bit of a surprise, but I really didn't think it required the level of scrutiny that Seren was giving me. I passed the flagon along more often than I drank from it. If I got drunk and made an ass of myself, I just knew Seren would give me that look again. That disgusted little narrowing of the eyes that made me feel like I was only eight inches tall.

Just as the party was starting to kick into high gear and Asher started dancing—wow, he had drunk way too much—I headed off towards the tower once more.

It took some real effort to haul the bits and pieces of Talon's statue outside by hand, but I felt like I needed some good manual labor about then. The strain of my muscles against heavy objects. It felt clean.

It was only once all the big stone fragments were laid out on the dirt that I turned inwards. Seven hundred and seventy-seven experience became four hundred and seventy-seven when I bought out Shrine Construction. I'd deal with the pillars and all the rest in a moment, when my head felt clearer. The last thing I wanted to do was make any snap decisions that I couldn't reverse later.

Building the shrines was simple enough, just slapping together the stone in the required shapes. Imbuing them with the right inscriptions to attract our essence so that they could serve as our anchor to the physical world was the tricky bit. I was kind of surprised that it didn't come under Aether, really. But, apparently, it was the physical shape of the stones that did the trick, somehow. File it under rules I didn't understand.

I'd worried that the other two would have to build their own shrines, but it seemed simple enough to dedicate them. The gods only gave out names to Eternals once, so that there couldn't be any confusion. So I carved each of our names into the rock and then stepped back to look at the cemetery I'd just built for us on the doorsteps of Talon's Keep.

Okay, maybe that was a little bit morbid, but what would you describe a cluster of stone blocks with your names written on them as? I kind of expected to feel some magical connection when I finished work on them but nothing. I guess they only kicked in when you died. I sincerely hoped that I was never going to find out if they worked.

Seren was standing watching me when I turned around. "Was the haste in construction necessary? Did you suspect that you would be murdered in thy sleep?"

"Why?" I grinned. "Did you have plans?"

She did not smile. "Should the time come that I must dispatch you, it shall be in an open field of battle in a fair and even match."

"That's sort of comforting, I guess?" Gods help me, it actually was.

"Still my question has not been answered." She stepped up beside me. "Your kin are by the fire, sharing tales of thy prowess, yet you find no joy in it. Was it my accusation of bravado? I do not truly believe that..."

"No." I stopped her before she somehow made this even more awkward. "No. It isn't your fault, Seren. I just wasn't in a party kind of mood."

Her fingers brushed over mine at our side, and I nearly jumped.

"Was there some other celebration that you would rather partake in?"

I did a double-take, trying desperately to work out if this was another culture shock problem and she was going to be mortified when I had to explain to her that it sounded like she was inviting me to bed with her.

"I am inviting you to bed with me, in case my invitations were not clear enough."

I opened and closed my mouth a few times before finally managing to squeeze out, "Yes. Please."

"I understand that Talon had a bed chamber. Perhaps even a mattress. Shall we retire to his tower?"

"Okay." I couldn't stop grinning. Any minute now I was going to wake up to Mercy slapping me or something. "I mean. Uh. Also very much yes, please."

She set off towards the tower, our interlaced fingers drawing apart as she hurried ahead with a bounce in her step.

I couldn't believe that this was really happening. Out of some ancient, long-forgotten habit, I reached for my wallet and the long-expired condom that had been there since I was fourteen years old, then I realized that I didn't even have a wallet in this world, let alone ancient relics of a teenager with considerably more confidence in his romantic abilities than I had now. Instead, my hand hit the cold weight of the shard in my belt-pouch.

Seren had vanished out of sight into the tower, but I knew that if I didn't do this now, I'd contrive to forget all about it.

I poured glory into the pillar of aether, brightening it up again despite the dimness that had crept in since I last soul-bonded something. When it hit the second tier, it thickened up considerably. Looking more like a solid bar of crystal now than any of the narrow spindles that comprised the rest of my Eternal being.

Back out in the real world, I took a tighter grip on the shard in my hand and waited for Chernghast's growling voice to ask me if I was sure about this. It didn't come. Instead, I could hear my own much more pleasant voice whispering behind my ear. "This is a permanent decision, with irreversible consequences. Are you certain?"

I let out a breath of relief that I hadn't cocked up somehow. "Yes."

The light in my eyes blinked out.

For one awful moment I thought that I had gone blind, but then my eyes adjusted. There was the jungle, there were the partying Dvergar, and there was the tower with the hot Alvaren girl that wanted me to join her for the night. Why was I standing around out here worrying about the lights in my eyes going off again?

I set off towards the tower and nearly tripped over my feet. I had no light to see inside the tower anymore, but it was as though there were no shadows inside it at all. Okay, maybe this was just my eyes adjusting even more. Everything was fine. Totally fine.

Picking up the pace again, I scurried up the stairs after Seren, grabbing onto the handrail as I went. What the hell was that? My hands. The back of my hands were mottled with darkness. The black veins that had been visible beneath my skin seemed to have spread out in a capillary bloom until that darkness inside me was everywhere I looked. In truth, it probably wasn't much bigger than it had been before, but you try getting weird wrong-colored veins appearing on your arms and see how calm and sensible you feel about it.

I closed my eyes and turned my attention inward once more. There had to be some explanation for this, some reason that bonding things was making me change. The pillars of divinity loomed up out of the darkness, and I was about to turn away and search through for the description of soul bond to properly scour it for any hidden details when I froze. There were more pillars than the last time that I'd looked.

The pillars that I'd started out with were dimmed, the same darkness that had spread through my body ran through them now, thick marbling veins of black in the moonlight. But in between them in that grand circle, I could make out the shapes of others now. Between Aether and Cosmos, directly opposite Creation, there was a thin line of absolute darkness. The same black as the Inimicus had been. The darkness of the void.

Annihilation, *the destruction of worlds.*

I darted around the rest.

Empyrean – *The breaking of reality.*
Occult – *The knowledge of impossible things.*
Corruption – *The accumulation of power.*
Slaughter – *The ending of life.*
Devouring – *The consumption of souls.*
Entropy – *The unmaking of materials.*

Every pillar had a dark counterpart. Every counterpart blossomed out into tier after tier of new divine powers that I'd never been warned about.

I snapped back into my body in shock, stumbling on the stairs and barely catching myself. I had no idea what any of this meant, and I had a sneaking suspicion that telling the others about it was going to end badly for me.

They hadn't been happy to learn that I was a Lunar Eternal. How were they going to take it when they found out that I'd unlocked some sort of Void Eternal powers too?

Jumping back to what Mercy called my character sheet, I searched for any evidence of my suspicions. There was no longer any sign that I was an Acolyte of Chernghast. The only perks that I had were *Psychopomp* and *Relentless*. Nothing looked like it had changed since the last time I checked. Except that something obviously had.

Maulkin – Chagnar Faun of the Lunar and Void Court –
6th Tier of Glory

Statistics:

HP: 890/890

Devotion: 240/240

Attributes:

Potency: 46

Celerity: 21

Vitality: 18

Piety: 4

Divinities:

Aether – Rank 2: Soul Bond

Aether - Passive: Psychometry

Ascension – Rank 1: Ascendant Brutality

Ascension – Rank 2: Potency Surge

Artifice - Rank 1: Rough Hewn Architecture

Artifice - Rank 1: Rough Hewn Weapons

Artifice - Rank 1: Rough Hewn Armor

Artifice - Rank 1: Rough Hewn Shrine Construction

Artifice– Passive: Sphere of Influence

Primal – Rank 1: Restoration

Primal – Passive: Lifesense

Skills:

Combat: Rank 10/10

Sword: Rank 10/10

Mace: Rank 1/10

Polearm: Rank 1/10

Phalanx: Rank 7/10

Brawling: Rank 10/10

Brutality: Rank 10/10

Acrobatics: Rank 7/10

Climbing: Rank 1/10

Poison Resistance: Rank 10/10

Airstrike: Rank 3/10

Bestiary: Rank 3/10

Dungeoneering: Rank 2/10

Ancient History: Rank 1/10

Traits:

Relentless: *The Faun are the greatest hunters on Amaranth, known for pursuing prey for days or even weeks at a time before closing in to strike.*

Effect: Faun are immune to fatigue, their Attributes do not degrade over time without rest.

Psychopomp: *You are a conveyor of souls, a guide or guardian akin to the reaper, who may push their incorporeal victims beyond the limits of the world and on into the next.*

Effect: If you so choose you may guide those who have been slaughtered to the afterlife of your choosing. Sundering whatever connections they have to their mortal shell.

Invest your remaining Glory to continue your Ascension.

There it was in the very first line. So obvious that I'd have to be blind to miss it. Whatever echoes of the Void God were still attached to the shards of the rusted blade must have done this. I'd bonded them to the core of my being. I'd infected myself with this corruption. But still, I couldn't bring myself to worry about it too much.

What could be more appropriate than throwing the power of the Void God right back in his stupid face?

I opened my eyes, feeling better than I had since Talon. This was power, and it was mine. Why should I worry about it?

From up above me in the tower, Seren's voice echoed down. "I do not care to be kept waiting."

I took off after her at a jog, my grin coming back unbidden.

Drawing both shards from my pocket pouch as I ran, I held them up to examine them together for the first time, working out where they'd slot together—if they even did. I hadn't even noticed that I'd left my gloves outside on top of the shrines until that moment.

The whispering came, all the millennia that had passed since the Void God's defeat whipping by in an instant. Insignificant compared to the one moment where this sword had become what it was now.

Nobody knew who had killed the Void God, but with psychometry, I could find out right then and there. Shadows whipped all around me. The brief lives that had been lived around these shards. All of them irrelevant.

There in the distance, I could make out a shadowed figure. I tried to focus in on him, tried to bring him to the fore. My skills with psychometry were far from exact, but even so, I could feel him there. The one who'd done it. The hero of the ages who'd been forgotten the moment of his greatest victory.

The figure stepped forward out of the shadows, slick and jet black from the tip of his pointed tail to the top of his smooth head. Featureless as the void itself. *"I began to wonder just how long it would take before you realized that we could commune. Little matter, I do not require intelligence, only obedience."*

I dropped the shards, and in an instant, the black figure disappeared. I was back in the tower. I was standing on a stairwell. It all came back to me. Everything that the cold darkness had stripped away in just a few brief words.

My hands shook as I bent down to retrieve the shards. There was no avoiding touching them. I could not leave them here—as much as it pained me.

It took only a moment for me to scoop them up and shove them back into my pouch but that was all the time required for the voice to hiss into my ear, *"You know who I am."*

I let the shards go and they fell like a leaden weight into the pocket. Clanking together. The name spilled out of my lips without my permission.

"Araphel."

Thank You All! Please Read!

Hi everyone! Thank you so much for taking the time to read *Savage Dominion* and joining us on this brand new (and hopefully awesome) LitRPG adventure! We both hope that you all had a blast and are excited to see what happens to Maulkin and the others next! It's only because of all of your support and excitement that we're able to work on these stories and continue to improve.

On that subject, a few notes:

First: **Please, *please*, consider rating and reviewing *Savage Dominion* on Amazon, as well as any of your other favorite book sites.** Many people don't know that there are thousands of books published every day, most of those in the USA alone. Over the course of a year, a quarter of a million authors will vie for a small place in the massive world of print and publishing. We fight to get even the tiniest traction, fight to climb upward one inch at a time towards the bright light of bestsellers, publishing contracts, and busy book signings.

Thing is, we need all the help we can get, and that's where wonderful readers like you come in!

Second: If you want to join our growing community, be sure to join Wraithmarked Creative's private readers' group on Facebook! Both of us are active participants in the group, so tag us with any questions, check out all the other awesome books Wraithmarked is publishing in the coming months, and chat with those authors as well!

Regardless of whether or not you choose to review, reach out, or support us elsewhere, thank you again for taking the time to read *Savage Dominion*, and we will see you in the sequel!

Thank you all so so much,
Luke & GD

CPSIA information can be obtained
at www.ICGtesting.com
Printed in the USA
LVHW040314030822
725066LV00001B/198

9 780999 192078